Praise for *The Early Birds* and *The Future Homemakers of America*

'Please do me a personal favour and buy (and read!) both
these books. You will not regret it' Sarra Manning, *Red*

'This wonderful book about friendship is full of
warmth, wit and winning characters' *Daily Mail*

'She has wit and insight to match Nick Hornby,
and the entertainment value of Helen Fielding, as well as
depth . . . It amounts to a picture of the way women's
lives have changed, without ever sacrificing the particular
to the generalisation' *Independent*

'Superlative. The writing sparkles from first
to last' *Sunday Telegraph*

'This novel crackles with energy and snappy
American dialogue. Laurie Graham conjures
tough, funny, mouthy women, through
American airbase in Norfo
off an absolute triumph; the
the redoubtable Peggy, never falters as she unfolds
forty years of friendship' *Daily Mail*

'Laugh-out-loud funny, intelligent, moving; has
more delicious roll-off-the-tongue one-liners than
Seinfeld. One of those books you buy six copies
of to send to all your old friends' *Scotsman*

A former radio script writer and journalist, Laurie has been sacked by both the *Daily* and *Sunday Telegraph* and by a raft of glossy women's magazines. Nothing daunted she now gives vent to her opinions on her own excellent website, www.lauriegraham.com. She lives in Dublin.

Also by Laurie Graham

The Ten O'Clock Horses
Dog Days, Glenn Miller Nights
The Dress Circle
Perfect Meringues
The Unfortunates
Mr Starlight
At Sea
The Future Homemakers of America
The Importance of Being Kennedy
Gone With the Windsors
Life According to Lubka
A Humble Companion
The Liar's Daughter
The Grand Duchess of Nowhere
The Night in Question

The
EARLY BIRDS

BIRDS

LAURIE GRAHAM

Quercus

First published in Great Britain in 2017 by Quercus

This paperback edition published in 2018 by

Quercus Editions Ltd
Carmelite House
50 Victoria Embankment
London EC4Y 0DZ

An Hachette UK company

A CIP catalogue record for this book is available
from the British Library

PB ISBN 978 1 78429 793 0

10 9 8 7 6 5 4 3 2 1

Typeset by Jouve (UK), Milton Keynes

Printed and bound in Great Britain by Clays Ltd, St Ives plc

To Connie
Yet another writer in the family

1

Sometimes, on a bad day, I think if it hadn't been for Tucker Hoose's broken tooth we could still be in Texas, living in God's own country. Other things have happened, of course. Life's never simple even when you have your health. One thing goes wrong and the whole house of cards can come tumbling down, and all for want of a horseshoe nail.

'Mixed metaphor,' says my darling friend Grice, who has no business peering over a person's shoulder when they're trying to tell a story.

Strictly speaking it wasn't Tucker's tooth that was the start of things going bad. The start of it was his legs. Legs were a noted weakness in the Hoose family so we might have seen that coming. They called it claudication of the arteries. Tucker's mother lived to a hundred and three but as long as I knew her she walked with a cane and then eventually she took to an invalid carriage. If Tucker wasn't available to push her, the help was required to do it or Grice, as a last resort. Not me, though. I did it once, when I first started visiting with them, trying to be a helpful guest an' all, but she said I had a hasty, unmannerly way of pushing, so that was that. The house would have had to be

1

burning down before she'd ever have consented to be pushed by me again.

By 1998 Tucker's legs were failing. His mother's old stair lift was still in place, kept as a sacred memorial to her, but it had seen better days. It'd start up, no problem, but then it'd stall and Tucker'd be left halfway up, halfway down, neither here nor there, cussing and talking of suing for his money back, which was wasted breath. The warranty on that contraption must have been older than the Declaration of Independence.

So we began to talk, me and Grice, in a roundabout way, of the advantages of single-level living. Tucker made a show of resisting but not for long. One of the realtor's brochures caught his eye and he took the bait.

It was a corner lot on a new build, about five miles from our place in Corinth. Eagle Colony, very select. Four beds, gas fireplaces, granite counter tops, hardwood floors and a great view of Lewisville Lake, which isn't a lake at all. It's a reservoir, very clean, very neat. As Grice said, if a proper lake was a coat it would be an old Afghan goatskin, infested with creatures and none too fragrant, whereas a reservoir would be more like a good wool overcoat from Neiman Marcus. Grice comes out with these fanciful thoughts from time to time. He's talked of writing poetry too but I believe it's an empty threat.

Moving from Corinth to Eagle Colony was some project. There was too much stuff for the new house, big old pieces that had been in the Hoose family since BC, so Tucker, being a fair and generous man, gave his relatives first refusal before he sent anything for auction. Nieces and nephews and second cousins three times removed, people I'd never heard of before. I don't believe Tucker even received Christmas cards from them but they came crawling out of the brushwood anyhow. It was like he'd wakened the dead, and one of the nephews, Sawyer Hoose III, developed an interest in more than the furniture. He wanted to know about our domestic arrangements.

Sawyer came blustering in from Lubbock, supposed to be appraising a mahogany bureau. First thing he wanted to know was did I have marital expectations of his uncle Tucker? Grice nearly choked on his lemonade.

I said, 'Sawyer, I think you know your uncle's not the marrying kind. We're all friends here. We're just three long shadows watching out for each other.'

Grice said, 'Less of the long shadows, if you don't mind, Peggy Dewey. I'm hardly out of my fifties.'

When Grice turned sixty it hit him very hard. He ever gets to seventy I fear he'll fall into a depression.

'Well,' said Sawyer, 'that's as maybe but I won't see my uncle Tucker preyed on. I'll be keeping an eye on things from now on, just so's you know.'

And that was the real start of our troubles.

'Not troubles,' says Grice. 'Changes.' He can't resist looking over my shoulder when I'm writing.

We were all packed ready for Eagle Colony, rugs rolled, cartons everywhere, when I received a call from Crystal.

She said, 'Mom, I think you should know Dad has twenty-five cases of canned meat in his basement. That's approximately three thousand servings of Good 'n' Hearty Beef Stew.'

Now, it had been been forty-three years since me and Vern

Dewey got divorced. I said, 'I guess there's some reason you think this is any of my business?'

'Dad's losing his grip,' she said. 'He's not been right since Martine passed away.'

Vern could never have stayed single for long. After we split he'd gone back up to Maine, started a bait farm, Vern's Vermiculture, and married a plus-size widow called Martine. She had a boy, Eugene, a few years older than our Crystal. One of Eugene's greatest pleasures in life also happened to be raising leather worms and night crawlers so you could say he was the perfect stepson for Vern.

'And,' said Crystal, 'the Missing Link just makes matters worse.'

She has often referred to her step-brother as the Missing Link. I used to think she was suggesting he had a screw loose, but Grice informed me it referred to a lower form of human life, the kind that drags its knuckles along the ground.

Crystal said, 'Eugene's convinced Dad the end is nigh. December thirty-first, all the computers'll crash, there'll be anarchy in Safeway. End of civilization. He's stockpiling food and ammo.'

A lot of people seemed worried about 1999 turning into 2000.

I said, 'Funny you should bring that up. Gayle's predicting the coming of the Antichrist that very same day.'

'Gayle?' said my darling daughter. 'Remind me again. Which one is Gayle?'

'Clairol Light Ash. Three husbands. TV healer.'

'Got it.'

Gayle, Lois, Audrey, Betty and me. Future Homemakers of America. When it came to domestic skills some of us hadn't been honor students but one thing did unite us. We were all 96th Bomber Wing wives, posted to Norfolk, England, in 1951. A lifetime ago. You needed friends when you were married to the military, when your menfolk were away, patrolling the skies at 510 miles per hour, aiming to be Jock of the Week, and you were trying to turn a Wherry house into a home. You stuck together. There was nothing else to do, nowhere much to go. They say it's different now. Tell me something that isn't different now.

Back then if you got along with a few other wives you made the most of it, but you never allowed yourself to get too close because you knew you'd soon be moving on. Uncle Sam might have different plans for you next year. Like towards the end of 1952, most of our boys got orders for Wichita, Kansas, to train on the B-47s. Not Audrey's husband, though. Lance Rudman got a promotion. I was going to say we left Audrey behind at the Norfolk base but, seeing her husband was the only one ever made captain, I guess it was Audrey who left us behind.

January 1953 the rest of us were reunited at USAF McConnell, Wichita. Another tour of duty, another cinderblock row. Betty was the first to arrive. She was five, maybe six months pregnant, swaying around like one of those stately Spanish galleons, but she had her drapes hung in no time. Gayle pitched up next. She and her darling Okey had been given quarters next door to me and Vern. I kind of looked out for her a bit. Seven years younger than me, she seemed no more than a kid. Now we're both seniors. Funny how that happens.

Lois's husband, Herb, was already on the base but Lois had gone to stay with his folks in Hoosick Falls, New York, for her confinement so she followed on later. 'Confinement's about right,' she said. 'Herb's mom believes in two weeks lying-in, to stop your insides prolapsing, plus maple syrup pancakes every meal, for iron loss. Then she had me churched. You ever heard of that?'

We were all so happy to be back in the US. People say if you're on base you're in the US no matter where in the world it happens to be, but it's never quite the same. Sure, you have the commissary and the PX but outside that perimeter fence you're in foreign parts.

Drampton in Norfolk, England, was the only overseas posting I went on with Vern. It was a windswept saltmarsh, no mistake, but I wouldn't have missed it for the world because that was where we all met Kath Pharaoh. And that was where we saw how those poor English folk lived. Post-war austerity, they called it. My days, what an eye-opener! Our meeting Kath, chumming around with her, that changed a lot of lives, Kath's included.

But to get back to Wichita, that was where I first made close acquaintance with tragedy. Air Force wives were always braced for it. You might not know the particulars of what friend husband got up to when he climbed into that cockpit but you sure as hell knew it wasn't a country walk. When Vern was flying an F-84 he used to call her the Groundhog, on account of her reluctance to get airborne.

I used to say, 'Vern, I don't want to hear about it.'

There were accidents. Incidents, we called them. It was considered a more delicate word. And Wichita was where there was An Incident and Gayle's Okey bought the farm. A B-47 was a skittish plane to land. If you deployed the drag chute, she was

6

liable to bounce. If she bounced she was liable to dip a wing, and if she dipped a wing then over she'd go, might have six thousand gallons of jet fuel in her.

When death came to your squadron you needed your friends, to keep you from falling to pieces and help you pack your bags. That roof over your head was only there as long as your man was alive and flying. An airman's widow was no one at all. They gave you three weeks to clear the post. Thank you and goodbye.

So, now I calculate it, I've known Gayle more than fifty years. There were two more husbands after Okey. I've seen her up, I've seen her down. Slinging hash in a diner, fronting her own TV church, on the wagon and off it again more times than I can count. That's Air Force friendships for you: you might not see one another for years but it's till death do you part.

2

When a person passes I can never bring myself to cross their name out of my address book. Don't get me wrong, there's plenty of names I have scratched out. People I lost touch with, some I grew to dislike, some I could hardly remember. But when a friend dies I just leave them there. Like Betty, who's been gone since 1981. In fact, not only did I not strike out her entry but when my old address book fell to pieces a few years back, I copied her name into the new one, which, as my daughter Crystal said, was pure insanity.

And the really crazy thing is, I wasn't even that fond of Betty. But out of them all I knew her the longest because we went back as far as high school. She was a Future Homemaker, I was captain of the softball team. We really didn't have a darned thing in common until she married Ed Gillis and I married Vern Dewey and we found ourselves on the same transport out to Ladd Field, Alaska, both Bomber Wing wives. Summer nights when the boys were standing the duty, we used to put the kids to bed, my Crystal and Betty's two girls, top to tail in one bed, and then we'd sit out together in the gloaming. Betty'd read out handy household tips from her magazine. I'd swat mosquitoes with the Sears catalogue.

I won't speak ill of the dead but I wasn't the only person to find Betty the tiniest bit irritating. She was one of those girls had everything taped, housekeeping-wise. It was Lois who christened her the Pie Crust Queen and Betty took it entirely as a compliment.

We all thought her dainty, homemaking ways were amusing before we knew any better. Later on we realized there was nothing very peachy about Betty's life. Her kids were ingrates — leastways the first two were. Ed Gillis was a bully. And then she went and got an adenocarcinoma. Times like that you find out who your real friends are. Betty was back in San Antonio, Texas, but Lois came from down New York to see her, and Kath came all the way from England. Not Audrey, though. She was still over in England and I wondered if she'd come. But Audrey and Betty never were all that. Maybe they were too much alike. Chin up, best foot forward, wash those windows.

Gayle would have visited Betty too, I'm sure, but at that particular time she and Lemarr were on the road, on a healing tour, laying on hands in Tennessee and Kentucky. Anyway, with a gift like Gayle's all she had to do was offer up a prayer. If God had wanted Betty to live Gayle would have been the one to fix it. I guess Betty's time had come. And Gayle did send a very nice video eulogy.

So poor Betty was still there in my little book when I sent out my cards, end of 1999, with my change of address. Gayle was in North Carolina, a widow again. She reckoned she's through with marrying.

'Thy will be done, Lord,' she said. 'But I've had three good husbands and it'd be greedy to ask for more.'

Audrey was in DC. I didn't hear a lot from her, but she always sent out very nice cards for the holidays, very tasteful, Baby Jesus or some olde English coaching inne, and Lois'd go out of her way to find a real garish one to send her back. She said, 'I just love to think of all that glitter mussing up Audrey's good rugs.'

Lois and Herb were back in White Plains, New York, by 1999. They'd tried retiring to Florida, but Lois said it was one long bad-hair day, and Herb didn't settle. He couldn't find a lumber yard worthy of the name. All plywood and laminates, he reckoned. Kath and Slick were in Eastchester, not far from Lois and Herb. Now there's something I never would have dreamed. When I think back to the first time we met Kath, that freezing Norfolk morning waiting to see the King's coffin go by on the Royal Train. February 1952. The world's least likely woman to end up in New York with a five-bed colonial and a husband who calls her 'Sweetchops'. Kath Pharaoh.

Kath flew over when Betty was near the end, wanted to see her one last time, and then she found she had a reason to stay on, to help Herb and Lois when their boy Kirk got sick. I guess Kath had realized before any of us that Kirk wasn't Herb's son. Lois fell pregnant when we were at USAF Drampton in Norfolk. She'd had a mad five minutes with Kath's brother, John Pharaoh, and Kirk was the outcome. Trouble was, John Pharaoh landed her with more than a baby. He had an illness in his blood. It killed him and it killed Kirk in the end. Huntington's chorea.

I'll never forget that day when it all came out. Sitting with Kath in the parking lot outside Lois and Herb's building, getting up the courage to go in and face certain facts. If it had been me I'd have left well alone. As far as we knew, Herb believed that boy was his child. Of course we underestimated Herb.

Anyway, Kath was determined to have it out, and when she saw Kirk for herself, saw he was going exactly the same way her brother had gone, she was heartbroken. I remember her saying, 'I should have put a stop to it, Peg. I knew what was a-going on. I should have said something.'

But she had nothing to blame herself for. Lois had been itching to get off the base and have a bit of fun. She was bored. Well, we were all bored. The difference was, the rest of us didn't go looking for trouble in trousers.

As soon as Kath had seen Kirk and confirmed her worst fears she started figuring how to stay on. She said, 'He's got the Huntington's. I feared as much. Now Herb and Copper-knob are going to need all the help they can get.'

Kath had called Lois 'Copper-knob' when she first knew her and the name stuck even though the colour has been out of a bottle for many years now.

I said, 'It's not your job to help. They'll have to get a nurse in.'

'They will,' she said. 'But that don't mean I can't help as well. Prior experience, see, Peg? It's the least I can do. And it won't be the first mess John Pharaoh left me to mop up.'

'Are there other children?'

'Not so far as I know. No, I just meant his general shenanigans.'

'My boy,' she took to calling Kirk, which I guess was near enough the truth. Strictly speaking, he was her nephew. But she worried that the US authorities wouldn't see it that way. She used to say, 'What if I can't prove Kirk's got Pharaoh blood? If your immigration people come after me they'll probably chuck me out. I could end up on a slow boat to China.'

But before that could happen Slick Bonney put a wedding band on her finger. I never saw that coming and I don't think Kath did either, but she soon got over the surprise and set out her terms. She said, 'I've told him I can't live in Texas. I've got to be up here, with Lois and Herb and my boy.'

And Slick agreed. He said he'd let one good woman get away, by which he meant poor Betty, who he'd courted in vain because she was still lawfully wedded to Ed Gillis even though she was in Texas and he was in Indiana, and he didn't intend losing another. He was willing to sell up and relocate. He was very ardent. When I asked Kath if she was going to accept him, she said, 'Well, he's a proper gent, and he's got a bob or two himself, so it's not my money he's after.'

'What money? You won another of those Premium Bonds?'

'No. I'm just saying, Slick's not a gold-digger. No cause to be.'

I said, 'So is that a yes to marrying him?'

She laughed. 'Wait till they hear about this at home,' she said. 'Wait till I write to May Gotobed.'

May was Kath's best friend, another spinster, another of those tough old birds they breed in the wilds of Norfolk.

'When May hears, that'll be all over Brakey before teatime. "Have you heard? Kath Pharaoh's took leave of her senses. She's marrying a Yank." One good thing, Peg, at my age at least they won't say it's a shotgun affair. They won't say I must be in the pudding club.'

Slick and Kath were married in the spring of '82, in San Antonio. It was one of the nicest weddings I ever organized and

12

definitely the smallest. Just me and Grice and Tucker, Lois and Herb's girl Sandie, who attended on behalf of the Moon family, and Slick's neighbours, Mr and Mrs Komisky. There was another neighbour on the guest list, a Florence Melon, but she declined. I think Miss Melon was a disappointed woman.

So that was how things stood towards the end of 1999. That's what had become of the old crowd. Herb and Lois and Kath and Slick got together as usual for Thanksgiving up in White Plains. Audrey was being cheerful about spending the holidays on her own. *Lance Three's vacationing in Thailand*, she wrote. She called him Lance Three because he was Lance T. Rudman III. *Mikey just remarried, did I tell you? They have their own lives. I'm just fine. I'll probably volunteer for something.*

Gayle was in Fayetteville, North Carolina, steeling herself for the coming of the Antichrist. And I was at Eagle Colony trying to remember which packing case the stemware was in while Grice and Tucker did something real important, like argue over tree ornaments.

3

I left it till 5 January, then called my darling daughter. I said, 'Well, the world didn't end in Texas. How're y'all doing in Maine?'

'Okay,' she said. 'No sign of the Antichrist in Waterville. No looting in Safeway. But Eugene says the Millennium bug wasn't the half of it. Him and Dad are still sitting on their stash of canned beef and they won't be breaking into it any time soon.'

I told her not to worry. That stuff probably lasts for ever.

She said, 'Then I guess I'll just think of it as part of my inheritance. It'll be something to look forward to. You finished unpacking?'

We hadn't, nowhere near. I'd get up, look at the pile of boxes and, more often than not, I'd go out for a drive instead. I seemed to have run out of steam.

She said, 'Grice not pulling his weight?'

It wasn't that. Grice'd willingly open a box and make a start but then he'd spend all day deciding where to place one vase.

I said, 'I'm not getting any younger.' I was seventy-five, to be precise.

Crystal said, 'Uh-oh. Here we go. I hope you're not going to start playing the old-lady card. Bad enough I've got Dad driving me nuts. He's getting real forgetful. Asking the same question over and over.'

As I pointed out, at least she was nearby to keep an eye on him. From her place to Belgrade Lakes couldn't have been more than twelve, fifteen miles.

She said, 'You call that an advantage?'

I said, 'Those cans of beef stew? Every time you go over there you could take a few away with you. Like drawing down on a pension ahead of time?'

'You mean enter the basement and breach a double-wrapped pallet? No, no, no. Eugene might take a shot at me. "Step away from the survival rations, Crystal. Hands in the air. Nice and slow." Anyhow, they're moving all the stuff to Eugene's bunker. Did I tell you about the bunker?'

'You mean like a bomb shelter?'

'Bomb shelter. Survival pod for the End Times. Play den for grown men. By the way, Marc's gone vegetarian so I don't have much call for beef stew, these days.'

That didn't surprise me. My son-in-law always was a bit different. The day they got married he was wearing leather bracelets.

Now, my daughter is a taxidermist by profession so I had to wonder how a vegetarian was living with that. I said, 'How's he coping with your workshop full of body parts? All those moose heads. Does he want you to go in for a different line of business?'

'He's got more sense than to ask. Besides, I don't get so many moose heads nowadays. I'm doing a lot more salmon.'

'Don't fish count? To a vegetarian?'

She said it depended.

I always hated to get off the phone with Crystal. We're neither of us sentimental types but Texas to Maine is a great distance between a mother and her only child.

'Could be worse,' she always joked. 'You could be in Arizona.'

That day she said, 'Mom, I didn't mean it, about you playing the old-lady card. I do think of you. You know I'd be there for you if you needed me. Just right now, Dad needs me more. Miss you. Love you.'

So then I had to go out, drive to Lake Park for a quiet cry and an Old Faithful Peanut Cluster.

By April we were just about straight. We had to be because Kath and Slick planned on visiting us for Easter. Slick was looking forward to fishing for crappie. I'm sure they have plenty of pan-fish up in New York but Slick was always drawn back to Texas.

Kath did a tour of inspection of our new house. 'Very nice,' she said. 'It's bigger than I expected, but I suppose you need it with the three of you. We should get a smaller place but Slick does like his space. We've got a three-car garage and I still have to park out front. You heard of this eBay business? He's on there all the time bidding for things. I never know what's going to turn up next. Pre-war tractors, that's the latest.

'May Gotobed's got a council bungalow now, did I tell you? She's got bad knees. Can't manage stairs like she used to do. That'd be caused by all the damp of the fens, I suppose, and the cold, and wearing no stockings. However did we manage? Well, we're paying for it now. I get a few twinges myself.'

'Foo' was how she pronounced it. A foo twinges. Kath has never lost her Norfolk way of speaking.

She said, 'You're still going on all right, though, Peg. You're still sprightly.'

Kath was my source of information on Lois and Herb. Lois was a lousy correspondent, and if I phoned, I hardly ever caught her at home.

Kath said, 'You know what she's like. She won't stay in. She goes to a seniors' centre. One day they have singing. Another day she does Step.'

'What's that?'

'Search me. She tried pottery but she never seemed to make anything. They do all sorts. Book club. Well, of course that doesn't interest Copper-knob. Tee Chai. That's supposed to stop you falling over and breaking your leg. The trouble with Lois is she doesn't stick at anything for long. She's like a flea at a fair. And, you know, the older she gets, the lairier she dresses. Purple plimsolls. Great dangling earrings.'

'No law against that, Kath.'

'But Herb's such a quiet soul. He sits there in his cardigan, doing his whittling. He has the patience of a saint, that man.'

Easter Sunday we went to the Pooch Parade in Robert E. Lee Park, me, Kath and Grice. Slick didn't hold with dogs wearing bonnets so he elected to go fishing instead. Tucker was feeling fatigued so he stayed home. They didn't have winners at the parade, lest any non-winning dogs might get their feelings hurt. The taking part was all.

Grice said, 'I don't know that I follow the psychology of that.

You dress a Doberman as a bumble bee you must be inflicting untold damage to his feelings anyhow. Seems to me the least you should do is award him a year's supply of beef-hide chews. For bearing his humiliation with dignity.'

We headed back to Eagle Colony around five. I'd made a baked ham and a potato salad, thinking we could sit outside to eat, but it had commenced to rain.

I remember Grice saying, 'Slick'll be home before us. He won't stay out fishing in this.'

Kath said, 'Don't you believe it. A spot of rain won't stop him.'

But Grice was right. Slick's rented SUV was on the drive when we pulled in. I remember every bit of what happened next. Kath was out of the car, Grice was reaching back inside for his roll of Lifesavers, I still had my belt fastened. The front door opened and Slick came out. He didn't look right, somehow.

'Kath,' he said.

'What?' said Kath. 'What's up? Have you scraped the paint-work on that car?'

Slick shot a look at Grice.

So then we were all out of the car, getting rained on, and Slick stood barring our way.

He said, 'It's Tucker, Kath. I found him when I got back. He was on the floor.'

Grice went running into the house. 'Tuck!' he was shouting. 'Tuck!'

Kath said, 'How long ago? Where's the ambulance?'

I said, 'You did call nine-one-one?'

'No, Peggy,' he said. 'I didn't. There's no point. He's gone.'

Kath said, 'What, are you a doctor now? Get on the phone. No, don't bother. I'll do it.'

She ran in after Grice.

Slick looked at me, kinda defeated. He said, 'He's definitely dead, Peg. And I didn't want y'all to pull in here and see an ambulance. I thought it was better this way.'

Slick had done right. Grice agreed and even Kath did, eventually, although she gave him a hard time for a while.

'Do you find a person out cold on the floor you call an ambulance,' she kept saying. 'Not for you to say if it's too late.' She grumbled on like a dog that wouldn't quiet down. 'You ever find me passed out like that,' she said, 'you get on that phone. You hear that, Peg? You're my witness. I'll have one of those paratroopers certifying me dead, thank you very much, not you, Slick Bonney.'

Grice managed a smile. He was very calm. He said, 'Put it that way, Kath, if there isn't a paramedic available I wouldn't mind getting the kiss of life from a paratrooper myself.'

They said Tucker had suffered a coronary thrombosis and that it had likely happened not long after we'd left him to go to the parade. It would have been sudden, they said. Like a thunderclap. He wouldn't have suffered. But as the evening wore on Grice started with the what-ifs. What if he hadn't gone out to that fool parade and left Tucker alone? What if something could have been done to save him? And if only he hadn't been short-tempered with him the day before, when Tucker left the milk out of the icebox.

All a bunch of nonsense. Tucker had had his three score years and ten and then some, and he and Grice hardly ever quarrelled. If one of them had a monkey mood on him he'd just go off to the other end of the house until it passed.

Grice took a pill to help him sleep. Kath and Slick were meant to be leaving next morning, heading to San Antonio for a few days. I said they should stick to their plans. Maybe come back for the burying. It wasn't like there was anything they could do.

Kath said, 'That's a good thing Grice has got you, Peg. I mean, they were like a proper married couple, him and Tucker. Funny, really.'

There was a time when it had seemed funny to me too. I don't recall such a thing existed in Converse where I grew up. I guess men like Tucker and Grice didn't have sleepovers in those days, or maybe they just moved away, somewhere folks wouldn't know their private business.

Kath said, 'We used to call them jessie boys. There was one in King's Lynn, in the fifties. He was considered a bit of an oddity. No interest in the football. Never went to the pub. People used to have a laugh about him. Well, the men did. I wonder what became of him. Tucker never seemed jessified to me, though. Grice is, a bit, isn't he? The way he talks. Some of the things he comes out with. But Tucker was just a gentleman, through and through. You're going to miss him, Peggy. And thank the Lord you'd moved before this happened. Just think, if you'd still been out at Corinth in that great barn of a place, all that land, all that big, heavy furniture. That'd have been too much for you. At least you're set up here nicely. You'll be all right, you and Grice.'

And so we thought. We purchased a burial plot at Garland Memorial, with second interment rights for Grice. It's very pleasant out there, very scenic, and although the grave was in a different section from Tucker's mother's, it wasn't far from it. As Grice said, 'Close enough. Eternity's a long time. You need to be careful who your neighbours are.'

He picked out the casket and the flowers and the hymns. 'Blessed Assurance', 'Amazing Grace'. The only thing he asked me to do was to make the calls to all those Hoose cousins and the Van Stoffels, who were Tucker's mother's kin, she having been Ladybird Van Stoffel before she married Tucker's pa. There were some people on the list called Bearpaw, from out of state, in Hot Springs, Arkansas.

I said, 'What kind of name is Bearpaw?'

Grice said, 'The kind Miss Lady never spoke about, but you may remember she did pride herself on her high cheekbones and her good, thick hair. I'm sure the Bearpaws won't come but we should let them know anyway.'

Well, they did come, more even than were listed in Tucker's address book, and very pleasant they were too. Kath still talks about them. 'The Red Indians,' she calls them. I've told her time and again we're not supposed to say that in the twenty-first century. They're Native Americans. But she just laughs.

'Like on *Rawhide*,' she said. 'After we got a telly that was John Pharaoh's favourite programme. What would he have made of it, I wonder, seeing a real Cherokee in a suit and a black tie?'

After the burying everyone came back to Eagle Colony for a finger-food buffet. We had it catered. The Van Stoffels and the Bearpaws were soon on their way, having travelled quite a distance, and so were most of the Hooses. Only Sawyer lingered on.

Kath whispered to me, 'Why's he hanging around like a bad smell?'

Slick said, 'I'll tell you why. He's got expectations. He's waiting to hear the will read.'

Grice said, 'Then he'll be disappointed. Tucker's attorney's got the will.' And as he said it his voice went very quiet. Then he walked away, out into the garden.

Kath said, 'He's held up very well today. He'll want to be on his own for a bit.'

But I know Grice. I can read his mind, practically. I followed him outside. I said, 'The will? Are you worried about it?'

When he turned to look at me he was pale as a church candle. He said, 'Peg, I think we might have a problem. Tuck never signed his will. Remember he was going to the lawyer's office a few weeks back and then he cracked that tooth? Had to cancel the lawyer and go to the dentist's office instead. He never rescheduled.'

I said, 'Then his previous will still stands. You'll be all right. He intended everything to go to you. Everybody knows that.'

'No, Peg,' he said. 'That's the trouble. There was no previous will.'

4

In the state of Texas, if you die without leaving a signed will your assets pass to your next relative, in accordance with the law of intestate succession. Real estate falls outside this law, if the property is held in joint tenancy, such as Tucker might have entered into with Grice. Except he hadn't. I guess his attorney never thought to suggest it. And that was why Sawyer Hoose III inherited the house at Eagle Colony and I, in my seventy-sixth year, ended up in a one-bed rental with Grice Terry, sleeping on a pull-out couch.

Sawyer pulled quite a punch for such a ponderous barrel of blubber. As we learned, he had had his lawyer lined up and ready to fight even before Tucker was in the ground.

I said, 'Tucker and Grice were together more than twenty-five years. You can't take the roof from over Grice's head.'

'Ma'am,' he said. 'I don't care if they were together fifty years. Hooses don't give family property away to faggots. Never have, never will.'

Sawyer didn't need Tucker's house. He owned a couple of grain-storage facilities. He had a home in Lubbock, four beds, three and a half baths and an acre of yard, and only him and his pug-faced wife living in it. Every October they partook of a luxury cruise, Galveston to Cozumel. I heard that from another Hoose. A decent, Christian type of Hoose, a kind of cousin, but too far removed to be in the inheritance line. Lavinia.

She said, 'Sawyer wouldn't give you his nail clippings. He's always been that way. When he was a boy he wouldn't share a damned thing. He'd sooner sit guarding his Dinky cars than allow anybody to join in and play a game with them. And now he's set on getting that house. Poor Tucker'll be turning in his grave.'

Sawyer was prepared to go to law to get what he believed was rightly his but, thanks to Tucker's cracked tooth and that cancelled appointment with the attorney, he didn't need to. It was handed to him on a platter.

Grice blamed himself. He went through a patch where he'd have blamed himself for anything. 'I should have reminded Tuck,' he kept saying. 'I should have made sure he went and signed that will. I don't know what I can do to put it right for you, Peggy.'

But I didn't expect him to put anything right for me. Since I'd moved in with them I'd paid my way but I hadn't sunk money into any property. I'd had ten good years with them, at Corinth and then at the new place. If I'd thought about it, I'd have known it couldn't last for ever. I've lived so many places. I guess I never lost the military frame of mind. No sense worrying, no sense wondering. When it's time to move on just pack your bags and pull the door shut behind you.

The one-bed was in Lake Highlands, just inside the Lyndon B. Johnson Freeway. It was a nice neighbourhood. Grice agreed with me, better to have a small place in a good location than more space and be afraid to venture outside. It was handy for the expressway into the city and there were buses too.

Grice said, 'I do not do buses.'

But he did. After all those years as Tucker's pampered darling, he learned to economize. 'Hard times,' he'd say. 'Throw some grits in the microwave, Peg.'

And to think gas was only a dollar fifty then. Those were the days. We're paying two twenty now.

Grice and I have always gotten along but a small apartment is no place for two people with time on their hands. We became like those little figures in a weather house. If he looked like staying home, I went out. If it got to eleven and I was still in my bathrobe, he'd go out. Then one day he was gone so long I began to worry about him. When he turned up he looked brighter than I'd seen him since Tucker passed.

'Good news,' he said. 'You are looking at a working man.'

I was astonished. Once you're past sixty nobody wants you.

He said, 'I won't lie. They were desperate. They'd have taken anyone.'

It was a temporary position. Well, come to think of it they're all temporary, some just more so than others. Grice had gotten a start at a call centre. He just had to sit in a cubicle and make calls on behalf of Governor George W. Bush, who was campaigning to become the next President of the United States.

Well, then I was even more astonished because Grice was as true a blue Democrat as I was a thorough Republican. He thought I was sadly misguided and I thought the same of him, and we have never allowed this fact to spoil our friendship.

He said, 'I told them I won't do any of that dirty-tricks stuff, not even against another Republican. But they said that was all finished since McCain dropped out. Mission accomplished, you might say. So now it's just a question of calling the faithful, reminding them their vote matters.'

I said, 'Wouldn't you feel happier campaigning for Gore? There have to be a few Democrats in Texas. How about Lloyd Doggett? Doesn't he have a call centre?'

He said, 'This may sound strange but I kinda feel I'm helping the Democrat cause. I mean, those phone calls are real annoying. So, you know, pester enough Republicans, maybe some of them'll get so mad they won't bother to vote.'

Grice often has a different way of looking at situations. He said, 'It's called "thinking outside the box". Or, in this particular case, "thinking outside the cubicle".'

To my mind the race for the White House was all over anyway. Even if Gore's team kept those Clintons bound and gagged, Gore was never going to win. Still, election night we stayed up with a bottle of Yellow Rose, and as the results came in it was a closer call than either of us had thought. There were some surprises too. George W. took New Hampshire, which caused Grice to throw a pillow at the TV screen.

I went to bed, and by the time I surfaced the next morning everything hung on the Florida result. George Bush was ahead by a whisker, Gore was about to concede and Grice had been out to buy muffins. Comfort eating. I had just stepped out of the shower when I heard him shout, 'Yes! Recount!'

If he'd realized how long that recount would be dragged out, I doubt he'd have thought it a cause for celebration. It was mid-December before we knew for certain who was going to be the next President and then I feared I might have to endure four years of cries of 'Foul play', but one thing about Grice Terry, he doesn't hold grudges for long. Not against George Bush. Not even against Sawyer Hoose III.

He said, 'I'm not wasting my life wishing bad luck on that pit viper. Someday he'll get what's coming to him.'

But so far as we know it didn't happen yet.

What a difference a year can make. In 1999 we'd made our last Thanksgiving at Corinth with a good cotton damask cloth on the table and Miss Lady's Villeroy & Boch dinnerware, which was only ever brought out for high days and holidays. Thanksgiving 2000 we sat at the card table and had Cornish hens and a pecan pie from Henk's deli.

Grice said, 'Next year, the soup kitchen.'

'You thinking of volunteering? I heard they get more volunteers than they can use. Same at Christmas. February, that's when they need people.'

'Not volunteering,' he said. 'I meant that's where we'll be dining.'

He was feeling low, missing Tucker. Tucker loved the holidays. Every year he'd pick out new Thanksgiving garlands for the doors, cornhusks or vine leaves or bittersweet. Middle of December, down they'd come and the Christmas wreaths'd be put up in their place.

I said, 'You need to buck up. Make a plan. Have a reason to get up in the morning.'

'I know,' he said. 'You too. What's your plan?'

'I'm thinking about it. You're younger than me. You go first.'

'I should look for another job. Home Depot are hiring, but I think you have to know about power tools. And then there's the uniform. That apron. I don't know if I could wear orange.'

We watched the Minnesota Vikings humiliate the Cowboys, 27 to 15, and as I recall it was Grice who fetched a second bottle from the kitchenette. As he recalls it I was the one who weakened first. Doesn't matter. The point is, when the telephone rang later that evening I wasn't quite myself.

Crystal said, 'Happy Thanksgiving.'

I said, 'You got a head cold? You sound congested.'

'No,' she said. 'I don't have a cold. I've been crying. Mom, I just can't do this any more.'

5

My daughter's no cry-baby. When me and Vern split up in '54 she never complained, though I know there were times she pined for her daddy. She didn't complain when I hauled her out of her dungarees and made her wear an organdie dress to Gayle's wedding. Gayle's second wedding, that was. And when Betty left Ed Gillis and needed a place to bunk down for a while, it was Crystal who offered to give up her bed. Weeks she slept on the couch.

Veterinary-nursing diploma, taxidermy school, she just went off and did it all by herself. True, she did go through a phase, smoking herbal cigarettes, marrying that Communist, running off to California, address unknown, but she came out the other side. Since she married Marc she hadn't given me a moment's worry, so when I heard her snuffling on the other end of the phone I couldn't think what was troubling her.

I said, 'Tell me.'

But she couldn't speak for sobbing so the conversation turned into a guessing game. It wasn't about Marc. She wasn't sick. Neither of her beloved dogs was sick. Then when she was all cried out we got to it.

'It's Dad,' she said. 'He's just getting worse and worse. What am I supposed to do? He's getting senile.'

I said, 'Isn't Eugene helping?'

She said, 'His idea of help isn't the same as mine. All he's interested in is his stupid bunker. He takes Dad up there, then he forgets about him. Dad wanders off and I have to go searching for him. Anyway, Eugene's not family. Not proper family. I'm all Dad's got.'

I said, 'So what are you saying? Do you need to put him in a facility? You need some money?'

Then she got really mad. She said, 'I'm not putting him in any facility. I just need help. And who else am I supposed to turn to? Not my fault you omitted to have any more kids.'

Fifty-three years old, and it was the first time she'd ever complained about being an only child.

I said, 'Do you want me to come up there? Spell you a while?'

It was a fool thing to offer, but after five or six glasses of Duck Pond I wasn't thinking too clearly.

'Yes,' she said. 'That's what I want.'

Vern was in Maine. I was in Texas. And he was my ex. I couldn't see him being happy having me around.

I said, 'Did you discuss this with your dad?'

'Mom,' she said. 'You can't have discussions with Dad. He's beyond that.'

That was when she said the Alzheimer's word.

I said, 'Has he seen a doctor? Or is this just your idea?'

'It's what the doctor thinks.'

'Did he get tests?'

'Yes.'

30

'Is it definite?'

She said it didn't really work like that. She said time would tell. 'Far as I'm concerned it doesn't matter what name they give it. He's not right, Mom, and he's worse now than he was six months ago.'

I said I'd sleep on it, think what I could do, call her in the morning. I said, 'I'm sorry. About everything.'

'Sure,' she said. 'How was your Thanksgiving?'

'Good. Quiet. You make turkey and all the fixings?'

'Yep, eighteen pounds of Heritage Bronze, which, considering Marc made himself a lentil roast and Dad only wanted dessert, is an awful lot of meat between me and the Missing Link.'

I thought Grice had fallen asleep in his chair but I was mistaken. He'd been listening. He said, 'Well, that wasn't your normal Happy Holidays conversation.'

'Vern has Alzheimer's.'

'Shit.'

'Right.'

Like I'd promised Crystal, I slept on it. Woke up Friday morning, I was still darned if I knew what I was expected to do.

I said, 'She could find someone to come in for a few hours a day, to help out. Senior Home Care.'

Grice said, 'She could.'

He was preparing a prairie oyster. He always has to brace himself to drink it down but he swears by it. I don't know why. Two Advil and a cup of coffee work just as well. 'Does Vern have family?'

'He had three sisters. All dead, I'm pretty sure. Anyhow, they

31

didn't get on and I couldn't blame them. Vern was his mother's blue-eyed boy. He could do no wrong and his sisters could do no right.'

'Meanwhile, Vern needs nursing and Crystal can't do it alone.'

'There might even be someone local be glad of the job, someone Vern knows.'

'Yes,' said Grice. 'There might.'

'They could live in, like the help Tucker's mom had.'

'Windolene. She was a treasure.'

'Gwendolene. She was like one of the family.'

You'd be lucky to get one like her. But you're giving them bed and board so I figured it didn't need to cost a pile of money, and if Marc and Crystal couldn't afford it I could send them a little each month. Plus Vern has his pension. That way he could stay put. And so could I.

I said, 'One thing, Crystal won't hear of putting him in a facility. No use even bringing it up to her again because she'll just get mad. But it's been forty-seven years, Grice. I don't see I have any obligations.'

'Peg,' he said. He was zipping up his Puffa. 'Sometimes the best person to argue with is yourself so I'll leave you to it. I'm going to Dillard's Black Friday sale. I thought I'd see what they're giving away in the pants' department.'

And off he went.

Vern Dewey. What went wrong between us? Nothing much. Nothing terrible. The thing about Vern was he was married to the service – United States Army Air Force it was called back then. When a guy spends your second date telling you about the lift-to-drag ratio of the B-29 you get the picture. But he looked so cute in his Ike jacket and his garrison cap. People used to say he looked like Robert Mitchum's kid brother. It was on account of the dint in his chin. And I couldn't get enough of him. He was training at the Randolph base, came into town to a Saturday hop at the Braun, and found himself a Texan sweetheart.

Would we have gotten hitched if I hadn't fallen pregnant with Crystal? Maybe. Far as I know he never looked at another girl after he met me, and I didn't look at another guy. His mom didn't approve of me but then Ma Dewey didn't believe there was a woman born worthy of her Vernon. Fact of the matter is, me and Vern got along great until it was time for him to leave the service. He went through a rough patch then. He was like a bear with a sore backside. It happens. All those years of the military telling him, 'Go here, go there.' He gets out into the normal world, he doesn't know what the hell he wants. As it turned out Vern got his mind made up for him. Pop Dewey electrocuted himself doing a little home electrics to save on the cost of buying a new twin-tub, so Vern had to go up to Maine for the burying. He stayed on for a while, to give his mom a hand. I took Crystal back to Texas, got a job stacking shelves at the Piggly Wiggly. There were no big fights. Just one broken beer bottle. We just kinda fizzled out, I guess. Stupid, really.

Grice was gone till evening.

'Well?' he said. 'You figured out what you have to do?'

I said, 'If I was taken sick I wouldn't expect Vern to come running.'

'True. But you'd certainly hope Crystal'd come.'

'No, I wouldn't. She has her own life.'

'Also, you have me. As back-up.'

'You gonna look after me when I get old?'

'You're already old.'

'You gonna care for me when I get sick?'

'If I'm spared.'

'I gave that man the best years of my life.'

'No, you didn't. You had the best years of your life after Vern.'

'You don't know.'

'Well, that's what you always said.'

'Maine, Grice. He's in Maine.'

'Yes.'

'He lives on a worm farm. With the Missing Link.'

'So you keep telling me.'

'Did you buy any pants?'

'No.'

'What's in the bag?'

'Fruit of the Loom thermals.'

'Thermals?'

'I heard it gets cold in Maine.'

He had a Rand McNally road map in the other bag. Spent the evening lying on his belly, studying the Interstates. He said, 'We could do it in five days. That'd be pushing it, though. If we're driving a truck we should allow at least a week.'

'A truck?'

'You wouldn't leave all your stuff here, and storage costs money.'

'Depends how long we'd be away.'

'No sense going all that way for a few weeks, Peg. If Crystal's right, about Alzheimer's, Vern's not going to get better. And the worse he gets the more she's going to need you. If we put our stuff in storage while we're gone, when are we ever going to see it again? It's just money down the drain.'

'Are you really willing to come with me?'

'Sure. Nothing else in the diary.' He took out a highlighter pen and commenced drawing on his new book of maps. 'First leg,' he said, 'Route 30 to Little Rock, Arkansas. Now, are you going to call your daughter and put her out of her misery or are you just gonna set there watching me?'

6

They say moving house is a highly stressful event and, now I calculate it, me and Grice moved three times in a year. Corinth to Eagle Colony, Eagle Colony to Lake Highlands, then from Texas all the way to Maine, and every time we moved I cared less and less about what we took with us. Every box I packed, I'd think, Why am I keeping this? Grice rented a ten-foot truck from U-Haul but we hardly needed it.

I said, 'There'll be room for us to sleep in there. That your intention? Save paying for motels?'

'Sleep in a truck?' he said. 'In Arkansas? Are you kidding? You ever watch *Deliverance*?'

'That was the Appalachians.'

'Same thing.'

The plan was simple: to head north-east and stop whenever we got tired. Crystal was worried. She said Grice should do the lion's share of the driving.

I said, 'Oh, yes? And what year did you hope we'd get there? Grice drives like an old woman.'

'Well, just be careful,' she said. 'Know your limits. Drive a day, take a day off. You'll be no help to me if you end up in a hospital bed.'

I wouldn't have minded making a couple of detours. I was in no great hurry to get to Maine. We could have visited with Gayle in Fayetteville and Audrey in DC but Grice wouldn't hear of it. He said Gayle was way off our route, and by the time we got to Washington we'd be within striking distance of Kath and Slick's place in Eastchester, New York. He was happy for us to rest a couple of days there, maybe see Herb and Lois too, then push on for one last day of driving to Belgrade Lakes.

He said, 'Roads run in both directions, Peg, and as far as I recall, this Audrey's never visited with you.'

'I don't think she drives any more. I don't think her eyes are so good.'

'There's planes. Isn't she the one got a millionaire son? Same thing with your friend Gayle. She's never visited. The money she's made I'll bet she could have flown here in her own Learjet.'

'It's just . . . we go back a long way and there's no telling when I'll ever get to see them again.'

'I know that,' he said, 'but this isn't a pleasure trip. You're on a mission, right? Help Crystal in her hour of need. As soon as possible.'

'But you're willing to stop over in New York.'

'Yes. Because Kath's been a good friend to you, the kind that visits, and Lois makes me laugh. And because we'll need a lay-over. Wash a few clothes, sweep the Subway crumbs outta the cab. Smoke the pipe of peace.'

'You think you and me are gonna fight?'

'Fight? Driving from Dallas to Maine? I'd say you can take it to the bank.'

Not true. We never really fight. We bicker is all.

Crystal had told Vern I was coming.

'What'd he say?'

'He just smiled.'

'What about Eugene? He okay with this?'

'Sure. It's all the same to him. He's busy weather-proofing his bunker.'

'That because we're coming? Is he taking refuge?'

'No, not unless you're members of the Illuminati. Did you know they're planning to take over the world?'

'That's like a horror movie, right? Aliens and stuff?'

'Not aliens. The Illuminati are people, apparently. They're going to control everything, any day now, and we'll all just be their slaves. See what I have to live with?'

'Are they Communists?'

'No. They're all mega-rich.'

'Eugene's a Republican, right?'

'Yes.'

'So maybe he'll feel easier in his mind if George Bush gets confirmed.'

'You'd think. But get this. He says the Bushes are all part of it. The Illuminati. They're in on it.'

I told Grice. 'Just so's you know what you're letting yourself in for.'

'The Bushes?' he said. 'What, even Barbara?'

'That's what Crystal told me.'

He said, 'Sounds to me like this Eugene has a hole in his screen door.'

We left Lake Highlands early on Christmas Day 2000. It was Grice's idea. He said there'd be no traffic to speak of and he was right. We stopped for breakfast at a Taco Bell.

He said, 'This feels pretty darned radical. Burritos on Christmas morning. Tuck'd have a fit.'

Tucker was always very particular about Christmas breakfast. Mimosas, eggnog French toast, black coffee. Actually, Tucker was particular about most things. What he'd have thought of the chicken fried steak we ate that night in a Dixie Diner I dread to think but Grice was treating it like some big adventure and I'll admit his cheerfulness was rubbing off on me.

TUCKER HOOSE'S FESTIVE FRENCH TOAST

20 December: tell the help to put aside a good white loaf to allow it to get stale.

24 December: have her cut it into good, thick slices.

Christmas morning: pour eggnog (store-bought is just dandy) into a soup dish. Dip the stale bread both sides and fry in sweet butter till golden. Don't let the flame get too high now or it'll be ruined.

We'd crossed the state line at Texarkana. Grice was driving.

He said, 'Here we go. Into the great unknown.'

I said, 'It's only Arkansas.'

'Maybe so,' he said, 'but it's still quite a step for Grice-kind.'

He hadn't travelled much, for a younger person. A couple of cruises, when Tucker was still alive. Venice, Italy. Grand Cayman. He's never lived in another country, like I have.

I could see the waitress trying to figure us out. Not husband and wife, not mother and son. Grice hasn't aged well. I'd say he looked older than his sixty-two years but when I first knew him he had such a boyish appearance. That was March 1970. I'd quit working at the Bridal Registry and set up on my own, Peggy Dewey Weddings. And business was so good I was hiring.

I must have seen a dozen girls; not one of them had an opinion about anything. It was like interviewing jelly doughnuts. Then Grice Terry walked through the door. Weddings were an unusual line of work for a boy but I knew right off he was the one to hire. I guessed the mothers would love him for his charm and the brides would love him for his original ideas.

Bubble-blowing was one of Grice's innovations. That was the Jenneau–Carson wedding. Each guest got a bubble pipe and a little tub of liquid soap. I remember Grice saying, 'I believe I've persuaded Miss Jenneau that doves are so last year. Plus there's always the soilage factor. A guest drops seventy-five bucks on a silk two-piece, she doesn't want dove shit landing on her shoulder.'

Of course, bubbles are commonplace now. Nobody realizes it was Grice Terry started it.

Thirty years we've been together, and getting personal information out of Grice is still like pulling teeth. Pretty much all I knew was he grew up in Amarillo. But he told me a bit more on that long drive.

He said, 'It wasn't the most accommodating place back then, Amarillo. Not for a boy like me. My daddy got me a start at the meat-packing plant and he didn't take it too kindly when I turned it down. He blamed my gramma. Said she'd girly-fied me, allowing me to read her ladies' magazines.'

'Did she?'

'Let me read her *Modern Homemaker*? Why not? Where was the harm? And there was no point her passing them along to my mother.'

'Your mom not a homemaker?'

'Home-wrecker, more like. Mom liked to play Doctors and Nurses with guys before they'd even been properly introduced.'

'Did your dad know?'

'Peg, the whole street knew. She might as well have hung a shingle out front. "Buy a fuck, get one free. Enquire within." Dad just didn't come home a whole lot. Truth is, I don't even know for sure he was my dad. He wasn't a bad man. He did his best. He just didn't want a fag for a son.'

'But you had your gramma.'

'Yes.'

'You never told me about her.'

'What's to tell? She was old. She loved me to the moon and back. She died. The usual gramma story.'

He'd drifted across to Dallas after his grandmother passed. He figured he'd be happier in a bigger city. I told him what Betty had said when she heard I was moving to Dallas from San Antonio: that she didn't know how I could bear to live in such a bloodstained place. Keep in mind it wasn't long after President Kennedy had been shot there and Betty had taken it very personally, as a Texan. I couldn't see why. That guy, Lee Harvey Oswald, he was from Louisiana. And some people think he didn't even do it. But the way Betty looked at it, every Texan shared the blame.

Grice worked in an upscale rug store when he first moved to Dallas. Then he saw my ad for a personal assistant and we've been together ever since. He stuck with me in 1975 when Peggy Dewey Weddings hit the rocks, no fault of mine. All it took was one misunderstanding and one alley-cat of a bride's mother. Lola Dekker. She thought I'd been messing around with her husband. Ha! Like I should be so desperate. Randy Dekker was all hat and no cattle. But Lola was on the phone spreading slander faster than a duck on a June bug, and I'm afraid too many people listened to her. All those happy customers we'd had didn't seem to count for a damned thing once Lola Dekker got started. I heard Randy left her a couple of years after that. I'm not a vindictive person, but I will say, what goes around very often comes around.

For two pins I'd have given up trying to run a business. If it hadn't been for Grice, Swell Parties would never have happened. I didn't have the heart to start over but he pushed me to do it, just like he'd pushed me to drive to Maine to help Crystal.

He said, 'Nudged, Peg, not pushed.'

We did a lot of talking on that trip. You think you know a person but when you have two thousand miles to cover you have time to fill in the gaps. For instance, I'd never known how he met Tucker.

'Sold him a rug,' he said. 'Remember the red and blue Persian used to be in Miss Lady's sitting room at Corinth?'

'No. I was never in Miss Lady's sitting room. I was never invited. So you already knew Tucker when you came to work for me?'

'I guess.'

'I didn't know that. Why did I think you met him just before we started Swell Parties?'

'Well, being acquainted with him and moving in with him were two different things. I suppose you could say we got off to a slow-burning start.'

'Did you have other friends? You never used to talk about anyone. Never told me what you did on weekends.'

'Weekends? When I worked for Peggy Dewey Weddings I didn't get weekends. But, heck, Peggy, I wasn't a monk if that's what you mean.'

'You and Tucker, were you waiting for Miss Lady to die?'

'That's a terrible suggestion.'

'I'm sorry. I just wondered.'

He laughed. He said, 'Well, Tuck and I knew she was liable to live long. It's what Hoose women do. I guess we just waited for her to get accustomed to my being around. And she did. In the end I think she quite liked me.'

'She didn't like you. She loved you.'

'There y'are, then. Patience was rewarded.'

'The money you put into Swell Parties? Was that Tucker's?'

'Don't remember. Probably. It's a long time ago.'

'He was a generous man.'

'He was.'

'You must miss him. I know I do.'

'Stop right there,' he said. 'It's Christmas Day. Strictly no blubbing.'

He beckoned the waitress. She had a length of tinsel garland in her hair. I suppose the management had required her to wear it, to add a festive touch. Grice enquired about the Christmas Surprise Dessert Special.

'Icebox pie.'

'Flavour?'

'Black bottom and peanut butter.'

'And what's the surprise?'

'That'd be telling.'

We ordered one to share.

He said, 'Taking bets now. Will the surprise be a red and green candy cane or a cake-top sparkler?'

It was a sparkler.

He said, 'It certainly added to the gaiety of my Christmas.'

The waitress asked if we were travelling to visit with family.

'Sure are,' said Grice. 'Any luck we'll be there by 2001.'

I believe the only other guests at the Econo Lodge that night were a working girl and her john and, boy, did she give him his money's worth. 'Oh my God, oh my God, oh my God.'

Grice said, 'I guess she's on automatic. Probably thinking about a pair of shoes she wants to get at Aldo's. You'd have to, wouldn't you, to stay sane? Working Christmas night, balling some sad-sack creep in a motel.'

We endured an hour of it, then everything fell quiet. Two a.m. she started up again.

'New client,' said Grice. 'That's it. I'm going to the office, get her moved.'

He was gone a long time. I began to think he'd run into trouble. Those girls don't work for themselves. They have men who mind them. I looked out a couple of times, quite expecting to see Grice lying in the car park, beaten to a pulp. She was still at it. Oh my God, oh my God. When he reappeared he had a fifth of Knob Creek in his hand.

'Nobody in the office, of course,' he said. 'That's probably him she's working on right now. Night manager's perks. So I thought at least this'd help us to sleep.'

'You went to buy bourbon?'

'On Christmas night? No, you chump. I knew it was in the truck. It was just a question of locating it.'

'How many boxes did you open?'

'Never mind. Fetch those paper cups from the bathroom. Tomorrow night we'll find somewhere a little more salubrious. With a fireplace. And no hookers.'

7

We crossed the Mississippi river at Memphis. It was the first time I'd ever seen it. Grice said he'd seen it in *Tom Sawyer* but that doesn't count. I saw it in *Showboat*. Everybody did. But that's not the same thing at all as seeing it for real. I wanted to stop and take a proper look but there was no viewing platform. If it had been me I'd have pulled up anyhow and looked over the side of the bridge, but Grice was at the wheel and he lives in fear of getting a ticket. Me, I'm too old to care about traffic citations.

We left the highway somewhere around Crossville and looked for a country inn. Grice had picked up a list at a welcome centre. 'This sounds nice,' he said. 'Breathtaking mountain views, rocking-chair porches, free swimming, free tennis.'

I said, 'Grice, it's December twenty-sixth. And neither of us plays tennis.'

'Also, wood fires and fine dining.'

I didn't care about fine dining. We'd spent the day counting road kill. A couple of skunk, one raccoon, about a thousand rabbits, one unidentified, could have been a possum, could have been a squirrel. So I wasn't too hungry for meat. A baked potato would have been fine with me. What I really wanted was a hot shower and a good night's sleep.

They asked did we have a reservation. The place was packed with families.

Grice groaned. He said, 'They're full. We're going to end up dining at Big Boy's Barbecue. I can feel it in my bones.'

But Tennessee folk seemed as eager to oblige as Texans because they cleared off the condiment table and fit us in.

I called Crystal after dinner. I said, 'I believe we're in the Crab Orchard Mountains.'

'Sounds nice,' she said. 'Where the heck are they?'

'Tennessee. We'll be into Virginia tomorrow. Grice reckons to stop somewhere round Harrisonburg, maybe even press on into Maryland, to Hagerstown.'

She said, 'Don't sweat it, Mom. Tell Grice. A day or two here or there makes no difference. I feel better just knowing you're coming. Enjoy the scenery.'

'How was Christmas?'

'Same as any other day.'

'You got a tree?'

'Yes.'

'What did Marc get you?'

'Pair of Wiss shears.'

'Romantic.'

'We don't do "romantic". And as skinning shears go they're the absolute best.'

★

If you're heading north you leave the Interstate 40 after Knoxville, join Route 81. The 40 continues east into North Carolina. We could easily have gone to see Gayle.

Grice said, 'I don't get it. Why would you put yourself to the trouble? You hardly ever mention her. Seems to me you can't have been that close.'

None of us girls was ever close to Gayle. Her menfolk, her husbands, were everything to her. The sun rose and set by them and she'd only turn to us when she had no choice. Like when Okey was killed.

Grice didn't know the particulars about Okey. He thought it had happened when we were at Norfolk, England, but it was after that, at Wichita. The boys were flying Stratojets, top speed of 600 m.p.h. and liable to roll, taking off or landing, if there was a crosswind. But wives didn't discuss things like that. Anything occurred, if there happened to be An Incident, we each had our own way of changing the subject. Betty'd bake, I'd go for a drive, Gayle'd drink.

That day, I reckon it was early summer, we'd gone to the Cowtown Drive-In, me, Lois and two Combat Crew wives, but they were still showing *The African Queen*, which we'd seen twice already, so we went shopping instead. Lois wanted to get a sweater like one she'd seen Marilyn Monroe wearing in *Moviegoer* magazine, except the tight-fitting look hadn't arrived yet in Wichita. She said, 'I guess I'll just hot-wash that abomination Herb's mom knitted for me.'

Funny, whenever there was a fatality you always remembered little things. What you were wearing. Where you were when you heard.

We were on our way home, nearly at the base, when we saw the smoke. Nobody said anything, but as we got closer we could smell fuel and burned rubber. We all wound up our windows, but we still didn't say anything. There was no sign of any crash trucks, they'd already gone down, and there was nobody out on the street. When there was An Incident officers' wives didn't run around like headless chickens. It wasn't done. You waited by the phone and, if you were that way inclined, you said a prayer.

Betty had heard it was a crew from 96th, but that was unconfirmed. She was as taut as a piano wire. She tried to get me to call the squadron office for information. She knew damn well I wouldn't. Wives did *not* call the squadron office. Lois got the next scrap of information. It was definitely a Stratojet that had crashed, no survivors. That meant three men. Pilot, co-pilot, navigator. I was pretty sure it couldn't be Vern. He wasn't meant to be flying that day but I went out front anyway, away from the telephone, so if it was him I wouldn't have to hear the actual words. Not yet, at any rate. Those were the crazy games you played inside your head.

I was standing there, trying to remember the last thing Vern had said to me that morning, when a vehicle pulled up and the chaplain got out. He had a woman with him, Red Cross, but it wasn't me they were looking for. It was Gayle. Her darling Okey, First Lieutenant Carl 'Okey' Jackson, had flown his last sortie.

It hit Vern hard. Okey had been like a kid brother to him. They used to shoot hoops and snicker at jokes only aviators could understand. He didn't say a lot about the accident and he kept himself together at the funeral, even when the bugler sounded 'Taps', but I know he cried, in bed, when he thought I was asleep. And sometimes I'd catch him gazing at Crystal. I guess he was thinking of what might have been. That was one blessing, I suppose, that Gayle had never managed to fall for a baby.

She quit the base and went back to Winston-Salem, got a job packing smokes. We kept in touch, every year a different address, c/o The Coffee Can, c/o The Stay a While, but I didn't expect I'd ever see her again. Christmas of 1960 she wrote me that she was getting married, to a marine called Ray, and she wanted all of us to be there, the old Wichita and Norfolk, England, gang, Kath included. I couldn't see Kath making the trip but she did. John Pharaoh had died and she'd spent some of the insurance money on a kind of lottery they have over there. Premium Bonds. She'd only had her numbers a few months and she won a big prize. 'Hundreds, Peg,' she said. 'I'm in the money.'

So when she heard Gayle was getting married there was no stopping her. She bought herself a roll-on corset and an airplane ticket to Fort Worth.

Ray Flagg was based at Camp Lejeune, which is where they had the marrying. My days! We went all the way from San Antonio, Texas, to Jacksonville, North Carolina, by Greyhound bus. Me, Kath and Betty, plus Crystal, and Betty's youngest girl, Carla.

That was some journey. Crystal was in a sulk because she wasn't allowed to wear dungarees to the wedding. Betty was in a high state of readiness for racial unrest and dirty bathrooms. And that was when, somewhere near Wilmington, Kath dropped the bombshell that John Pharaoh, who we'd all thought was her husband, wasn't any such thing. He was her brother.

We laugh about it now.

Kath said, 'That's just how it was in those days. We only had the one room. That's how we used to muddle along and we weren't the only ones. The Jexes, in Waplode, they must have been head to tail and stacked like firewood. But there wasn't any funny business between me and John. Strike a light, Peg, if I'd gone in for a husband I'd have picked somebody better than John Pharaoh. He smelt like an old eel trap. Even after he'd had his Sunday wash.'

Ray Flagg was an E-4 corporal and a Baptist teetotaller so Gayle was off the drink and as wrapped up in him as she'd ever been with Okey. We were so happy to see her moving on. They had three days honeymooning at Cape Hatteras, then Ray was deployed, an extended float out east somewhere. You marry a marine, you may not get to see much of him. As I recall, Gayle went on one accompanied tour. How many days and nights they had together I don't know, but March of 1965 Ray was listed MIA, at some place called Da Nang. It was October before he was confirmed dead, but Gayle had already quit the base.

'I knew, Peggy,' she said. 'I didn't need to wait for them to find his dog-tag. What are we doing out there anyway? Where the hell is Vietnam? Other side of the world. None of our business. What a stupid waste.'

December of '68 she called to tell me she had found Jesus and also another chance of love. She was marrying Lemarr Passy, a widower and pastor of his own Sidewalk Ministry and radio station. I went to that wedding too. In fact, I helped style it. Her colours were green, white and grape.

After that we lost touch for a while. When exactly Gayle discovered her gift for healing, I couldn't say. All I know is, by 1974 Lemarr and Gayle had their own TV show and they were touring the country, laying hands on the sick and the dying. When Betty told me they were appearing in San Antonio I wouldn't have missed it for the world. It was a thrilling thing to see somebody you know standing in the spotlight on a great big stage. It was the greatest pity Gayle and Lemarr left town straight after the show without saying hello but they had their reasons, I'm sure.

Lemarr passed over, him being an older man, and after that Gayle quit touring and doing all those public appearances. She still had the healing knack so she started doing the TV healing. People sent money, then put their hands on the TV screen to get healed. She had a whole bunch of testimonials.

'It's not really me,' she said to me one time. 'God heals, I just deliver.'

Grice didn't hold with it. He said if she was just God's delivery girl she shouldn't be cashing poor folks' cheques. He said if I wanted to go visit with her he wouldn't be going with me. Same thing with Audrey, but I wasn't so eager to see her anyhow. We go back a long way but Audrey didn't pal around quite the same as the others. The Officers' Wives Club was more her style. She knew Lance was colonel material.

Lois used to say, 'You noticed how Audrey's been keeping her distance lately? I reckon she don't care to hear the scraping of cheap flatware. I could like her a lot more if everything she did wasn't so damned perfect. Wouldn't you just love to hear her make a duck call with her armpit?'

Audrey even managed the neatest way of breeding: twin boys, Lance Three and Mikey. Two for the price of nine months. After that we'd get a family group every year on the Rudman Christmas card, all wearing their matching holiday sweaters and their matching holiday smiles. Those boys were so good-looking, and straight-A students, heading for great things in the military too, according to Audrey. Well, that didn't work out, as I learned when I flew out to Beale for Lance Junior's funeral. Those boys had failed to come up to the expected Rudman standards.

Of course, Audrey would never have admitted it. But I got the scoop from one of the 366th Squadron wives. She told me the Rudman boys had their own ideas about where they were going in life and it wasn't the Officer Training School at Maxwell. All they did was argue with Lance and Audrey. And that was how Lance had come to choke on a piece of steak and expire at the tragically young age of fifty-four. He had made colonel, though.

Audrey went a bit haywire after that, but she got back on track eventually. Bought herself a little apartment in Alexandria, Virginia. Lance Three was still single. Mikey did enough marrying for both of them. He seemed to upgrade to a new wife every few years.

No grandbabies yet. I keep so busy I don't know how I'd ever find the time to be a granny. Que sera, sera. That's what Audrey always wrote. I hadn't seen her in twenty-five years so that was how I pictured her, still striding out in penny loafers and a pea coat, shiny hair, pearl ear studs.

Grice said, 'You'd get a shock if you did see her. She probably wears extra-wide orthotics these days. Anyway, if you really want to reminisce with her, tell her to come up to visit with you in Maine. She knew Vern, right?'

'Not exactly. I wouldn't say she *knew* him. It wasn't like that. The husbands hung out and the wives hung out, but not together. Fourth of July we'd have a cook-out and a softball game. That was the only time we socialized and even then the guys'd congregate near the cold beers and talk barbecuing technique. A jock'd never converse with another jock's wife. Not unless he was looking for trouble. Anyway, I don't know if Vern's fit for visitors. He might be drooling and stuff.'

Grice said he didn't think Alzheimer's made you drool. He said, 'But Kath'll come up, I bet you. I don't think you'll keep her away.'

I wouldn't have wanted to keep her away. Some visitors are more trouble than they're worth but not Kath. Wherever she goes she just fits in, rolls her sleeves up if there's something she can do to help and, if not, she's good company anyway. The truth was, I didn't know quite what we were going to find when we got to Maine. I hoped Vern wasn't too bad. On the other hand I didn't want to go all that way and then discover I wasn't really required.

Grice said, 'You will be required. Crystal requires you. And you'll require me. Now, concentrate because this is the Dandridge interchange coming up. We want the I-eighty-one.'

I called Kath from Pulaski, told her we'd be a day later getting to Eastchester.

'You take your time, Peg,' she said. 'A day or two makes no difference to us. You all right? You sound a bit anxious.'

Me and Grice had had words. It wasn't my fault we'd missed

55

the exit. Not really. If he hadn't been going on so about slowing down, getting into the right lane and *not* going to North Carolina. He just got me flustered.

I said, 'I think Grice needs a break.'

'Course he does,' she said. 'That's a lot of driving, even for two people. Anyway, Virginia's nice. You have a tootle around, see a bit of the scenery.'

'Tootle' is one of Kath's English words.

'And while I think to ask you,' she said, 'do you both do normal dairy? Only Slick's gone semi-skimmed. Something he read on the computer about his arteries.'

Grice spent the day in bed, reading *Empire Falls*. I drove out to some lake, maybe it was a reservoir. The older I get, the more I like to sit by water. We were pals again by dinnertime.

'Tomorrow's the big one,' he said. 'I reckon we should make an early start and push on to Slick and Kath's. Once we get to Eastchester, we'll have broken the back of this trek. And I promise not to yell if you'll do likewise.'

We managed it without war breaking out. Route 81, you just keep your foot down, cross the Susquehanna at Harrisburg, at the Union Township interchange take the 78-E, cross the Delaware just after Allentown, then take the Phillipsburg–Newark Expressway. Virginia, Maryland, Pennsylvania, New Jersey. Grice was ticking off the states like a schoolboy.

He said, 'I'm collecting states so today's a bumper day. Never been to New Hampshire. I don't suppose I ever will. Never been to Idaho. Tucker did talk of taking a cruise to Alaska but I wouldn't want to do it without him.'

I said, 'You didn't miss much, unless you like glaciers. Tucker'd have been bored. There's nothing to buy up there. Leastways, there wasn't when I was there.'

But, as Grice pointed out, that was fifty years ago. They probably got malls and everything by now. One state I haven't been to is Hawaii. If there's one thing I envy Lois it's Herb's posting to Hickam Field. But considering the rest of the hand life dealt her, I won't begrudge her her year in Hawaii.

Audrey always said Lois has nobody to blame but herself, taking foolish risks for a five-minute thrill. Well, true, nobody forced her to go with John Pharaoh, but there's something in her, a wild thread, and I don't think she can help herself. She wasn't particularly good-looking. Gayle was prettier. Audrey had a look of Grace Kelly about her. But men always noticed Lois. Herb's a diamond but that didn't stop her getting restless. I don't know if John Pharaoh was the first time she strayed but, boy, did she pay for it.

When Kirk was born he seemed normal. A bit peevish maybe, but he did have terrible colic. It was only when he was in grade school things started to go bad. Behaviour problems, they said. When we all met up for Gayle's wedding the only way Lo could keep him under control was feeding him Dramamine. By the time he was twenty the writing was on the wall. Huntington's chorea is a one-way street and Lois knew what lay along it. She knew what had become of John Pharaoh.

She did say to me one time, 'I still get plenty of chances, you know.'

She was selling real estate by then.

'Empty apartments. Some lonely guy viewing. Wifey's back in Illinois so he's not getting any action. I don't, though, Peg. It's nice to be asked, but I've lost my appetite for it.'

8

We got to Kath's in the nick of time because the following morning we woke up to deep snow. The first thing I heard when I opened my eyes was the sound of Slick out on his snow plough.

Kath was watching him through the kitchen window. 'There's a happy man,' she said. 'He went all the way to Norwalk to get the best deal, July it must have been, or August. He's been dying for some real snow so he could try it out. You ready for pancakes?'

Kath Pharaoh making pancakes.

I said, 'You've really gone native.'

'No, I harn't,' she said. 'No offence, Peggy, America's a wonderful place but you can't get proper bacon here. It just shrivels away to nothing. When I go over to see May Gotobed, I shall bring some proper bacon back with me, the kind as looks like it came off of a pig.'

'I didn't know you were planning a trip.'

'Nothing definite. I keep threatening. I should go. May's not so chipper, these days. I should go and see her one last time.'

'I don't think they'll allow you to bring bacon back here.'

'That's what Slick says. Well, they'll have to catch me first. I shall hide it in my dirty drawers. A couple of packets of streaky. That's not going to be the ruination of American hog farmers, is it? Did you hear the phone go first thing?'

I'd heard nothing.

'Copper-knob. Seven o'clock she rang. They're snowed in and she's fit to be tied. They were going to drive down here today to see you.'

'I'm surprised Herb doesn't have a snow plough.'

'He shouldn't need one. That building they live in, the superintendent's supposed to clear the snow.'

Lois and Herb's super had gone AWOL so Lois had sent Herb out with a shovel but it was still snowing in White Plains. Didn't matter how fast he shovelled, the snow was gaining on him.

Kath said, 'She was in a right old mood. You know what she's like when she's cooped up. Whether they'll get here today I do not know. Any road, you and Grice won't be going anywhere in this weather. You'll stay here a few days and rest up. Lois can come another day.'

The smell of pancakes brought Grice out of his room, big smile on his face. 'Best night's sleep I've had since we left Eagle Colony,' he said. 'The apartment we've been renting, Peg made me sleep on a pull-out. She wouldn't even spell me, you know, maybe one night a week? She can be such a selfish creature.'

Kath said, 'And you're such a gentleman. I don't know why you didn't just creep in beside her. What is it they say? Fortune favours the brave.'

He looked out of the window. 'Now that's what I call real snow,' he said. 'I may just go break out my new Fruit of the Loom thermals. What time is the Moon landing scheduled?'

I said, 'It's cancelled. Lois phoned to say they're snowed in. If this keeps up we might not get to see them.'

'You'll see them, never fear,' said Kath. 'I can see Slick Bonney pondering whether to go up there with his Snow Bear and dig them out hisself. I can hear the cogs creaking and clanking between his ears. But Lois'll get here even if Herb has to drag her on a sled. She'd find a way to break out of Alcatraz, that one.'

And so it turned out. New Year's Day Herb and Lois made it over in time for lunch but we spoke before then on the telephone.

Lois said, 'A bit of news for you before you hear it on CNN. I'm going to be a great-grandmother, middle of June. Tell me I'm too young.'

'You're not. But I'm sure you look it.'

'Okay,' she said. 'I'll settle for that. Herb's happy as a flea in a dog pound, of course. All very well for him. He don't have to keep his roots retouched. Men have it so easy.'

'Who's expecting?'

'Pat's girlfriend. They're not married. I don't know if they intend to. Nobody bothers about that, these days, or they have the brats first, then wait till they're old enough to be flower girls before they have the wedding. She's a nice girl. Dental nurse. And they're up on Cape Cod so I won't be asked to babysit.'

'You've overtaken the rest of us. Crystal's gone through the change so I'll never be a granny now. Gayle won't, Kath won't. I suppose Audrey might.'

'Peg,' she said, 'you're forgetting about Betty's lot. Last I heard the Gillises were breeding faster than blackfly. If Betty was still alive she'd probably be a great-great-great by now.'

Somehow that was always on the cards for Betty. Babies and homemaking were all she ever cared about. But not Lois. Sandie was a whoops baby.

'Not that I don't love her,' Lo used to say. 'She just came a bit sooner than I'd planned.'

When we were posted to Drampton, Norfolk, England, 1951, little Sandie was still in a stroller so she was two or three years younger than my Crystal. Then Lois had her mad five minutes with John Pharaoh and along came Kirk, may he rest in peace. Kirk got a girl in trouble and she had a little boy, Cory. He was Lois and Herb's first grandbaby. That was before they knew about Kirk's disease. There's a test they can do now and Cory took it a couple of years ago. He got the all-clear, so that was a prayer answered. He moved out west, to California. I don't think Lois and Herb hear from him much.

Sandie married Gerry Carroll and for the longest time it seemed like they couldn't have a family. Sandie's womb was upside down or back to front or something. Then she had Patrick, her 'miracle baby', as she called him, so Lois and Herb got another grandson. And now Patrick was all grown-up and going to be a father. How time does fly.

New Year's Day the snow had cleared enough for Herb and Lois to drive over.

Slick said, 'You want to borrow a pair of ear mufflers, Grice? When Lois gets started they could use her as a fog horn on Long Island Sound.'

How long had it been? Way too long. Kirk's funeral was the last time I'd seen her. 1991. She'd shrunk a bit.

'Except for her voice,' says Grice, who will read over my shoulder.

She said she hadn't really shrunk. It was an optical illusion because she was wearing flats. 'Tits have sunk, though,' she said. 'Pardon my French. I woke up one morning and they'd gone. It happens. Tits go to your waist, waist goes to your hips, hips go to your ankles. I'd have it all lifted but Herb's got a padlock shackled to his billfold. You look great. Did you get work done?'

Herb just stood there grinning. He shook my hand. None of this modern cheek-kissing for Herb. 'Peggy,' he said, 'I'm glad to see you.'

His hair had gone, just a few strands left, but I could still see that young airman we knew at Drampton. Vern always rated him as an aviator. He used to say, 'Ed Gillis is all balls and no brains, Lance Rudman's all brains and no balls, but Herb's got it all. If I was in a tight corner, Herb'd be my man.'

Kath had made an English dish, Toad in the Hole. Sausages baked in a kind of batter. It was interesting. She's trained Slick to eat all kinds of foreign food. Plum Duff. Bubble and Squeak.

Slick said, 'Gotta show willing. We're a mixed marriage.'

Kath said, 'But then once a month he gets an order of barbecue ribs delivered from Texas. Federal Express. That's his treat.'

Lois said, 'Herb's treat is this chicken thing I make in the crockpot. He can smell it cooking all day. I get home all I got to do is microwave some Bob Evans mash and we're set.'

Herb made a point of sitting beside me when Kath served

coffee after lunch. He said, 'So you're going up to see Vern? Lo says he's not doing so good.'

'They say he's got Alzheimer's.'

He was quiet for a while. He said, 'I don't know that I believe in this Alzheimer's disease. Sometimes these doctors don't know what the problem is but they put a name on it anyhow.'

'Crystal seems convinced.'

'Yeah? Could be he just needs more company, Peggy. How long has he been on his own now?'

'Martine passed in 'ninety-five. So five years, nearly six. But he's not alone up there. Martine's son lives with him, and Crystal and Marc aren't far away.'

'Still, it's not the same as a wife. Like losing one of your shoes. Anything happened to Lois I reckon I'd go downhill fast.'

'You wouldn't. You've got Sandie and Cory and Patrick, and now you've got this great-grandbaby to look forward to.'

His face lit up. 'Oh, yes,' he said. 'We're real excited about that. Pat's in the service, you know. In the Air National Guard. He's based at Otis, training on the F-15s. How long do you reckon on being in Maine with Vern?'

'No idea. You see the truck outside? All my worldly goods – well, mine and Grice's. If they're right about Vern I guess we'll be up there for a good while.'

'I'll come up and see him.'

'He'd like that.'

What did I know? Vern might not even remember Herb.

'When the weather improves,' he said. 'You tell him when you see him. We'll drive up, take him out a bit, go fishing.'

'Lois won't be too thrilled about that.'

'She can go shopping. They got malls up there?'

'I don't know what they have. I'm heading into the unknown, Herb.'

I was helping Kath load the dishwasher. Lois came up behind, gave me a hug.

'How are you, girlfriend?' she said. 'It's been a long time since we talked.'

'Not Peggy's fault, I'm sure,' said Kath. 'You're never at home.'

'Secret of a long marriage, Kath. As you'll find out. You can't sit watching a man whittling for fifty years. You have to get out. Then when you come home you'll have something to talk about. You can talk about world events and he can talk about whittling.'

I suddenly remembered something from the Drampton days. Lois's birthday, 1952 it must have been. Herb was standing the night duty with Ed Gillis and Vern so we decided to make a birthday party for Lois in Betty's quarters. Popcorn and beer. I'd heard a whisper that Herb was preparing a surprise present for her. He was carving a giraffe. Then Vern came home from Beer Call one night and said Herb was carving a roebuck for Lois's birthday but it was a big secret so not to say anything.

I said, 'You sure it's a roebuck? I heard it was a giraffe.'

'That's what Herb said. Roebuck.'

Came Lois's birthday, we were all round at Betty's, kids squeezed in together in the bunks. Gayle was nipping on something stronger than Schlitz and so was Lois. We gave her some little presents, I don't recall what. There was damn-all to buy in King's Lynn.

Audrey said, 'What did Herb get you?'

'Thought you'd never ask,' said Lois. She fetched her pocket-book. 'See?' she said, 'There's more to Herb Moon than meets the eye. He surmised that I was probably bored with silk panties and French perfume. He surmised I'd appreciate something different. A hand-crafted item that would make me the envy of Soapsuds Row. Hold on now, girls. And I don't want to hear no jealous remarks.' She dug into her bag and brought out the little wooden creature. 'You want one of your own? Then drop a hint or two to your darling husband and maybe he'll commission Herb to make one for you. Form an orderly line now.'

Gayle said, 'But what's it meant to be?'

'Gayle,' said Lois, 'are you blind? Have you taken too much liquor? It's a dachshund-type animal.'

And Betty said, 'So it is. Though I will say, the head's not quite right. That head's more like a giraffe's. But still. A home-made gift is always appreciated.'

Lois and Kath were looking at me. Lois said, 'What are you smiling about?'

I said, 'It was just you talking about Herb's whittling. Do you remember the dachshund?'

'No,' she said.

'At Drampton? For your birthday? It started out as a giraffe?'

'Hellfire, Peg,' she said. 'You have some memory.'

'You still got it?'

'The dachshund giraffe? No idea. I doubt it. How many times have we moved? McGuire, Hickam Field, Kirtland, Drampton. Where did we go after Drampton?'

'McConnell. Wichita.'

'Wichita. You need to recall anything, Kath, apply to Peg Dewey. She's a walking almanac. Tell me about Vern.'

'Not much to tell. Crystal says it's Alzheimer's.'

'He seen a doctor?'

'I guess.'

'You're a saint, going up there. He's not your responsibility. How long have you been divorced?'

'I'm not going for Vern. I'm going for Crystal.'

'Still.'

Kath said, 'And if Peggy needs help, later on, we'll all take a turn, won't we?'

Lois looked at her. Then she said, 'Sure we will. Herb's got big plans for Vern. He thinks he just needs an interest in life. He'll probably try to start him whittling. Just one thing, Peg. Is he in diapers?'

Vern in diapers? It hadn't crossed my mind.

She said, 'Only I don't mind sitting with a person for an hour, you know, conversing and stuff, but I can't change diapers.'

I said, 'On an ex-husband, neither will I. If it ever comes to that it'll be a job for Eugene.'

'Who's Eugene?'

'Vern's stepson.'

'Right. You ever meet him?'

'Only at Crystal's wedding. Sounds like he's gone a bit weird. Apparently he thinks the Bushes are planning to take over the world.'

'You mean like *Day of the Triffids*?'

'No, not bushes. *The* Bushes. George H. George W.'

'So this Eugene's not playing with a full deck.'

'But harmless. Well, I hope he is. He's built a bunker, got it stockpiled with canned goods and batteries and bottled water. He's preparing for the End Times.'

'Wow, a bunker. Don't tell Herb. He'll want to drive up there tonight. Do you think you'll be allowed in it? Supposing you're up there when the End Times come? How many does it sleep?'

'No idea. I don't think I'd go into it even if he invited me. Bunkers are kinda underground, right? I wouldn't like that.'

'Me neither,' said Kath. 'I was in a shelter one time, 1942. We'd gone into Lynn, me and May Gotobed, looking for our John. He hadn't been seen all day and Mam was fretting about him. We looked for him in all the pubs, no sign of him, and we were just going to start for home when the sirens went, so we got shooed down into a shelter. It was horrible. It stunk to high Heaven. And you didn't know who you were sitting next to. May swore she caught fleas off somebody down there. But at least we didn't get pancaked. We had to look at it that way. That would have been the last straw, get killed searching for that little varmint. The Eagle got hit that night. That was a terrible thing. There were dozens killed in there. The only thing you can say is they probably died happy, in the boozer with a pint in their hand.'

Lois doesn't like us talking about John Pharaoh but, as Kath says, that's her problem. You make your bed, you lie in it.

I said, 'And where was John when you did find him?'

'At home, messing with his blessed eel traps. He was lucky he hadn't been in the Eagle. So you won't get me in any bunker. If the world's going to end I'll sit in my armchair with a bar of chocolate and wait for it to happen, thank you very much. Oh, and a glass of that Bailey's Irish Cream. That'll do me. I've had my innings.'

Lois said, 'I'm with you, Kath. A bubble bath and a bottle of Gentleman Jack and they can pull my plug. But what I don't understand is how the Bushes are supposed to bring about the End Times. I thought that was up to God.'

I said, 'I haven't got the full story. When you and Herb come up to visit with Vern you can quiz Eugene about it.'

'Can't wait,' she said. 'As long as the world don't end before we get there. Grice is a good sort, Peg, going up there with you. It's not like he's family or anything, is it?'

'He feels like family.'

'Anything happens to Herb, I reckon I'll find myself a nice fruit.'

Kath said, 'You mustn't call them that.'

Lois rolled her eyes. 'Not you too, Kath. Bad enough I have Sandie correcting me. You can't say "fags". Can't say "blacks". You gotta say "homosexuals". You gotta say "people of colour". You get that from Crystal, Peg?'

'She tries. I think she's decided I'm a hopeless case.'

' "Slope". That's one really sets Sandie off. She says, "Mom, either say 'Oriental' or say what they are, like Korean or Vietnamese." I say, "Sandie, I don't know what they are. They just do my nails. And they don't know I call them 'slopes' so what does it matter?" Gerry always winks at me when Sandie's telling me off. I don't think they call them "homosexuals" down the fire house. I don't think they call them "people of colour".'

'Is Gerry still working? I thought he'd be retired by now.'

'He could be. He's done enough years. But he loves it, Peg. You know what firefighters are like. Same as our boys used to be. Work's like family to them. Take that away, what are they gonna do?'

It was true. Vern was lost when he left the service. Didn't know what to do with himself. Same thing with Ed Gillis. He'd go a week without shaving and Beer Call got earlier and earlier in the day. Betty used to urge him to smarten up, and that was when he started throwing things, including his fists.

'Plus,' said Lois, 'may I remind you, my son-in-law plays the tuba. Gerry ever retires from the Fire Department he's liable to drive Sandie out of her mind.'

Kath said, 'Doesn't Sandie play too?'

'She used to. The cornet. That's how she met Gerry, in a marching band. But not any more. She's studying. Counselling.'

'What's that?'

'Darned if I know but she's always got her head in a book. And when you're talking to her she sits looking at you, so intent, listening to every word.'

'That's nice.'

'Is it? It spooks me. Okay, enough girl-talk. Let's go back in to the boys. I want to ask Grice if he minds being called a fruit.'

He didn't, of course.

LOIS MOON'S CHICKEN CORDON BLUE

Skinless chicken breasts – Herb'll eat three, one's enough for me.

Piece of Swiss cheese for each chicken breast.

10 oz can of mushroom soup.

Whack the chicken breasts flat with a hammer, or similar. Roll up with the cheese inside and secure with toothpicks. Stick them in the crockpot, pour the soup over, plus water if the soup isn't enough to cover the meat. Cook for 5 hours on the lowest setting.

For this idiot-proof dinner I almost forgive Herbert Moon for buying me a kitchen gadget for my birthday.

9

We left Eastchester for Maine first thing on 2 January. I hadn't slept well. Kath said we should stay another day but Grice wouldn't hear of it. He said we had a job to do up in Maine and it was time to get there and do it. Slick helped him put our bags in the truck.

Kath said, 'What's up? You getting cold feet about going?'

I was. If I'd been travelling alone I swear I'd have turned round and driven right back to Dallas. I was worried what I was going to find when we got to Vern's place.

I said, 'I should have asked more questions. I could have called Vern's doctor, found out the score.'

Kath said, 'That's Copper-knob got you worried, talking about diapers and suchlike. She had no business. She's got such a big mouth on her. Don't cross your bridges before you get to them, Peggy. Go up there and see what's what. If you can help, good. If you can't, you don't have to stay. Road runs both ways.'

'Crystal seemed desperate. If I don't help her, who else is there?'

'If it is the Alzheimer's, it won't be for ever, you know? There's

71

a person Slick knows from the tractor club, Mr Luckman. His wife had it and he cared for her, but then it got that he just couldn't do it any more. Nobody blamed him when he put her away. Well, a few did. But they should have walked a mile in his shoes before they started criticizing. I know what I'm talking about, Peg. I looked after John Pharaoh.'

'But you never put him away.'

'Know why? Because there wasn't a place to put him. There wasn't anywhere in those days. I was on my knees, I can tell you. And then just when I thought I'd have to do the pair of us in, turn the gas on and be done with it, he obliged me by dying, poor soul. I shouldn't complain about him. All said and done, he didn't have much of a life. I reckon King's Lynn was the furthest he ever went.'

'Did he know he got Lois pregnant?'

As soon as I'd asked it, I knew the answer. It came back to me, what I'd seen that hot afternoon, Lois's last day in Norfolk before she came back Stateside for her confinement.

Kath said, 'Course he knew. And he blummin' near killed her over it. You remember. If we hadn't walked in, you and me. Another five minutes and we'd have been too late. Copper-knob'd have been dead and so would that little baby.'

I'd given Kath a ride to the doctor's office that day. It wasn't really an office at all, just the back room of a pub where the doctor came once a week and everyone could hear your private business. When I dropped Kath home, there was broken china on the floor, like there'd been a fight, and we could hear their voices, John and Lois. They were in the outhouse where he kept his eel traps. Lois was backed against the wall and John was holding an eel spear to her belly. A 'glave', that was what they called it. Kath shouted at him to drop it, threatened him if he did any harm he'd end up in jail, and when he ignored her, she grabbed the glave from him.

She said, 'Copper-knob was a-crying. Well, she only had herself to blame, getting him roiled like that. Whatever was she doing, coming out there in her condition?'

'Saying goodbye, I suppose.'

'Saying goodbye! John must have been glad to see the back of her. He didn't care for her, Peg. He didn't care for any of them. He was just getting his oats.'

I said, 'You probably saved her life.'

'Yes,' she said. 'I probably did. What is it they say? No good deed goes unpunished. And she's still here, getting on my pippin.'

'I drove Lois back to the base.'

'You did. And after that I didn't see you for a good while. You stayed away. I didn't blame you. It must have shook you, seeing John like that. Any road, all I'm saying is, don't pay too much heed to Lois. She don't know anything about Vern's condition. She opens that great cakehole of hers without thinking.'

Grice was driving the first stretch. I was going to take a turn after Hartford.

Kath said, 'You mind how you go. Stop off for a night if you get fatigued. Where was that nice place we went, Slick? Near Boston?'

'Plum Island,' he said. 'But they're not on vacation, Sweetchops. They want to get to Maine now.'

'Well,' said Kath, 'taking two days instead of one wouldn't do any harm. You get tired, Peg, you take a break. And watch your speed. Every time you cross a blummin' state line it's a different speed limit.'

I said, 'Kath, remind me, who was it taught you to drive?'

She laughed.

We did stop, at a Howard Johnson somewhere in New Hampshire. Grice said, 'One last night where I'm guaranteed a hot shower. No telling what Vern's facilities are like. Could be a bucket on a rope, like in the army.'

'You were never in the army.'

'No. But I saw Mitzi Gaynor in *South Pacific*.'

Crystal said she'd rendezvous with us in Augusta, to guide us in. 'Park at the Marketplace Center,' she said. 'I'll meet you in Red Robin. It's a burger joint.'

I said, 'How will I know you?' I wasn't entirely joking. It had been quite a while.

She said, 'Bean boots, tan field jacket, and a Vern's Vermiculture camo hat with earflaps.'

Turned out she wasn't entirely joking either. I said, 'I hope you're not letting yourself go.'

'Mom,' she said, 'this is Kennebec County. I warned you not to pack a bunch of formal wear.'

Grice perked up when he heard where we were to meet her. He loves a mall but he'd been expecting to become a mail-order shopper once we were living in the country. Crystal gave him a withering look when he told her that.

She said, 'Welcome to Augusta, dear boy. State capital. We

have electric light and everything. See here, you can even get guacamole with your burger. How's that for sophistication?'

Crystal was born in 1947. That made her, what, fifty-four. Her hair was salt-and-pepper. Her skin wasn't bad, considering how she'd always gone out of her way to neglect it.

I said, 'You still using Nivea?'

'No,' she said. 'I changed to Otter Boot Wax. I like a multi-purpose product.'

Grice asked her about Eugene.

'He's okay. He's nuts, but he's outta the house mostly.'

'Does he know we're coming?'

'Yes. He's cool.'

'What happened to his wife?'

'She left, years ago. I don't know what happened. She used to help out in the yarn store and Gramma wasn't very nice to her. Maybe that was it.'

'Your gramma wasn't very nice to anybody, excepting your daddy. She thought the sun rose and set on him.'

'Right. Anyhow, Filomena walked and Eugene didn't seem too upset. You won't see any framed photos of her lying around. You ready to make a move?'

I said, 'There are a few things I should have asked you.'

'Right. You mean about diapers?'

'How did you know what I was going to say?'

'Kath Pharaoh called me yesterday. She said Lois has a mouth like the Lincoln Tunnel, no new information there, and she'd got you worried about bathroom issues. Relax. Dad doesn't need a diaper. He doesn't always remember where the bathroom is but he just requires directions. Anything else on your mind?'

'What are the sleeping arrangements?'

'Well, you don't have to sleep with Daddy, if that's what you mean.'

'We brought most of our stuff with us. My bed. My vanity. Grice's chairs. You got space for all that?'

'Of course. We've cleared Dad and Martine's old room for you. I didn't get time to redecorate so it's a bit seventies, but you'll have your eyes closed most of the time you're in there, in the dark, so low priority. Grice gets one of the guest houses. He can choose which one he'd like.'

'Guest houses? How many of those do you have?'

'Six. Martine used to do bed and breakfast, for fisher-folk. Maybe you'd like to revive the business. Not this time of year but in the spring? It'd give you an interest.'

'I think I'll leave that to you.'

'No, it has to be someone who's on the spot, to meet and greet and change the sheets and cook breakfast.'

That was when it really hit home, what I'd agreed to. It was gonna be just me and Grice and Vern and the Missing Link. My heart sank and Crystal read me.

She said, 'Mom, that's the whole point of your coming. Dad doesn't need both of us at the same time. You and Grice'll cover Monday through Friday. Weekends I'll come over and spell you.'

'But I don't know the house, I don't know the neighbourhood. What if something breaks down?'

'Eugene's pretty good at fixing things. And tomorrow when

you've unloaded your stuff he'll go with you to Waterville, drop off the rental truck. He can take you round the car lots too, if you want to get your own wheels, but you don't need to. You can use Dad's station wagon. He had a couple of close calls so he's not allowed to drive any more. We've hidden it, back of the worm shed.'

'You're not leaving us on our own tonight?'

'No. I'll stay. But tomorrow I really have to go home. I've got orders backed up since September. Last I heard I've got a husband too.'

We followed her to Vern's. There was a sprinkling of snow. Grice was very cheerful.

He said, 'I'd forgotten how much I love Crystal. She's like you but without the lipstick. It's going to be great seeing more of her. I'm feeling very positive about everything, Peggy.'

I said, 'All very well for you. You get to live in a guest house. If I need you in the night you won't even hear me.'

'We'll install a bell. Or an intercom. Eugene'll do it. You heard what Crystal said. Eugene can fix anything. Do you remember what he looks like?'

'The only time I ever saw him was Crystal's wedding and that's more than twenty years ago. He had a beer gut and a straggly moustache. I don't believe I ever heard him speak. Mind you, with his mom around he didn't get much chance. Martine could talk for the Union.'

We turned onto a dirt road.

Grice said, 'Oh, my gosh. Bear country. So, Peggy, how do we feel about fir trees?'

I said, 'They smell nice. Like Vicks Chest Rub. Why? They troubling you?'

'No,' he said. 'Not really. Just so long as they don't tap on my window at night.'

The house was called Marvern.

'Martine plus Vern, see?' Crystal explained.

It was quite a spread. The main house, a couple of barns, the bait store, the guest houses. I'd had no idea.

Crystal said, 'Did you think you were coming to a log cabin?'

I said, 'I didn't realize there was money in worms.'

'There isn't,' she said. 'But we also sell maggots and fly patterns. Just so's you know.'

The land had belonged to Martine's family and her first husband had built the house.

She said, 'Dad and Martine built the guest houses. Martine was full of ideas. And you see the deck? That wraps all the way round, and the dock's on the other side. We keep our runabout here and Marc's canoe. You like boats, Grice?'

He said, 'Only the kind that has dining options and a multi-screen cinema. You have any neighbours here?'

'Well, there's Cooper's. We just drove past the gate but it's so overgrown you probably didn't notice it. You can just see the house through the trees there, but it's all closed up. Cort's never here this time of year. Since his wife died he goes to his sister in Florida for the winter. Next nearest neighbours would be Merle and Corky's place. About three-quarters of a mile.'

We went in. A little terrier dog came yapping around our ankles.

'This is Banjo,' said Crystal. 'Head of vermin control. He'll try to sleep on your bed but he has terrible gas so don't let him.'

She went ahead of us, called out Eugene's name.

I heard her say, 'Daddy, you decent? We got company. Do you remember who I told you was coming?'

'Yes,' said Vern.

I was real nervous. I could hear my heart pounding.

He was sitting in an armchair by the window, looking out at the water. He hadn't changed so very much in twenty years. A bit heavier maybe, hair a little thinner.

Crystal said, 'Where's Eugene?'

'Out,' said Vern.

'See what I'm up against?' she said. 'He was supposed to sit with Dad till I got back.'

I said, 'Heya, Vern.'

'Heya,' he said, but his eyes never left Crystal. He said, 'I remember somebody was coming but I forgot the name.'

She said, 'It's Mom and her friend Grice.'

Then he did look at me. 'Hi, Mom,' he said.

Crystal said, 'When I say "Mom" I mean Peggy. My mom, not yours.'

'I know that,' said Vern. 'You okay, Mom? Everything okay at the store?'

I smile when I think of it now, that Vern could have mistaken me for his mother and that I could have cared enough to make a scene about it.

I said, 'Crystal, can we talk?'

We went into the kitchen to have our first disagreement. Crystal called it a discussion. I thought we should make sure right from the get-go that Vern understood who I was. Crystal said the word 'understood' didn't really apply. Sometimes he might call me Mom, sometimes he might call me Crystal. He might even call me Martine. Or Peggy, once he got accustomed to my being around. She said, 'Just go with the flow. If he thinks you're Gramma, so be it. It might even make things easier, might make him more amenable.'

I said, 'What do you mean, "more amenable"? What happens when he's not amenable? Does he get violent?'

'No,' she said. 'He doesn't. He just gets uncooperative. Sometimes. Not often.'

Grice kind of sided with Crystal. He said, 'Vern seemed happy enough to see you. So what does it matter who he thinks you are?'

I said, 'You didn't know Vern's mother.'

My days, what an old witch she was. She only ever referred to me as 'your wife'. Martine probably handled her better, having more maturity than me and a hundred-pound body-weight advantage over Ma Dewey.

Crystal was right, I'll own to that. I still had everything to learn about Vern's disease. I went back in and sat with him awhile. I told him I'd seen Herb Moon.

'Yeah?' he said. His eyes lit up. 'I haven't seen him lately. I've been flying night missions. Is he back? He say if he's on the roster for tomorrow?'

I said, 'Did you know Herb's grandson is an aviator now? Patrick. You remember Herb had a daughter? Sandie? Well, Sandie had a boy, Patrick, and he's at Otis, Massachusetts, now, Air National Guard.'

'That right?' he said. 'Otis. That where you seen Herb?'

'No, I saw him New Year's Day, in New York. And Lois. Remember Lois?'

'Sure. She's Herb's girl. Red hair.'

'That's right. Herb doesn't change much.'

'No,' said Vern. 'He wouldn't. Otis. He say if he's on the roster for tomorrow?'

And so it went. My first lesson in Alzheimer's talk.

Eugene didn't appear till dinnertime.

Crystal said, 'And where the hell were you? You were supposed to sit with Dad.'

He shrugged. He said, 'I did sit with him. Then he fell asleep. I ain't no babysitter.'

Eugene was thinner than I remembered but he still had that wispy moustache. There were no niceties, no 'How was your trip?' He'd known we were coming, we'd arrived, so what? He'd been checking the insulation on the worm bins.

'We bring them into the barn end of the fall,' he said, 'but you get a sudden drop in temperature you can still lose them even when they're indoors.'

Grice showed a polite interest in the best way to keep worm bins warm in winter. Pieces of an old stair rug, apparently.

I said, 'Grice used to sell rugs.'

I was just making conversation. Eugene looked at him. As Grice said, if I'd announced that he used to be a Diana Ross impersonator in Las Vegas Eugene couldn't have been more dumbstruck. Selling rugs! What kind of work was that for a man?

Eugene said, 'Been reinsulating the bins today, Vern. You want to come out tomorrow, see what I've done?'

'Might do,' said Vern. 'We're flying night missions this week. You happen to know if Herb Moon's on the roster?'

'Nope,' said Eugene.

Crystal said, 'You know I'm leaving in the morning, Eugene? Mom and Grice'll be taking over.'

'Yup,' he said. 'You told me already.'

It was Wednesday. She said she'd swing by Saturday, see how we were doing. Anything urgent, I could get her on her cell. Daytime, if Eugene was out of earshot and I needed help, I could let off a distress flare to get him home. She showed me where they were kept, quite a supply of them in the kitchen.

She said, 'Eugene won't use a cell phone. He thinks the government listens to people's calls.'

She said it real quiet but he heard her.

'I don't *think*. I know,' he said.

Crystal said, 'All I can say is, that's an awful lot of boring calls to listen to.'

'What I'm saying is, they have the capability. I'm not saying they're listening to you. I'm not even saying they're listening to me. But they could do, if they wanted.'

Eugene ate his dinner like he had somewhere to go in a hurry.

I said, 'You'd better tell me what you like to eat, seeing I'll be doing most of the cooking.'

'Anything,' he said. 'I ain't fussed.'

Then Grice had to go and say, 'Well, I guess we know you like beef stew. We heard about your bunker and all.'

Eugene put down his fork. He said, 'You heard nothing about anything.'

'Okay,' said Grice.

Vern was studying me.

Crystal said, 'Don't be so touchy. Mom and Grice aren't gonna tell anyone about your damned bunker. They just got here. They don't even know where it is.'

Eugene resumed shovelling in food. 'Good,' he said. 'Let's keep it that way. No sense in preparing for a situation if everybody around knows what you're doing. You lay yourself open to theft. Jim Coffin already got his generator stole. You lay yourself open to invasion. A situation arises, you'll get folk clamouring to be let in. You'll get looting. Because they know you got supplies and they don't.'

'Yes,' said Grice. 'I can see the sense in that. Absolutely. You could be overrun with people. If any kind of situation should ever occur.'

Eugene took the bait. 'Not a question of if,' he said. 'It's just a question of when.'

Grice said, 'Gosh. You really think so?'

'I know so.'

'And do you think it's imminent? A situation?'

'Could be,' said Eugene. He was quiet for a minute. He was weighing up Grice. Then he said, 'You ever considered how the government interferes in your affairs, where it don't have no business? You aware how they're brainwashing you and chipping away at your liberties? You familiar with the concept of the New World Order?'

Grice didn't miss a beat. He said, 'Not exactly, but I've heard of it and I've been intending to find out about it. Isn't it something to do with the Bushes?'

'Damned right it is,' said Eugene. 'Not so much George W.

LAURIE GRAHAM

He's just an idiot. But the others, going back, like his grand-daddy. Then there's Kissinger. And Rockefeller, of course. And that Queen.'

'The Queen of England?'

'No, the other one. Dutch. Queen Beatrix. The English one could be in on it too. I wouldn't be surprised. They're all related. Take it back far enough they're all cousins.' He got up from the table, left the room.

Vern said, 'Who's minding the yarn store?'

Ma Dewey used to have a yarn store in Skowhegan.

Crystal said, 'The yarn store was sold, Daddy. Remember?'

'Oh, yeah,' he said. 'It was sold.'

Eugene came back with a book in his hand, looked like it had been read many times. He dropped it in front of Grice. *Who Pulls the Strings?* 'You read this, my friend,' he said. 'This will open your eyes.'

Our first night at Marvern. Crystal showed me the ropes. Vern had a night light so he could find his way to the bathroom. She said, 'Sometimes he gets up, takes a leak, then forgets where he's going. Keep your door open. If you hear him wandering just take him by the elbow, guide him back to bed. You don't need to say a word.'

'How about we get one of those baby intercoms?'

'Tried that. He kept turning it off.'

The smell of Vern took me back. Vitalis hair tonic. My husband, long ago and far away. How would it have been if we'd gritted our teeth and stayed together? There'd have been no Peggy Dewey Weddings, no Swell Parties, no Grice. Even Crystal might have turned out different. But, then, I wouldn't want her any different.

I said, 'It doesn't seem right, does it? He used to put you to bed. You shouldn't be putting him to bed.'

'No,' she said, 'but that old wheel of life keeps turning. Nothing you can do to stop it. Thank God you didn't get old yet. I have to say, you're still looking pretty nifty. What are you taking?'

'Whatever I feel like. Wine, bourbon, Danish, ribs, potato chips.'

'I meant pills.'

'I'm not taking any. Should I be?'

'Not even statins?'

'What are statins?'

'Pills. Everybody's taking statins.'

'You only get pills if you go to see a doctor. Go to a doctor's office at my age, guaranteed he'll find a pile of things wrong with you. So I just stay away.'

'You're something.'

'Should I take that as a compliment?'

'Asked and answered. I don't know who'll look after me when I get old. Marc says he's going to outlive me, being a vegetarian. He thinks he'll make it to a hundred. He says I'm full of toxins because meat sits rotting in your guts for days. Makes you wonder how the human race ever got to be a going concern. But if Marc goes first, who'll look after me? I mean, right now we've got a schnauzer that can do high fives and a retriever that can open the icebox but I doubt we could train either of them to get us into our pyjamas.'

Vern settled, good as gold. He said he'd just get his head down for an hour before he went to the hangar.

'Copy,' said Crystal. 'And tomorrow morning I'm leaving early so you'll report to Mom here, okay? She'll be OIC.'

He smiled. Whenever he smiled I could really see the old Vern. 'Crystal!' he called after her. 'But if Mom's here who's minding the yarn store?'

The guest houses hadn't been used in a long time. They were cold and bleak but Grice was upbeat. He chose the one nearest the house and Crystal got the wood stove burning. I thanked him for being such a good sport.

He said, 'Everything's gonna be fine, darl. We'll unpack tomorrow. When I've hung a few pictures and put my Designers Guild pillows out you won't recognize the place. And after we drop off the truck there are a few things I'm gonna buy. An electric underblanket. A draught excluder. And some camouflage apparel.'

He was serious.

'Never more so,' he said. 'I reckon if I wear a camo shirt and I read this book he gave me, I'll have Eugene eating out of my hand.'

'But he's nuts.'

'All the more reason to make friends with him. You want to get on the wrong side of a man who owns an assault rifle?'

I said, 'I'm Texan. Doesn't trouble me if people keep guns.'

'I'm Texan too,' he said. 'But this is the first time I've lived up a dirt road with a man who thinks Barbara Bush is a threat to civilization. Anyhow, tomorrow I'm definitely shopping for a capsule camouflage wardrobe.'

10

There were days after we first got to Maine when I wondered what we were doing up there. Vern didn't seem too bad at all. Just forgetful, just stuck in the past a bit. Oftentimes he'd tag along with Eugene and Eugene's friend Jim Coffin. Jim was a bachelor, also the owner of a survival bunker. He had an Abe Lincoln beard. They seemed to like facial hair, those bunker enthusiasts. Grice thought they were probably preparing for the End Times, when you wouldn't be able to get Burma-Shave for love or money.

Eugene and Jim would take Vern with them, trapping or fishing or doing some top-secret bunker-fixing work, and apart from putting his boots on the wrong feet, Vern seemed just fine. But then Crystal would say, 'He's not fine, Mom. You're getting used to him is all.'

The evenings were the hardest. Around five o'clock he'd start to get an attitude. You could almost set your watch by it. Then he'd argue black was white. Sometimes he wasn't interested in dinner and all he'd take was a glass of milk and a few cookies. Sometimes he'd eat enough for three. And after he'd eaten he was liable to nod off. We'd try to keep him up a while, maybe watch a movie, but that wasn't always a success. He didn't like

Airplane!. He didn't understand it was meant to be funny. And, then, how many times can a person watch *Top Gun*?

Bedtime, there was no predicting how he'd be. He could go like a lamb or he could fight you every inch of the way, pyjama bottoms on front to back, throwing off the covers, cussing and kicking. And that was one thing Grice couldn't help me with. In the early days Vern wouldn't let Grice touch him, not even a gentle touch on the arm to guide him to the bathroom.

'The faggot's interfering with me,' he'd yell, but Grice'd laugh it off.

'In your dreams, Vern,' he'd say. 'In your secret dreams.'

We dropped into a kind of routine. We traded in Vern's old station wagon and bought a '97 Chevy four-wheel drive and once a week we'd take him into Waterville to get the all-day breakfast. Always Waterville, always the same diner, always the same breakfast. Red flannel hash, two eggs sunny side up, white toast, coffee. Crystal said not to try coaxing him to go some-place else or order something different. 'Stay on the same page,' she'd say. 'Keep it simple.'

Eventually Vern got that he'd call me Peggy, but not always. Sometimes he'd call me Mom and sometimes he'd just give me a sideways look, like he didn't know what the heck to call me. The weirdest thing was his attitude to Grice. As long as Grice didn't touch him they were the best of friends.

Grice said, 'Well, he did ask me a couple of times why I got put in here, like this is some kind of institution.'

'What did you say?'

'I told him I couldn't remember. He said, "Me either." So I guess he just thinks we're both in the same leaking boat.'

Weekends Crystal'd drive over. Occasionally Marc came with her and went out in his canoe. Not often, though. He seemed to travel a lot with his work. When they were first married and he was editing that cranberry magazine he never went anywhere. Crystal said globalization was changing everything.

I hardly knew my son-in-law. I could count the number of times I'd been in his company on the fingers of one hand. He seemed like an easy-going man. He needed to be, married to my daughter. And he never seemed to get any older. Crystal said it was since he'd hit fifty. He'd decided to get into better shape. He'd joined a gym, got his teeth fixed. Grice swore he had a sun-bed tan too but Crystal said it was natural weathering.

Our first winter, January through March, seemed to last about a century, then suddenly there were sweet violets in bloom and people started talking about visiting us. Kath was first. She wanted to know if Slick'd be able to fish if they came in early May. I put Eugene on.

'Smallmouth bass,' he said. 'Water'll still be cold but they'll be rising. He won't be disappointed. We got good fishing here. Tell him we recommend Sneaky Petes or Bass Dusters. We got everything he'll need.'

Kath asked me if I'd heard from Audrey. I hadn't.

'Well,' she said, 'I thought it was funny I hadn't had a Christmas card from her. Then I got a letter. One of her boys has been badly. Lance Three. It's something to do with his blood. Audrey thinks he must have picked it up on one of his holidays. So, any road, I phoned her and had a nice long natter. She was very sorry to hear about Vern.'

'Is Lance in hospital?'

'In and out. The Johns Hopkins. She'd just got him at home when I talked to her. She said he'd gone as thin as a rail and he'd had a bad go with his chest. Bronchitis. There's a lot of it about this time of year.'

'She could have taken him down to Florida for the winter, to his brother's.'

'That's what I thought but Audrey said they don't really get on. She said Mikey's always travelling, because of his businesses, and he's got this new wife they haven't met yet. She models swimsuits. How old would those boys be now?'

'Late forties. That must be Mikey's third wife, or fourth. He likes them young so he doesn't keep them long. But he's made a pile of money, Kath, so I hope he's helping with Lance's hospital bills.'

'Audrey didn't say. But you know what she's like. Always cheerful, always busy doing something. Computers, that's her latest thing. She's been going to a class, learning how to work computers. She said, "You should do it, Kath. If we don't do it we'll get left behind." I told her I got left behind a long time ago. I leave all that computer business to Slick. The only thing ever seems to come out of ours is bad news and adverts for vintage tractors he's tempted to buy.'

It was April. First time I'd gone out without my down coat. I was just setting off for Waterville when a car pulled out from a side opening, nearly slammed right into me. The driver stopped, got out and walked over. 'Apologies,' he said. 'My fault. Middle of the morning we don't get a lot of traffic along here.'

I said, 'I know. I live here.'

He was a tall man. He stooped down to take a closer look at me. 'That so?' he said. 'Where are you at?'

'Marvern.'

'Then we're neighbours.' He pulled off his beanie. 'Cortland Cooper. Call me Cort. I've been away. Can't hack Maine winters any more. So did Vern and Eugene sell up?'

'No. I'm Vern's ex. I've come to help look after him.'

'Is he sick?'

'Alzheimer's.'

'I didn't know that. I'm very sorry to hear it. He has a daughter, right?'

'Crystal. I'm her mom.'

'Crystal. Okay. Drive safe now. Watch out for careless neighbours.' He started to walk away. Then he came back. 'Did you tell me your name?'

'Peggy. Dewey.'

'Peggy. I'm sorry I nearly ran you off the road, Peggy Dewey. It won't happen again.'

He had a nice lop-sided smile and a kind of saddle-leather smell about him. Crystal said it was the little cigars he smoked. 'When the wind's in the right direction, you know when Cort's home. You can smell his cigarillos. His wife trained him to smoke outdoors. I don't know why he keeps that place on. He's hardly ever here.'

'He didn't know about your daddy.'

'Why would he? He's not the type to visit with neighbours. He keeps to himself. I think he used to teach college, Colby or somewhere. The house is full of books.'

'You've been inside?'

'After his wife's funeral. It was a real mess in there.'

She was right about Cort Cooper keeping to himself. I smelt his smokes once in a while and I saw him in Waterville one time, going into a liquor store, but that was all. He might as well not have been there.

Kath and Slick drove up to Maine the first week of May. She said they wouldn't come for Easter in case it brought back bad memories for Grice.

'Slick still talks about it,' she said. 'Coming back to the house and finding poor Tucker. How's Grice going on up north?'

'Better than I'd ever have thought. He even tried his hand at ice-fishing. And he's taken a couple of trips, on weekends when Crystal's been here to help me. He's been to Québec and Montréal. But he seems happy here and Vern doesn't mind him.'

'What about the other one?'

'Eugene? Yeah, they're getting along pretty good. Grice has even been allowed into the bunker. Got a guided tour. Of course, he strings Eugene along. He pretends to believe all that crazy talk about the end of the world.'

I wondered how Vern'd be when we had company. He'd known Kath by sight when we were at Drampton, but he'd never met Slick. Turned out it was Kath he took exception to. He was okay when they first arrived. Next morning he accused her of wearing one of Martine's blouses.

'Is it?' she said. 'Well, I must have mistook it for one of mine. I'll go and change it directly.'

'You'd better,' said Vern. 'Before Martine gets back.'

Slick, being a patient man but not a great conversationalist, was perfect company for Vern. Sometimes they'd pretend to play checkers, sometimes Slick'd talk about tractors and Vern'd listen, sometimes they'd just sit. It was tractor talk that caused a ruckus between Slick and Eugene. Slick said something about the tractor factories getting turned over to make tanks and turbines and aircraft parts after Pearl Harbor, and Eugene happened to overhear.

'Not *after* Pearl Harbor,' said Eugene. 'Before Pearl Harbor. Which Roosevelt knew was on the cards. And allowed to happen.'

Slick said, 'What are you saying, my friend?'

'That Pearl Harbor wasn't no surprise. They knowed it was coming. It was all a charade to get us into the war. Means to an end. Ask anybody who's looked into it.'

Slick got quite flushed. He said, 'That's treasonous talk.'

'You call it what you like,' said Eugene. 'I call it the truth and I'm not the only one. That war was none of our business but Roosevelt was determined to get us into it. Course, he wasn't his own man. His wife was a Commie. She was the one pulling his strings.'

Slick left the room. He's not a man to get angry but he looked fit to blow. I guessed that'd be the end of their bass-fishing days. I was so mad at Eugene.

I said, 'That man's a war vet. It ever occur to you to show a bit of respect? You meet an older man, doesn't it occur to you he might know more about the war than you do? You were hardly even born.'

Slick never talked about his war but I do know he was at Utah Beach on D-Day.

Kath said, 'Peggy's right. My husband did his duty. And so did his brother. He was in a Jap camp, took prisoner on Java. He was like a skeleton when they got him home. Slick reckons he was never right after that.'

Eugene slurped his coffee. 'Nothing disrespectful about speaking the truth,' he said. 'And as far as I remember this is still my mom's house so I'll speak as I please. Point of information. He's not the only one had a war. I'm a vet too. Anybody remember Vietnam?'

After that quarrel Slick went away for a couple of days, left Kath with me. He said he was going to Albany to see about engine parts. I felt terrible, like Eugene had ruined their visit, but Kath said, 'Slick's all right. He's not one for grievances. You're the one I'm worried about, Peg. If it's right what Eugene said, that this was his mam's house, does that mean he owns it now? I'd have thought it was Vern's.'

I didn't know. I should have.

She said, 'Well, you'd better ask your Crystal. Because if this house doesn't belong to Vern where does that leave you? Fellow-me-lad could turf you out any time.'

'He wouldn't, though, because then who'd look after Vern?'

'He'd put him in a home.'

'Crystal wouldn't allow it.'

'So you say. But, any road, Vern won't live for ever. Then what will you do?'

'When Vern dies, me and Grice'll leave. You think I want to stay up here the rest of my days?'

'Crystal's up here. I'd have thought you'd want to be near her. You're not getting any younger, Peg. You reckon you'll go back to Texas?'

Fact was, I didn't know. I couldn't think further than the end of the week. I said, 'I've worked all my life, Kath. Run two good businesses, and here I am, no security, living on a bait farm with my ex, liable to be put out on the street by a nutcase who sees government plots everywhere he looks. Where'd I go wrong? End of the year I'm going to be seventy-seven, Kath.'

'I know,' she said. 'Me too. But never fear, you can always come and live with me and Slick. And so can that jessie boy. It'd be handy to have a younger man around. Somebody to change the light bulbs. Clambering up step-ladders – I'm frit of falling. Get to our age, do you bust your hip you're finished.'

Slick came back from Albany, very happy with his purchases, and his quarrel with Eugene was forgotten. It was their last day with us and I was dreading their leaving. I was feeling low. Then Crystal called, all excited. 'Quick!' she said. 'Turn on *Jenny Jones*. You'll never believe who's on the show today.'

I said, 'You're watching TV? I thought you were working.'

'I am working,' she said. 'I'm mounting a seven-pound bass. The dogs like to watch this show. Now get off the phone. They'll be coming out of the commercial break any minute. Deana Gillis is back in show business.'

My days! Three generations of Betty's family. Her daughter Deana, her granddaughter Delta, and her great-grandbaby Destiny Rae. It wasn't the first time the Gillis family had appeared on television. Deana and Delta had been on *Ricki Lake*, on a show about when a daughter steals her mother's sweetheart.

Grice has advised me to lay out the Gillis family tree in full before I go any further. 'All those begats,' he said. 'A person can easily lose the thread.'

Betty was married to Ed Gillis and they had three girls, Deana, Sherry and then Carla, who was a bit of an afterthought and the best of the bunch by a mile. She was the only one I kept in touch with after Betty passed. Last I heard of Sherry she was in New Mexico eating magic mushrooms, losing touch with reality.

Deana grew up real fast. Up and out. She'd had three kids by the time she was twenty-one and she never seemed to shed her baby weight. Also, as Grice says, that was where it got confusing because Deana's brats all had names began with D. Delta, Dawn, Danni, Dixie. Then Delta continued the tradition because she named her first Destiny Rae.

Who Destiny Rae's father was I don't recall but I do know that at some point Delta took up with her mom's live-in, Bulldog, so maybe it was him. So then Deana kicked Bulldog to the kerb and found herself a new beau, TeeJay, and gosh, darn it if he didn't run off with Dixie. So lightning can strike the same place twice although, as Crystal says, 'In the case of the Gillis family, not always fatally, unfortunately.' My daughter can be very judgemental.

We tuned in to *Jenny Jones* just in time to see Destiny Rae get a slap from Delta. The audience was howling at them, calling them names. Destiny Rae took a swing at Delta. Then another girl joined in. Turned out she was Dakota Lee, Destiny Rae's kid sister.

Kath said, 'I thought Crystal said Deana was on. I can't see her.'

She'd no sooner said it than Deana came into view and joined in the fight. It was like tag wrestling.

The story was that Destiny Rae had had a fling with Delta's

ex, a guy called Skeeter, and gotten herself pregnant. While Destiny Rae was at the hospital giving birth, young Dakota Lee had stepped into her shoes, so to say, and been a comfort and consolation to Skeeter until Gramma Deana found out what was going on and reported him for having sex with a thirteen-year-old.

So Deana blamed Delta. She said the apple hadn't fallen far from the tree. Delta blamed Destiny Rae, and Destiny Rae blamed Dakota Lee, and they all cursed out Skeeter but he couldn't appear on the show. He was in the Big House doing time for aggravated assault. Grice said I should draw a diagram.

We did laugh but I felt sad too.

Kath said, 'That's all got up by the telly people, of course. They egg them on. All that fighting and swearing. It's done to keep the audience happy. But I'm glad Betty didn't live to see it. She was always so proper.'

She was. Betty never cursed, never raised her voice.

Kath said, 'I shall never forget the first day I saw all of you, waiting to watch the old King go by in his coffin. Remember, Peg? That was a freezing cold morning. Everybody'd got their mufflers on and their tam o' shanters but not Betty. She was wearing a little black hat and lacy gloves. She must have been frozz, but she did look nice. Very respectful. She'd hang her head in shame if she could see this shower.'

Grice said, 'What went so horribly wrong?'

It was a good question. I don't blame Betty. I don't even blame Ed. I didn't much like him and he let himself go after he quit the service, but he was a straight-shooter and I'm sure he loved his girls, like any father would. Carla has turned out aces. Got her nursing certificate, married a nice, steady type. One out of three isn't bad. Two out of three, even. Sherry went what they call New Age, but there's no harm in that. Deana's been the problem. Crystal agrees with me.

She called back when the show was finished.

'Well?' she said. 'Everybody who thinks Deana's tribe oughta get their tubes compulsorily tied, raise your right hand.'

The longer I live the more I think raising kids is a crapshoot. There's just no telling. Carla grew up under the same roof as Deana. How do you account for that? Crystal's theory is that the more you neglect a child the better they'll turn out – not that she has any personal experience. For sure Carla didn't get attention danced on her the way Deana did. By the time Carla came along things were starting to go bad between Betty and Ed. Betty kept the lid on it for a long time, making excuses for him. She was a long-suffering soul, no mistake. Carla grew up seeing all that. You could say it was Lee Harvey Oswald who finished it. Ed Gillis threw one of his hissy fits, jealous because Betty was griev-ing so much over President Kennedy. That was when she left him. We none of us thought she had it in her.

Crystal said, 'Okay, so now you know my shameful secret. I allow my dogs to watch train-wreck TV. Do you think Carla Gillis will have seen the show? You got her address? I recorded most of it. I could send it to her.'

I said, 'Deana will have told her. If they're still speaking.'

'Yeah, you're right,' she said. 'Deana'll probably have sent out announcement cards, like for a baby shower. Save the Date for the next televised Gillis brawl. And if she didn't, so much the better for Carla. Ignorance is bliss, so they say. How's Daddy?'

*

Truth was, there were no two days the same with Vern. Some mornings he'd get up, all smiles, and wash and dress himself, after a fashion. Other mornings he'd wake up in a monkey mood, and if I tried to help him with his shoes he'd fly into a rage. The only good thing was, his bad moods soon passed. Five minutes and it'd all be forgotten. Everything got forgotten. If you didn't watch him he'd eat three breakfasts. That mystified me. I'd have thought his stomach would have told him to stop eating but, the way Crystal explained it, the message just didn't get through.

She said, 'You ever tried calling Comcast? Or AT&T? You're on hold, on hold, on hold. Then the line drops. Get the picture? That's what happens with Dad's brain. The line drops.'

I was just worried Vern was piling on weight. He'd always kept himself so trim. Push-ups, squats, lunges, every morning without fail. You had to if you were an aviator. When Lance Rudman got promoted, I remember Vern saying, 'He'll go to seed, just watch. He's in the chair force now.'

Crystal said, 'You mean you're worried Dad'll get fat and risk shortening his life? Think about it, Mom. If he wants three breakfasts, let him have them. Whatever makes him happy.'

What made Vern happiest was to go to work. 'Well,' he'd say, 'I can't sit here chewing the fat with you folks. I gotta get down to the briefing room.'

If Eugene heard him talking about flying sorties he'd correct him. He'd say, 'There ain't no briefing room, Vern. You can come out back, help me box up some night crawlers.'

But Grice'd play along. He'd ask Vern what the day's mission was likely to be and Vern'd answer, 'Not at liberty to say.'

Crystal believed Grice had the right approach. She said, 'I don't get it with Eugene. There's no shortage of imagination when he's going on about the New World Order. But when it comes to communicating with Dad, he's clueless. Seeing as Dad's unlikely to re-enter the real world we might as well all join him on Planet Vern. Where's the harm?'

Grice even suggested buying Vern a flight suit but Crystal drew the line at that. 'Nice thought,' she said, 'but I foresee zipper issues.'

11

Eugene's bunker was in a clearing up through the trees. I had no idea exactly where and that suited me. But Grice had seen it. He'd been invited to view it, after he'd read *Who Pulls the Strings?* and a couple of other funny-bunny books. Eugene seemed to think he'd made a convert.

I said, 'You don't really buy that nonsense?'

'No,' he said. 'Well, some of it, maybe. A lot of it is really far out, but I'm good at pretending. You want to read something? Then you can get the bunker tour too. But you don't really need to. I can tell you what it's like. It's just an old shipping container, underground mainly. Eugene rented an excavator, dug a hole, dropped it in. It's got a pile of brushwood over it so it's pretty well hidden. You could walk past it and you might not notice it.'

'It must be damp.'

'Yeah. It's a kinda work in progress. He's figuring how to heat it without the vent shaft giving its location away.'

'Does it have electric light?'

'Yes. There's a generator, but of course that could be a problem too because it's noisy. It'd draw attention to your secret location. And then, what happens when you run out of propane, which could easily happen? It depends on how long you're going to be down there. It depends on the nature of the SHTF scenario.'

With Grice you can never be sure if he's spinning you a yarn. He can keep a straight face longer than most.

I said, 'Okay, you got me. What's an SHTF scenario?'

'Shit Hits The Fan.'

'Such as?'

'Germ warfare. Invasion by flesh-eating zombies. Repeal of the Second Amendment. Compulsory bar codes.'

'Bar codes?'

'Yes. Eugene reckons it won't be long till we all have to get bar codes. You know, like cattle have ear tags? Everybody'll get a tattoo and a computer chip. Then everywhere we go we'll get scanned. Like groceries at Costco. And eventually babies'll get a bar code soon as they're born.'

'He really is nuts.'

'I don't know, Peg. He might be right about bar codes. You can see how they'd be useful. You wouldn't have to worry about leaving home without your billfold. Or losing your passport. Just walk past a scanner and you're set. Groceries paid for. ID verified.'

'Has he got a shower and stuff down there?'

'There's a chemical toilet. I don't know if it's up and running. Eugene always takes a leak in the bushes. There's gallons of bottled water. But a shower? That'd be low-priority.'

'Did you see all those cans of beef stew Crystal told us about?'

'Stew. Beans. Peach halves. It's all on metal shelving. He had trail mix but critters got in and ate it. Instant noodles. Ketchup. Rifle ammo. Hershey bars.'

'In that case, better not show me where the bunker is.'

'You mean the Hersheys?'

'Yes.'

'That thought crossed my mind too. I'd be hopeless at stock-piling. I'd keep raiding my stores. But lead us not into temptation, O Lord. And don't forget, Eugene also has a Glock, a Luger, a crossbow and two Bowie knives. You go pilfering his chocolate stash you're liable to become a tragic statistic.'

I prefer a murder mystery myself but I did try to read one of Eugene's books. If I understood it right, it was saying that we don't own the Federal Reserve. It owns us. Well, I had to call Eugene out on that. Everybody knows the government runs the Federal Reserve.

But Eugene said, 'Nope. Other way round, Peggy. Don't be fooled by that word "Federal". Damned clever name. Government agreed to it, way back. Act of Congress, sure. But that don't mean they ever controlled it. Federal Reserve's a law unto itself. It's private. Bankers, that's who owns it. And you know what most of them are? Jews.'

'I don't like to hear bad talk about Jewish people. Look what that led to. Adolf Hitler.'

'Don't get me wrong. Sammy Ward, used to live up the road a piece, he was Jewish. He made very good bread. I got no problem with anybody works hard and minds his own business. No, I'm talking about bankers. They make money off the back of folks like you and me. Charging interest, that's not honest labour. Besides, they're not all Jews. The Rockefellers, they ain't. Tell you another thing about the Federal Reserve. It's never been audited. Any time Congress dares to talk about an audit, the Fed threatens mayhem. How d'ya like them apples?'

Eugene's a queer duck. I doubt he graduated high school but he's got a bunch of opinions, and quite a library too, according to Grice. He'd been admitted to the inner sanctum. I even wondered if there might be something going on between them. Grice nearly gagged when I asked him.

He said, 'Peggy! The very idea! Eugene is a stranger to the nail brush. But he's a very interesting guy, you must admit. And the reason I braved his boudoir was I was invited to see his war mementos. He's got a Vietcong water canteen and a rice bowl.'

Eugene served in the infantry, got through it in one piece, unlike some. Perry Kaiser, who was Crystal's first sweetheart, he came home minus his legs. Don't ever get Crystal started on Vietnam. She went on a big protest march up to Washington and that was when she started using the F-word.

I said, 'So that was it? A canteen and a bowl? I thought he must have had something really interesting to show you.'

'Well,' said Grice, 'there were some photos too. Girls in garter belts and such. I think he was testing me. I think he was making sure he'd got me rightly figured out.'

'And had he?'

'I think I confirmed his worst suspicions. Anyway, he's not stupid, that's for sure. He may be a little crazy but he's certainly a thinker. I wouldn't try to get anything past Eugene without him examining it every which way. You tell him two plus two makes four, he'll check it for himself.'

I got so I was careful what I said in Eugene's hearing because he was liable to give me one of his pitying looks. You could make an innocent remark, about the price of gas, about the Navistar shooting in Chicago, and he'd commence one of his lectures.

Did I really think Pearl Harbor happened out of a clear blue sky? Did I really believe Lee Harvey Oswald was a lone Communist assassin? Hadn't I ever wondered how a nonentity like Jimmy Carter got to be President? Grice enjoyed it, but when Eugene turned the talk to secret committees and plans for world domination he just made me plumb uncomfortable.

One time I said to him, 'Eugene, I don't care for this kinda talk. I'm a patriot.'

He said, 'I'm a patriot too, Peggy. Let's hope one of us don't end up feeling let down.'

Then one day he asked me if I'd care to see his survival preparations. Maybe it was because I'd told him nothing'd ever get me into a bunker. Not even little green men from Mars. Maybe it was because he was about to excavate a connecting tunnel from the backyard and he was just buttering me up before he started bringing mud into the house on his boots.

Jim Coffin was over that day so we all went there together. It was up through the trees, no path marked, no handrail, because that would draw people's attention. I had to cling on to Grice and Jim.

I said, 'Do you plan on putting lights along here? In case you suddenly need to get here in the dark?'

'No lights,' said Eugene. 'Just a head torch. No sense building a bunker and then advertising your whereabouts.'

He'd bought the container from Salvage and Surplus and painted it camo-effect.

I said, 'How did you get it into the ground?'

'Rented a crane, dropped it in. Thanksgiving two years ago.'

Jim said, 'Crane cost extra, it being a holiday, but you don't got people snooping around on Thanksgiving, see? We done mine the same day.'

'Why don't you just share the same bunker?'

'Because Jim lives up the road a piece. Shit hits the fan, he might not have time to get here. See this door? This is a special door. Fourteen-gauge steel. Blast-proof.'

'You really think people'd try to break in?'

'Is a duck's ass watertight? You get civil unrest, a major grid outage maybe, you're gonna get looting. And when they've emptied the stores of TV screens and running shoes, they're gonna come looking for food.'

'Would you shoot them?'

'Damned right. Next job, after the tunnel, is to cut a kinda gun turret. Retractable. You want to take a look inside? If you can't manage the ladder we can lift you down.'

I said, 'I'm sure it's great but I don't care for confined spaces. If one of those SHTF scenarios occurs you can leave me in the house with my hairdryer and my box of wine. I'll take my chances.'

Eugene laughed, which was a rare thing. 'SHTF scenario!' he said. 'I see Grice has been educating you. Now you're getting the idea, Peggy. Now you're smelling the coffee.'

At the end of June Lois and Herb became great-grandparents. Their grandson Pat and his girlfriend had a baby girl, thirty-six-hour labour, ventouse delivery. They named her Madison.

I thought she wouldn't thank them for a name like that when she got older, but Crystal said, 'Seeing you raised the topic, what kind of name is Crystal?'

I said, 'It's a pretty name.'

'Not when you're in your fifties, it isn't. Not when you're in the male-dominated profession of taxidermy.'

'Your daddy chose it.'

'Sure, blame a man who can't defend himself.'

Herb and Lois had gone up to Cape Cod to see the new arrival. Lois said the baby was cute. She said, 'Well whatya expect me to say? Head shaped like a red Sharpie marker? She's family. I know how to make the right noises. I just hope she gets my build. We met Pat's in-laws and they're all real low-slung.'

'What's she gonna call you?'

'Ma'am. I dunno, Peg. I haven't thought about it.'

'Time you did. She'll be talking before you know it. Did you get to hold her?'

'A bit. Herb was really into all that. Him and Gerry did most of the cradling. Me and Sandie hardly got a look in. But that's okay. You know me and babies. When she gets older she can come to me for fashion notes.'

I'd hoped Herb and Lois would continue on up to Maine after they'd visited the new grandbaby, spend some time with me and Vern, but they'd headed home instead. Some days I felt real lonesome.

Grice said, 'You've got me.'

I said, 'I know. I never thought I'd say it but I miss a bit of girl-talk.'

'Well,' he said, 'at the risk of repeating myself, you've got me.'

There was a ladies' club in town, had bridge afternoons and a knitting bee. Once in a while they'd go see a movie but you don't need company for that. You can't converse in a movie. I'd rather go alone. Grice fidgets so. He's always getting up to buy candy or take a leak, then when he comes back to his seat he has to ask me what he missed.

Well, I don't knit and I don't play bridge. Fact is, I'm not really one for joining clubs. Audrey was a leading light at the Officers' Wives Club, and she'd try to get the rest of us interested. Of course, Audrey was always thinking of Lance's career, 'brass-polishing', Lois used to call it, scheming to get him those five-star-general's shoulder boards. The rest of us preferred just hanging out in each other's kitchens and Vern didn't give a damn if I went to tea parties with the CO's wife. I don't think he even cared whether he made captain. He just loved flying. Second time the promotion panel passed him over he started to lose heart. He was thirty and the young jocks were getting all the training on the new Thunderstreak. That was when he got paunchy and morose, and then he quit. Quit the service, quit the marriage.

So I didn't care to join any ladies' club but I'd sure have liked a neighbour to call on once in a while. There was an older woman at the Clark spread, and one time we were driving back from Waterville and she was fetching in her mail. Grice said, 'Let's be neighbourly,' and he pulled up. He said, 'But you do the talking.'

I introduced myself.

'Oh, yeah,' she said. 'Martine's place. I heard there was flat-landers moved in up there.' She was peering into the back of the car where Vern was sitting. 'I heard he'd gone strange. He's missing Martine, I guess. That woman was his rock.'

She never did tell me her name.

Grice said, 'Well, I don't think we'll be going to any soirées at her place.'

Lois said they definitely planned on visiting, early September.

I said, 'Why don't you come in August? They have a whole lot of stuff going on then, for tourists.'

'Such as?'

'Bean Hole Suppers. Also a loon-calling contest.'

'Right. Just remind me how that goes?'

'A loon is a kind of bird. Like a duck. They make this sound, at nightfall. Real spooky.'

'So they get a bunch of them together and see which duck makes the spookiest sound? Winner gets a year's supply of duck chow?'

'No, the contest is for people. For imitating loon calls.'

'Wow. They get more than one try? Like heats and quarter finals?'

'I don't know. I'm new to this.'

'They test them for steroids? You know what, Peg, I'm really tempted but I'm gonna resist. We'll come in September. You got proper heating in those cabins?'

Like I told her, we called them cabins to appeal to the fisher-folk, but they were actually good brick guest houses with en-suite facilities. Grice had made his real cosy.

I said, 'I'll put you in the same unit Kath and Slick stayed in. Didn't Kath give us a good write-up?'

'She did, but let's face it, Peg, Kath's very easily satisfied. She grew up in a shack. Remember that outside john?'

'That's a long time ago. Since she married Slick she's gotten accustomed to the finer things in life. This isn't the Ritz-Carlton but you'll be comfortable. Grice has a spare sheepskin. How about that under your little toes when you get out of bed?'

'Okay,' she said. 'Sounds good. Can we get twin beds? Herb has Ruthless Leg Syndrome.'

'You sure that's not Restless Leg Syndrome?'

'Whatever. How about a hot tub? I love a hot tub.'

'No, no hot tub, no manicurist, no masseuse. But we do have a survival bunker, in the event of any shit hitting the fan.'

'Yeah,' she said. 'Kath mentioned you were living with a lunatic. He sounds like fun. Well, listen, I'm gonna tell Herb we'll be staying in a cabin. It's one of those words makes his eyes light up. Cedar decking, that's another one. That's two words but you know what I mean.'

August was stifling and the house, which never got properly warm in winter, never felt cool in summer. It was one of the mysteries of Marvern. One afternoon, when Eugene was doing some kind of mindless hammering and Vern kept taking his pants off, I just lost it. Grice advised me to go for a drive and I ended up at the Regal in Augusta. They were showing *Captain Corelli's Mandolin*. The girl at the ticket booth didn't know what it was about but she said it was popular with seniors and the cinema had air-con, so in I went.

The place was nearly empty. I had a whole row to myself. Then somebody came in and sat plumb behind me, started rustling the cellophane on a box of candy and talking to himself. They hadn't even started the ads. I was just thinking I'd move when he leaned forward and spoke to me. He said, 'Good afternoon, neighbour. Can I interest you in a jelly bean?'

It was Cort Cooper.

He said, 'I have watermelon flavour, juicy pear and berry blue. Guaranteed kosher and dairy-free. Also strawberry daiquiri flavour, which, it turns out, contains no alcohol.'

I took a berry blue, to be polite.

He said, 'I have a confession to make. I've forgotten your name.'

'Peggy.'

'Peggy. Did you read the book?'

'What book?'

'*Captain Corelli's Mandolin*,' he said. 'The movie is always a let-down after the book.'

'I only came in to get cool.'

'Very wise. You haven't set yourself up for disappointment. How is your husband?'

'Ex. Vern. He's as well as can be expected.'

Back and forth we talked some, then the ads started and the next thing I knew, Cort Cooper had moved to my row. Not to the seat next to me, though. He put a bag on that seat, a kind of sports' holdall.

We'd just gotten to the bit where Nicholas Cage kisses Penélope Cruz for the first time when something wet touched my bare arm. I jumped so high I nearly hit the ceiling. Then I heard Cort Cooper say, 'Herk, settle down.'

There was a dog in that bag, tiniest thing I ever saw. It was one of those cute little Yorkies, sometimes have ribbons in their hair, but this one was grizzled and scruffy.

As soon as the movie ended Cort Cooper was on his feet. He jammed an old straw hat on his head and picked up the holdall. 'Sorry if Herk got fresh,' he said.

111

'Did you say Herk?'

'Short for Hercules. He was the runt of the litter and my wife thought a big name would help raise his self-esteem. But he doesn't like me hollering "Hercules", not in Maine.'

'Did it raise his self-esteem?'

'Funnily enough he's never had a problem in that department.'

I asked him if the movie had disappointed him.

'Oh, yes,' he said. 'Too much singing, too much dancing. And why must they always have their happy ending? Do they think we're children? Do they think we can't take tragedy? Well, I never learn. But, as you said, it was pleasantly cool in here. Good day, then.' He paused for a minute. 'Peggy,' he said. 'Right? So, good day, Peggy.'

And then he was gone.

The week before the Moons came up to Maine, Lois was on the phone every day. How many skirts should she bring? Was there a good dry cleaner nearby? Should she bring her fur?'

I said, 'We have seventy degrees up here.'

'Same here,' she said, 'but still, Maine. You're in the Arctic Circle practically. We could wake up to snow. I reckon I'll bring the fur. You got animal-rights people up there?'

'I guess there must be some. They'll be outnumbered, though. This is trapping country.'

'Did I tell you what happened to me last time I wore fur into the city? This kid starts screaming at me, "Animal murderer, animal murderer!" right there on Broadway.'

'What'd you do?'

'Told her to fuck off. Manhattan, Peg. No sense trying to

have a polite exchange of views. Who has time for that? Stupid thing was, it wasn't my fox coat. It was my *faux*-leopard. I mean, it's made of polyester or something. Still, if she'd had a paint spray she could have ruined it.'

Grice helped me prepare for their arrival. The usual cabin décor was framed displays of fishing flies on the wall. We should have hung an Elvis poster for Lois but I thought of it too late. Nearly twenty-five years since he died and she's still in mourning for him. The day before they were due to arrive I put the finishing touches to their accommodation. Good towels, a CD player, a basket of toiletries, like you get in a hotel. Vern sat on the bed and watched me. I reminded him who was coming. I said, 'You remember Herb Moon?'

'Course I remember him,' said Vern. 'Kinda question is that? You think I'm pixilated?'

I heard the phone ringing in the house so I ran across to answer it. It was just someone selling something we didn't need. I came back out and there was Vern coming out of the cabin carrying a pile of stuff: the framed dry flies, the alpaca throws Grice brought from Canada, the apricot body butter I'd picked out for Lois.

'Some fool left all this behind,' he said. 'Well, finders, keepers. I'm taking it for Martine.'

12

They arrived Saturday afternoon. Lois was wearing purple sneakers.

'I got them in three colours,' she said. 'Lime, orange and these. Hell, Peg, you're really in the boonies here. This reminds me of Herb's folks' place, upstate. You got wolves up here?'

Grice said, 'No wolves. They say there's black bears but I've never seen any. And there's moose, but they won't trouble you.'

She said, 'You mean not unless they jump out at you and total your vehicle.'

Herb said, 'Lo gets nervous, soon as she's away from the city lights. Me, I feel the exact opposite. Funny thing that.'

'Not funny at all,' said Lois. 'In the city you know there's douchebags. They wear hoodies and cargo pants halfway down their ass. You can see them coming. You cross the street. Get your Mace spray ready. But bears. They blend into the scenery, and they can get real mean. Any bears come snuffling round our cabin, we're leaving.'

Grice said, 'You'll be okay. Just don't leave any cookies on the windowsill.'

We went in to find Vern. He'd been napping.

I said, 'See who's here? You remember who I told you was coming to visit?'

He looked at Herb. 'Son of a gun,' he said. 'Herb Moon.'

As I calculated, it had been forty-seven years.

Vern said, 'When'd you get posted?'

'Just blown in,' said Herb.

'You standing the duty tonight?'

'Nope. I was hoping you'd be up for Beer Call.'

'Sure thing. Boy, am I glad to see you. You up from McConnell? I don't know what you're gonna make of this outfit. I've been here a week now and I still ain't seen any other jocks.'

Herb screwed up his eyes to try to stop his tears, but he still had to leave the room.

'See who that was?' said Vern. 'Herb Moon. Son of a gun.'

Sunday, Crystal and Marc came over, took Vern and Herb up to Messalonskee Lake in their runabout while me and Grice and Lois went shopping at the outlet mall. The intention was to buy her a cheap pair of pants, in case she decided to change the habit of a lifetime and take a country walk. She bought a pair of tourmaline earrings and a toy moose for the great-grandbaby. No pants.

I asked her how Vern seemed to her because I didn't know any more.

She said, 'Well, he's not good, but he's not real bad. I was kinda prepared for him to be worse. More to the point, how are you?'

I thought I was looking okay. Lois said I looked like shit.

I said, 'Thanks for that. I'm just a bit tired is all. Vern's worst at night.'

'You always do the night shift?'

'Except if Crystal's over, Friday and Saturday, then she takes a turn. But she can't always make it.'

'That sucks.'

'She has a life.'

'It's like you got a baby again.'

'Yeah. Sometimes I yell at him. I shouldn't. He can't help the way he is.'

'No. But you can't help not being Super Woman. I used to yell at Kirk sometimes. Herb never yelled. He'd just punch the door. I smacked Kirk a few times too. You ever smacked Vern?'

I couldn't lie. But I only did it once. 'It was nothing much. He had his boots on in bed and every time I tugged them off he pulled them back on. Stupid thing was, he didn't remember, even the next morning. I felt terrible for days but he was like it never happened.'

She said, 'That's something. Kirk used to look at me like a beaten dog sometimes. It'll get too much for you, Peg. You do know that? There'll come a time.'

'Crystal won't ever give up on him.'

'You mean two-nights-a-week Crystal? Okay. We'll see. You're a star, though, Peg, doing what you're doing. After all those years. He left you, Goddamn it.'

'Not really. We left each other.'

'Still, it's not like you owe him.'

'Herb say anything? He filled up when he first saw Vern.'

'He did. You know, all the way coming here he was worried Vern wouldn't remember him and then – ba-boom. It was just like they'd never been apart.'

'That's the military for you.'

'Yeah. Band of brothers. Hey, have you been watching it on TV? That Damian Lewis is so cute. Band of brothers. I guess that makes us the band of sisters.'

I said, 'Band of old crones, more like.'

'Speak for yourself,' said Lois. 'I'm a walking testimonial for Cold Cream. Pond's oughta pay me a commission. Thing is, Herb really rated Vern. Okey Jackson and Vern, best aviators he ever flew with, Herb reckons, and he says you never forget that because you were putting your life on the line every time you flew a mission. Look what happened to Okey. Herb's always said if Okey had been at the controls that day instead of riding back seat he'd have used the flaps, landed that bitch of a plane in one piece.'

'That was Vern's version too. Okey was like a kid brother to him.'

'It was different for us. The dependants. Didn't you just hate that, Peg? Being a DP? I was glad when Herb quit. I couldn't wait to move on, join the real world. And all those other DPs we knew. Saw them every day of our miserable DP lives and I've forgotten most of them. You're the only one I've really kept up with. You, and Ida Batten and Lorene Bass. That's about all.'

'What about Audrey, and Gayle?'

'Not really. Sending a Christmas card, that's not keeping up.'

'You hear Lance Three's sick?'

'Yeah, Kath said. AIDS, I guess.'

'Are you serious?'

'Why not? He never married, did he? We know what that means.'

'Lots of people don't get married, these days. Your Pat's not married and he's got a baby now.'

'But you know what I'm getting at. I always wondered how those boys'd turn out. I mean, they had their whole lives planned out for them from the minute they were born. All those top-drawer godparents. Remember, Peg? Nothing lower than brigadier. It must have killed Lance Junior, watching them ignore the flight plan.'

'It did kill him.'

'Did it?'

'You know. The reason he choked on that piece of steak was he was arguing with the boys about something.'

'I thought he had a heart attack.'

'That was the official story. But I got the lowdown from Yvette Franklin.'

'Who?'

'Yvette Franklin, 366th Squadron. She was at the funeral. Doesn't matter. Yvette knew some of the wives on the base at Beale so she found out what really happened. I'm sure I told you. They were having dinner, Lance was arguing with one of the boys, choked on a piece of meat. Curtains.'

'Fuck. He needed that Heimlich thing.'

'Anyhow, Audrey didn't want the boys blaming themselves so she had it put out that it was a heart attack. But from what I saw at the funeral they didn't look too grief-stricken.'

'Relieved to be out from under, probably. So the little worms turned. Good. You can't plan your kids' lives like it's a fucking NATO exercise. Ask me, Lance had it coming. He was such a stuffed shirt. I never liked him, did you?'

'I hardly knew him.'

'Me either, but I still didn't like him. Good-looking, though. He reminded me a bit of Tab Hunter. T-bone or sirloin?'

'What?'

'The steak he choked on. Probably filet mignon, knowing Audrey.'

'So you *think* Lance Three might have AIDS? But you don't actually know?'

'Call it an educated guess. A middle-aged guy, hangs out with his mom, vacations in the Far East, suddenly he gets sick.'

'I think you're running way ahead of yourself. We should call Audrey, find out.'

'You call her. She doesn't like me.'

'She sends you a Christmas card.'

'Peg, the Lexus dealership sends me a Christmas card. Don't mean anything.'

'No, but I just thought if Lance Three's really sick, you'd understand what that's like. All you went through with Kirk, you'd know the right thing to say.'

'Not really. I'm as clueless as anybody else. I don't think there is a right thing to say. Plenty of wrong things, though. Like, "God doesn't send you more than you can handle."'

'Did somebody say that to you?'

'Oh, yes. Also, "Everything happens for a reason." That was a neighbour. Course, she couldn't tell me what God's fucked-up reason for Huntington's chorea might be. "Time heals." That's another one.'

'Doesn't it?'

'A bit. If you never pick at the scab. But it's been hard not to

119

do that, Peg, after what I did to Herb and Sandie. And Kirk. He didn't ask to be born. All that, for a few fucks.'

Lois had always been so defiant. It was the first time I'd heard her say she regretted what she'd done. First and last.

I said, 'Everybody makes mistakes.'

'Yeah?' she said. 'Tell me one you made.'

I could think of plenty – not being a good scholar at school, marrying in haste, allowing that ocean-going bitch Lola Dekker to destroy my first business – but none of them seemed in the same ballpark as what Lois had done.

'See?' she said. 'Got you there.'

'I still think we should call Audrey. She knows Kath'll have told us about Lance Three being ill. She'll be expecting to hear from us.'

'Go ahead, call her. Just count me out. You got one of those speakerphone doofers? I'll listen in and write down helpful conversational suggestions.'

As soon as we got back to Marvern I called Audrey. I got her machine. *We're sorry, there's no one home chez Rudman right now. Please leave your message after the tone.*

'Chez Rudman!' said Lois. 'Give me a break.'

They came in sunburned from Messalonskee.

'Windburned, more like,' Crystal said. 'Dad should sleep well tonight.'

I'd planned to make dinner for everyone but Crystal said they had to make tracks. Marc had a big week coming up. He had an early flight next day, going down to New Jersey for some big meeting.

Lois said, 'So, Crystal, when's your mom gonna get a vacation?'

Crystal looked at her. 'Vacation?'

'Yeah. You know? Time off?'

Crystal said, 'I come over Fridays and Saturdays. You got a problem with that, Mom? Something you want to tell me?'

I said I was okay. But Lois said, 'Bullshit. Nurses get time off, domestics get time off. Even fucking jailbirds get recreation time. When did you last get your nails done, Peg?'

Crystal snorted. She said, 'We don't care about nails up here.'

Of course my darling daughter was speaking for herself. Hair like chewed twine, hands beaten up with chemicals. Marc was giving her the big hurry-up.

'I'll talk to you later,' she said. 'Without your friend butting in.'

Marc was gunning the engine.

Lois said, 'Well, would you look at that? That's not the Crystal I remember. That was pure Betty Gillis, the way she went running just because friend husband snapped his fingers. Is he always like that?'

'No. I don't know. All those years and I still hardly know him. They seem happy. None of my business.'

'You're right. Getting a vacation, *that*'s your business.'

The plan for Monday was that there was no plan. We'd just hang out. Herb'd talk fighter jets with Vern. If Lois got restless I'd take her into Augusta, show her the sights.

'Okay,' she said. 'And what would they be?'

'State Capitol. And there's an arboretum.'

'What's that?'

'Trees. I think there's a Holocaust Center.'

'Oh, man!'

Grice was looking on his computer. He said, 'Also there's a place highly recommended for rock-hounds.'

'Now you're talking,' said Lois. 'They got any Elvis stuff?'

'Oh,' said Grice. 'Hold that thought. It doesn't mean that kind of rock. It means the other kind. Like geology. Could be interesting, though.'

'Yep. Or we could paint a wall and watch it dry. Let's just go out, drive around. We could go to some realtors, view some properties.'

'You can't do that.'

'Sure you can. When I was selling real estate I'd get plenty of time-wasters, but you don't always know. You gotta give people the benefit of the doubt. They could be bona fide buyers. Anyhow, in a place like this, people come up for a vacation, have a good time, maybe win a loon-calling contest, and they get the crazy idea they could live here year-round. They're time-wasters but they don't realize it yet. Realtors are used to it.'

I agreed to do a few drive-bys, but no viewings. Lois and Grice said I was a spoilsport because poking around in other folks' bedrooms and checking out their drapes was the most enjoyable part of it, but I stood firm.

Lois was surprised by what we saw, I could tell. There were some real handsome waterfront properties. She said it was a pity you couldn't tow them two hundred miles south. Plenty of cabins too. Fixer-uppers. Lois said, 'Properties with potential, as we call them in the business. In need of a little TLC. Don't tell Herb what you can get for fifty thousand up here. He'll start dreaming. How much do you reckon Marvern's worth?'

'No idea.'

'Is it Vern's? Or Eugene's?'

'I don't know.'

'You need to find out. When Vern goes into a nursing-home they might have to mortgage it. Those places cost big bucks.'

'He's not going into a nursing-home.'

'That's what everyone says. I reckon Marvern's worth half a million. With the guest houses and the dock. It's got potential. You could turn it into an upscale fishing destination.'

Grice said, 'We couldn't have Eugene on the front desk, though. Except maybe for a Hallowe'en holiday special.'

We met Cort Cooper along the road. He pulled over to let us pass, wound his window down, said, 'Good day.' His little dog was standing on his lap.

I said, 'Who's driving?'

He said, 'Herk's learning. It's the written test trips him up every time.'

We drove on.

Lo said, 'He was cute.'

I said, 'He's in his seventies. How can he be cute?'

'I meant the dog,' she said. 'But the guy was okay too. Kinda Jimmy Stewart gone to seed. Where'd you meet him?'

'He's our nearest neighbour.'

'Married?'

'Widowed.'

'He was flirting with you.'

'He was not.'

'I'm telling you.'

★

It had started to rain.

'Hellfire and damnation,' said Lois. 'Now we can't go to the arboretum. I am truly devastated.'

And Grice said, 'I know. Let's have a party.'

Lo unclipped her seatbelt so she could reach into the back seat and give Grice a kiss. She said, 'Peggy, I love this guy. You ever tire of him, send him to me. I'll pay carriage and packing. Okay, we'll need booze, we'll need nachos. You got a boom-box at the Bates Motel? I have plenty of CDs in the car. Big Bopper Mega-mix. Rosemary Clooney.'

We stopped off and bought soda and beer, Gallo wine, JD, franks, nachos, ice cream, butter pecan and rocky road. When we got home Herb and Vern were still sitting exactly where we'd left them.

Lo said, 'Looks like it's been a quiet day at USAF Marvern.'

'That's all you know,' said Herb. 'Just after you left a couple of MiGs wandered into our air space so we got scrambled. Prob-ably a navigational error but we set them straight. We gave them a friendly reminder, didn't we, Vern? Waxed their Russky tails and sent them on their way.'

Vern chuckled. He could have been humouring Herb. You could never be sure with Vern.

Lois said, 'So Uncle Sam's had his money's worth out of you for today. Good. Now move these chairs and roll back this rug while I go change my earrings. It's party time.'

She whispered, 'We oughta invite Jimmy Stewart. Get to know your neighbours, Peg.'

I said, 'He's not that type. He reads books.'

'What a bore. So are you gonna dance with Vern? Do you think he remembers how?'

I'd met Vern at a dance. That was how you met guys in those days. He was in the officer training school at Lackland, came in from the base one Saturday night, looking for a little R&R in San Antonio, and the rest is history. He wasn't a great mover, he just kinda shuffled in place, but I thought he was nice-looking and apparently he thought the same of me. We didn't have the Pill in those days, of course, and Vern hated using rubbers so three months later I was pregnant with Crystal.

I said, 'I'll just bop around by myself. See if he wants to join in.'

I didn't want him getting frisky. He had been known to call me Martine. I didn't mind that, but I didn't want the sap rising. It was okay, though. He pushed me around some to a couple of slow tracks, like I was a shopping cart at the Piggly Wiggly, then we just twitched and shimmied in the vicinity of each other and Grice made it a threesome.

Lois was changing the CD.

Herb said, 'You enjoying yourself, Vern?'

Vern said, 'Sure. Who're the women?'

Herb said, 'The redhead's Lo. She's mine. The other one's Peggy. You gonna ask her for her number?'

'I don't reckon so,' said Vern. 'She's old.'

The phone rang. It was Audrey.

'Peggy dear,' she said, 'you sound breathless. I hope you didn't run to the phone.'

I told her what we were up to.

'How super,' she said. 'It's so important to keep active. Oh, my, and is that Lois Moon's voice I hear in the background? So distinctive. It sounds as though she's still the life and soul of the party.'

I offered to put Lois on but Audrey said she'd speak with her some other time, she must dash, and she'd just wanted to return my kind call. She said she was pretty well, considering how many miles she had on the clock. She had an appointment with a new eye doctor, the absolute top man in DC, Mikey was paying for it. He and his wife were in Sardinia, staying at a very exclusive resort, and Lance Three was in Johns Hopkins again but doing much better. She said he had some kind of anaemia.

'Anaemia my ass,' was Lois's verdict.

Eugene looked in on us a couple of times. First he just peered round the door, went away, second time he stood in the doorway for a minute.

Herb said, 'We disturbing you, Eugene? Music too loud?'

Eugene turned away.

Grice said, 'Why don't y'all come in and join us? You want a beer?'

'You got Bud?'

'We got Coors.'

'Okay, then.'

He came in like he was doing us the biggest favour and, of course, he didn't dance, but after a while I noticed he began tapping his feet. Grice was in a world of his own, punching the air, shaking his head, shimmying his butt. He did the same moves whatever music was playing.

Lois said, 'Grice darling, I didn't know you couldn't dance.'

Vern was starting to fade. It was past his usual bedtime. Herb and Lois were slow-shuffling to Perry Como.

I said, 'You lovebirds ready for ice cream?'

Lois said, 'Shoot, we forgot to buy toppings. Who's good to drive?'

Nobody was good to drive. We'd all been drinking since five o'clock.

Lois said, 'Herb loves that marshmallow fluff on his ice cream. Probably made the same place they make roof insulation. I'm sorry, darling.'

Herb said it couldn't matter less.

Eugene said, 'There's sprinkles, back of one of the cupboards. Mom always kept sprinkles.'

He didn't know I'd gone through those cupboards and tossed anything that had been there since before Martine died. I'm not an overly fastidious person but when I see a rusty can or an ancient carton I err on the side of caution. Heck, I don't think they even make Jell-Well Pudding Mix any more.

Grice said, 'And I'm sure I've seen a jar of Smucker's some-where around.'

'Smucker's'd be good,' said Herb. But I knew damned well we didn't have any. Then I noticed Eugene giving Grice the evil eye.

I said, 'Eugene, you got Smucker's in your store? You got any-thing we can use? Chocolate syrup? Fudge topping? Anything at all.'

He said, 'I told you, there's sprinkles in the cupboard.'

So then I confessed. I said, 'Eugene, those sprinkles must have been there since Eisenhower was President. I'm afraid I tossed them.'

And Grice said, 'Maybe I misremembered the Smucker's.'

But the cat was out of the bag.

Lois said, 'C'mon, Eugene. Don't be a party pooper. What's the point of keeping a store of stuff if you don't draw on it in an hour of need? The world's not gonna end tonight.'

I said, 'And we'll replace it first thing.'

I never saw a man move with such a heavy heart. As Grice said, it was his fault. Eugene didn't like people knowing what he had in his survival store.

Lois said, 'You leaked classified information. Man, oh, man, you'll be shot at dawn. Not just you, though, Grice. Peg's in the dog house too. Throwing away those sprinkles. What were you thinking, Peggy Dewey? Just because a person has passed over that doesn't mean you can dispose of their baking requisites.'

We laughed till my ribs ached.

Eugene was gone a long time. Herb wanted to go look for him, make sure he hadn't fallen in the dark, but I knew Eugene wouldn't take kindly to that.

Grice said, 'You have to ask yourself, in a Shit Hits The Fan scenario, would you even be eating ice cream, with or without topping? He doesn't have a freezer down there. Not yet at any rate.'

'Good point,' said Lois. 'You'd just be sipping bottled water, eking out your energy bars. Periscope up, watching out for flesh-eating zombies. And how much marshmallow fluff will he need? Who's gonna be down there with him anyhow? Does he have any friends?'

'Jim Coffin. But he's got his own bunker.'

'So who's gonna eat all that stuff? Is Vern on the list? Won't be you, Peg, that's for sure. You blew it, you sprinkle-tosser.'

When Eugene returned he'd brought two jars of topping: one of marshmallow and one of pineapple flavour. I thought the walk in the evening air had calmed him and he was making an effort to show some good Maine hospitality. But after Lois and Herb had gone to bed he resumed his scowling. He said, 'I'll thank you to leave my mom's stuff alone. This ain't your place. You're just a blow-through.' He came right up close to me. He had pineapple topping on his moustache. 'Point of information,' he said. 'Sprinkles don't go bad. They last for ever.'

The drink and the dancing took their toll. We slept late, even Vern. It was a quarter of nine before I made a start on breakfast and there was no sign of Herb and Lois. The rain had cleared and it was a perfect morning.

Grice said, 'Thank heavens. I was worried what we'd do with Lois if the weather was bad. Not exactly a Solitaire player, is she? How about driving to Penobscot Bay?'

The phone rang.

Crystal said, 'Mom, are you watching TV?'

I said, 'No, I'm making waffles.'

'Turn the TV on,' she said. 'Now.'

I said, 'Not Deana Gillis again?'

But she'd rung off.

13

Grice said, 'Not those Gillis throwbacks again! Not with my waffles.'

But there'd been something in Crystal's voice. My first thought was, Somebody shot the President. I turned on the kitchen TV. There was a story breaking in New York. A fire was burning in one of the World Trade Center towers, black smoke billowing. They said there had been a fireball. Some people who'd seen it thought it was a gas explosion. Others said a small plane had flown into the side of the building.

Grice said, 'That doesn't look good. There'll have been people in their offices already.'

Herb came in, looking for breakfast. 'Whoah!' he said. 'What's happening there?'

As we watched a helicopter flew behind the tower.

Grice said if he was in a building like that and a fire broke out he'd go up to the roof, wait to get winched off.

Herb said, 'You might be out of luck if you did. Fire Department don't usually do rooftop rescues and they don't like it if the police do them. Remember what happened there in 'ninety-three?'

In 1993 a bomb exploded in the garage underneath those same towers. I remembered that much.

Herb said, 'Fire Department likes to evacuate people down the stairs, see? They like to get them into the street. A roof can cave in or a wall can come down. So, get people out, that's the main thing. But in 'ninety-three some people headed up to the roof anyway. That's human nature. They were trying to get above the smoke. But that roof wasn't intended for a helipad. There was a whole bunch of antennas and stuff up there. So what happened was, a police pilot flew over and dropped a couple of guys down to clear a place for him to land. Time it took to do all that, they could probably have evacuated the whole building. I don't know how many the police rescued off the roof that day but the Fire Department got bent out of shape about it. Said it was needless showing off when evacuation to the street was a proven procedure. Number of times I've had this discussion with Gerry. "Glory boys", that's what he calls the police pilots. You get to hear it all when you have a firefighter in the family.'

As we watched, the helicopter flew away. Too much smoke, Herb said, and too many antennas.

I said, 'Aren't they supposed to have a bunch of high-speed elevators in those towers? That's what I'd do. I'd grab my pocket book and I'd be outta there.'

'Not when there's a fire, Peggy,' said Herb. 'You don't want to get in any elevators. You sure they said it was a small plane? That's some hole in the side of the building.'

Grice said, 'Well, it can't have been an accident. You can't not see those towers.'

131

Herb said, 'No, no. Must have been deliberate. Probably some failed tycoon, about to file for Chapter Seven, decided to end it all, take his Cessna with him. Don't wait breakfast for Lo. She's still out for the count. Jesus Christ, what was that?' As he spoke there was another fireball. 'You see that?' He kept saying it over and over. 'Did you see that? Mother of God, that was no Cessna. What do you say, Vern? 767?'

'Yup, 767,' said Vern. 'Did I get my coffee yet?'

They said a plane had hit the other tower. I didn't see it. I'd turned away to get OJ from the fridge. People were calling in to the TV station on their cell phones, been on their way to work and seen the whole thing. They said there were pieces of paper raining down on the street like confetti. A guy who'd been driving up from the Battery Tunnel said a plane tyre fell out of the sky and nearly hit his car.

'Should we wake Lo?'

'No, she gets madder'n a wet hen if you don't leave her to wake naturally. I might give Sandie a call, though. See if Gerry's working today.'

Gerry was with a fire house in Brooklyn. Sandie said it was his day off but they'd just seen what was happening at the Twin Towers so he was going in anyhow.

Herb said, 'You can understand it. What's he gonna do? Stay home and watch TV, see if he can spot any of his company? Sandie thinks he's getting too old to go out. She thinks he's a silly old fool who don't know when to quit! But that's firefighters for you.'

They said there was an unconfirmed report that an American Airlines plane had been hijacked and that it might have been the plane that hit the building. Everything was 'might have' and 'could have been'. Those TV guys have to keep rolling even when they don't have anything definite to tell you. They were even talking about the time the Empire State Building got hit by a plane. That was 1945.

Herb said, 'It was a different case altogether. That was in thick fog.'

'B-25,' said Vern. 'Flying out of Hanscom. Did you forget to make the waffles?'

A reporter in Washington said all seemed quiet at the White House. President Bush was out of town, in Florida. The Pentagon said no military planes had been scrambled as yet.

'Hunh?' said Herb. 'As yet? What are they waiting for?'

Grice said, 'Seems a bit late now anyway.'

'You think so? Two hits in the space of, what, half an hour? Not even. There could be more on the way. There could be another twenty. Frigging Russians. They could hit the Chrysler Building, the Rock Center, that new Trump tower. And they didn't put any fighters up yet? What the hell's going on? Plane gets hijacked, plane goes rogue, you scramble. The very least you do is get up there, take a look-see. Remember Payne Stewart?'

The name meant nothing to me. Herb said Payne Stewart was a golfer, killed when his Learjet crashed, except he was dead already along with everybody else on board, because their oxygen failed.

'When Payne Stewart's plane went off course they had F-16s tail him, to fly alongside and give the pilot a friendly warning. Only in that instance the pilot was dead and they just had to let the plane fly on till it ran out of fuel and crashed.'

'What do they do if the pilot isn't dead and he ignores the friendly warning? That ever happen?'

'I guess you shoot him down.'

'You guess?'

'Well, if it's a hijacking he'll be making demands. Saying where he intends landing, what he wants, that kinda thing. But if he's not talking to you, you got to be prepared to shoot him down.'

'Even if it's an American Airlines plane full of people?'

'If you get orders, yes. But first you need planes in the air. First you need to get close to him, to figure out what his game is.'

'Did you ever shoot anyone down?'

'No. But I would have done. If you're gonna debate orders you don't belong in the military. President signs off on it, you gotta do as he says.'

I tell you, I wouldn't be President if they begged me on bended knee.

The Pentagon said there had been no indications an incident like this was about to happen.

I said, 'What does that mean? They expect to get sent a postcard?'

Herb said sometimes they get what they call 'chatter'. He said, 'This is something, though. This looks like war. Bush better be ready to drop the big one.'

Grice said, 'And where's Eugene? This is real SHTF and he isn't even here.'

Eugene was always out of the house early. He was likely to be out all day. Grice wanted to let off a distress flare to get him home. He said, 'I've been longing to do that.'

I said, 'Don't you dare. Last thing we need is him sitting here saying, "I told you so."'

Next thing was, Kennedy and Newark and LaGuardia were shut down, no planes leaving or landing until further notice, and they started closing the tunnels and bridges into Manhattan. Only emergency vehicles allowed. President Bush came on. He said those responsible for the attacks would be hunted down.

'Not a great speaker, is he?' said Grice. 'He reminds me of a ventriloquist's doll. Bad colour too. Is that sunbed or Man Tan?'

I said, 'The man just received shocking news. Look at him. He hardly knows what to say.'

Grice said presidents always have paid staff to tell them what to say.

We were flipping between channels. NBC said American Airlines had just confirmed that one of their flights, Boston to Los Angeles, had been hijacked. It had veered off course, heading for Kennedy, then disappeared off the radar. They kept showing the second plane coming in and hitting the tower. Over and over they showed it, and every time Herb said, 'No way. No frigging way. What do you say, Vern? How'd he do that?'

'That was some pilot,' said Vern. 'Hit it right on the nail. He musta had some balls.'

'Even so,' said Herb. 'There's no frigging way. What's the wing span on a 767 would you say?'

'Hundred and fifty,' said Vern. 'Give or take.'

'I'd say you're about right. And how wide is that building? Vern, we just seen a plane flown through the eye of a needle.'

The TV anchors were switching back and forth, talking to people on the street in Manhattan, talking to reporters in Washington and Florida. Everybody had a different version of what was going on and none of it amounted to a row of beans. 'All the indications are that this was a terrorist attack but there has been no official statement.' How many times did we hear that?

Grice said, 'I guess they don't want people panicking.'

I said, 'Are you serious?'

'No,' he said. 'Ironic. I'm at a loss.'

Next thing was, all civilian planes were grounded, not just around New York. Right across the country. Nobody landing, nobody taking off. In-bound international flights were being diverted to Canada. The President was on his way back to Washington. Then an NBC guy came on from the Pentagon. He said they'd just felt a slight explosion in the building. The windows of the press office had rattled. He went off air to go investigate.

Herb said, 'See? I told you there'd be more. I hope somebody got off the stick and gave Bush a fighter escort. Now they put it out where he's headed, Air Force One's gonna be a sitting duck. And I hope they got Dick Cheney someplace safe too.'

The Pentagon reporter came back on and said something had definitely happened there but no one was sure what. One of the rumours was that a bomb had gone off at the heliport. He said they hadn't heard any sirens, inside the building or outside, but the Pentagon's a very big place.

It was about a quarter of ten.

There were stories coming in from all over. More planes hijacked. The President wasn't going to DC after all. Nobody knew where he was, or they just weren't allowed to say. A bunch of FBI anti-terror experts were in California, supposed to be taking part in a hostage rescue exercise, and now they were stuck there because all flights were cancelled. The only way they could be of assistance was by telephone but a lot of phones weren't working. Staff were being evacuated from the Capitol and the White House. An unmarked plane had been sighted over Lafayette Park.

Herb said Lafayette Park was pretty much in the backyard of the White House. He said, 'So where in tarnation's the Air Force? Langley should have planes up there by now. Andrews should have planes up there.'

Whenever they ran out of new stories they flipped back to New York, to the World Trade Center. They said there was masonry falling off the side of the South Tower. They said people were jumping. I saw one. Then I couldn't watch any more. I went to make fresh coffee.

Then Grice said, 'Am I going crazy or has one of the towers disappeared?'

Herb said it was just the smoke and the camera angle.

Vern said, 'It's fell down.'

'No,' said Herb, 'that cannot be. That's a steel-frame building. You'll see it when the smoke clears.'

And even when the TV people said the South Tower had collapsed Herb just kept shaking his head and saying, 'No way.'

The story from the Pentagon changed. It wasn't a bomb at the heliport that people had heard. It was a plane hitting the building.

Herb said, 'White House. That'll be next.'

I said, 'Who's doing it?'

'Russians. Has to be. Or North Korea. Who else hates us?'

Grice said, 'Could be Cuba.'

'Cuba!' said Herb. 'They don't even have gas to put in their cars.'

'How about the Palestinians? Or the ones who bombed the US embassy?'

'Al Qaeda? I don't think they got any ace pilots, Peggy. Car bombs, that's about their limit. But this? Somebody really knew what they were doing. I mean, this is frigging out-and-out war. And my money's on the Russians.'

I called Crystal. The line was busy.

The door opened. Lois said, 'Peggy, do you have anything stronger than Advil?'

Herb said, 'Come and sit down, darling, see what's been happening.'

Vern said, 'We're getting waffles but I don't know when.'

Lois said, 'Nothing for me. Just a hair of the dog with a side of Tylenol. What's occurring?'

We brought her up to date.

Herb said, 'I spoke to Sandie.'

'Why?'

'Because all the fire houses are likely to be sending rigs. To find out if Gerry was working.'

'Is he?'

'He was going in.'

'Why didn't you wake me?'

'Because you get in a bad mood if I wake you.'

'Well, now I'm in a bad mood because you didn't.'

I made a pile of toast. Vern bellyached a bit about the waffles but he ate the toast anyhow. It was around ten thirty. I tried Crystal again but her line was still busy.

Lois watched the replay of the second plane hitting.

'See that?' said Herb. 'See the way it banked and then hit the side of the building? I'd sure like to know who the hell was flying that baby.'

'Whoever he was he's dead,' said Lois. 'Was that a regular plane? With passengers and everything?'

'American Airlines.'

'What about the other tower? That a regular plane too?'

'We don't know. Nobody filmed it. They think it was a flight out of Boston.'

'Fucking hell. Don't ever try to get me on a plane again, Herbert Moon.'

Then there was a rumble and a mushroom cloud of dust and the North Tower fell down, before our very eyes. It just kinda sank to its knees.

Banjo ran in and dropped something at my feet. A dead mouse. I always think of those two things together now. Tower fell down. Dead mouse.

Lois said, 'The people in the buildings? Did they get everybody out?'

Herb said, 'I doubt it. Folk from the offices, they might have. If they started evacuating soon as the plane hit. But there'll have been first responders in there. There'll have been firefighters going up to put the blaze out. There's bound to be casualties.'

'Do you reckon Gerry's down there?'

'Could be. Depends if he got to the fire house before the rig set off.'

'What time did you talk to Sandie? Was he still home then?'

'He was just going in. I heard him give her a kiss. What time would that have been, Peggy?'

'It was after the second plane hit.'

'That was around nine o'clock. Half ten now. I'll call her again.'

Lois said, 'Don't call her again. She's been married to the Fire Department years enough. She's accustomed to worrying. Like we used to be, eh, Peg? We used to hear the siren, see smoke down the flight line, wonder if we were gonna be Widow of the Week. We just stayed home, stayed calm.'

Well, we did and we didn't. We certainly used to make a few calls, just between ourselves. Betty'd usually have us all round to her place for coffee and cookies while we waited to hear what exactly had happened. Waited to find out whether the news was real bad, and who'd be getting it. Safety in numbers. That's how we kidded ourselves.

Herb did call Sandie again but he couldn't get through. On the TV they said telephone communications were severely disrupted in the New York area. He said, 'What do you think? Should we go home?'

'Hell, no,' said Lois. 'Nothing we can do.'

We never did drive to Penobscot Bay. We just sat all day staring at that TV screen. They kept showing the same stuff over and over, the second plane flying in, the two towers falling down, but the furthest any of us ventured was to the bathroom, not wanting to miss any further developments.

Every time they showed a shot of the rescue services Herb and Lois tried to spot Gerry. The firefighters have their name on the back of their turnout coat, in high-vis tape, so we were looking, looking for CARROLL, but you couldn't read many names because those guys were covered with thick dust. You could see them pouring water into their eyes, get the grit out.

They said there had been a car bomb outside the State Department. Then they said it was a false alarm. They said another plane had crashed somewhere in Pennsylvania but not into any buildings. There was a lot of surmising but the bottom line was nobody knew what the heck was going on.

Herb said, 'We've been caught with our pants down. No two ways.'

'America will never be the same,' they kept saying. They got that right. A lot of things changed that day.

14

It was midday before I got Crystal. She picked up, first ring.

I said, 'I guess you're not working. We can't settle to anything here. Do you want to come over?'

I heard her take a deep breath. She said, 'Mom, to be honest, I wouldn't be great company.'

I said, 'You know anybody works in those towers?'

'No,' she said. 'But I'm not sure what I know any more. My husband's not where he's supposed to be.'

Marc had a meeting in Newark, New Jersey. He'd mentioned it at dinner on Sunday night because he was flying down on Monday. Something to do with the various fruit and vegetable trade magazines. 'We're looking at going on-line.' That was what he'd said.

Crystal had called his hotel straight after the first tower was hit but there was no reply from his room. When she tried his cell phone it was out of service.

I said, 'It'll be because of the towers falling down. Herb couldn't get Sandie the second time he called her.'

Crystal said, 'Well, let me finish. So I called the office to find out where his meeting was. And do you know what Claudette said? "Hi, Crystal! I thought you'd be up at Moosehead by now. You hear the terrible news from New York?"'

'What does that mean? Why'd she think you'd be at Moosehead?'

'Because Marc told the office he was taking vacation and he told me he had a meeting and none of it's true. It means he's cheating on me. And don't say there's probably some innocent explanation. Just don't.'

I didn't. I didn't know what to say. Marc, cheating? It didn't seem possible. But when I told Lois she said, 'I dunno, Peg. It was the first time I'd met him but I thought he looked pretty hot. No offence, but Crystal doesn't exactly make an effort, does she?'

Grice said, 'Maybe he's gone for a big job interview and he wanted to surprise Crystal.'

He was trying to be helpful.

Herb said, 'You want to go over to be with Crystal? Sounds like she needs you. Vern'll be okay with us.'

I called her back.

She said, 'No, thanks. I don't want anybody here when he gets home.'

I said, 'They're saying all flights are grounded. He won't be home tonight.'

'I know,' she said. 'Still, I just prefer to sit here and fester. And when he does get home I don't want anybody here, cramping my style. Is Sandie Moon's husband still in the fire service?'

'Reserve. Herb spoke to Sandie this morning. She said Gerry had gone in as soon as they heard the news. They'll need all the hands they can get.'

'Yes. Surreal. Is Dad okay? Has he been watching?'

'Watching and paying close attention. He's still in his bath-robe. I guess we'll forget about showering and shaving today.'

'Eugene gone to the bunker?'

'I don't think so. He's out shooting woodchucks with Jim Coffin. He probably doesn't even know what's happening.'

Crystal said, 'The long-awaited shit hits the fan and Eugene doesn't even know about it. I could find that amusing if I was in the mood.'

I said, 'Sweetheart, let Marc get home and explain himself. Don't cross your bridges.'

'I'm afraid Marc's the one already did the bridge-crossing. I hope Sandie's husband's okay. They reckon there were a lot of firefighters in the towers when they came down. Tell Dad I love him.'

I said, 'Well, if you change your mind we'll be here. I've got a quantity of ham and potato salad.'

'Mom,' she said. 'I love you too. It seems like a good day to make sure you know.'

It was late afternoon when Eugene walked in, whistling. We all turned to look at him.

'What?' he said.

Vern said, 'Russians bombed New York, knocked two great buildings down, hit the Pentagon too.'

Eugene said, 'That right? You didn't bother getting dressed today, Vern? You having a pyjama party?'

He thought Vern was having one of his imaginings.

Herb said, 'You'd better sit down. You have some catching up to do. What Vern said is right. Only thing is, we don't know who done it. Russians haven't claimed it. In fact, they just said Putin called off his war games supposed to be going on this week. Gesture of goodwill. I dunno. He could have been bluffing. Then they're saying it couldn't be the Russians cos they don't have the capability, these days. The Palestinians say it wasn't them. As if. North Korea haven't said anything. Whoever it was, they've thrown away three ace pilots, four if the Shanksville story's true. The way those planes hit. It's beyond belief.'

Eugene joined us at the kitchen table and watched the TV screen, all the stuff we'd seen over and over and still couldn't believe. It was his turn to say, 'No way.'

They had begun saying that the finger of suspicion pointed to Osama bin Laden.

Grice said, 'I thought he lived in a cave.'

Herb said, 'They mean his people. Al Qaeda. Well, if they were bin Laden's sand monkeys I'd sure like to know where they learned to fly like that.'

Lois said, 'You can't call them sand monkeys, Herb. Sandie'll have a conniption fit.'

'Not if they've killed her husband she won't. Anyhow, Sandie's not here,' said Herb. 'And I'll call them what I damn well please.'

'Go for it, Herb,' said Lois. 'I've got your back.'

It took Eugene a while to get the story straight in his head. Little wonder. None of it made any sense even when you'd seen it happen. The first building to get hit was the North Tower but the first building to fall down was the South Tower. Plus, the plane that hit the Pentagon had flown through restricted airspace and no US military had tried to intercept it. Plus, George Bush was everywhere except Washington DC where he should have been.

Vern said, 'You sell much today, Eugene?'

'Yes. No,' he said. 'I didn't open up today. I went hunting with Jim Coffin. How many people in those towers?'

'Could be thousands.'

'Did they get them all out?'

'I doubt they had time.'

'And the buildings just fell?'

'You saw them.'

'They must have been built pretty shoddy to fall down so easy.'

Grice said, 'Is that the kind of scenario you've had in mind? For the bunker?'

Eugene didn't answer. He said, 'And they flew a plane right into the Pentagon? How'd they do that?'

'Good question, Eugene.'

'I wouldn't have thought they'd get anywhere near the Pentagon. I'd have thought they'd use missile launchers. Knock that plane clean out of the sky.'

'Yes, you would have thought so.'

'I'd better call Jim.'

Jim Coffin didn't have a TV but he'd been listening to the radio. We heard Eugene say, 'I don't know. I haven't decided. I'm thinking on it. You want to come on up here, see it on the television?'

We ended up quite a crowd. Crystal drove over with her dogs. 'Figured I might as well,' she said. 'Nobody to make dinner for.'

She hadn't heard from Marc. She hadn't even tried his hotel again. 'Thing is, Mom,' she said, 'he might not even realize he's busted. Planes are grounded, cell phones aren't working. He probably thinks he's covered his ass. I mean, this has even gained him a bit more cheating time. So I'll just wait till he gets home. When somebody lies to me I prefer they do it to my face.'

I said, 'I'm still hoping there's been a misunderstanding. I thought you and Marc were rock solid.'

'Me too,' she said. 'The "rock solid" bit. By the way, I dropped his tofu in the trash before I left. I enjoyed that. Did Lois hear from Sandie yet? They're saying a lot of firefighters are missing.'

Herb kept trying Sandie's land line. Lois said he should call Patrick, see if he had any information. He said, 'I'm not calling Pat. He's a serving airman. He won't be taking calls on a day like this. He'll be suited up in case they get scrambled.'

Then Jim Coffin arrived. He watched all the replays.

Eugene said, 'What do you reckon?'

Jim just shook his head. He said he'd need to pick the bones of it.

Eugene said, 'Tell you what I think? The way those towers came down? Demolition job.'

Grice said, 'What are you talking about? They were hit by planes.'

'Maybe so,' said Eugene. 'The planes didn't knock them over, though. They didn't topple over, bit at a time. You ever see one of those demolitions on TV, when they're clearing a building in a built-up area? They bring them down neat as you like, so nothing else gets damaged. Highly skilled business. It's all depending on where they put the explosives and how they have them on timers. They take out one floor at a time, boom, boom, boom.'

Crystal said, 'So you're saying not only did two planes get hijacked and hit the towers but somebody went into those buildings and laid explosives and timers? Have you ever been in those buildings?'

'No. Have you?'

'I don't need to have done. Those kind of buildings you don't just stroll in with a bag of dynamite.'

'I'm just saying that's what it looked like. You got a better explanation?'

They were showing it again on the T V.

'See?' said Eugene. 'Look how neat it goes down.'

Crystal told him he was nuts.

'Well,' said Eugene, 'if they could hijack a bunch of planes and fly them into a bunch of buildings I don't see why they couldn't have laid explosives too. That'd probably be the easiest part. I'll bet they got workmen in and out of those buildings all the time, fixing stuff.'

The TV wasn't turned off all day and the air got bluer and bluer. Herb Moon wasn't usually given to cussing but every time we saw that second plane bank towards the tower his language got riper. Lois was quiet. She kept going to the phone and trying Sandie.

Then another tower at the World Trade Center came down that hadn't even been hit by a plane. Building Seven.

'Look at that!' said Eugene. 'A demolition if ever I saw one.'

Crystal said it could have been weakened by falling debris.

'Yup,' said Eugene. 'Or hit by flying pigs.'

About five thirty Lois got through to Sandie. She gave Herb the thumbs-up sign. We heard her say, 'And when you get him home tell him it's time to hang up his helmet. Tell him I said so.'

Sandie asked to speak to her daddy. Lois came back to the table. She said Gerry'd arrived at the site just before the second tower came down, breathed a lot of smoke and dust, but he was okay. They'd all gone back to the fire house to muster and rest for an hour, then they were heading back to search for survivors. They were putting up klieg lights so they could work all night.

Herb got off the phone. Lois said, 'I've never heard her like that before. All the years Gerry's been in the service. You'd think she'd be used to it by now.'

He said, 'She'll be all right. She's just shook up, and you know why? Because Gerry's shook up. There's more than three hundred firefighters not accounted for and that's like family to him. He won't rest till they're found. None of them will.'

Lois said, 'I know that. But after that it's time he took up golf.'

I put food on the table. I had no appetite but Vern and Eugene made a dint in it. Jim Coffin too. He said it was a pretty good dinner. He said he'd been on his own seventeen years, since his mom passed, and mainly he had Corn Pops for dinner. Only cooking he did was when he was driving a distance. I didn't understand.

Eugene said, 'You never cooked anything under the hood of your vehicle, Peggy? You haven't lived.'

JIM COFFIN'S EXCELLENT
MANIFOLD CHILLI DOGS

Wrap a bunch of Hebrew National franks in aluminium foil, nice and snug. Start your vehicle and drive around for five minutes till the engine's warm. Pull over. Stop the engine. Tuck the franks and a can of chilli beans on the exhaust manifold or on top of the engine block. Resume your journey.

Cooking distance: 20–30 miles.

I tried to persuade Crystal to stay over. She could have had one of the guest houses. But she said Shorty wouldn't settle. Shorty's her schnauzer.

Grice said, 'Not even on my bed? He can come in with me. I love to wake up to the smell of Ol' Roy breath.'

And with that she burst into tears. I guess she'd been holding it in all day. Vern saw her crying and he started, like his heart would break.

I said, 'Vern, what's wrong? Why are you crying?'

'Because that little girl's crying,' he said. 'And I don't know how I'm gonna get home.'

Crystal put her arms around him, told him everything was just fine.

He said, 'Is it? Did I do wrong?'

And that set me off. I didn't feel much for Vern but I hated to see him like a child. It pained me to think of the man he used to be, flying those fighters, keeping us safe in our beds. Then there were all those people dead or missing. Including my son-in-law, whatever his story was. All up, it had been a very upsetting day.

Herb went out for a smoke. Jim said he'd better be making a move and Eugene said he'd walk him to his pick-up. As Lois said, there's nothing like a couple of weeping women for clearing a room.

Crystal said, 'You didn't do wrong, Daddy. You never do wrong. It's been a bad day, that's all. A bad day all round.'

Grice said, 'So, who thinks Eugene and Jim'll be sleeping in their bunkers tonight? I don't.'

I didn't think so either. Eugene'd want to be where he could watch TV, in case of further developments.

Crystal said, 'Did he even put a bed in there yet?'

'Bunk frame and a sleeping-bag,' said Grice. 'Last I saw, there wasn't a mattress. Know what I think? I think Eugene and Jim are just playing at bunkers. Remember when you were a kid, building a hideaway in the yard? Down in the bee brush? A stash of *Mighty Mouse* comics and emergency Oreos?'

Crystal said, 'We didn't have that kind of yard. I'm a military brat, don't forget. I grew up in Quonset huts.'

'You poor child,' said Grice.

Crystal said she used to hide under the table sometimes. I don't recall that.

Vern said, 'Did we see a movie today?'

I knew how he felt.

I didn't sleep much. I was up at one, then again at four. Herb and Lois's light was burning and so was Grice's. I reckon Vern was the only one slept that night. He was worn out with all the company and all the day's events. Only thing was, when he woke up on Wednesday morning, he didn't remember any of it. It wasn't just the TV showing replays over and over. It was Vern too.

'Plane just flew plumb into a skyscraper, Herb. 767. Son of a gun.'

How many times did we hear that?

It was still early, not even eight o'clock, when the phone went.

It was Marc. He said, 'Peggy, do you know where Crystal is? Her phone's turned off.'

I took a deep breath. I've never gone in for play-acting but I thought I'd better make a good job of it for Crystal's sake.

I said, 'She's probably still sleeping. She was here for dinner last night and we all felt wrung out, watching all that horror yesterday. You okay?'

'Yeah,' he said. 'I can't get a flight home, that's all.'

'Crystal knows that. Your meeting go okay?'

'It was cancelled. Under the circumstances. Some people couldn't get in.'

'A wasted trip, then?'

'You could say.'

I really wanted it to be a big misunderstanding, for Crystal's sake, but I couldn't read him. I said, 'If I speak to Crystal I'll tell her you were trying to get her.'

He said his cell phone still wasn't working.

'Does she know which hotel you're at?'

'Oh, yes,' he said. 'But tell her not to worry. I'll probably go out, get breakfast. I'll try her again later.'

Grice said, 'Did he sound guilty?'

'I don't think so.'

'Did he sound like he had someone there with him?'

'What would that sound like?'

'I don't know, but I'm sure it sounds like something. What's your female intuition telling you?'

My female intuition wasn't telling me a darned thing. I said, 'Just don't talk about this in front of Herb. I don't want him reminded about Lois's carrying on.'

'That's a very long time ago.'

'But he's had enough reasons to remember it without us piling it on. He didn't just forgive her, Grice. He raised another man's child. You know what he said to me? He said he knew the minute Kirk was born it wasn't his child but as soon as he held him in his arms he fell in love with him.'

'Did he know who Lois had gone with?'

'I don't know when he figured that out. All I know is when Kath brought it all out in the open Herb didn't bat an eyelid. All he cared about was doing the best he could for Kirk.'

'And he forgave Lois.'

'She moved out for a while. I don't think Herb asked her to. She was just feeling mad at Kath, for speaking out, and mad at herself for what she'd done. I think she was even mad at Herb for staying so calm. And then she went home and they carried on as before.'

'They're an odd couple.'

'They are. But it works.'

Wednesday, the TV was on all day again but only Herb and Vern and Eugene were watching. They were calling the site Ground Zero. Just a mountain of smoking rubble. Relatives had started posting photos of people who hadn't come home. They were calling the attacks 'another Pearl Harbor'. They were saying Al Qaeda had done it.

Eugene said, 'Yup. That sounds about right. Another load of bunk. Next thing, we'll be going to war. Where is it they reckon this bin Laden's hiding? Afghanistan. Just watch. We'll be sending troops there before you know it.'

Herb said, 'What do you expect? We *are* at war. You think we should take this lying down?'

Eugene said that wasn't what he thought at all. He said he'd just like to know how a bunch of ragheads from the other side of the world were supposed to have pulled off everything that had happened. 'Where'd they learn to fly like that?' he said. 'You'd know better than me, Herb. You were an aviator. And where was the military yesterday? You telling me this adds up?'

Lois whispered, 'Let's go out, Peg. Herb's been awake half the night going on about those planes. I can't take another day of him and Eugene picking over this.'

We drove over to Crystal's, me, Lois and Grice. She had a three-bed clapboard Cape-style near Maquoit Bay. It needed a bit of fixing up when they bought it and after twenty years it still did. We found her in her workshop, hair in a bandanna, spring-cleaning in September.

I said, 'Did you hear from Marc?'

'I'm not answering my phone.'

'I know that. He called me.'

'Oh, yeah?' she said. 'Did you tell him he's been found out?'

'I did not. I played along. He said his meeting was cancelled but he doesn't know when he'll be able to get a flight. There'll be a backlog even when they start flying again.'

Lois said, 'He could get a Greyhound. Or a train. You got trains up here?'

Crystal said, 'Yes, Lois, we have trains.'

We went into the house to get coffee. There were bags of trash lined up by the front door. 'Marc's stuff,' said Crystal. 'Soon as he gets home he's going to have to turn right round and go shopping because all he'll have is the clothes he's wearing.'

I thought she was being over-hasty, and so did Grice. He suggested she hide the bags somewhere, just in case there had been a misunderstanding.

She said, 'I don't know why you're all so inclined to give him the benefit of the doubt. Did you ever get caught cheating?'

Grice jumped right in. He said, 'I did. But I wasn't married, of course. I was just kinda multiple-dating. Keeping my options open. I'm not saying it was the same thing.'

Lois said, 'Grice is just trying to distract you from the elephant in the room. It's okay. Everybody and their uncle Walt knows what I did. Well, all I'll say is, if Herb had put my clothes in the trash I wouldn't have blamed him. I reckon the wronged party is entitled to let rip. No sense bottling it up. You'll end up with an ulcer, or blood pressure. Whether you patch things up, that's another matter. I guess that depends on what you have to work with. I got lucky with Herb. He drives me nuts with his whittling and his plane talk, but he's pure gold, and I was the silliest fool on earth to cheat on him. But you know? That God-damned toothpaste, once it's out of the tube you can't put it back. Once you know something you can't stop knowing it. I hope you don't mind, Crystal, but I'm going to put some chest hairs on this coffee. Anybody else?'

She had two miniatures of Gentleman Jack in her purse.

Crystal's dogs hadn't been out. Grice took them for a run.

Lois said, 'He's a little sweetheart. Are there any more where you found him?'

Crystal said, 'Maybe we could take little Grice cuttings of him, like with one of those schefflera houseplants.'

Lois said she had a neighbour who was always giving her plant cuttings. 'I've tried to stop her,' she said. 'They take one look at me and die. Plants are nothing but trouble. We had a potted palm, don't ask me what it was, and when our old spaniel went a bit senile – no offence, Peg, but I reckon he had doggie Alzheimer's – he started cocking his leg and peeing on it. So that had to go. The palm tree, not the dog. We've got a fake fern now. Sandie got it for me for Mother's Day, and the only way you'd know it's not real is I haven't killed it. All you have to do is dust it about once a century. I leave Herb to do that.'

Crystal said, 'Know what I suddenly thought of last night? That time when we were kids and Sherry Gillis cut her foot. She was dripping blood everywhere and we had to drive her to the dispensary. Was that in England?'

It was at USAF Drampton. Lois said she didn't remember it.

I said, 'You were expecting Kirk. It was just before you were coming back Stateside for your confinement. You'd gotten really big so me and Gayle and Audrey were helping you clean your quarters, and Crystal and Sandie were out front selling Kool-Aid to passers-by.'

'That's it!' said Crystal. 'A nickel a cup. And there was a boy with us.'

'Was it the Kurlich boy?'

'Joey Kurlich, yes. He was a bit of a scaredy-cat.'

'He was killed in Vietnam.'

'Shit.'

Lois said, 'Well, it's kinda coming back to me now. The reason you had to drive Sherry to the dispensary was because Betty was grounded.'

'Wasn't me drove her. It was Audrey.'

'Whatever. Because Ed had taken the car keys. That was it.

Betty was being punished for some crime against humanity. She'd probably omitted to iron a good, sharp crease on Ed's PJ trousers.'

'No. It was because we'd been to the seashore, remember, the day before? And we were late getting back to the base.'

'Dinner not on the table,' said Lois. 'Like I said, a crime against humanity. Was Ed Gillis an ass-wipe or what?'

We were still reminiscing about that day when Grice came back with the dogs. 'Oh, excellent,' he said. 'I love it when you talk about the olden days.'

We'd been to the shore, the 'seaside', as Kath called it. I couldn't remember the name of the place, only that there was more side than sea. When the sun came out you could just about make out a line of water glinting in the distance.

Betty was on edge all day because Ed had made such a big deal out of her coming along with us. Where exactly were we going? What time would we be home? She sat knitting, kept looking at her watch. She didn't even bother to hike with us to find the ocean, and then when we did start for home she insisted on leading the way, and then she got us lost. I had to take over and drive the lead car.

I said, 'You know, as I recall we weren't very late. Maybe an hour?'

'Not even,' said Lois. 'And then that knucklehead decided she needed punishing. Went off on assignment and left her without transport.'

'And he took her ID. Two kids to feed and she couldn't even go to the commissary.'

'Remind me, when did that worm turn?'

Betty endured Ed's bullying for a long, long time. Every step she took, every dime she spent, it all had to be accounted for. And she wouldn't hear a word against him. She said he was a good provider and he just wanted to keep his family safe. Then one day she woke up.

'1963. It was President Kennedy ended that marriage.'

Lois roared. She said, 'I know they say Jack Kennedy'd screw anything with a pussy but Betty Gillis? Really, Peggy!'

'You know damn well what I mean. Betty loved those Kennedys. She went into full mourning when the President was shot so Ed's nose was out of joint. It was the week of Thanksgiving. A million and one things to do and Betty was sitting around weeping.'

'Turkey still in the freezer. Cranberry sauce not made. Don't bear thinking about. How come you know all this, Peg?'

'Because we were back in San Antonio by then, me and Crystal, and so were the Gillises. The day of the funeral Betty turned up on our doorstep in such a state. Ed had thrown their TV out of the window, to stop her watching.'

'Did it hit anybody?'

'No. Everybody was indoors watching the Requiem Mass.'

'So then she left him?'

'Yes. She just snapped. She moved in with us for a while till she figured out what to do, her and Carla. Carla was still a kid.'

'Didn't Ed try to stop her?'

'Oh, yes. On bended knee. Tears, promises, the whole nine yards, but credit to Betty, she was done with him. And I think the longer she stayed with us the more she realized what a short rope she'd been kept on all those years. Sometimes you have to get out from under before you even realize you've been there. Then Ed went back to Indiana, Betty moved back into their apartment and that was the end of that. She blossomed a bit, after she split from Ed.'

'Blossomed?' said Lois. 'Betty? Hardly.'

'She took up with Slick. And she was doing well selling those cleaning products.'

'Never going anywhere, though, was it? Betty and Slick? She was such a priss. I doubt he ever got past first base.'

Grice said, 'How did Slick 'n' Betty turn into Slick 'n' Kath?'

'Betty got cancer, Kath came over to visit with her, Betty died, Kath stayed on.'

'She stayed to help me and Herb nurse Kirk.'

'And Slick fell for her. At Betty's bedside. Now that is a love story.'

'Brilliant woman, Kath. She's the best. And tough. I don't know what she's made of but they should sell it to Boeing. How the hell did we get onto this?'

'My fault,' said Crystal. 'It all started with Sherry Gillis's cut toe. Still, it's better than talking about what happened yesterday.'

Lois said, 'You're right. I don't want to keep watching those buildings coming down. And I dread to think what Gerry's gonna be like, scrabbling around in that heap of rubble looking for bodies. He'll be dwelling on that the rest of his life.'

Crystal said they were still searching for survivors.

'Yeah,' said Lois. 'Searching but not finding any.'

We sat quiet for a while. Crystal has her place quite pretty. She tiled the kitchen herself. She's quite handy, my daughter.

Lois said, 'Another thing about Kath, she looks younger now than she did fifty years ago. Well, okay, not exactly. But you know what I mean. Remember how rough she looked, Peg, when we first knew her? We thought she was middle-aged.'

'She'd had a hard life.'

'And no stockings. It was a raw day and she was out with bare legs. All to see a stupid coffin go by.'

'Well, it was the King's coffin. It was a historic moment.'

'Which we didn't see.'

'Betty was certain she saw the Queen and Princess Margaret.'

'Yeah, sure.'

Grice said, 'But what exciting lives you had. And there I was thinking you military wives never got off the base.'

'Grice,' said Lois, 'we were in Norfolk, England. It was just nature and stuff. Birds. Sugar beet. Eels. Where was the nearest movie house, Peg?'

'King's Lynn.'

'We ever go there?'

'*The Lady with a Lamp*. Anna Neagle.'

'Are you serious? Do you actually remember that?'

I did remember it. I don't know why.

Lois said, 'This is going to sound really bad but I was just thinking, with what happened yesterday, if somebody wanted to disappear it'd be the perfect opportunity. You know? They're not finding many bodies.'

Crystal said, 'You're right. It does sound bad.'

'Well,' said Lois, 'I'm just saying.'

15

When we got back to Marvern, Herb and Vern and Eugene were sitting just as we'd left them. Jim Coffin had joined them.

Lois whispered, 'He's looking for another dinner.'

The TV was still on but they weren't watching it. Herb was drawing planes on a piece of paper towel, explaining what he thought had happened.

Lois said, 'Let it go, darling. There'll be a big investigation. They don't need you to figure out how it happened.'

'Maybe so,' said Herb. 'That don't mean I'm not allowed to think about it. I spoke to Sandie.'

'She okay?'

'Yeah. She's at the fire house with the other wives. They're helping out. They've got a lot of people bringing stuff in. Cookies and soda and stuff.'

'What for?'

'To show their appreciation.'

'Pay rise. That's the kind of appreciation firefighters need, not cookies.'

'People want to do something. It's only natural. They're not allowed on the crash site. They can't help with the search. People feel helpless.'

'So they make cookies?'

'And give blood. There's people lining up to give blood.'

'Only nobody needs it,' said Eugene. 'They're not going to find anybody now. It's nothing but steel and dust down there.'

Herb said, 'Sandie spoke to Pat. And you know what? That first plane, the first one that hit? When they realized it'd been hijacked they scrambled Otis. Only Pat wasn't there. He was on his way to the Westover base.'

Lois said, 'Where's Westover?'

'Over by Springfield. There was a big training exercise going on Tuesday morning. Some of them got sent to Westover, some of them got sent to a base down by Newburgh. So the Otis base wasn't even at full strength. Sandie said Pat's spitting nails. Otis went to Battle Stations and he was at Westover moving body bags.'

'Why was he moving body bags?'

'Part of the exercise, I guess. And Pat reckons the Otis guys who were scrambled, they didn't know for sure if it was the exercise or Real World. They sent two F-15s up but they didn't know where they were supposed to go or what they were supposed to do when they got there. Sounds like it was a real mess.'

I said, 'Then I guess they learned a few things yesterday. More than if it had just been an exercise.'

Eugene said, 'Like, if you've got three, four hijackings you need to put more than two fighters in the air.'

Vern said, 'Otis? Fuck didn't they scramble Langley?'

Just when you thought Vern'd nodded off he'd come out with something.

'Damn right, Vern,' said Herb. 'NORAD's got some questions to answer. You get a hijacking you've got standard intercept procedures. But that's not what's really bugging me. What I want to know is how they managed to hit those buildings.'

The way Herb explained it, the only way you could aim a plane the size of a 767 at a target not much wider than its wing span was to slow it down to landing speed. He said, 'And if you slow down to landing speed without landing, you're gonna stall. Anyway, that plane wasn't at landing speed. That plane was travelling. It turned, banked, hit the bullseye. Think of it like this. The door to your worm shed? Could you drive your pick-up through that opening at a hundred miles an hour? Eighty miles an hour even. You want to try it?'

Grice said, 'But, Herb, we all saw it. How can you say it's not possible when somebody proved it was possible, three times in one day?'

Lois groaned. She muttered, 'Cheers, Grice.'

Jim Coffin said, 'See, this all puts me in mind of Operation Northwoods.'

Lois said, 'Shall we go out again, Peg? Go shopping? Go shoot ourselves?'

But I didn't want to go out. I was interested in what they were saying. Herb knew about flying. He's a sensible guy. But Grice was right too. There was no point saying something couldn't be done when somebody had already gone and done it and we'd seen it live on TV. And I'd never heard of Operation Northwoods.

Jim said it was a plan dreamed up back in the sixties. 'What they call a false flag operation,' he said. 'You mount an attack or let somebody else mount an attack, then you blame it on the bad guys.'

'Why would you do that?'

'Because then you got an excuse to declare war.'

'Like Pearl Harbor,' said Eugene.

Jim said, 'Operation Northwoods, that was about Cuba. They had a bunch of plans, Lemnitzer and the top brass, and one of them was, make a drone to look like a passenger plane, unmanned, fly it by remote control, know what I mean? Then shoot it down and blame the Cubans for the loss of American lives. That was one of their ideas. Then you've got your *casus belli*. That's Latin for an excuse to bomb the shit outta somebody.'

'How do you know? That'd be classified information.'

'Not any more. Declassified some time back.'

'But they never did it.'

'No. Kennedy wouldn't buy it.'

Grice got very excited. He said, 'Hold on, hold on. Are you saying maybe those weren't real planes yesterday? But we saw the second one.'

'I'm saying it could have been a drone. Like a guided missile. Right, Herb?'

Herb was rubbing his eyes. Too much watching TV.

'I guess,' he said. 'That'd take some know-how, though, Jim. I don't think Al Qaeda's playing at that level.'

Grice said, 'No, I'm sorry, but those were real flights. There's a list of passengers. It's in the papers. Those were real people, with families. Where are they if they weren't on that plane?'

Eugene said, 'They're probably sequestered some place.'

'Sequestered? What, like for ever? Are they suddenly going to reappear? Families grieving for them and they turn up alive and well?'

Neither of them had an answer for that.

'Plus,' said Grice, 'what about all the people in the towers? And the firefighters? Nothing imaginary about them. There's a lot of people dead. That Northwoods thing, that was the US military, right? The US military planning to make it look like Cuba killed US citizens? So what are you saying about yesterday? That it was our own guys did it?'

Jim said, 'I guess time'll tell.'

'What does that mean?'

'See if we go to war. See who they decide the bad guys were.'

'No,' said Grice. I'd never seen him so hot under the collar. 'You haven't answered me. Are you telling me you think America'd kill thousands of its own people? Because that wasn't what the Northwoods thing was about. You said the Northwoods plan was going to be a fake plane, no real casualties. And, anyway, they never went ahead with it because it was a crazy idea.'

'All I'm saying is, if they thought of it forty years ago, no reason they couldn't think of it again. They got the know-how. Right, Herb?'

And Eugene said, 'Just because Kennedy wouldn't allow it don't mean George Bush wouldn't. Maybe they didn't even bother to run it by him.'

Grice said, 'I've heard enough of this. I'm going out.'

Lois said, 'And I'm coming with you.'

I followed them. Vern called after me, 'Peg, where's the bathroom?'

It made me happy when he remembered my name. I said, 'You're having a good day.'

'Gotta be,' he said. 'We're doing War Games.'

I waited while he did what he had to do, in case I had to mop up. Sometimes his aim wasn't so good.

I said, 'I was over to Crystal's this morning. She sent her love.'

'Yeah?' he said. 'You tell her about the War Games?'

Grice and Lois were sitting in the car.

Lois said, 'Thought you'd decided to stay in there with the lunatics. We were just going to leave without you.'

'Where are we going?'

'Anywhere. Just as long as I don't have to hear any more of that BS.'

'Herb wasn't saying much. Was he being polite?'

'Not necessarily. He was thinking. I haven't heard the last of this, trust me. He'll be awake all hours again, figuring out who did what. Find me a liquor store. I require anaesthesia.'

We drove into Waterville, looked around some. It was real quiet. The shops all had flags in their windows. People were stopping to talk on the street and we all knew what about. Lois bought bourbon. She said, 'I have a feeling it's going to be a long, long night.'

Grice said, 'We need to get rid of Jim Coffin. He's the trouble-maker. So, we won't show any sign of making dinner till he's gone. We'll starve him out.'

Lois said, 'You reckon? Didn't he say he lives on Coco Pops?'

'Corn Pops.'

'Same thing. He'll hang around like a bad smell, waiting for another Peggy Dewey special.'

Grice said, 'I know! Let's stay in town and get Chinese.'

I said, 'What about Vern?'

'Don't worry about Vern,' said Lois. 'Herb won't let him starve.'

'He remembered my name, just now, when I was leaving. He called me Peg.'

'He's been great since yesterday. Joining in and following what Herb was saying. Anything to do with flying, he's ace. So now you know what to do with him. Get him one of those Janes books. Herb's got one. Find out if there's a magazine. Herb'll know. It's a pity you can't get reruns of *Sky King*.'

Grice had never heard of *Sky King*.

Lois said, 'You young thing! Kirby Grant as Schuyler "Sky" King. He was like a cowboy, only with a Cessna instead of a horse. The boys all used to go crazy sending away for the gadgets – remember, Peg? A glow-in-the-dark signalscope. You had to send in a peanut-butter label and a quarter, or something like that.'

Lois and Herb were due to leave on Sunday.

Lois said, 'Don't be downhearted. You're going to come down to the city, get a little R and R.'

I didn't see how I could talk to Crystal about a vacation when she had husband trouble.

Lois said, 'No, but as soon as she's dealt with him. You can't put your life on hold, Peg. And if you don't fix something I'll be on the phone to her.'

Grice said, 'What do you think's going to happen when Marc gets home? Is he going to come clean? Is he going try to bluff his way out of it?'

Lois thought Marc would pretend it was all a mix-up. 'He'll say the girl at the office got it completely wrong and he never said anything about taking vacation. He'll probably call her an idiot. Then he'll buy her a box of candy on the quiet.'

Grice thought he'd own up but make it seem like nothing had actually happened.

'Could be,' said Lois. ' "Honey, I just needed time to think. Sure, I get offers. There was somebody, but as soon as I got down to Jersey I realized she didn't mean a thing to me. I'd have turned right around and come home if flights hadn't been grounded." Or, how about this, maybe he went to get a jowl lift? Guys can have all kinds of reasons for being secretive.'

It rained while we were in the Peking Panda. Nothing much. Just a light shower.

Lois said, 'When we get back to Marvern, if Jim Coffin's still sitting there we have to do something drastic. We gotta get rid of him.'

Grice said, 'How about stripping off?'

Lois said, 'I will if you will. Not Peggy, though. I reckon Mr Coffin's a bit sweet on her. He wouldn't take much encouraging there. What do you think, Peg? Did your cherry-cola ham get his juices flowing?'

The ground was slick with the rain.

'Okay,' said Lois, 'back to Conspiracy Central. Cleared for take-off.'

She was running to the car, doing an airplane impersonation, like a kid, but with old-lady legs and lime green sneakers. Over she went. She was still laughing when we reached her, and trying to get up, but her right leg wouldn't move. It was kinda rolled out to the side. A young couple came over to see if they could help. They couldn't. Then she stopped laughing. If we tried to move her even an inch she screamed.

Grice called 911. The rain came on heavier. Someone held an umbrella over Lois. I don't know how long we waited. It seemed like a very long time and Lois had started using the F-word. We called Herb and he said he'd drive over, but I told him to wait till we knew where they'd be taking her.

'Augusta,' somebody said. 'If she's busted her leg they'll take her to Augusta.'

It wasn't her leg, it was her hip. The paramedics asked her if she had insurance.

'Course I've got insurance,' she said. 'What do you think? I'm some fucking illegal? Some fucking fence-hopper?'

They said it was probably the shock making her aggressive. That's all they knew.

We followed the ambulance to Augusta, and Herb met us there. He said he'd left Vern with Eugene and Jim. 'I hope I did right,' he said. 'Vern seemed happy enough.'

I went in to see Lois for five minutes. They'd made her comfortable, told her they'd operate in the morning.

She said, 'Tights are ruined. They told me I'll most likely need a new hip. There's probably not enough good bone there to mend it.'

I said, 'You'll be like those gymnasts when they're done with you. You'll be doing the splits and all.'

Then she started crying. I don't believe I'd ever seen Lois cry.

She said, 'I hate this being-eighty shit.'

I said, 'You're not. You're seventy-seven.'

'Same thing,' she said. 'What's the point? Why am I still here, Peg? I've eaten junk all my life. I drink too much. I should be dead by now.'

'Nice talk. I thought you were going to stick around till that great-grandbaby was ready for some fashion notes.'

She blew her nose. 'I'm just not cut out to be old. Some people are old when they're fifty. It suits them. Maybe I'll get pneumonia. That can happen.'

'Well, it's not going to happen to you. They told Herb they'll have you up and out of bed within twenty-four hours.'

'You serious? And then I can go home?'

'I don't know about that. I expect you'll need rehab.'

'You mean like a drug addict?'

'No, to improve your personality.'

She managed a smile.

I said, 'Do you remember what you said to Betty when you visited her, just before she passed?'

'That's cheerful. No, I don't.'

'You asked her what she thought she was doing, lying in the sack in the middle of the day. You said, "Call yourself a home-maker? I want to see you outta that cot, floors waxed and gear squared away."'

'Did she laugh?'

'Eventually. She was upset because she'd peed in the bed. You told her she was making a vital contribution to full employment in the hospital laundry.'

'I said that? To a dying woman?'

'More or less. You told her she was helping to keep some nose-miner off welfare.'

'Peg,' she said, 'if I don't make it, tell Sandie she has to have Herb go live with her. He can't stay on his own.'

I promised I would, though as a matter of fact I think Herb Moon would manage very well on his own. I said, 'Anything else? What's your secret number for the ATM?'

She smiled, then she drifted off.

It was after dark when we got back to Marvern. House lights blazing, nobody around. I called Kath to talk about Tuesday's events and tell her what had happened to Lois.

She said, 'I couldn't sleep last night, for thinking about it. Specially them that jumped. You ever been up there in those towers? I have. Slick took me for dinner, for my seventeenth. Windows on the World, one hundred and sixth floor. It gave me the hoo-hahs, being so high up, and we didn't even sit near a window. I hardly ate a thing. And now I keep picturing us sitting there, up in the sky. How bad would it have to be, Peg, to jump? And then Sandie's hubby, I keep thinking about him too. I pray he's not one of the ones that's missing.'

I told her Gerry Carroll was alive and working at the rescue site, Ground Zero. And that Lois was convinced she was going to die under the anaesthetic but she didn't mind because she didn't think old age suited her.

Kath said, 'Who does it suit?'

Vern's mom suited old age. So did mine, come to that. I'd say she was only in her fifties when she started acting cranky and having people run around after her.

Kath said, 'Lois'll be right as ninepence if they give her one of these new hips.'

'Right as ninepence' is English for 'just fine'.

She said, 'But you'll have her there with you longer than you thought, Peggy. You'll have her convalescing and then she'll get on your pippin.'

'They said she'll be up and walking by the weekend.'

'She will. But she won't be able to go home. They'll want to see her back at the hospital, to make sure everything's all right, before they sign her off. And even then, how's Herb going to bring her all that long way? She won't be able to sit in the car all those hours. I know about it because there's a lady goes to my hairdresser who had it done last year and she couldn't drive for weeks, and even with her seat tipped back she couldn't sit in a car for long.'

I told her I didn't care how long Herb and Lois stayed. The longer the better, as far as I was concerned. I said, 'Herb's been terrific with Vern.'

'Yes,' she said. 'He would be. He was good with Kirk, too, and that was a hard row for anybody to hoe. He doesn't allow things to rile him.'

'Lo was cussing at the nurses.'

'She'll still be cussing when they screw the lid on her casket. She'll give St Peter a mouthful, that one.'

Half an hour, and Kath called me back. She said, 'Now, I don't know what you're going to think of this but I was telling Slick about Lois's accident and he said if she's allowed to travel and she needs to stretch out he can drive up there and bring her home in the Buick.'

I didn't know Slick had a Buick.

Kath said, 'He's got all sorts. If it's old and it's got wheels Slick'll buy it. But here's the thing, Peg. The Buick's not a regular motor. It's an old hearse.'

'You mean, like a funeral carriage?'

'Yes. But it's very nice. Not black. More of a dove grey. And we could give her a mattress, slide her in, bring her home horizontal.'

'Dead or alive.'

'Don't say it. She'll be all right. It'll take more than a broken hip to finish old Copper-knob. Any road, mention it to Herb. Tell him Slick's willing. All he has to do is say the word.'

Grice thought it was the best idea ever. He said, 'And I call dibs on riding with Slick. I've got a black tie.'

About nine o'clock Eugene walked in, carrying a generator battery. He was alone.

I said, 'Where's Vern?'

He looked at me. He said, 'Probably in his bedroom.'

I knew Vern wouldn't be in his room. Since Crystal moved him into a single he can never remember where it is. I said, 'He's supposed to be with you and Jim.'

'Yeah,' he said. 'He was. We had to go out, check on something and he didn't want to come with us. He said he'd be okay for five minutes.'

'But it wasn't five minutes. Me and Grice have been home nearly an hour. So where the hell is Vern?'

Eugene stood there, scratching his greasy head. He said, 'I guess time got away from me. But he'll be around. He won't have gone far.'

'In the dark? Up dirt tracks? Where insane people are digging tunnels? He's probably out there, broken his neck.'

'Or fallen off the dock,' said Grice. 'Can Vern swim?'

I said we should call out the sheriff's department right away but Eugene said he wasn't having no deputy poking around on his land when there was no good reason. His land! Then Grice suggested we search a bit, try to find Vern ourselves first, because it might not look good if it came out that he'd been left unattended.

I said, 'One hour. Then I'm reporting him missing. And get Jim Coffin back here. The least he can do is help us to search.'

The phone rang. It was Crystal. She said, 'What's up? Bad moment?'

I guess I sounded stressed out. I said, 'Lois fell, broke her hip. She's in Augusta, getting surgery in the morning.'

Crystal said, 'I'll bet she turned the air blue. Well, let me know if she needs visitors. I'm sitting here, can't settle to anything. You know what I'm worried about? If Marc doesn't come home soon I'll have burned up all my fury.'

She was feeling low. She just wanted to talk. I said, 'Can I call you back? I need to get off the phone.'

'Mom?' she said. 'You okay? Is there something else?'

Well, then I had to tell her.

She said, 'I'm on my way.'

I didn't want her to drive in the dark and the rain. We'd already had two mishaps in one day. Kath always says bad things come in threes.

Crystal said, 'I think that old rule got canned on Tuesday. I reckon it's the open season for bad things. Don't worry, I'll drive carefully. I want to see Eugene, tell him what an inconsiderate asshole he is.'

'Grice already told him.'

'Did you ask Banjo where Dad is? He's a pretty smart dog.'

Banjo had been out all day.

'He's probably getting laid. I'll bring my mutts. Dad loves Browser. If he hears Browser barking he'll call out.'

Me and Grice went around the yard and the outhouses and the dock with flashlights, calling Vern's name. We checked all the guest houses, and Eugene went up through the trees to the bunker. Jim Coffin said he'd be right over.

Grice said, 'What about the guy next door? We should ask him to check his barn and stuff.'

'Okay. You go. His name's Cort Cooper.'

'No, you go. He knows you.'

A Maine night can be very, very dark. I overshot the turning to Cooper's and had to back up. Cort had heard the car and come out onto his stoop. His little dog was fussing.

I said, 'It's Peggy. From Marvern.'

'Yes,' he said. 'I see you now.'

'Vern's gone missing. Could I take a turn round your yard, see if he's here?'

'Certainly not,' he said. 'That's no job for a lady. This is bear country.'

'I've never seen a bear.'

'But they've likely seen you. My wife used to have bird-feeders all over. Nothing in them now but the bears still drop by, on the off-chance. They won't hurt you. Give you a fright, though. Just hold on while I find my boots.' He was wearing an old bathrobe.

I said, 'I'm sorry to get you from your bed.'

'You didn't,' he said. 'This is my casual evening wear. There's a chair up on the deck. You go sit down while Herk and I check the outhouses.'

They didn't find Vern.

I said, 'It was a long shot.'

'Has he gone missing before?'

'Never. He hardly gets out of his chair all day.'

'That's what I thought. I never see him. Even when his wife was alive, she was the one you'd see out and about. I don't suppose you'd care for a vodka martini?'

'I would, but I need to get back. Report Vern missing.'

'Of course.'

He opened the car door for me, like a southern gentleman would. Since we left Texas, Grice is the only person I know with any manners.

I said, 'Terrible events yesterday.'

'Indeed,' he said. 'Beyond belief.'

Herb came in from the hospital. He looked beat, but as soon as he heard what had happened he pulled on his slicker and came out searching too. He said he felt bad, seeing he was the one who'd left Vern with Eugene.

I said, 'Herb, it's not your fault Vern has an idiot for a stepson.'

Then two women turned up with Jim Coffin. Merle and Corky. I'll tell you the truth, out there in the dark I thought Corky was a guy. She doesn't dress pretty, even for Maine. Merle and Corky had brought their hounds with them, redbones, Eugene said, which is a kind of coon hound. They used them to take flatlanders out hunting for black bear. City folk mainly, people who worked in offices and wanted a taste of the wild.

Jim said, 'They'll need something Vern's been wearing. Give the hounds a scent.'

It seemed to me that bear hounds might not be interested in tracking a person. One whiff of a bear and they'd be off, going about their rightful business, but Eugene said I underestimated what a well-bred redbone could do.

I said, 'Well, the hour's nearly up. Just so's you know. You don't find him real soon I'll be calling it in.'

I went to fetch something of Vern's for the dogs. I don't know what made me look into my bedroom. We'd already searched the house. It was all in darkness. I was just about to close the door when I heard a voice, muffled: 'Heading one three zero. Dewdrop One, got a target twenty right.'

Dewdrop was Vern's call sign when he was flying. I turned the light on. There was nobody there. I even looked under the bed. I called his name.

Next thing I heard was, 'We got a man down. Man down. Seven right.'

I opened the closet door and there was Vern, curled up in his singlet and his Y-fronts. 'Dewdrop One, I see a chute, ten right,' said Vern. 'Beeper, beeper. Come up, voice.'

I said, 'Vern! What are you doing in there?'

'Got a man down,' he said. 'I reckon it's Herb Moon.'

I said, 'No, Vern, Herb Moon's driving up and down the road searching for you.'

'You sure about that? I thought I saw a chute but I can't raise him.'

I said, 'Herb's fine. Eugene's out on the water looking for your drowned body. We've got hounds out there, waiting to track you.'

He was shivering. I called Grice and he came in to help me haul Vern out of the closet. We took him into the kitchen, put him in his bathrobe and sat him next to the wood-burner. Merle and Corky loaded their hounds back onto their truck and came in for a cup of coffee. That was when I realized Corky was a gal.

Grice offered to go out and holler for Eugene to come in off the water but I said to leave him out there. Let him catch his death. It was all his damned fault anyhow. The main thing was to let Herb know we'd called off the search. I knew there'd be no settling Vern until he saw that Herb was okay.

Crystal arrived and Herb pulled in right behind her.

Her first words were, 'Where's that brainless bag of shit?'

I said, 'It's okay. We found your dad. He was hunkered in a closet, thought he was flying a mission. But, Herb, he's convinced you got hit and ditched. You'd better get inside and show him you're still in one piece.'

Well, of course joy broke out when Vern saw his old buddy. 'I knew it,' he said. 'I told them I seen a chute. Man, you had me worried, though.'

Jim Coffin was pouring coffee when Eugene came in. 'Come and set yourself down,' he said. 'Vern's found and coffee's brewed.'

You'd have thought it was his kitchen, the way he carried on. I was so damned tired I just wanted them all to drink up and leave, but Eugene commenced looking for cookies, making a party of it, and Crystal was squaring up for a fight. The way I looked at it, in the end there was no harm done. Vern was okay. I'd have left it at that. But not Crystal.

She said, 'What was so damned important you had to leave the house, leave my daddy unattended? What do you think Martine'd say if she could see you being so neglectful?'

All he said was, 'You leave my mother outta this.'

Then she said, 'I suppose you were up at the bunker. Well, now you've had your catastrophic event. You've been preparing for it long enough. All that canned stew. How come you're still above ground? What are you waiting for? Why don't you just go down your rat hole and stay there?'

Well, that touched a nerve. Eugene came out fighting. He said, 'When things escalate you'll be begging to be let in.'

'Escalate?' said Crystal. 'Escalate? Three thousand dead not enough for you?'

'That was just the start,' he said. 'Now Bush'll do anything he likes and he'll tell you it's for your own good. He'll have Big Brother watching you. He'll try and take your guns away. He thinks he can take mine he'd better think again. He'll start a war, you watch. He's already said he will, near as damn it. And my bunker ain't no rat hole.'

So the one called Merle said, 'But who's Bush gonna go after? He says he's gonna hunt them down, but Al Qaeda started it and nobody knows where they're at.'

'You believe that?' said Eugene. 'Al Qaeda? Don't make me laugh. Last I heard they'd only just discovered the wheel.'

Corky said, 'I didn't know you got a bunker set up, Gene. You get one of them survival pods? I'd sure like to see it some time.'

Eugene ignored that. For one thing he doesn't like people calling him 'Gene'.

Grice said, 'Who did it, then? If it wasn't Al Qaeda?'

'Think,' said Eugene. 'Who's got the technology? Who's got the balls? Who's got a sticky finger in every American pie?'

Nobody said a word.

'Israel,' he said. 'You folks all asleep? The Israelis, that's who.'

'Whoah,' said Crystal. 'I've heard a lot of craziness from you but that beats all. Israel? They're our ally, you nut.'

'Tell you what,' said Eugene, 'we can talk about this again a year from now. See who was right. And regarding Vern, if you ask me you all make way too much fuss about him. Just because he's gone a bit strange don't mean he needs watching every minute. You all right there, Vern?'

Vern said, 'Yup. Didn't get dinner yet, though.'

Eugene said, 'And Herb agrees with me, don't you, Herb?'

But poor Herb had fallen asleep where he sat, chin on his chest.

Merle and Corky got ready to leave. They said they'd swing by Cooper's, let Cort know Vern had been found.

I said, 'He told me he gets bears on his spread.'

Crystal said it was because he let the place get so messy. She said he'd forget to bring his trash out front, let it pile up for weeks. 'I don't know why he doesn't sell up,' she said.

'Sentimental attachment,' said Corky. 'Don't forget now, Gene, I'd sure love to get a look at your pod some time.'

But Eugene just carried on rolling a cigarette and never gave her an answer. Crystal went to see them off. She came back indoors.

'They gone?' he said.

Grice said, 'Did Corky do something to offend you? There some reason you ignored her? They turned out to help search for Vern.'

I said, 'That was a real neighbourly thing to do. Are they sisters?'

Crystal said, 'Mom! They're not sisters!'

Eugene growled, 'Pair of lesbeens. We never used to get those types around here.'

Well, how was I supposed to know what they were? We didn't get a whole lot of that in Texas.

Eugene said, 'I'll bet they vote Democrat too.'

There was no pleasing him.

I said, 'You don't trust George Bush. You don't like Democrats. So who do you want people to vote for?'

'I just want folk to think for theirselves,' he said. 'Before they pass a law against it.'

16

Saturday my son-in-law arrived home and showed his sorry face, though I didn't hear about it till Monday morning. Crystal phoned to see how Lois was doing. Lois was doing fine. She hadn't died under the knife, like she'd predicted, and they'd had her out of bed, torturing her with physiotherapy. They'd told Herb she'd be discharged the very minute she was fit. Grice said that was hospital-speak for 'Get this trouble-maker out of here.'

I said, 'Any sign of Marc?'

'Oh, yes,' she said. 'He got home Saturday afternoon.'

'And?'

'How long do you have?'

'Tell me the end first. Did he confess? Have you forgiven him?'

She said, 'How can you forgive a person when they keep changing their story? First you need to know what you're forgiving.'

'Is he there? Did he go to work today?'

'Yes.'

'So he walked in and what happened?'

'Okay, I'll give you the short version. He walked in and I could tell straight off he knew he was busted.'

'He look guilty?'

'No, but he spent way too long greeting the dogs.'

'Did he kiss you?'

'Mom! We've been married more than twenty years. So I asked him if he'd eaten, and he had, and then I asked him if he'd called the office and he pretended he hadn't heard me.'

'Playing for time.'

'Yes. Waiting to see how I was going to play it. So I asked him why he'd told people he was going on vacation. He said, "I didn't." I said, "Well, that's what Claudette said." So then he says Claudette's a moron. Claudette! Who's been there as long as he has and practically runs the place. He's always said so. "Don't know what we'd do without Claudette." Then he backed off a bit and said, well, she must just have misunderstood. And I said it was hard to see how anybody, even a moron, let alone a very experienced office manager, could mix up "going to a big meeting in Newark" with "taking the kayak up to Moosehead Lake".'

'What'd he say to that?'

'He went for a shower.'

'Playing for time again.'

'Yeah. Then he came out of the shower with a new story. He'd gone down to Newark for a physical. He hadn't told me and he hadn't gone locally because he didn't want to worry me. He said he'd been having urinary issues.'

'What does that mean?'

'Getting up to pee a lot in the night. It happens to men when they get to a certain age. Prostate. I pointed out that I wasn't the kind of woman to get into a flap about her husband's health problems. I'd just have asked around about urologists. Offered to go with him to the doctor's office, more than likely. He said he'd just preferred to check it out without my knowing. So I said, "Okay, who's the doctor and what did he say?" Dr Abrahams, and everything was normal.'

'You believe him?'

'Of course not. I said it seemed an awful long way to go to have a guy stick his finger up your backside.'

She could have spared me that information.

'Per rectum, Mom,' she said. 'That way they can feel if the prostate's enlarged. I asked him if they looked at his PSA levels. Yes, all fine. Which is surprising because that's a blood test and you wouldn't expect to get the result of that for at least a week. So I asked to see the report but you know, surprise, surprise, Dr Abrahams is going to mail it.'

'Did you let it drop?'

'Kind of. I said we should schedule a follow-up, maybe a year from now. And I'd go with him next time. Or, even better, just find a doctor closer to home instead of wasting money on flights and hotels. I could see him figuring how he'd finagle his way out of that. You could almost hear the cogs turning. Know what cracked it? Know what put a stop to all the bullshit? When he opened his closet and saw his clothes were gone.'

'Did you take everything?'

'Everything. Some of it was still in trash bags under my work bench but he didn't know that. I told him he could stand there in nothing but a towel until I got the truth. Her name's Mia. You know what that means? It means she's a child practically.'

'How'd you know that?'

'Mia. Mom, nobody called their kid Mia until Mia Farrow came on the scene. I'd say she's twenty-five, tops.'

'Where did he meet her?'

'I don't know. Don't care. Some trade thing, I guess. She probably works for *Citrus Fruits Monthly*. *Apple Farmer Weekly*. He said he was sorry but it couldn't come as a surprise to me, considering how things had been lately.'

'You been having problems?'

'Not that I was aware of. He said we didn't have anything in common any more. I said, "Well, we've got a mortgage and two dogs," and he said I was just being obtuse. He told me to stop being infantile and give him his clothes. I told him I'd have them sent on to wherever he was going to be living.'

'Are you sure? You don't want to cool off, try starting over?'

'Not after he called me a vindictive, dried-up old bitch.'

'That doesn't sound like Marc.'

'Nothing sounds like Marc any more. I guess I must be a dried-up old bitch compared to young Mia. The "vindictive" bit was because of his Armani bomber.'

'Marc has an Armani bomber?'

'Had. I took it to Goodwill.'

Like Grice said, there are some things a person can forgive and then there's giving away designer apparel.

Marc moved into the Comfort Inn in Portland.

'Until I see sense,' said Crystal. 'Ha! He's dreaming.'

If Vern had played around, would I have given him a second chance? I don't know. He was never a skirt-chaser. Crystal didn't ask for my advice anyway. She had it very clear in her mind. She said, 'If it had been a one-off, you know? Office party, too many beers, it might have been different. But he booked a hotel, Mom, and a plane ticket. So now I wonder about other times he's been away. He lied to me, lied to people at the office, made me look an idiot. And then he had to go and play the went-to-see-a-doctor-didn't-want-to-worry-you card. I hope she was worth it.'

She said she wasn't missing him but I know my daughter. It took me back to when she was a kid. If Vern yelled at her she'd stick out her chin, determined not to let him see her cry.

On 21 September Maine General discharged Lois.

'Bundled me out the door, more like,' she said. 'Look at me. I'm a cripple.'

She wasn't. She was getting around just fine on crutches.

Herb said, 'There's no pleasing you. You cussed them out for keeping you there and now you're complaining they sent you home.'

Of course they hadn't sent her home. They'd sent her back to Marvern until they saw her again, first week of November. Sandie called me. She said, 'Do you want me to come up there, Aunt Peggy? You've got enough to do looking after Vern and I don't imagine this has made Mom any easier.'

She was right about that. We were on egg shells around Lois. One minute she'd bite your head off, next thing she'd be sobbing and saying all she was fit for was the breaker's yard. They said it was the anaesthetic had caused it. But every day she hobbled a bit further, and if she turned the air blue, we just stopped our ears. There was no point in Sandie making that long journey. It sounded like Gerry needed her more than Lois did. When he wasn't on watch he was still doing turns at Ground Zero, picking through the dust for remains. And then there were all the funerals.

Sandie said, 'Gerry's fire house didn't lose anyone but Brooklyn Heights lost six and he knew them all. They were caught in the

Marriott when the South Tower came down. Then there's six killed from Bed Stuy, seven from Red Hook. He's worn his dress blues more this month than in all the years he's been in the service.'

I said, 'He must feel grateful to be alive.'

'No,' she said. 'He just feels guilty as hell. Well, you let me know if you need me up there.'

But we coped.

As Grice said, 'New hip, bigger mouth. It's a well-known phenomenon.'

Lo's argufying was mainly aimed at Eugene, who had left off digging the access tunnel to his bunker and bought a bunch of legal pads, which he was filling up with his theories about the events of September 11. Every time their paths crossed Lois told him he was a raving effing lunatic and he'd hold up one grimy finger and say, 'The day I get a straight answer to just one of my questions, just one, I'll be happy to reconsider. Right now, seems you're the one that's raving. Rest of the time you appear to have your head in the sand.'

He was calm as a clam when she started in on him, which made her even madder. She threw a coffee mug at him one morning, broke the handle off and caused Vern to cry. Even Herb wouldn't stand for that. He told her to get out of the kitchen until she remembered her manners, and I don't know who was more shocked, Lois or me and Grice, but she did leave and made a meal of it too, groaning and banging about with her crutches.

I left it a few minutes, then went after her. She was out on the dock. I asked her if she was pain. She said of course she was in effing pain.

She said, 'Do you think drowning's an easy way to go?'

I said, 'No. I think it'd be a terrible way to go. You did once talk of shooting yourself. A long time ago.'

'And you stopped me?'

'You didn't have a gun.'

'I shouldn't have given up so easily. I'll bet I know where that was. I'll bet that was at Drampton, Norfolk, backside of the eff-ing moon.'

'It was. They were having a Fen Blow. Remember that?'

A Fen Blow was a horrible whistling, whining wind that blew so hard it lifted the earth off the fields, like a sandstorm. They couldn't fly sorties in weather like that so the jocks were mostly at home, driving us wives crazy.

Lois said she kind of remembered.

I said, 'You offered to shoot me and then you changed your mind, told me to shoot you first.'

'I guess I had my reasons.'

'Mine were better. I'd stove in my collar-bone. I was strapped up, couldn't really drive. Getting dressed was quite a project. Then the Blow started and flights were grounded. Vern kept going to the window every five minutes hoping to see a patch of sky. Betty kept dropping by with food, like Vern was liable to starve because I was cooking one-handed.'

'The Betty Gillis Food Wagon. Delivering to a disaster zone near you. Remember when Okey Jackson bought it? Betty was round at Gayle's three times a day wearing her oven mitts. Pot roasts. Pasta bakes. God almighty, all Gayle wanted was strong drink and smokes. Canned turkey chunks with macaroni and Velveeta. Betty ever bring you that?'

'Something like. The turkey chunks sound familiar.'

BETTY'S FIVE-CAN COMFORT CASSEROLE

1 can turkey chunks

1 can condensed chicken-noodle soup

1 can sweetcorn

1 can peas

1 can whole white potatoes

Mix everything together and bake in a medium oven for 1 hour. Always appreciated by a shut-in neighbour or a hubby coping on his own.

'Of course, that was before we had this five-a-day bullshit.'

Lois swore that five-a-day was just something dreamed up by carrot farmers. She said the more they preached about what people should eat the more inclined she was to live on Milky Ways and booze. She said, 'The government should mind their own Goddamned business, which is to stop Al fucking Qaeda flying planes into our buildings, not telling me to eat more salad. Oh, no, not Al Qaeda. I forgot. Those planes were empty. They were guided by remote control. Rumsfeld did it. Or little green men from Mars. That Eugene is certifiable, Peg. We gotta get you out of here. You're coming down to civilization and you're getting a manicure and a shoulder rub.'

'Does that mean you changed your mind about drowning yourself?'

'It remains an option.'

'You've got an awful lot to live for.'

'Yeah?'

'You've got Sandie. Two grandsons. And now this little great-grandbaby.'

'I guess.'

'You've got a brand new hip.'

'Okay. You made your point.'

'And I'll tell you something else. As a friend. While you're up here recuperating you could let your natural hair grow in. Nobody around here cares what you look like.'

She said, 'You mean stop colouring it?'

'Let the white grow in. You'll look real pretty. Herb'll think he's got a new woman.'

'Sure,' she said. 'And why don't I get me some orthotic shoes too? Fuck off, Dewey. I came into this world Radiant Auburn and I'm going out the same shade. And Herb don't need a new woman. All he needs is me and a good lumber yard.'

Keen as she was to get home, Lo didn't see the funny side to Slick's offer of the Buick funeral car. She said she'd wait till Maine General signed her off and then she'd go the regular way.

Grice said, 'You mean having to stop every half-hour, thereby taking about three months to get to White Plains and generally tormenting Herb.'

He was disappointed. He'd been looking forward to riding in Slick's hearse. He said, 'She's such a spoilsport. Couldn't you just picture it? A recumbent Lois giving people the finger all the way through Massachusetts and Connecticut.'

Eugene ceased going to the bunker. He spent his days sitting at the kitchen table with Jim Coffin, chewing over what had happened on September 11 and filling up his yellow pads with craziness. Where was the wreckage at Shanksville? Where was the wreckage at the Pentagon? How come none of the pilots had Maydayed? Every day he had more questions.

If a customer came and rang the bell for the bait counter he'd get real annoyed about having to leave off his scribbling. He wanted to put Vern in the store but Vern couldn't have managed the money side of things and Grice couldn't do it, even though he did offer. Grice didn't know his Mickey Finns from his March Whites.

I don't know if it was hearing Lois talk about going home, but it was around that time Vern started asking to go home. He'd be perfectly happy, napping out on the dock, checking his eyelids for light leaks, as Herb called it, and then he'd suddenly get it into his head that he had to be someplace else.

'You *are* home,' we'd say, but he didn't believe us. We'd show him his room and the photo of Martine on his night-stand. We'd take him out and show him the worm sheds and the bait store and he still wouldn't have it. He'd get so mad. It was Crystal who figured out it might be Great Moose he was thinking of, where he'd grown up.

The Deweys used to farm out there, sheep mainly. I was only ever there once, must have been 1951, just before Vern was posted to England and we brought Crystal up to Maine to meet his folks. I'm no expert but I don't think Pop Dewey was a big success as a farmer. There always seemed to be some hard-luck story – livestock'd come to a bad end, prices'd gone down. Plus Vern's mom was a quarrelsome woman so by the time Pop had accidentally wired himself to the electric mains she hardly had a single neighbour willing to condole with her or come to the burying.

Vern seemed so determined Marvern wasn't his home I wondered if we should drive him out to Great Moose some day, let him see there was probably nothing left but a vacant lot, but Crystal said that wouldn't be a good idea. She said we just needed to find other things to distract him, until the moment had passed.

Lois said to her, 'You're so full of bright ideas, you come and distract him. Peggy's been doing it for nearly a year. Look at her. She needs a rest.'

Crystal didn't like that.

Then Lois said, 'I told you that the night you and your husband were over to dinner but I guess you weren't listening. Friend husband snapped his fingers and you went hurrying off like a good little wifey. Lot of good that did you.'

Crystal didn't say a word. She just went out, pretended the dogs needed walking, which they didn't. Poor old Browser looked at her as if to say, 'Hunh?'

I said, 'That was below the belt.'

Lois said, 'Hey, I speak as I find. Otherwise you might as well say nothing.'

And Grice said, 'Yes, and that's always a good alternative to keep in mind.'

When Crystal came back I heard her loading the dogs into her hatchback. I ran out to her. I said, 'You're not leaving without saying goodbye?'

She said, 'It's not you, Mom. It's Big Mouth. Does she ever keep her opinions to herself?'

Like I told her, the years didn't mellow Lois. I said, 'You used to like her when you were a kid. At Drampton and McConnell, you were always round at the Moons' place.'

She said, 'That was because I liked Sandie. And they always had better cookies than we did. Look, I know you need a rest. I'm not taking you for granted. I just need to get my head straight about Marc.'

'And how's that going?'

'I don't know. Money and stuff. It's a big mess.'

'Are you talking?'

'He wants to come home.'

'Do you want him to?'

'I thought I might move in here for a while.'

'I'd like that.'

'But not while Lois is here because I wouldn't last a day without throttling her. After she's gone home. And then if you want to go away, take a breather, I'll look after Dad. Grice can go too, if he wants to. It's time Eugene got off his butt and helped out.'

Grice wasn't sure.

I said, 'I thought we could go to Kath's. She'd put us up and she's handy for the city. We could catch a couple of shows. *Mamma Mia* sounds like fun.'

He said I should go ahead, fix it up with Kath, but just for myself. He said he might make other plans. Montréal. That'd make his third trip there since we moved to Maine.

I said, 'What's with Montréal?'

'Nothing in particular,' he said.

'Did you meet someone?'

'At my age?' he said. 'No. But it's still nice to do a little window-shopping. Know what I mean? You don't mind if I don't come with you to Kath's?'

I told him I didn't, but I did. We've been together so long I don't feel quite right when he's not around.

Kath said, 'Grice knows he's always welcome but what would he do, sitting around with a pair of old ladies? And Slick's got a new toy so he wouldn't be much company. It's a 1963 diesel tractor. He went down to Rhode Island to collect it and since he got it back here he's hardly had his head from under that bonnet.'

'Bonnet' is English for 'hood'. They call the trunk 'the boot'. Don't ask me why.

At the end of October they brought in something called the Patriot Act. That was like throwing kerosene on a blaze for Eugene. 'What did I tell you?' he said. 'Now they can walk right into your home, go through your private papers, tap your phone.'

Seemed to me it had been done for our own safety but Eugene
went on and on about it. How they could throw a person in jail
without charging them or even bringing them to trial.

'Even if you're a bona fide American citizen,' he said. 'And
that's contrary to the Constitution.'

I said, 'What about foreigners?'

He said, 'What about them? I don't care about them. We should
deport the whole damn lot. Let them go back where they came from.'

Lois said, 'Good thing Kath got neutralized. Eugene ever gets
to be President he won't be able to lay a finger on her.'

Jim Coffin said, 'This Patriot Act, they can even check what
liberry books you take out.'

Grice said, 'You mean they'll know if you borrowed *How to
Build a Bunker and Resist the New World Order*?'

'Yep,' said Jim. 'Excepting I didn't borrow any such book. I
don't even use the liberry, so they've got nothing on me there.'

Grice said, 'Well, you're in the clear. But you have me worried
now because when Sawyer Hoose took the roof from over my
head I confess I searched on the Internet for "undetectable poi-
sons". I hope that won't come back to haunt me.'

So it was agreed that I'd go to Kath's for a week in December
while Grice went to do whatever it was he got up to in Montréal. I just hoped my going wouldn't set Vern back because
when anything changed it upset him, even Lois's leaving.

'Where's that woman gone?' he kept asking. 'The one with
the striped hair.'

Herb was the one he really missed, though, and Herb knew it.
He was quite choked when it came time for them to leave. He

said, 'Peggy, we'll come up here once a year, minimum. As long as Vern knows me, we'll keep coming and that's a promise.'

We'd told Vern that Herb had orders for Carswell. Didn't matter that the Carswell base had closed. Where Vern was living, in the Long Ago, Carswell was still active.

He said, 'You training on the B-58?'

'If I make the grade,' said Herb.

Vern said, 'Carswell. Son of a gun, that's Texas. You should look up Peggy while you're down there. Remember my Peggy? She's in Dallas.'

Herb winked at me. He said, 'Well, I don't know that Peggy'd want to see me but I'll keep it in mind.'

Lois had her seat reclined plenty so as not to strain her new hip. She put her window down to give me a kiss. 'You've been a darling,' she said. 'And I've been a bitch. But you'd miss it if I ever changed. I'll make it up to you when you come down to the real world. Nails, shoulder massage, eyebrows.'

I said, 'I don't have any eyebrows.'

'That's what I mean,' she said. 'Get them tattooed. Semipermanent. Everybody's doing it. Pencil makes you look like Marlene Dietrich. You want a body wrap? Leave it to me. We'll get the works. Okay, gotta go. Herbert is getting antsy.'

They went off singing.

> *Off we go, into the wild blue yonder,*
> *Climbing high into the sun.*

Vern was whistling that damned tune for days.

17

When I got to Kath's she said, 'Bit of a surprise for you, Peggy. We've got company coming tomorrow.'

I thought she must mean Lois.

'No,' she said. 'I wouldn't call Lois company. Lois is family, like it or lump it. Somebody else. Who do you think?'

Audrey.

Kath said, 'She buried her boy, beginning of November, and never let me know. I phoned her to see how he was going on, and she says, "Oh, Kath dear, Lance passed away." Pneumonia, apparently. How that came about she didn't say. I thought they could cure pneumonia, these days. They brought May Gotobed's auntie back from the grave's edge and she was ninety-three. She probably didn't want bringing back. Well, anyway, I felt terrible when Audrey told me about Lance. If she'd let me know I'd have gone down there for the funeral, but she said she hadn't wanted any fuss. So, any road, I told her you were coming for a little holiday and if she wanted to see you we've got room to put her up. I never thought she would, but she said she'd love to and she'd get the train.'

*

I hadn't seen Audrey Rudman in more than twenty years. The last time was in England when I'd gone over to visit with Kath, 1976. Audrey had been having what Kath called 'a funny five minutes'. After Lance Junior died she seemed not to know what to do with herself. It was understandable. Twenty-five years an Air Force wife, fifteen postings, a leading light at the Officers' Wives Club, then it was all gone, overnight. Of all the places in the world, she'd decided to go back to England, to Norfolk. She said all she wanted to do was walk and walk, and Norfolk was a place you could do that without getting murdered or somebody calling the cops because you were acting weird.

Things didn't work out too well for her, though, in Norfolk. We'd always thought Audrey was the brains of the outfit but she hooked up with a man called Arthur and it was clear as rock-water he was only after one thing. Well, two things because Audrey was still a good-looking woman, but mainly he was after her money because, as Kath said, he didn't have a pot to pee in. Arthur had a little shop, a kind of art gallery, but there were many days when he might as well have closed up and gone home, and if he did happen to get a customer he probably scared them off. He was a very opinionated man, very sarcastic. Audrey had taken up painting – in fact that was how she'd met Arthur – and I thought her little pictures were very nice but, according to Arthur, they were just 'Sunday daubs', whatever that meant.

So the Arthur thing didn't work out and she came back Stateside, but she was in DC and I was in Texas and we just never got together. We had a lot of catching up to do.

Kath said, 'Now, I know Lois has got plans for you this week and I don't fancy her and Audrey being in the same room for more than five minutes so I shall have to keep them apart. I don't want you going home more frazzled than when you got here.'

I was sure things would be fine. Audrey was a proper lady. If Lois crossed her path and happened to say something tactless, Audrey would just change the subject.

I could recall a few fights from the Drampton days, just words and most of them from Lois, but Audrey could stand her ground. One time there was An Incident, when a crew from 366th Squadron had had to eject and a sergeant died from his injuries. His widow got notice to clear the post. We all felt so sorry for her but regulations were regulations, as Audrey reminded us.

She said, 'Do you realize how many E-5s are waiting to get on base? You can't have widows hanging around occupying valuable married quarters. And, anyway, it's not good for morale. There's no place for sentimentality in the military.'

So then Lois called her a smug, apple-polishing piece of work and Audrey just smiled and went off to her bridge club.

Then there was the John Pharaoh business. I was with Audrey the day we discovered what Lois was up to with Kath's brother. We'd guessed what might be going on because Lois was hardly ever home. Betty thought she had suddenly got the taste for country drives but that was because Betty's imagination didn't run to messing around with men.

One day Audrey cornered me, asked me if I'd help her do something about the Lois Situation and I agreed. We each had our reasons. Audrey's first consideration was always the good name of the squadron. She was worried about a scandal. I was thinking about Herb and little Sandie. I just wanted Lois to stop before Herb found out. Of course, Herb wasn't quite the fool we took him for.

So, me and Audrey drove out towards Kath's house, parked at an old gas station and then walked some. There aren't a lot of hiding-places out on those fens, it's like a prairie, only England-sized, but Audrey seemed to have somewhere in mind. We set off towards a stand of willow trees and we'd just gone past a tumbledown old barn when I happened to look back and saw the tail of Lois's Chevy.

'Caught her!' said Audrey, and she went striding over, calling Lois's name. My days, what a scene! They both tumbled out of the back of the car. John Pharaoh was buttoning up his pants and laughing. Lois had her drawers and her nylons round her ankles.

I turned and ran, but I could hear Lois yelling, calling Audrey names, and then me. 'You, Peggy Dewey,' she bellowed. 'Snooping around. I thought you were my friend.'

As far as Audrey was concerned it was a good morning's work, but I felt sick to my stomach. I wished I'd never agreed to go along. I was fond of Lois. I was fond of Herb and Kath, too. A suspicion is one thing. Knowing it for a fact is something else. I didn't see Lois for days after that. I don't know if she was avoiding me but I was definitely avoiding her. Then she made the first move. She came to my door and said we oughta clear the air. She swore she'd only been with John Pharaoh one time, the very day Audrey and I had found her, and I pretended I believed her. Peace broke out. As I recall it was Betty's birthday and, as the boys were flying night missions, all hatchets were buried so we could make a little party for her.

If only it had been just the once. Whether she ever went with him again after that day I don't know. All I do know is, Fourth of July she cried off the barbecue and the softball game, said she had a migraine but we saw through that. She had all-day morning sickness.

It was one of those topics I'd always danced around with Kath: how much she'd known at the time, when she'd guessed Kirk wasn't Herb's child. I'd waited till she brought the matter up herself, and when she did, it was clear Kath had it all figured out

It was all so long ago but I could see Kath was anxious about Lois and Audrey's paths crossing again.

I said, 'Don't worry. We'll keep them apart. And if we can't, never mind.

'You know, the biggest quarrel they ever had was about Lois and your John. Audrey tried to put a stop to it, for the sake of the good name of the US Air Force.'

'She could have saved herself the effort. There was plenty around our way didn't like Yanks. It was from the war years. They didn't like the way your boys had come over, turning girls' heads, giving them nylons.'

'Did you ever get your head turned?'

'I might have. A bar of chocolate could tempt a person.'

'You're a dark horse.'

'That wasn't normal times. Boys going off to get killed. You couldn't begrudge them a kiss and a cuddle. And we had the blackout, you know. We did things in the blackout we'd never have done with the lights on.'

'About Lois and John. Did you know all along? Do you know when it started?'

'Not exactly. I wasn't John's keeper. He was hardly ever at home. He'd be in and out with his eel traps. He wasn't no saint, Peggy. He did have an eye for the girls, but so far as I know he never went in for the married ones. Not as a rule. He didn't go looking for trouble. So I'm sorry to say it but I reckon Lois must have handed it to him on a plate.'

'And when she fell pregnant, did you ever wonder?'

'I did. And when she went home for her confinement I was glad to see the back of her. Because I used to think if ever I saw that little baby I'd know straight off if it was our John's. And then, of course, when John took badly and the doctors said there was no cure for it and it was a good thing he'd never married and passed it on to any kiddies, I hoped and prayed Kirk wasn't his boy. Well, that ship had already sailed.'

Audrey was getting the train to Tuckahoe. Kath and I drove to the station to meet her.

I said, 'Do you think we'll recognize her?'

Kath laughed. She said, 'We might shrink a bit but none of us changes that much. She'll be the one wearing a nice wool coat and a scarf with horseshoes on it.'

Kath was right on every count. There aren't many getting off the train at Tuckahoe at two o'clock on a working day and there was only one wearing a Burberry trench and an Hermès scarf. I guess she had shrunk some, but the biggest change was how she walked, very slow, very careful, looking kinda sideways.

She said we were darlings for picking her up. She said she perfectly hated not being able to drive but her eyes were so bad it was out of the question. She said, 'You're still very confident behind the wheel, Kath.'

'Oh, yes,' said Kath, 'but, then, I had a good teacher, didn't I, Peggy? Up that lane, back of Waplode? Changed my life and no mistake.'

I'm not very good at timing. When a person has suffered a loss I never know if I should mention it right away when I see them or talk about other things first. Kath's plan was to give Audrey the chance to bring it up. She said to me, 'We'll get back, let her freshen up and then I'll put the kettle on. If she's not said anything by the time the tea's brewed I'll speak up.'

Finding an opening wasn't so easy, though. Audrey was rattling away, a mile a minute. She said she wanted to catch up and hear all about everyone. 'Specially you, Peggy dear,' she said. 'Kath's been telling me what sterling work you're doing with Vern.'

Slick put his head around the door. He said, 'I'm all grease so I won't shake your hand right now. I just wanted to say hello.'

'It was so very kind of you to invite me,' said Audrey. So gracious. You can see why she was always a big hit at the OWC.

Kath said, 'Don't you get sump oil on my towels, Slick Bonney.'

'Cross my heart,' said Slick. 'And, Audrey, I was very sorry to hear of your loss.'

So then we had to get on with it.

I said, 'We didn't realize how sick Lance was.'

Audrey dabbed her lips with a paper napkin. She said, 'No,

people didn't. He preferred it that way, and he went very quickly, at the end. He was ready. In and out of hospital, one infection after another. He'd had enough, the poor lamb.'

I said, 'Was it cancer?'

'No, Peggy dear,' she said. 'It was AIDS. I thought you'd probably have worked it out.'

'Well,' said Kath. 'You don't seem to read about that as much as you used to.'

I said, 'Lois guessed.'

'Did she?' said Audrey. 'Yes. She would.'

I said, 'Do you know how it happened?' Which, of course, didn't come out quite right. It made it sound like a car crash. But then Kath's cat came in to see what was what. He went straight to Audrey and jumped on her lap. I didn't think Audrey was a cat person but it got us over a sticky moment.

She said, 'He probably caught it on one of his vacations. He liked to have fun, you know? He had a lot of friends but he never settled down. I wish he'd settled down. He was quite lonely towards the end. He had me, of course, but it would have been nice if there'd been someone special in his life.'

Kath said, 'Peggy's friend Grice is a homo sexual, you know. He's a lovely lad but he doesn't have anybody, not since his special friend died.'

I don't know if it was the way she said 'homosexual', like two separate words, or the way she just came out with it, sitting there pouring tea, but Audrey started laughing and then I did, and we just couldn't stop. And poor Kath kept saying, 'What? What have I gone and said now?'

She'd put a box of pastel tissues on the side, anticipating Audrey might shed a tear or two, but as it turned out we used them for the happier kind of tears.

Audrey said, 'Oh, Kath, I'm so glad you used the homo word. I hate "gay". There was nothing gay about Lance Three's life this past year.'

Then the old Audrey kicked in. She sat up straight, the cat dived off her lap and she smoothed her skirt over her knees. She said, 'But he was a wonderful, wonderful son and I'm lucky to have had him for fifty years so I'm not going to be a drooping violet. Now, Peggy, I want to hear all about Crystal. It's so good that you're close to her now. Texas to Maine was way too far.'

I'd thought I might keep the Marc drama to myself, in case they got back together, but when it came to it I didn't have the energy to tell a lie. So out it all came, how he'd been caught playing away.

Kath said, 'Well, I'll be jiggered. He seemed such a pleasant type. And just think, if it hadn't been for everything that happened that terrible day, Crystal might not have found out. He might have sown his oats and then thought better of it.'

I wondered if Crystal's ears were burning. Three old ladies sitting in Eastchester deciding what she should do about Marc. Audrey thought he deserved a second chance. She said, 'All things being equal. I mean, if this is the only time he's strayed. One has to be practical. What about money? What about their house? Divorce can leave you a lot poorer.'

Kath thought money was the least of it. 'Can she ever trust him again?' she said. 'That's the point. What use is money in the bank if you're always wondering what he's up to?'

Easy for Kath to say. She's very comfortable, these days.

I said, 'Okay, Audrey, if you'd ever caught Lance messing around would you have taken him back?'

'Oh, yes,' said Audrey. 'Not that he ever did, of course. But when you have a position in life you don't throw it away because of one silly indiscretion. Lance was in line for brigadier general, you know. Before he died.'

I said, 'I know. I came to his funeral.'

'Did you, dear?' she said. 'I don't remember anything about that day. So many people. You've all been such faithful friends to me, even though we're so scattered. And after so many years too.'

Audrey said she'd take a little rest before dinner. It had been a long day, with the travelling an'all. Kath took her up. She wasn't so good on stairs. 'It's my eyes,' she said. 'That's why I bought a first-floor apartment when I moved to Silver Spring. It's such a bally nuisance, though. I'm going to have to give up my bridge club.'

Kath came back down. She said, 'Well, that went off all right. Now all we have to do is keep Copper-knob away till Audrey leaves on Wednesday.'

18

It was a cloudy day, but not too cold. Kath asked Audrey if she wanted to go into the city.

Audrey said, 'Thank you, I do not. I took a cab from Penn to Grand Central and that was as much as I wanted to see after those terrible events. When I think how our boys risked their necks every sortie they flew, keeping us safe . . . and now this. Where were our air defences? I'm sure glad Lance Junior didn't live to see the day.'

Slick said, 'They say there was a big exercise going on, very same time. You can see how there'd have been confusion. One minute you've got your pilots responding to a make-believe attack, next thing you're telling them cancel that, it's for real.'

Audrey said, 'Yes, but that's the thing about military pilots, Slick. They're trained to respond. They follow orders. And, from what I understand, nobody gave them any. It wouldn't have happened in our day. And I must say I'm very disappointed in President Bush.'

Slick, being a Texan to the bone, thought quite highly of George Bush, but he has good Texan manners too so he didn't stay to argue about who exactly had failed us on September 11.

He excused himself and said he had a fuel hose to clean. He was on his way out when he called, 'Sweetchops, are you expecting the Moons?'

'No,' said Kath.

'Well, they just pulled in,' said Slick. 'You'd better roll down the hurricane shutters.'

We heard Lois come clattering in. 'Surprise, surprise! Did Peggy get here yet?'

Audrey said, 'Is that really Lois Moon? Why how lovely!'

Kath groaned. 'There goes our nice quiet morning.'

Lois was using a cane but she was walking pretty nifty. She stopped in her tracks when she saw somebody else sitting with us. 'Oh,' she said. 'I didn't know you had company.'

'Yes,' said Kath. 'And do you see who it is?'

Lois didn't recognize Audrey at first. Afterwards she swore she'd just been kidding us but I know what it is. She thinks she still looks thirty so she expects everybody else to look the same too.

Audrey said, 'It's my white hair that's thrown you. Aim high, Lois. Fly, fight, win.'

'No!' said Lois. 'Audrey Rudman. Is it? Audrey effing Rudman. Well, I'll be damned. Did I know you were coming?'

'The thing is . . .' Kath said. She was trying to get Lois's attention, trying to get her to calm down and think before she spoke, but Lois wasn't listening.

'Herb Moon!' she yelled. 'Get in here. You'll never guess who's visiting.'

Herb came shambling in.

Lois said, 'Recognize anybody?'

'Peggy,' he said.

'Not Peggy, you knuckle-head. Somebody else from way back.'

He looked at Audrey. 'Drampton,' he said. 'Rudman's wife. And your first name's on the tip of my tongue. It starts with an A.'

'Full marks,' she said. 'It's Audrey. And you haven't changed one bit.'

Kath said, 'Only the thing is, Audrey's had a sad loss recently, so she's come up for a day or two, for a bit of company.'

Lois dropped her cane. 'Not your boy?' she said.

'Yes. At the beginning of November.'

'See?' she said to me. 'I told you it was something serious. Fuck!' She pulled up a chair. 'Audrey,' she said, 'we had our moments, back in the day. Had a few fights, didn't we? Chalk and chips.'

'Cheese, dear,' said Audrey.

'Whatever,' said Lois. 'Different as cheese and chips. But we've got something in common now. We've both buried our boys.'

Audrey said, 'How long has it been since Kirk?'

'Ten years. People tell you time'll heal. You know what? That's bullshit.'

I said I didn't think that was a very helpful thing to say. Lois told me to butt out. She said, 'I'll bet Audrey's got words of comfort and wisdom up the wazoo. Right, Audrey? Time heals. He's gone to a better place. He's only slipped into the next room. At least you've got another child. People talk like your other kid's a spare tyre.'

Audrey didn't say anything but she took Lois's hand. Kath got up to make fresh coffee.

Lois said, 'Was it AIDS?'

Audrey nodded.

'Thought so,' said Lois. 'Well, then, that's a double whammy. If it was cancer the neighbours'd be having bake sales, raising money for Sloan-Kettering, but AIDS? Uh-oh. There'll be talk. You had remarks? Like we had with Kirk, because nobody had ever seen Huntington's before. Only Kath here. The things I heard said about my boy. There's some ignorant fuckwits in this world.'

Audrey said, 'Well, I must say everyone has been so very kind to me. Lance Three was well liked, you see? All my neighbours, everyone at church, I haven't heard anything unpleasant.'

Herb said, 'We didn't have it so bad, Lo. There might have been one or two, when Kirk was having trouble at school, but that was before we knew the cause of it. Some people thought he just needed more correction. But once the doctors had put a name to it most people were very kind.'

Lois said, 'All I'm saying is, some people are too damned quick to open their mouth.'

'True,' said Kath. 'I reckon we all know somebody like that.'

Herb asked after Vern.

I said, 'He puts his boxers on backwards nine times out of ten but he talks about you all the time. Funny that.'

'Eugene still theorizing?'

'Oh, yes. Never stops. Building Seven, that's the latest bee in his bonnet. Jim Coffin knows somebody who used to do demolitions, says it was a perfect drop if ever he saw one. So now Eugene says, considering the CIA had offices in that building and the Secret Service and the IRS and considering the Mayor's crisis management centre was in there too, how the heck could terrorists have gotten in there to lay explosives?'

'It's a fair question,' said Herb. 'You'd think it'd have been secure as Fort Knox.'

And Lois said, 'Herb! Enough about all that.'

Audrey said, 'Oh, my! What's all this about?'

'Peg's living with a lunatic,' said Lois. 'Vern's stepson, raving, I mean off the chart. His name's Eugene and he's got all kinds of wacko ideas about 9/11. And he has guns.'

And Audrey said, 'Well, even I have a gun, dear.' She said she had a Baby Glock. Mikey had got it for her, in case of an armed break-in or getting car-jacked. He said as long as bad folk had guns good folk had to have them too.

Lois said, 'And would you actually, like, fire it? Some jigaboo breaks in, trying to steal your good Rudman silver, would you kill him?'

'I wouldn't be trying to kill him. I'd be hoping to scare him off, wing him at most, to discourage him. I was never a great shot. Mikey paid for me to go to a range. I'd be hopeless now, with my eyes. I just keep it in my safe. I guess I should sell it.'

Herb said, 'Well, now, Peggy, here's something for you to tell Eugene. Do you remember Walt Petie?'

Lois groaned.

'I remember a Pearl Petie. Were they at Kirtland?'

'McConnell. Walt was Combat Crew.'

It came back to me then. The day Okey Jackson was killed. Me and Lois, Pearl Petie and Ida Batten, driving home from a movie and seeing the smoke.

Herb said, 'I've kept up with Walt over the years, and here's the thing. His boy was in the service and now his grandson. Three generations. He's a tech sergeant, the grandson, and last year he was working at Marana. You know where that's at? Arizona. Back in the fifties they used it for Special Activities Training, top secret. Far as I knew it was closed. I thought it was just a boneyard where old Boeings went to die. But Walt says they renamed it and there's a bunch of other stuff been going on there. Commercial refits. And the military have been testing remote-control planes. Walt's, well, what can I say? He's got a questioning type of mind. Him and Walt Junior, they don't see how those jets hit the towers right on the nose and I don't either. The stuff that went down at the Pentagon, Walt's as sure as dammit that wasn't no plane. Anyhow, tell Eugene Marana, Arizona. It might be worth looking into.'

Lois said, 'See what I have to live with? No offence, Peg, but since we came up to Maine friend husband has really lost the thread.'

'Not *lost* the thread, sweetheart,' said Herb. 'I'm just following a few stray ones. No harm in that.'

Kath said, 'Sit down, Herb. Have a cup of coffee.'

He said he'd have a quick one. He was on his way to Pelham.

'Got a new lumber yard to check out,' said Lois. 'He hardly slept last night he was so excited. So I'll stay here, catch up with you gals. You got plans for today?'

I helped Kath to clear some of the breakfast things.

'Looks like we're stuck with her,' she whispered. 'Still, Audrey seems happy enough to see her.'

There was no telling with Audrey. She'd put on a pleasant face whatever she was really thinking.

Herb downed his coffee and made a move. He said, 'Lo, you okay to get the train home? I thought I'd go on down to Sandie's after Pelham. Leave you girls to reminisce.'

I said, 'When you speak to Walt remember me to Pearl. We used to go to the movies sometimes in Wichita. *Creature from the Black Lagoon.*'

'Oh, Peggy,' said Herb, 'I'm sorry to tell you Pearl passed away a good while back. Ten years ago, could be more. Walt remarried. After Pearl died he took to eating at the diner, save cooking for one. He only ended up marrying the lady who runs the place. So he's set.'

'Yep,' said Lois. 'No more boil-in-the-bag dinners for Walt. I'll bet he gets seconds too. Go check out the lumber yard, Herbert, but do not buy anything. Not even a bag of nails. And if you go to Sandie's, ask her what she's decided about Christmas.'

Kath asked Audrey if she'd be going down to Florida for the holidays. Audrey said Mikey and his wife always went away for two weeks, until after New Year's.

Lois said, 'I thought the whole point of living in Florida was so you didn't have to go away in the winter. I couldn't stand the place myself. It gave me flat hair. Didn't matter what product I used I couldn't keep any volume. So we came back north. Herb didn't mind. He liked the sunshine down there but he missed Sandie and everybody. Where's Mikey at?'

Audrey said he had a beautiful Gulf shore condo in Naples. She had some pictures in her pocket book. The view from the living room, Mikey and his wife poolside in matching leisure-wear.

Lois said, 'Wow, she's had work.'

Audrey said, 'She's Latvian. They have good bones.'

'Maybe so,' said Lois. 'She's still had work.'

There were photos of Lance Three as well. One in a tux where he looked pretty good, the image of his daddy, Lance T. Rudman II. The other one was more recent. He'd dropped a lot of weight. You wouldn't really have known it was the same guy.

Kath said, 'How's Mikey taken it?'

'Okay, I think,' said Audrey. 'We knew it was coming. It wasn't like a sudden death. And they were never close, you know. People think twins are always close but they're not.'

Kath said, 'I wonder you didn't go back with Mikey after the funeral, get a bit of sun on your face. That looks like a smashing place he's got.'

'No, no,' said Audrey. 'They didn't come for the funeral. Mikey had meetings and Gizela had bookings. She's a model, you know. It's a cut-throat business. If you let people down they won't hire you again. It would have been too complicated for them to rearrange everything.'

Lois put her cup down. She said, 'Audrey, darling, are you telling us Mikey didn't come to his brother's funeral?'

Audrey said, 'Heavens to Betsy, it was just a cremation. It was over in ten minutes. To come all that way would have been too silly. And I wasn't on my own.' She said quite a number of Lance Three's nice friends had attended, and people from bridge, people from the glee club. After the cremation they'd gone to the Jefferson Hotel for afternoon tea. She said, 'Don't look at me like that, Lois Moon.'

Lois said, 'You mean don't look at you shocked because you

just buried your kid and his big-shot brother was too busy to be there? That the look you mean?'

Then Audrey's stiff upper lip quivered and her face just crumpled.

Kath said, 'Now look what you've gone and done.'

But when Audrey stopped sobbing and blew her nose she said, no, Lois was right, Mikey should have been there. She said she hadn't wanted to make a fuss about it. She said Mikey could be difficult.

Lois said, 'Go get your coat, Rudman. You and me are going for a turn round Kath's yard. We'll talk about our lovely lost boys and have a damned good cry.'

Audrey said something about helping with the dishes.

'Fuck the dishes,' said Lois. 'Kath and Peg can do them. Come on. I have Kleenex. I have magic concealer stick for droopy red eyelids. I have liquor in my purse.'

We watched them from the kitchen window. Like Kath said, just when you were ready to crown Lois she'd turn round and do something good, even if it was just making you laugh, or cry, if that was what you needed. When Kirk had died I'd thought she'd just be relieved. He must have been hard work towards the end, and a reminder, every time she looked at him, of John Pharaoh. I'd had the impression Herb was the one who'd really loved Kirk. That he was the one who'd taken it hard when he died. Kath knew more than I did. She'd been there. She'd helped them to nurse Kirk.

She said, 'Lois just acts gobby. I don't know why. She's the same with Sandie, always effing and blinding. And with Herb.

When do you ever hear her say a kind word to him? But she does love them and she loved Kirk. As a matter of fact, Peg, I think she got gobbier after he passed away. It's all a big act. Look at her out there now, blarting like a baby.'

Audrey and Lois, the least likely buddies ever, were out on the swing seat, weeping and nipping at a miniature of Gentleman Jack.

It didn't last, of course. The four of us went out for a drive and Lois was soon back to normal, telling us what she'd like to say to Mikey Rudman if she got him on the phone. Audrey said it really didn't matter, Mikey was Mikey, and she'd managed everything quite well without him.

Lois said, 'I guess he'll have an unlisted number. His kind always do.'

I said, 'Leave it, Lo.'

She said, 'No. I'm sorry, Audrey, but I never liked him even when he was a kid.'

Audrey said, 'You didn't like any of them when they were kids.'

'Not true,' said Lois. 'I liked Peggy's Crystal. I liked Lance Three, even though he was a bit of a whiner. I liked whassername, Betty's little afterthought.'

'Carla.'

'Yeah, Carla. She was okay.'

'Carla was aces.' I said. 'But have you seen Deana? She's been on TV a few times.'

'I thought her acting career didn't work out.'

'No, Sherry was the one tried to get into movies. She was the middle one. Last I heard she was in Santa Fe selling dream-catchers. And Deana was the oldest. You remember her with all her brats at Betty's funeral?'

'The Spandex freak show.'

'Exactly. And they've been breeding. There's another layer of them now, and they go on those TV shows. *Ricki Lake*, *Jenny Jones*. Betty would have purely died of embarrassment.'

Lois asked me to be sure to let her know next time they were on.

Audrey said, 'Anyway, Mikey has his generous side. He always pays for my vacations.'

'Sure,' said Lois. 'Just so long as you don't spend them at his place, eh? Anybody else hungry? My bellybutton's sticking to my backbone.'

We went to City Island and got fried clams and sodas at Johnny Reef's. December, but we sat outside and braved the wind, seagulls dive-bombing us.

Lois said, 'We can't have Mrs Colonel Rudman sitting inside. It's like a non-com chow hall in there.'

Audrey said, 'Lois, you misrepresent me. I'm happy to go anywhere and mix with anyone.'

'Oh, yeah?' said Lois. 'You ever been to Filene's Basement? You ever had a bare-knuckle fight over a cashmere cardigan?'

The sun came out. We got green-apple slushes. Lois got a piña colada. Audrey said, 'What must we look like? Four old coots sucking on ices in December.'

Kath said, 'Do you care? I stopped caring when I had to get Velcro shoes. After that I thought, Bugger it. And Slick don't mind. I could wear one of them gorilla suits and I don't think he'd notice.'

Lois said it depended what you meant by 'bugger it'. If it was doing things that people thought you were too old for, she was all in favour.

I said, 'You mean like doing plane impersonations on a wet sidewalk and falling and busting your hip?'

'I lived to tell the tale, didn't I? But letting yourself go? Never. Case in point, Peg thinks I should let my hair go white.'

Audrey said, 'Oh, but I agree with her. Absolutely. Why fight it?'

Kath said, 'If you don't want to be white you could get a nice apricot rinse. Do you remember when I went lilac?'

Lois said, 'I do. It was real pretty. You should do it again. Not me, though. Give in to white hair, next thing you're wearing compression hose. It's a slippery slope. Hey, Peggy, how's Jimmy Stewart? You dating yet?'

Kath and Audrey put down their drinks.

I said, 'I am *not* dating.'

Lois said, 'Well, that's because he needs encouragement. Land's sakes, Peg. A decent-looking guy living next door, single, still got his faculties, probably got money.'

Kath said, 'Is that the gentleman who goes away in the winter?'

I said, 'Cort Cooper. He lives next door to Vern's place. Winters in Florida and California. He's not interested in dating and neither am I. This is all in Lois's head.'

Audrey said, 'So who's Jimmy Stewart? I'm confused.'

'Cort Cooper has a passing resemblance to Jimmy Stewart.'

'More than passing,' insisted Lois. 'And he likes you, I could tell. Give him a bit of encouragement. Not too much. Keep him eager. But you gotta grab chances when they come your way.'

I said, 'Do you think you should be advising other people about their love life?'

Soon as I'd said it I wished I hadn't. But Lois didn't take offence. Things don't get through to her the way they do to normal people. In that respect she's like a Sherman tank.

And then Audrey stepped up, ever the diplomat. She said, 'Well, isn't this super fun? Who'd have thought we'd be sitting here together, how many years on? Fifty. Remember how we used to gather at Betty's for coffee?'

'There'd be a tray-bake. Betty made the best brownies.'

'And some new homemaking achievement. A bolero out of one of Ed's old shirts. A lovely necklace fashioned from elbow macaroni, to make you the envy of your friends. How did she ever find the time?'

'Rose early, went to bed late, and never put her feet up.'

Kath said, 'I thought it was smashing the way you all used to pal around. It's a pity Gayle's not here. Then you'd have the full set.'

'Gayle!' said Lois. 'You're right, Kath. We need little Gayle. Let's get her on the phone. Who has her number?'

Of course you never got Gayle. She was like a big corporation. The Lemarr Passy Tabernacle Ministry. You got a message service. Press one to make a donation. Press two to make a request for healing. Press three to speak with an adviser.

Lois said, 'Press one. That'll get you through quickest. Tell her we're sitting in the Bronx freezing our asses and wondering what to do with a hundred thousand spare bucks. That'll get her attention.'

I waited to speak with an adviser. She said Pastor Gayle was laying on hands in Greensboro but if I wished I could record a short message. I hate those machines. I passed my phone to Lois.

'Hi, Pastor Gayle,' she said. 'Lois Moon speaking. I'm sitting with Peggy Dewey and English Kath and Audrey Mrs Colonel Rudman and we wish you were here. Call us back, girlfriend. Angels on your fender.'

I said, 'Angels what?'

'Angels on your fender. It's what they say in some of those wacko churches. It's to keep you safe while you're driving. I saw it on TV. Shit, I should have asked her for some healing too, for Audrey's immaculate degeneration.'

We dropped her at Mount Vernon station. She hugged Audrey. 'Don't be a stranger,' she said. 'But go to Florida for the holidays. Tell Mikey I'm on his case. And get rid of that gun. Peg, Kath, I'll see you Thursday morning. Eat a good breakfast, wear your stab vests. We're gonna go through the discount stores like a plague of locusts.'

I was getting ready for bed when Gayle returned our call.

'Lois?' she said. 'Is that you?'

I said, 'Okay, it's Peggy. I'm visiting with Kath Pharaoh. We have Audrey Rudman staying over too, and Lois was with us this afternoon, which is how come you got a message from her but from my phone. Confusing enough?'

She laughed. 'Sounds like quite a party,' she said. 'I wish I could have been there.'

'Did you get that "angels on your fender" bit from Lois?'

'I did. Well, angels are always nice. So what's new?'

'You know I moved to Maine?'

'Right. I got your card. That must have been some move.'

'Vern has Alzheimer's and Crystal needed help. We've been up there nearly a year.'

'We?' she said. 'Did you get hitched again?'

'I did not. I meant Grice. He used to work for me. We've been together a long time. So when Crystal needed me he said he'd come with me. He's a good man. I was going to say boy but he's only a year off getting his Social Security so he's hardly a boy.'

'You should marry him, get a ring on your finger and God's blessing on your union.'

I said, 'Grice isn't the marrying kind.'

'I see,' she said. A bit cool, I thought.

I said, 'I guess you didn't know Audrey's son died? Lance Three.'

'No, I didn't,' she said. 'Well, he's safe in the arms of Jesus. Was it a car crash?'

'He got AIDS.'

'Oh,' she said. 'Well, that is a terrible, terrible thing. Before he passed, did he come to Jesus with a sorrowful heart?'

'He had pneumonia, Gayle.'

She said she'd pray to the Lord to have mercy on his sinful soul. I can remember a time at Drampton when she went on a bender, stayed in bed for days on end after there'd been a fatality and she was in a funk about Okey, afraid he was gonna get killed too.

I was about to say I thought we were all supposed to be God's creation. I've never been a big church-goer but I'm sure I'd heard that God loves us all, whatever we get up to between the sheets. But the words turned sour in my mouth so I just changed the subject.

I said, 'Audrey's losing her sight.'

'I'll pray on that too. Kath doing okay?'

'Kath's well. Do you ever get up to the city?'

She said, 'You mean to Charlotte?'

I said, 'No, I meant New York. Kath's in New York.'

Gayle said, 'I wouldn't set foot in the place. It's nothing less than another Sodom and Gomorrah, Peggy. Look what occurred September eleventh. Fire and brimstone.'

I used to be so fond of Gayle. She was such a kid when she first pitched up at Drampton and Heaven knows she's had her share of tragedy, first Okey, then Ray Flagg, KIA in Vietnam, then Lemarr, although she had a good few years of happiness with him. But since she got religion and healing an' all she's a changed person.

I said, 'I'll tell Lo you called back. Or do you want her number? I have it here.'

'I don't think so,' she said. 'It's been a long time. We wouldn't have much to say.'

I said, 'Yes. I know what you mean.'

19

When I got back from New York I swear Eugene was still sitting the exact same place as when I left. The only thing different was there were even more yellow pads on the kitchen table. I had quite a number of shopping bags, the haul from my day out with Lois. A pair of knee boots, couple of sweaters, half-price pants.

Crystal said, 'Wow, is there anything left on the rail in Century 21?'

I said, 'How's your dad?'

'All fine,' she said. 'Apart from the Milk Bones incident.'

Vern had been eating dog biscuits. It didn't appear to have harmed him. Well, he'd survived the early years of my cooking so I guess that stood him in good stead.

He was in the living room watching *Beat the Geeks*. 'Hi, hon,' he said. 'Where ya been?'

I had to mind what I said. I had to be careful not to let Herb's name crop up because Herb was supposed to be at Carswell.

I said, 'I went to see Kath Pharaoh. Do you remember her? She visited with us in the spring, her and her husband.'

'Nope.'

224

I said, 'She was the English girl we got to know when we were at Drampton. She lived out in the boonies, in the Fens.'

'Don't remember.'

'Doesn't matter. She's American now. She married Slick Bonney. So I went to see her and there was somebody else there from the Drampton days. You remember the Rudmans?'

'Lance Rudman? You seen him?'

'No, I saw Audrey. Lance died years ago, heart attack or something.'

'I never liked him.'

'I'm sure he thought highly of you too.'

He laughed. He said, 'I wouldn't have wanted Rudman watching my back. I wouldn't have trusted him. You're in a tight spot you need somebody like Herb Moon or Okey Jackson. You see Okey?'

I said, 'Vern, think, Okey's long dead too.'

'Okey?' he said, and his eyes teared up.

I said, 'At McConnell. He was in a B-47 that crashed coming in. Captain used too much rudder. You and Herb and Ed Gillis were honorary pall bearers.'

'That's right,' he said. 'I remember it now. Did we get dinner yet?'

'Crystal tells me you've been eating dog treats.'

'She's a liar.'

'That's not nice. That's your daughter you're talking about.'

'She's not nice. She's a ball-buster. Who died and left her in charge?'

'What did she ask you to do?'

'Get in the shower.'

'Sounds reasonable to me. You gotta keep yourself clean, Vern. You gotta have a little self-respect.'

'So where ya been?'

'Just out for a while. You hungry?'

'They never feed you in here.'

'Well, I know Crystal's making fried chicken. You up for that?'

'Sure. Where is it?'

'She's making it.'

'Crystal?'

'Yes.'

'She safe to be cooking?'

'I'd say so.'

'I don't want her catching fire.'

'No. But she's fifty-four years old. I think she's okay to fry chicken.'

He got up to follow me to the kitchen. 'She's a great kid,' he said. 'She's the best.'

He ate a good dinner. Sometimes he'd eat the pattern off the plate; others it was hard work to get a couple of spoons of soup into him.

He said, 'Glad you're back. Where were you again?'

I asked Crystal if she was staying over. Grice wasn't back yet from Canada. That meant if things kicked off in the night I'd have only Eugene to help me and he was as much use as a glass hammer.

She said, 'I can do.'

I said, 'You decided yet, about Marc?'

'It's complicated,' she said.

I said, 'That sounds like you're getting back together. Maybe.'

She fetched more soda.

I said, 'Whatever you've decided. None of my business.'

'Okay, okay,' she said. 'It's a case of being practical. Money's tight. I don't want to lose my house.'

'Pretty much what Audrey said.'

'Who?'

'Audrey Rudman. She was at Kath's. Mikey and Lance Rudman's mom.'

'I know who Audrey Rudman is. You mean you discussed my marriage with her?'

'We were just talking. About kids and stuff. I worry about you.'

'Anyone else? You been airing my private life on Advice FM?'

She kept on eating though I'm sure she couldn't taste a damned thing. I thought I might as well talk to Eugene.

I said, 'How's your investigation going?'

He said it looked like being a lifetime's work. He said the more he looked the more questions he found. But no answers.

I said, 'But it's early days. There'll be a proper inquiry.'

'For sure,' he said. 'Can't wait.'

I said, 'Did you ever hear of Marana, Arizona?'

He looked at me.

I said, 'It's just something I heard. It's an old air base, high security. There's a rumour that they've been testing remote-control planes there.'

Eugene wrote the name on one of his yellow pads. He said, 'You hear about that from Herb Moon?'

Vern was listening.

I said, 'No. Just on the old service grapevine.'

And, quick as you like, Vern said, 'Herb's not at Marana. He's at Carswell.'

He had seconds and thirds.

Crystal said, 'I guess my fried chicken passed muster.'

'You cook that?' said Vern. 'Martine show you how?' Then he said, 'That English girl you were talking about?'

'Kath?'

'Was she the one you let drive my Oldsmobile?'

'*Our* Oldsmobile. I taught her to drive in it.'

'Buncha breeds. How come they didn't get their own wheels?'

'Because they were poor and we were Americans. We had everything and they had nothing. Didn't hurt us to be friendly. Kath would have given you the coat off her back, even then, when she hardly had one to give. And, anyway, you changed your tune when you found out her brother was a fisherman. You remember going out to catch eels with Kath's brother?'

'No. He the one knocked up Lois?'

'We don't talk about that.'

'Been my wife I'd have killed him.'

'It takes two, Vern. Anyhow, Herb forgave her and John Pharaoh's dead. He died young.'

'Good. He was a retard.'

Crystal said, 'What rock did you crawl out from? We do not talk like that.'

I said, 'We're a different generation.'

'Tell me,' she said, 'is there any possibility that I got switched with some other baby at the hospital? Went home with the wrong parents?'

'None at all. You were born at Grandma Shea's house.'

'So there's absolutely no hope. I am your child. I have parents who think it's okay to say "breed" and "retard".'

She went home the next morning, said she had a caribou head to finish mounting, going to be somebody's holiday gift.

I said, 'I hope it's not for somebody who's expecting diamond earrings.'

She and Marc were going to sleep in separate bedrooms, see how things worked out. She said if it was okay with me she'd like to come to Marvern for Christmas.

I said, 'You know you don't need to ask. Will Marc come too?'

'I'll let you know,' she said. 'See how things are going. I wouldn't want us to dilute the festive joy.'

I said, 'What do you do around here anyhow? You send cards to the neighbours? You invite them over for hot punch?'

'Er, no, Mom,' she said. 'We don't do anything. Jim Coffin'll probably show up uninvited. Merle and Corky go skiing. Cort Cooper's left already. Middle of November he closes his place up, drives down for the Yale–Harvard game, then on to Florida.'

It was 15 December and there was no sign of Christmas at Marvern. Eugene said there was a tree in his closet if I wanted it.

I said, 'You have a plastic tree? In Maine?'

Eugene said it was his mother's tree. Martine hadn't cared to have pine needles messing up her floors.

I said, 'What about baubles?'

He said, 'They're hanging on the tree, of course. It won't take but five minutes to haul it out.'

Next thing I knew there was a moth-eaten Christmas twig

leaning against the living-room wall. It was bound up in a mile of silver lametta.

I said, 'You going to get bent outta shape if I bring in a new tree?'

He shrugged. He said, 'You want to waste money, that's your affair. I'll put this one in the lounge room. No sense putting it away again. That thing you were saying, about remote-control planes? Who'd you get that from?'

I said, 'From Herb, but I didn't want to say it in front of Vern. Herb got it from Walt Petie, used to be an aviator. Walt found out about it from his grandson. He's been working out there.'

'You got a number for him?'

I told him he'd have to talk to Herb.

He looked at me. He said, 'Cheers for the information, Peggy. I guess this means I've got you thinking now.'

I said, 'No. I was just passing along a message. If you want to show your gratitude, fill in that damned tunnel before there's an accident. You never go to your bunker, these days. Not since the attacks.'

'Don't mean I never will,' he said. 'You read the Patriot Act yet?'

'No. Have you?'

'Yup.'

'How many pages is that?'

'Three hundred and change.'

'That about the same as a John Grisham?'

'And some. Point is, this is just the start. They're watching us. Next thing they'll be able to jail you and throw away the key. Without due process. Just see if I ain't proved right. They'll come for your guns too. Well, let them try. People have any sense they'll arm theirselves while they can.'

I told him about Audrey's Baby Glock sitting in her safe.

'It's a nice lady's weapon,' he said. 'If she don't want it you should make her an offer.'

'I've never held a gun in my life.'

'And you're from Texas?'

'If I owned a gun I think I'd worry about it falling into the wrong hands.'

'Peggy,' he said, 'the wrong hands wouldn't need your pink Glock. The wrong hands already got guns. That's why you need to get one, to even up the odds.'

When we were at Corinth Tucker would start planning his holiday colours in September. By October he'd have been to Decorator's Warehouse, to get ahead of the rush. All I ever had to do was admire his handiwork, and maybe act as peacemaker if Grice interfered with his creative vision, like the time he put an armadillo in a Santa hat on the front lawn. Not a real one. It was fibreglass with glo-in-the-dark eyes. He said it was an ironic touch but Tucker didn't appreciate it. He said it drug the neighbourhood down. That was the year Tucker decorated with baby blue, vanilla and mint green.

I was down at Belgrade Falls buying a tree when my phone rang. It was Grice.

I said, 'Where the heck have you been? I thought you'd run out on me.'

'Any chance you could pick me up in Augusta?' he said. 'I'll be dropping off my rental car around three.'

I said, 'I'll have an eight-foot balsam fir in the tailgate. I should take that home first.'

'That's okay,' he said. 'I can wait. I'll be in Applebee's getting hammered.'

He hadn't shaved. He looked like he hadn't slept either. There was no excuse. It's not that long a drive from Montréal.

I said, 'We thought you'd forgotten where you live. You must have been having a great time.'

He said, 'I was, until I wasn't any more. Peg, do you mind if we don't talk about it right now?' He pulled his collar up, slid down in his seat and closed his eyes. He didn't open them until we were on the track up to Marvern. He said, 'Did you say you bought a fir tree?'

'Christmas is coming, Grice.'

'But we're surrounded by fir trees. Couldn't we have just cut down one of these suckers? It's not like anybody'd miss it.'

I said, 'Well, I'm a San Antonio girl. Chaparral brush an' all. I don't have a lot of experience of felling pines.'

'Why didn't you ask Eugene?'

'He's too busy.'

'9/11?'

'Of course. Plus, he has a fake tree, must have been in the closet since Martine died, so he doesn't see the point. I'd like to put it in a dumpster but I don't think I dare.'

'Like the sprinkles of sacred memory.'

'Yes. So we're having two trees. Did we bring baubles when we moved?'

'Some. I have them in my closet. We can get more.'

'Crystal's coming over for Christmas.'

'Good.'

'Marc might come too. They're trying to start over.'

'And what better way to mend a broken marriage than to spend the holidays with your mother, your demented father and your arguably deluded step-brother. And three dogs. And me. How is Vern?'

'Pretty good. He ate dog biscuits while I was gone. Cussed at Crystal when she made him shower and brush his teeth. The usual.'

I pulled in to Marvern, turned off the engine. He just sat.

He said, 'I'm old, Peggy.'

I said, 'Sixty-three is not old.'

'It is when the guys are all thirty-four.'

'Did you get your heart broken?'

'Cold shower, more like. All they want is sex, Peg.'

'Do I need to hear this?'

'They want lots of sex with a guy who doesn't have varicose veins.'

'What was his name?'

'Doesn't matter.'

'You're missing Tucker.'

'I always wondered what dog biscuits taste like.'

'Well, I'd say just ask Vern but he won't remember.'

The next day we drove to Bar Harbor to buy Christmas stuff. Grice was still very subdued. He said, 'What's to become of us, Peggy?'

I said, 'How about a bowl of chowder and an afternoon in Christmas Wonderland?'

'You know what I mean. Say, when Vern dies. What'll happen then?'

'Vern's in good shape, apart from his head. I reckon he'll outlive me.'

'Don't say that. That's even worse. What'll I do then?'

'Do you regret coming up here with me? You want to go back to Texas? I'd understand if you did.' Course, I was praying he wouldn't.

He said, 'There's nothing for me in Texas.'

Shopping cheered him up. I was thinking driftwood ornaments. They're very popular in Maine.

Grice said, 'So we're going the tasteful and understated route, are we? Well, let me see what I can do to ruin your day.'

I bought a garland for the door, cedar, reindeer moss, pine cones, blueberries. Grice disappeared for a while. He'd had something gift-wrapped. 'Peace offering,' he said. 'Sorry I'm being an old misery.'

An inflatable lobster in festive apparel. Santa Claws. I said I'd fix it to the mailbox.

'Better not,' he said. 'The neighbours might be consumed with envy and steal it.'

We stopped in Ellsworth on the way home, for coffee and cake.

I said, 'Are you unhappy up here?'

'No,' he said. 'It's different, that's all. Are you?'

I said, 'You know, I'm getting to like it. When I was down at Kath's I really missed it.'

234

'You didn't tell me about Kath's.'

'You didn't ask me. Kath was fine, Slick was fine. He was busy playing with his new toy. Some old tractor he bought. Audrey Rudman came up from DC for a couple of days. I hadn't seen her in so long. You never met Audrey. Her son died. Lance Three. He had AIDS.'

He whistled through his teeth.

'You know anybody had that?'

'A few, in Dallas. Just acquaintances. Not anybody that I ever, you know . . . It's not nice. It's not an easy way to go.'

'So Audrey's other son, Mikey, he didn't go to Lance's funeral. What do you think of that?'

'I guess they didn't get along.'

'But his twin brother? And what about being there for his mom?'

'Was Audrey upset about it?'

'She tried not to show it. She said Mikey was busy and it was a long way to come from Florida and a bunch of excuses, but then Lois put the arm on her to have a good cry.'

'Oh, no. Compulsory weeping. I hate that.'

'It was what she needed. I think Lois did the right thing. She does, sometimes. I'm sure Audrey's real lonely but she tries to put a good shine on things.'

'She'd have known Vern. Is she going to visit?'

'I don't think so. She's very pleasant but we were never that close. And Mikey pays for her to go on really swell vacations. Paris, France. Rome, Italy. She's been all over. Money's no object.'

He said, 'Damn. I should have had children.'

'They don't all turn out millionaires and pay for you to fly first class.'

'I can see that,' he said. 'You might get one who parked his car on cinder blocks.'

I said, 'There's something I'm going to tell you and you're probably going to be shocked but I don't want you making a scene.'

'I don't make scenes,' he said. 'Oh, my God, are you getting it on with Jim Coffin? Please tell me it's not true.'

Well, of course the whole coffee shop went quiet.

I said, 'It's about guns.'

He said, 'You're thinking of getting a gun, shooting Eugene and burying his body deep in the forest. And you want me to help dig the grave.'

'Close. I am thinking of learning to shoot.'

'I was kidding.'

'I know. I'm not. Audrey has a little pistol.'

'But she lives in DC, Peggy,' he said. 'I've heard you can't cross the street there without getting mugged. You're not serious?'

I said, 'I just think it'd be good to try it, find out what it feels like. I probably wouldn't actually get a gun.'

'You wouldn't need to. Eugene's got more weapons than Camp Stanley. Has he been getting at you? Has he been giving you all that repeal-of-the-Second-Amendment bull?'

'But what if he's right? He says the Patriot Act is just the start of it. He says they had that law oven-ready. That's how they managed to bring it in so fast.'

'They had to bring it in fast. Hello. We were attacked. And all those provisions, all that surveillance and stuff, that's not aimed at people like us, Peg. That's aimed at the bad guys, the terrorists.'

'If I learn how to shoot, will you hate me?'

'No,' he said. 'I'll just never turn my back to you.'

Crystal and the dogs arrived Christmas Eve just before dark. No Marc.

I said, 'I made a lentil thing for him, with chestnut mushrooms.'

She said, 'He wants to be on his own. He was never big on Christmas anyway.'

'He get you anything?'

'I don't want anything. He bought himself a book, though. *Find Your True North. Follow Your Inner Compass.*'

'What does that mean?'

'I guess it means he's lost.'

20

I was in Day's buying toothpaste when I ran into the redbone women, Merle and Corky. They could be sisters, I don't care what Crystal says. Corky's half the size of Merle but they have the same look about them, hair cut short, row of little ear studs, Carhartt work pants. They asked after Vern.

I said, 'Did Eugene ever show you his bunker?' I knew he hadn't. I was just making conversation.

Corky laughed. She said, 'That'll be the day. You going to put in a good word for us?'

Like I told her, I had no influence there. I said, 'Far as I understand it's just an old shipping container full of canned beans and bottled water.'

She said, 'Were you at Martine and Vern's wedding? I don't remember you.'

I said, 'No. I'm Vern's ex. I wouldn't have been on the guest list.'

'Oh,' said Merle, 'I'm sorry. We figured you were Vern's sister, way you came up here to look after him. So Crystal's your daughter? She's so cute.'

'Cute' was the last word I'd have chosen to describe Crystal.

Corky said, 'So who's the guy there with you?'

'Grice. He's a friend. He worked for me for years. Then we retired, ended up living together.'

'Radical,' she said. 'He's a queer, right?'

I thanked them for turning out that night to search for Vern.

'Any time,' said Merle. 'Hounds were disappointed they didn't get a run but I'm glad he was found okay. Vern's a nice guy. It's a crying shame. Good thing you came, though. Eugene's clueless.'

I paid for my stuff. I was on my way out of the store when I had an idea. I asked them if they knew of a place where I could learn to shoot.

'Sure,' said Corky. 'There's places will charge you, or there's us. We'll teach you. Long gun or pistol?'

I didn't know what I wanted. I said, 'I don't actually own a gun. I just wanted to try it.'

They said they had a Springfield, a Remington and a Mossberg, and I could drop by any time, get the feel of them, learn the basics. They were just up the road a piece, between Marvern and Jim Coffin's place. It was the turn-off that had the mailbox with a coonhound painted on the side. I said I'd think it over.

I got home and Eugene cornered me with a magazine in his hand. He said, 'Did you see this shit?'

Time magazine had named Rudy Giuliani their Man of the Year for the way he'd handled the 9/11 attacks.

Eugene said, 'Exemplary acts of leadership, my ass. I'll bet Herb's son-in-law'd have something to say about that. Ask the firefighters if he's their Man of the Year.'

Gerry Carroll had worked long shifts at Ground Zero. They all had. Firefighters pride themselves on bringing their dead home, even if it's only a finger. Even if it's only half a finger. But then Giuliani had said they couldn't carry on indefinitely because they were delaying the clean-up operation. He said a line had to be drawn. They had to accept that some of the missing wouldn't ever be found and he limited how many of them could be down there searching at any time. There had been quite a stand-off. The police had tried to enforce Giuliani's new rule and there had been scuffles between the firefighters and the cops. It was such an ugly episode after everything those boys had been through.

Eugene said, 'Herb reckons Giuliani's got it in for the Fire Department. Know why? Because the firefighters are the ones keep saying those towers were brought down with explosives. And they should know. A lot of them were in the buildings, lucky to get out alive. They're not stupid. It's their business to know a detonation when they hear one. Man of the fucking Year.'

I did think about Merle and Corky's offer to teach me to shoot. First we had snow and the track up to their place didn't get ploughed for days. Next thing Vern broke a glass and cut his thumb real bad so I was taking him to the doctor's office, getting it sutured, getting it dressed. Then Kath and Slick visited. They were on their way to Canada, making some big vacation across to Vancouver, sitting on a train for days. Kath said they'd decided it was time to spend a bit of money while they could. 'While we've still got the strength to lift a valise,' she said. 'No sense being the richest man in the graveyard. And it's not like we've got anybody to leave it to. Only Slick won't fly. But he's all right with trains and I can take my knitting.'

We were sitting out. First day it had been warm enough.

She said, 'Peggy, can you smell burning or is it somebody smoking cigars?'

Cort Cooper was back in town.

Kath said, 'Is that the chap Copper-knob was going on about? Looks like Jimmy Stewart?'

'Yes. Which he doesn't. Not much. And now, if I happen to see him, I'll feel awkward and all because of Lois's silly talk.'

'You just be yourself,' said Kath. 'She's half puddled, that one. Man-mad and half puddled. Well, I don't suppose she'll ever change now.'

It was the end of April before I drove up to Merle and Corky's place, and even then when I got there I nearly thought better of it. Playing with guns at my time of life. I didn't tell Grice what I was up to. I was coming up to the gateway, thinking I'd drive straight on and find a turning place, but Merle happened to be out front and saw me. She waved me to go on in. So that was that. Sometimes it's easier to let somebody else make a decision for you.

'Start you with a handgun,' said Corky. 'Semi-automatic. It carries sixteen rounds. First thing, point it down and away from you. Second thing, you're going to check it's not loaded. I know it isn't but you're going to check it anyway. Every time, Peggy. If you're going to be around guns you need good habits.'

She took me out back. They had a kinda range set up there, targets, earplugs, goggles, the works. She said I wasn't ready to do any shooting yet but she'd fire a few rounds, show me what it could do. She said I needed to get accustomed to the feel of the gun, make friends with it, stop gripping it like it was a pissed rattlesnake.

Folk in Maine aren't too familiar with rattlers but Corky said she was an Arizona gal, met Merle at a dog show, moved up to Maine and bought a parcel of land. Merle was from Bangor.

I wondered why they had guns when they had hunting dogs. Corky said they used the hounds for bear mainly, for rich types up from the city looking for an outdoors vacation, wanting something none of their friends had done so they could go home and brag about it. They used the guns to shoot woodchucks, and foxes too, if they raided the henhouse. And snow hare once in a while but only if they wanted one for the oven.

She said, 'I know Eugene uses traps sometimes but I don't hold with it. You trap a critter it can suffer for hours till you come along and put it out of its misery. Shooting's cleaner.'

I said, 'How about home defence?'

She laughed. Corky does not have good teeth. 'Not much call for that in Maine,' she said. 'Unless word gets round you've got gold bullion in the basement. Robbers won't waste gas driving out here. Even our TV isn't worth taking. Eugene still talking about the End of the World As We Know It?'

'More than ever since 9/11.'

'Yeah? Does he think bin Laden's coming to Maine? They say he's on dialysis. That'll clip anybody's wings.'

I said, 'It's not bin Laden he's worried about. It's this Patriot Act. He's predicting we'll be a police state before the next election. So he's ready for them, if they come to take his guns.

242

Whether he'd do it, whether he'd shoot a sheriff's deputy, I have my doubts.'

Corky whistled through her teeth. 'Gun fight at the Marvern Bait Store. He might. Eugene always was a bit touched. But I will say, if I was back in Arizona I'd see things different. I got brothers still down there and nobody's going to take their guns. You get Mexicans pouring over the border, you got to protect yourself.'

'I thought they were just hard-up guys looking for work.'

'I'm not talking about them. I'm talking about the ones running drugs. We're not talking about normal human beings, Peggy. We're talking about pieces of shit who'll kill you as soon as look at you. And there's no point calling nine one one, not when you live more than an hour from Tucson. By the time the police get to you you'll be dead, and so will your kids and your dogs. And that's if the police trouble to come at all. So, yes, if I was back in Rio Rico I'd own something more powerful than this old Remington. And I wouldn't let George Bush take it away.'

I tried it out, just to hold it, tucked right into my shoulder, cheek on the stock, both eyes open.

'Just to whet your appetite,' said Corky. 'Next time you come we'll get you squeezing that trigger.'

I was in my bedroom practising my shooting stance with an umbrella when Grice looked round the door. 'No!' he said. 'Tell me it's not true.'

I said, 'I got my first lesson. Merle and Corky are teaching me.'

'Who?'

'The women who brought their hounds the night we couldn't find Vern. House along the road called Slacks?'

'You mean Butch and Butcher? Guns. Lesbos. Peggy Dewey, what's happening to you? You used to be such a dainty Texan dame. That was Herb, by the way. I said you'd call him back.'

I'd heard the phone. Lois had busted her other hip. She'd been up a step-ladder, putting away the winter comforter, and lost her balance.

Herb said, 'It's not a nice clean break like last year. She's made a mess of it this time, Peg. And I told her not to climb up there. I told her I'd do it. Might as well have talked to the wall.'

I said, 'Shall I come?'

'Nothing you can do,' he said. 'I just don't know when we'll get up to Maine now. I'm real sorry. I was hoping to get some flying time in with Vern this summer.'

I was sorry for Lois but I was sorry for myself too. I'd been so looking forward to having them visit.

I said to Grice, 'This is how it's going to be now. Downhill all the way. Lois's bones are crumbling. Audrey's going blind. Even Kath's talking about spending her money before she dies. It'll be me next.'

'Yes, probably,' he said. 'There'll be a shooting accident at Slacks. Death by dyke.'

I went for my shooting lessons every Wednesday while Grice watched over Vern. He didn't like doing it but not because Vern was any trouble. He mainly just sat in an armchair or out on the stoop. He might ask where Martine was but if you told him she'd gone to the store that'd satisfy him. One time, though, he'd turned to Grice and said, 'No, Peggy's the one goes to the store. Martine's buried in Pine Grove. Perpetual Care lot. I'll be going in there too.'

As Grice said, it was like when you get gunk in a fuel line. You're driving up an incline and the engine's misfiring. You think, Uh-oh, more expense. Then next morning it turns over first time, no problem.

The reason Grice didn't like me going up to Slacks was because of the guns and because of my making friends with Merle and Corky. He didn't even know them but he'd decided to dislike them.

I said, 'I'd have thought you'd have something in common.'

'Ha!' he said. 'That's like me saying you should have gotten along with Lola Dekker. That's like me expecting you to be friends with every straight woman you meet. There's lesbians and there's lesbians, Peg. I prefer girls with a bit of elegance. I'll bet the only item on Corky's vanity is a Chapstick.'

Merle owned a Mossberg rifle but I never did more than pick it up and feel the heft of it. She said, no offence, but rifle-shooting wasn't for the older person. It required a steady hand. With a shotgun you've got a better chance of hitting the target and, true enough, with the Remington I learned to shoot clays, incoming and away-going. They said I was a pretty good student. But it turned out the pistol was my natural weapon.

With Corky's 9mm Luger I was hitting eights and nines, sevens if I got too hasty. And that was when I decided to quit.

Grice said, 'Well, that's plain nuts. Is it because of what I said? Don't give it up for me. Try a crossbow. Get a Samurai sword. Go for it. I'll keep my opinions to myself, promise.'

I said, 'It's not because of you. It's because I'm getting to like it too much. I feel like I've woken a monster.'

'Wow!' he said. 'The dark side of Peggy Dewey. When you pick up a gun do you, like, hear Ennio Morricone music? Do you ever get the urge to strike a match on the back of Eugene's bristly neck?'

Kath and Slick broke their journey on the way home from Canada. She said, 'We'll only stop for a day or two. We don't want to wear out our welcome. And, any road, Slick's itching to get back to his vehicles.'

Slick didn't seem his usual cheerful self.

Kath said, 'He's got the hump because I've decided I'm going to England this summer. He says we've had a nice time in Canada and that's enough. He says we're not made of money. But I'll stay with May so all it'll cost me is the flights and a few pub lunches.'

I said, 'I reckon it's not about the money. It's because he'll miss you.'

'Well,' she said, 'that'll only be a couple of weeks. And, Peg, when he's got a new toy to tinker with I hardly see him all day. He won't miss me. He's got a new transmission to put in the Dodge. Well, I'm determined to go so he'll just have to lump it. May turns eighty this year and that's a good age for a Gotobed. Get to our age, you don't know when you'll get another chance. Her mam died in her fifties.'

Grice said, 'How is it May never married?'

'Didn't want to,' said Kath. 'She had her chance. Nev Chaplin did ask her. He wore a boot, you know.'

'A boot?'

'A surgical boot. He had a withered leg from the poliomyelitis.'

'Was that why she didn't marry him? Because of the boot?'

'No, no. She just didn't fancy married life.'

'The sex and stuff?'

'Having to put a gravy dinner on the table every day for the rest of your life. May can't abide cooking. The day they brought in microwave ovens she was happy as a sandboy.'

Grice said, 'Tell us the genealogy of the Gotobeds. Start with Adelaide.'

He loved to hear Kath say those funny Norfolk names. Gotobed. Jex. Howgego. How many times had she recited that list to him? But she obliged him again.

She said, 'Well, Adelaide was married to Amos. He was one of the Waplode Gotobeds. She was a Napthorne. Amos and Addie had two girls, Winnie and May, and a boy called Tommy. He drowned in a ditch, half cut on parsnip wine. Winnie married Harold Howgego and they had a boy, Colin. He was a PoW in Burma. Colin married a Jex girl, can't recall her name, but she was one of the Smeeth Jexes. I don't think they ever had any kiddies. He wasn't a well person, Colin, after what the Japs did to him. And I'll give you a clip of the ear, Grice Terry, laughing at how I talk. Taking the mickey out of an olderly lady.'

He said, 'Kath, I love you. Will you marry me?'

'I'm spoke for,' she said. 'But I'll keep you in mind, if Slick gets bored of me. I wouldn't mind a younger man. What's good enough for Joan Collins is good enough for me.'

★

Kath had been back to Norfolk only once since she'd left. May had come Stateside to visit but she wasn't a great traveller. She didn't have Kath's get-up-and-go and she was a worrier. Kath always said May was born worried. They've been friends all their lives. Walked to school together, worked at the sugar-beet farms together, even dared to go to the pub together when Kath came into a bit of money.

Kath used to say, 'Lager and lime and scampi in a basket, champion! The old boys'd turn in their graves if they knew they were serving women in the Flying Dutchman.'

Fourth of July Crystal came over. We were expecting her anyway. We'd planned to take Vern to the parade in Augusta. Grice was watching from the window. He said, 'Is she sleeping over? She sure has a lot of luggage.'

She sure did. Suitcases, plastic sacks. She pecked me on the cheek. 'I'm moving in, Mom,' she said. 'Don't flap, don't ask questions. I'll take one of the lodges.'

Grice helped her with her bags then came back indoors.

I said, 'Did she tell you anything?'

'No,' he said. 'But there's a white-tail deer head in one of those boxes, a work in progress I'd say, so I guess she really is moving in.'

'So she's left him.'

'Looks like. Could be worse. Could have been Marc's head in that box. You make coffee, I'll put on my Listening Face. Pincer movement. We have to get the lowdown from her before we go into town.'

She came in, kissed Vern, told the dogs to settle. 'Okay,' she said, 'I see you both gagging to know so let's get this over with. I'm going to tell you what's happened and you're allowed one question each. Clear? Are you ready? Marc had a holiday surprise for me, which was that Mia – remember Mia? – has had a baby and she's coming after him for child support, which means he's completely fucked financially and the bank'll probably foreclose on the house and I really couldn't give a damn. Questions? Just one each, remember.'

I said, 'I thought Marc was the reason you couldn't have children.'

'That's not really a question,' she said. 'But I'll answer it anyway. We didn't have children because we agreed we didn't want them.'

I said, 'I ever see him again I'll kill him.'

'That's not a question either,' she said, 'but thanks, Mom. I appreciate the show of solidarity, specially now you're the fastest gun in Kennebec County. Grice? Just one question, mind.'

He thought for a minute. He said, 'Would you like a slice of my sweet potato cheesecake?'

GRICE'S SWEET POTATO CHEESECAKE

I make this without a crust. If you like a crust just bash up a mess of ginger snaps with melted butter and press it into the pie pan.

For the filling you will need:

3 eggs

1 and ½ lbs cream cheese

2 tablespoons maple syrup

¾ cup of sugar

1 cup mashed sweet potato, canned is fine

2 tablespoons flour

1 teaspoon each lemon juice and vanilla. You can add cinnamon if you like it. I don't.

Whiz everything in the mixer, pour the batter into the pan and bake at 325 degrees for 45 minutes. Then leave it to cool in the oven. Don't worry if the top cracks. Then people will know it's home-baked and not store-bought.

We saw Cort Cooper in town. He had a woman with him, ash blonde, white pants, white T, Miami Marlins visor. He waved.

I felt kinda flat and sad. Crystal had her troubles and Vern kept asking to go home. He always used to love a parade. It hardly felt like the Fourth.

We all sat on the deck till it got dark, had chicken and beer. Eugene and Jim Coffin let off a few firecrackers, then Crystal helped me get Vern to bed. He was acting out, wouldn't brush his teeth.

'Fine,' said Crystal. 'You get a toothache don't you come crying to me.'

Exactly what Vern used to say to her when she was a kid.

He asked for Martine. He often did at bedtime.

Crystal said, 'She's resting in eternal peace.'

'Okay,' he said. 'Those things were real pretty.'

'What things? You mean the marching bands?'

'No, the things. In the sky.'

'The firecrackers?'

'That's what I said. You going deaf?'

She said, 'I'll be here in the morning. I'm staying over. You happy about that?'

'Sure,' he said. 'You just better clear it with Martine.'

Eugene and Jim Coffin had come inside and resumed their note-taking. The holiday was over. They were going over every minute of September 11, questioning every damned thing. Flight 77 was what they were picking over that evening. That was the plane that crashed into the Pentagon.

Eugene said, 'Pentagon has to be the best guarded site in the country, bar none. How'd a plane ever get within a country mile

of it? And was there a plane? Where was the wreckage? Whoever heard of a plane crash without pieces of engine and fuselage?
And people's luggage?'

Jim said, 'There's always pictures of luggage. And some kiddie's doll.'

Crystal fetched more beers from the icebox. Grice whispered,
'I'm going to watch the Texas Rangers' game. I think Crystal
needs some mommy time.'

We sat out a while. I said, 'Want to talk?'

'I dunno,' she said. 'What's to say? I've been a sucker.'

'Do you think that baby's really Marc's?'

'Born in May. And we know he was with her September
tenth. You know what the Missing Link always says. If it looks
like shit and it smells like shit it probably isn't Shinola.'

'Boy or girl?'

'Who cares?'

'You deserved better.'

She looked at me. She said, 'Did I? You don't think it's my
own fault? For forgetting to use face cream?'

'I thought Marc loved you the way you are. Everybody did.'

'Well, it seems he was just faking it. He'd probably still be at
it if he hadn't been caught. He said Mia made him feel young
again. What's wrong with men? Who the heck wants to feel
young again?'

I had to laugh. Doesn't matter how old your kids get, you still
think of them as kids. But as the years pass there's less and less
difference between you. Live long enough, me and Crystal'll
both be old ladies. How weird would that be?

The no-see-ums were starting to bite.

She said, 'Let's go in and listen to the 9/11 loonies for a while. That's always good for a laugh. It was a boy, by the way. Named Quest Phoenix, apparently. So I guess he won't have a happy time in the Marines.'

Eugene and Jim were still at it. They were talking about Barbara Olson.

There had been a lot about her in the papers after 9/11 because she was famous. She'd been on TV, although I don't remember ever seeing her, and she was married to Ted Olson, the solicitor general. She was on Flight 77 and she'd actually called him from the plane and told him what was going on. That's how we knew about the hijackers. That's how we knew they had box-cutters. But Jim and Eugene didn't buy any of it.

'A and one,' said Eugene. 'Ted Olson kept changing his story. First he goes on CNN, says she called him from her cell phone. Then he goes on Fox and says she called him collect from the air-phone. Couple of hours later he's on *Larry King* saying it was her cell. Your lady wife calls you, fearing for her mortal life, I reckon you'd remember every detail.'

Crystal said, 'I disagree. He must have been distressed. The poor guy went on TV just after it happened. After a shock like that you wouldn't be thinking straight.'

'Bullshit,' said Eugene. 'You seen him. That was no nervous wreck. You know who changes their story? Liars, that's who. Anyhow, I'm not done. B and two, Barbara Olson couldn't have called from her cell. They don't work at altitude.'

Crystal said, 'Okay. So she called from an air-phone, like her husband said.'

Eugene beamed. 'You think so?' he said. 'Just one problem with that, Crystal. There weren't any air-phones.'

'On a 767? Sure there were.'

'Nope. They'd been deactivated, beginning of 2001. They might still have been on the seat backs, but they didn't work. And it was a 757, by the way.'

'How do you know about the air-phones?'

'Jim's cousin's granddaughter works for United. Cabin crew. Long haul.'

'But the Pentagon flight was American Airlines.'

'Makes no difference. If it was a 757 there weren't any air-phones and Ted Olson's story can't be true.'

I said, 'So what are you saying happened?'

'I'm not. I'm just asking questions.'

Crystal said, 'Well, I have some questions too. Why would a man like Olson go on national TV with a made-up story? You two sit here theorizing but you don't have all the facts. You don't have any facts.'

'We got some, and we intend getting a whole lot more.'

I saw where they were going with this. I said, 'You don't think Flight 77 hit the Pentagon.'

'A possibility well worth considering, Peggy,' said Jim Coffin. 'You looked at the hole it made, supposably?'

I'd stopped looking at those pictures by 13 September. I hadn't liked the way I was getting used to seeing terrible things.

Jim said, 'Whatever hit that building, it was no plane. Missile, more likely. And, like your friend Herb Moon said, it'd take some pilot to turn a 757 and bring it in, ground level practically, without stalling.'

Crystal was getting het up. She said, 'Okay, Einstein. So where's the plane? It took off from Dulles. Where's it gone? And where's Barbara Olson? She never made it to LA. And why would she make that call, why'd she say they'd been hijacked if it wasn't true?'

'All good questions,' said Eugene. 'Soon as we get any answers I'll let you know. So you're moving in again?'

'Yes. To help Mom. You have a problem with that?'

'No. So long as you chip in. Oil, food. Make a contribution.'

She said, 'I'll tell you what contribution I'm going to make. I'm going to make sure the bait store stays open, and not just hours that are convenient to you. Hours that are convenient to the customers. I'm going to get the bed-and-breakfast thing going again. Your mother'd have a fit if she could see how you're letting this place go.'

I lay in bed that night thinking of what might have been. I'd never been one of those moms always asking when they were going to get grandchildren. It'd have been neat, I guess. Vern might have gotten a boy. He'd have liked that. Take him fishing, tell him aviator stories. Not that Crystal was ever peaches and cream and playing with dollies. One time Betty made her girls a bedroom vanity out of a General Issue table. She had some of the pink cretonne left over, offered it to me to make one for Crystal's birthday. When we got home I could tell something was bugging her. Vern got it out of her.

She said, 'Auntie Betty says I have to get a princess dressing-table for my birthday.'

'Hell, no,' said Vern. 'Betty Gillis don't know what's she's talking about. I already ordered up the roller skates.'

★

I felt sad for Crystal, the way things were turning out. You get married, you make a deal. When I fell pregnant with Crystal there was never any question Vern'd do the right thing, put a ring on my finger. My side of the deal was I'd be a service wife, no belly-aching about where we got posted, no begging him to quit flying. Sure, the deal went sour later on but only when he left the military. Vern lost his way for a while then. It's not unusual. Ed Gillis went the same way, not shaving, not even doing his morning push-ups. But Vern was still a good father, and I only left him because I didn't care to have my furniture thrown across the room.

Marc and Crystal agreed they didn't want children. Fair enough. But then he should have kept his pants zipped. Getting a baby at his age, and with somebody young enough to be his daughter, that was downright cruel.

21

Kath phoned me the day before she left for England. She said, 'I went over to see Copper-knob. She's getting on all right. They've got her doing physiotherapy. She says it hurts like billy-oh but if she doesn't do it that'll be the end of her salsa dancing.'

'Billy-oh? I'll bet she didn't say it so politely.'

'You're right. She was using language. Oh, and listen to this. She's started making her own eyelashes. She reckons hers were getting so sparse there was nowhere to put the mascara. She tried the stick-on kind, only they don't do them in her colour.'

'I'm not surprised. Who'd want red eyelashes?'

'Lois does. So when she had her hair cut she got the hairdresser to put some of the clippings in a bag, for eyelashes. She's made a box full of them.'

'Are they any good?'

'Well, I wouldn't wear them. They looked like ginger cater-pillars. But you know what she's like. She doesn't care. Silver plimsolls. That's her latest. She got them off the computer.'

'You all ready for your trip?'

She said, 'I'll tell you the truth, Peggy, for two pins I'd cancel.'

'You worried about leaving Slick?'

'Not really. It's just such a long way to go. And all that argy-bargy at the airports now. No, Slick'll be all right. I've made him fourteen dinners. All he's got to do is take them out of the freezer. And I'll bet you when I get back he won't have eaten half of them. He'll be down at House o' Pancakes, pleading the poor abandoned husband. That Gretel in there gives him a tall stack for the price of a short stack, but only if I'm not with him. I'm not so green as I'm cabbage-looking. I know what goes on.'

'She trying to seduce him?'

'Could be. She's not his type, though.'

'What's his type?'

'Four wheels and leather upholstery.'

I said, 'Then off you go. Enjoy yourself.'

'Yes. I'm just being daft. It'll be nice to see May. She reckons everything's changed, though. All the old places, tidied up. Plastic window frames. She says the pork butcher's is gone. It's an estate agent's now. Well, what use is that? You'd buy sausages every week. How often do you buy a house? I know we were a bit ramshackle back in the old days but they were happy times, Peg.'

Crystal and Grice bought paint and made a start on sprucing up the empty lodges. I took down the drapes and washed them but they came out of the dryer in pieces.

Crystal said, 'Good. They were ugly anyhow. We should get blinds. Fishermen don't care about what's covering the window.'

Eugene said, 'My mother made those drapes.'

She said, 'Which tells us how ancient they are. Go do the inventory. It'll take your mind off your sad loss.' She'd been on at him for days to do an inventory for the bait store. 'Write everything down on one of those pads. What's on the shelves, which flies are your best-sellers and what time of year. The place is so run down. It looks like you had a fire sale in there.'

He said, 'Looks okay to me. What's in them boxes you got stacked in my worm shed?'

'Tools of my trade,' she said. 'I'll be doing my taxidermy out there.'

'You using chemicals?'

'Some.'

'Could be detrimental to my worms.'

'Eugene,' she said, 'worms are one of Nature's success stories. I'd say they're up there with fleas and mosquitoes. A whiff of formaldehyde won't even register.' She dumped the remains of the drapes in his arms. 'There,' she said. 'Send for a pastor. Go give them a burial. And then do that Goddamned inventory.'

He gave her a look. 'No mystery why your husband run off and left you,' he said.

'Matter of fact he didn't,' said Crystal. 'I left him. You must be mixing me up with that wife you had for five minutes. As I remember it, she ran away.'

'Nothing to do with me,' he said. 'It was old Mrs Dewey drove her away. Regular old witch she was, your grandmother. It must run in the family.'

Crystal laughed. She said, 'We all have our crosses to bear. What runs in your family? Allergy to soap? A big space between the ears?' After he'd gone she said, 'I hate to say it but he was right about Grandma Dewey.'

Grice said, 'Eugene does cling to his mother's things. He must have been a real momma's boy. What was she like?'

Crystal said, 'Martine was okay. I got along with her. She was a great cook. Everything from scratch, you know? Nothing store-bought.'

I said, 'Is that a dig at me?'

'Not at all,' she said. 'You were a career woman. Anyhow, there's no shame in using Jus-Rol.'

Grice said, 'He never mentions his father, though. You noticed that?'

'He hardly knew him. He was only about five or six when his daddy passed.'

It seemed like the moment. I said, 'This property? Who owns it?'

'Dad and Eugene. That's how Martine left it, when she got sick.'

'So when Vern dies?'

'I guess his share comes to me.'

'You guess?'

'Why? What's it to you?'

'Well, how about I gave up my life in Dallas to come here and help with Vern? He wakes up dead some morning, Eugene could give me my marching orders. That's what it is to me. And to Grice too. We already went through that kinda upset with Sawyer Hoose.'

'Don't worry about Eugene,' said Crystal. 'He can't do anything without my say-so.' She went to make a start on painting.

'Nevertheless,' Grice whispered to me, 'we should have a plan B.'

Herb called. He said, 'You spoken with Slick? I've been trying to get him. Lo's car's running rough. I thought he might take a look at it.'

I said, 'Kath predicted he'd be dividing his time between the garage and House o' Pancakes. Did you try his cell?'

'Don't have the number.'

'Neither do I.'

'Well, I'll maybe drive over there, see what he thinks. Ignition timing needs adjusting.'

We had a tricky afternoon with Vern. He kept asking for Martine. When he was in one of those moods we'd tell him she'd gone into town. Vern soon forgot what you'd told him so there was no harm done. Eugene had no patience with him. He'd yell at him that Martine was dead. A couple of times he even drove Vern out to the cemetery so he could leave flowers on her grave. Know what I think? By the time they got there Vern had forgotten he'd asked for Martine. He didn't know whose grave they were visiting, particularly seeing they'd never gotten around to giving her a headstone.

That particular afternoon he had a bad mouth on him. He accused me of stealing Martine's shoes. Then it was her pots and pans. He was pacing about the kitchen. 'These are Martine's,' he said. 'How'd you get them?'

Grice tried to distract him, get him out to the worm sheds, but Vern wasn't having it. In fact, the more Grice tried to coax him the more Vern squared up to him. It was Crystal defused the situation, accidentally you might say, because she came in and said, 'Mom, do you have any more strong garbage sacks?'

The word 'Mom' was like throwing a switch for Vern. He beamed at me, asked me how were things at the yarn store. I told him the yarn store was doing just fine. Stay in the moment. Keep Vern happy. That was my motto.

The phone went. It was Lois.

She said, 'Peg, I got something bad to tell you. It's Slick. He's dead.'

Herb had driven over to Eastchester and found him in the garage, in the repair pit. My first thought was the Dodge had fallen on him but Lois said, no, he was just lying there in his coveralls, like he'd fallen asleep. She said, 'What do we do about Kath?'

'We'll have to call her.'

'Do you think so? When's she due back?'

'Not for another week.'

'I'll bet her cell's turned off. We could leave it. Let her enjoy her vacation.'

'What, and then meet her at the airport, surprise, surprise, your husband's dead?'

'Kind of.'

'No, we have to call her.'

'Okay,' said Lois. 'If that's what you think, I'll leave you to do that.'

'I don't have May Gotobed's number.'

'Call four one one. Don't they have Directory Assistance over there?'

I said, 'Is Herb still at the house?'

'He's waiting for the funeral home to collect.'

'Tell him to look around. Kath will have left May's number. It'll be by one of the phones.'

'Okay,' she said. 'But I have to tell you, Herb's not real good at finding things.'

It took Herb all of ten minutes to find that number. Lois could have called Kath, but she said, 'It'll be better coming from you, Peg. You're closer to her than any of us.'

I could have said that Kath was family to Lois and Herb, as good as. Their boy Kirk had had Pharaoh blood. But I didn't. All said and done, I thought Kath'd sooner hear the news from me than from Lois.

It was late in Norfolk. I pictured they might be in bed already.

Grice said, 'Leave it till morning.'

I said, 'But we'll be asleep when it's morning over there. I can't sit up all night waiting.'

'Then call her when you get up tomorrow morning.'

'They'll probably have gone out by then. No, I'll have to do it now.'

May's phone rang and rang. Then she picked up. They don't say hi, the English. They don't say 'Hoose residence' like in Texas, or 'Yeah?' like in New York. They say their number, real slow.

I said, 'It's Peggy Dewey. Kath's friend.'

'Oh,' she said. 'Are you telephoning all the way from America? I'll fetch her. Only you'll have to hold on a minute. She's in bed.'

It was a long minute. Then I heard her coming to the phone.

'Peg?' said Kath. 'What's happened? Is it Vern?'

I said, 'No, darling. It's Slick.'

'Course it is,' she said. 'Why else would you be phoning me at this hour? Is he bad ? Is he dead?'

'Herb found him. He'd gone over to see if Slick could fix Lois's car. He was in the garage. Herb said he looked peaceful.'

She was quiet for a minute. 'Where have they took him?'

'I don't know. Herb called a funeral home. I can find out which one. Kath, you shouldn't rush back.'

263

'No. That'd probably cost me a packet. Changing my ticket. I suppose it was his heart. He'd had a touch of angina.'

'What was he, eighty-one?'

'Going on eighty-three. He was a good man, Peggy. None better.'

'I know. I'm so sorry.'

'Me and May went to Hunstanton today. Remember Hunstanton?'

'Was that where the tide went out so far you couldn't see the sea?'

'That's it. Sunny Hunny. You wouldn't know the place. They've got an Indian now. Curries and all that.'

'Did you eat a curry?'

'Not on your life. Fish and chips. And there's a place called Sea Life. They've got penguins and seals and you can watch them getting fed. Very comical. Perhaps I should change that ticket, Peg. I ought to come home. There'll be arrangements to see to.'

'Just tell Herb what you want and he'll take care of everything.'

'Poor Herb,' she said. 'He must be shook up. And he didn't even get Copper-knob's motor fixed. Time she got rid of it, if you ask me. The ashtray's full. Do you know what? I reckon I'll take Slick back to Texas. I reckon I'll have him cremated and take his ashes back to San Antonio. He'd like that. I knew I shouldn't have left him. Didn't I tell you, I nearly cancelled? My heart wasn't in it.'

'But you've seen May. That's important. And he went quickly, Kath. Herb said he looked like he was sleeping.'

'Oh, Peg,' she said. She was crying. 'He was on his own, though.'

'But he'd have been alone even if you'd been home. He was

out in the pit, working on the Dodge. You probably wouldn't have been with him.'

'I know,' she said. She blew her nose. 'All the same. I wish he hadn't been on his own.'

When I got off the phone Vern was standing in the doorway. He said, 'Did somebody die?'

'You remember Slick Bonney?'

'Was he 366th Squadron?'

'No, Bonney's Farm Vehicles in San Antonio. He was married to English Kath.'

'Martine died.'

'Yes, she did. You want a hot chocolate?'

'Sure.'

It was like old times, sitting across the table from him, just the two of us. The more Vern forgets, the younger he looks. I guess it's because he's done with worrying.

'Tell me again who died.'

'Slick Bonney. He was here a while back, did a bit of fishing. Heavy built, Texan. He was in the D-Day landings, infantry, I think.'

'Don't know him.'

'Do you remember Ed Gillis?'

'Did Ed die?'

'Not as far as I know. Ed was married to Betty. Right? They split up and then Betty dated Slick. But then Betty got a cancer. She died and then Slick married English Kath. You remember any of that?'

'Ed Gillis was an asshole.'

'I have heard it said.'

'Can I get marshmallows with the hot chocolate?'

Kath did change her flight. She said, 'I can't rest, Peg, not till I've seen him, so there's no point my staying here. May understands. And the airyplane people have been very nice, very obliging.'

Herb picked her up from Kennedy. He said, 'She had me take her straight to the funeral home. She insisted. Then I was meant to bring her to our place, just for a night or two, but she wouldn't come. She said she wanted to sleep in her own bed.'

I spoke to Kath the next morning.

She said, 'I know they meant it kindly, Peg, but I couldn't have stayed at the Moons'. Lois'd give me brain ache. I shall have to get used to sleeping in an empty bed so no sense putting it off.'

I said I'd go down to Eastchester for the funeral.

'You will not,' she said. 'You're needed up there. There's plenty of folk around here that knew Slick. He'll get a good send-off.'

I said, 'Then can I come with you to San Antonio when you take his ashes?'

'Now you're talking,' she said. 'I should like that. We'll go in the back end.'

'Back end' was English for 'fall'.

But that trip to my old home town didn't happen. Kath decided to keep Slick in a box on her night-stand instead. She said, 'I talk to him before I nod off of a night. And the thing is, Peg, when my time comes I should like us to end up in the same place. I know we'll only be dust but even so. Wherever they put me, they can bung Slick in with me.'

'You must be missing him.'

'Missing him terrible. Lois helped me take his good clothes to the Goodwill but I've kept his bathrobe hanging there on the back of the door. It still has his smell on it. You know, the first time I met him I didn't think much of him. He was doing that selling business with Betty. Remember that? Fat-Begone or something.'

'Pyramid selling. It was a racket. You had to get all your friends selling the stuff too. Lipo Buster. Was that it?'

'Slick was only doing it to humour Betty. He was very sweet on her but he reckoned she was a tough nut to crack. She'd walk out with him but she didn't like the idea of breaking her marriage vows. She was still married to Ed, you know? She didn't see him from one year's end to the next but as far as she was concerned he was still her lawful husband.'

'She was a fool. She might as well have grabbed a bit of happiness while she could.'

'Yes, well, her loss was my gain. It took me a while to warm to Slick. He was no Omar Sharif but he was a kindly-hearted man and he wasn't so bad in the sack neither.'

'Kath Pharaoh! You shock me.'

'Why? Did you think we was too old for all that?'

'Never thought about it. And I didn't know you had a thing for Omar Sharif either.'

'Oh, yes. I'd let him eat crackers in my bed any time. So who did you fancy? Film stars.'

'George Peppard.'

'Never heard of him.'

'Yes, you have. *Breakfast at Tiffany's*. He's dead.'

'That's the thing, Peg. Won't be long, we'll all have had our chips. So, any road, I'm keeping Slick here and when I go they can mix us up and dump us in the same hole. I've asked Sandie to see to it.'

'Why Sandie?'

'Younger generation. No sense asking you or Lois. I might outlive the pair of you.'

22

I think of 2003 as a year when everybody seemed to be on the move. The first thing was Lois and Herb's son-in-law Gerry retired from the Fire Department and they decided to relocate, to be nearer Patrick and the grandchildren. Madison was at the cute age – even Lois admitted that – and there was another baby on the way.

She said, 'Course, it's not just to be nearer the grandbrats. Sandie knows she'll never keep Gerry away from the fire house unless they leave town. Anyway, when Pat gets posted they can't just up sticks every time he moves. The week they closed on that house he got orders for Barnes. Talk about sod's law. Family's still on Cape Cod, waiting to see where he goes next. Well, we know all about that, don't we, girlfriend? Holding your breath and waiting on orders from Uncle Sam.'

Pat Carroll was away when the new baby was born, another girl, Lexi. She was a month old before he got to see her, just like when I had Crystal and Vern was away at Ladd Field, Alaska.

Pat was on rotation through AFB Barnes , flying patrols day and night over the Indian Point nuclear-power plant. Eugene said it was a case of locking the stable door after the horse had bolted. If anybody intended hitting Indian Point they'd have done it on 9/11.

Sandie and Gerry settled on Long Island. Lois said there'd be enough retired firefighters and Irish bars to keep Gerry happy. 'And there's Jones Beach,' she said. 'For when they get old. You ever noticed how old people like to sit gazing at the ocean, waiting till it's time to get the early-bird dinner? Now Sandie's started working on her dad, hinting we should get a place there.'

'Why don't you? Could be nice. Sea air. And you'd see the great-grandbabies when they come to visit.'

'Peg,' she said, 'we're happy where we are. And I do see the great-grandbrats. You know what Madison calls me? Orange Gan Gan. Because of my hair. She's a stitch.'

Kath was the next to move. She sold her house and moved to Long Island too, to Great Neck. It was called Green Glade Independent Living for Seniors. She said, 'I've had to give up the cat because they don't allow pets, but he's all right. He's gone to live with my old neighbour. He never liked me that much anyway. He was more Slick's cat. But this place, it's what they call Continuing Care. Do I get too frail then I can move across the lawn to the Sheltered Living. They give you a buzzer, in case you fall.'

It sounded similar to Audrey's arrangements in DC. Silver Spring. You provided your own furniture, did your own cooking if you wanted to, and if you didn't there was a cafeteria. Then if you got sick they had nursing facilities.

Lois said, 'Dumb names they give those places. "Green Glade" sounds like a burial ground. Why not be honest? Why not call it

270

"Departure Gate"? Why don't they call it "The Valley of the Shadow of Death"?'

Kath said, 'All very well for Copper-knob to criticize. She's got her husband, and Herb's still got his health and strength. He can get the top off a pickle jar. Anything happens to him, though, then she'll be lost. But I suppose she'd go to live with Sandie.'

'I don't ever see that happening. She'll never give up her own place.'

'But if it came to it, Peg, she could do. And that's the difference. I haven't got family to take me in. I have to think ahead. Any road, I like it here. They have coffee mornings and armchair keep fit, and I'm quite the novelty, being a foreigner. They all want to hear me talk Norfolk. I'm the entertainment. I shall never want for company here. And they have guest rooms, like a bed-and-breakfast, so you can still come and see me.'

Kath's move had been quite a project. From five bedrooms down to one. She'd rung me one day and said, 'I've got more pillow cases than Beales' Bedding. Do you know anybody that's running a hotel?'

So then she sent a big parcel for Crystal's fishing lodges. Grice wasn't sure about the pink and lilac but Crystal said fishermen didn't come in tired after a day on the water and start examining the bed linen.

All Slick's vehicles had to be sold too and they didn't fetch the kind of prices he'd imagined.

Kath said, 'Never mind. They were treasure to him. I thought I'd be glad to see the back of them but I had a little weep when that last tractor was loaded on the truck. Wherever he's gone,

271

I hope God's gave him an old combine harvester to tinker with. Now, Peggy, I've been thinking. I'll be eighty next year and so will you.'

'And Lois.'

'I know, but I dussen't bring it up to her. She kids herself she's still a teenager. But we should do something to celebrate. I've been looking at cruises. Caribbean. What do you think?'

'They can be expensive.'

'Not if you go in September.'

I said, 'There's a reason they're cheaper in September. It's the hurricane season.'

'Is it? Well, think about it anyway.'

'Would it be just the two of us?'

'No, the more the merrier. We could ask Audrey. And Lois, of course, so long as we don't mention about her turning eighty. She'd suit a cruise. They have dancing and beauty parlours and all sorts. And what about Gayle? We haven't seen her in a long while. She could afford it. I reckon she could afford to pay for all of us. Give her a call, Peggy. See what she says.'

Of course, I didn't want to call Gayle. I still had a bad taste in my mouth from what she'd said about Lance Three. 'I'll pray for his sinful soul.'

I put it off and put it off and then I was saved the trouble. Gayle wasn't likely to be available for a Caribbean cruise. It was Crystal picked up the story. 'Gayle Passy?' she said. 'That's your Gayle, right? She's on the news. Arrested. Charged with accounting fraud.'

The Passy Tabernacle Church and Television Healing Ministry

had been investigated by the IRS. Lois was on to me in no time. The old USAF drums were beating. She said, 'I spoke to Ida Batten. She remembers Gayle buying land in Costa Rica. And Lorene Bass heard she built a big house in Panama. I guess that's where she's been keeping her stash. Panama, though. Who the fuck'd want to live there? Herb watched a documentary about it. It's so humid your clothes rot.'

'Do you think she'll go to jail? Do they jail people of her age?'

'What is she? Seventy-three, seventy-four? Well, I guess they wouldn't put her on a chain gang. They wouldn't get her breaking rocks. Will you go see her?'

'No.'

'Why? Might be fun.'

'Because I don't have anything to say to her. And I don't think visiting a person in jail would be fun. It makes me feel sick to think of it.'

'They won't send her to Sing Sing, Peg.'

'Well, when you find out where she's gonna be, *you* go visit her. Not my idea of fun. By the way, me and Kath are thinking of going on a cruise next year. You interested?'

'Are you kidding? Of course I'm interested.'

'It's not definite. We just talked about it. We'll probably ask Audrey as well. Might not be her kind of thing, though.'

'Some of those cruise ships have art galleries. And educational talks. She loves all that shit. Well, definitely count me in but I don't want to share a stateroom with Audrey. I bet she's real tidy. I'll bet she puts her clothes on hangers before she hits the sack. Is Grice going? I'll share with him.'

I told Grice.

He said, 'Am I even invited? I thought it was going to be girls only.'

I said, 'Would you want to come?'

'Oh, yes,' he said. 'But I'm not sharing, not even with Lois. I'll pony up for a single cabin. In case I get lucky.'

Eugene's 9/11 papers were piled up everywhere. Crystal said they were a fire hazard. He said it was none of her Goddamned. But Jim Coffin went into Augusta and bought box files and Eugene stuck bait shop labels on them. He said it was in case the FBI came snooping. We had a laugh about that.

The labels were: *Bass Bugs*, which was anything concerning the World Trade Center; *Saltwaters*, anything pertaining to Flight 77 and the Pentagon incident. 'Pertaining' was one of Eugene's favourite new words. *Nymphs* was Shanksville and Flight 93. *Hoppers* was Flight 11, *Beadheads* was Flight 175, and *Muddlers* was NORAD and what in tarnation they'd been doing that morning. There was another, smaller, file, Manila, unlabelled and Eugene never left it lying around. I gathered it was information he'd gathered from Herb Moon and his grandson, Pat. 'Just protecting my sources,' he said.

Crystal said Eugene appeared to think he was living in a Tom Clancy novel. But I'll admit some of what he said was real interesting. Like one of his big ideas was that 9/11 had been a war game that had gone live.

According to Eugene, the week of September 11, there was a whole bunch of exercises going. Military, civil defence. The biggest exercise was a war game, Global Guardian. That was going on all week. Hijackings, chemical attacks, germ warfare, all sorts. It was like a dummy run for Armageddon. Then there was something called Northern Vigilance. That was to keep an eye on the Russians while they did manoeuvres over Canada, in the Arctic Circle.

Eugene said, 'See what they did? Tied everybody up with exercises, then they flipped it to a real attack. Clever.'

'Who flipped it? Do you mean Al Qaeda?'

'Forget Al Qaeda. They're just a CIA outfit. They're just Rent-a-Bogeyman. No, I'm talking about closer to home. The real power in this country.'

'You mean the President?'

He laughed. 'Chickenhawk George!' he said. 'He just does as he's told. You saw him, sitting in that schoolroom, like a coney caught in the headlights.'

'Who, then?'

Crystal was unloading the dishwasher. She said, 'Here we go. The dark powers. The global conspiracy.'

'Damned right,' said Eugene. 'And someday you'll wake up and wipe that smirk off your face.'

Crystal told him to kiss her backside. I really don't know where she learned that kind of talk.

The thing about Eugene was he'd tell you something that made sense, kind of, and then he'd top it with something beyond crazy. Like he said it was no wonder the air-traffic controllers got confused when planes started going rogue because they knew there was a war game going on. They knew NORAD could put fake radar bleeps on the screen to test their responses. He said,

'Everybody's pointing the finger at the air traffic controllers, saying the FAA dropped the ball. Seems to me they got played for fools. The military had them chasing phantom planes.'

But when you asked him about those planes that took off from Boston and got hijacked he'd just shrug his shoulders and smile.

I said, 'Eugene, those were real flights. What about the passengers? What about the crew? People don't just disappear.'

He said, 'As you may recall, Pat Carroll spent that morning at Westover, moving body bags.'

'Empty body bags. It was an exercise.'

'There we go again. Those damned exercises. Anyway, moving body bags is grunt work. You don't take fighter pilots away from their base to do grunt work.'

'So what do you say happened?'

'Most likely they switched the planes. Landed the real ones at Westover, then flew the fakes into the towers, remote control. That's the type of stuff they've been working on out at Marana.'

'Okay. And all those people who thought they were flying to California and landed at Westover? Where are they? You can't hide hundreds of people.'

'You can if they're dead. In those body bags.'

'But if they didn't die in plane crashes that means they were murdered. Who would do that? Nobody'd do that. There was a little kid on one of those flights. Three years old or something.'

He said, 'I see your problem. You're looking at this like a normal, decent human being. But you gotta understand, we're just the little people. We're the ants. We don't count for shit. You know how many people were on those flights? Ninety-some on the first plane, sixty-five on Flight 175, not that many on the other two flights and that's including the supposed hotshot Arabs that couldn't even fly a kite. So we're talking about three hundred people tops? That's chump change, Peggy. When you're taking over the world, when you're creating a reason to go to war, you gotta look at the bigger picture. You can't make pancakes less you break some eggs.'

I said, 'Okay, what about the call the cabin stewardess made? I heard that recording. She was desperate. So there must have been a hijacking. That much was real.'

'Glad you brought it up,' he said. 'Now I'll tell you a couple of things you probably don't know. Four hijackings, right? Not one of those pilots squawked. You know what I mean by that? Pilots got a procedure. Just one quick code, then the air-traffic controllers know they've got a hijack situation. September eleventh nobody squawked.'

'Maybe they couldn't. If you had a gun to your head. If you suddenly had a knife to your throat.'

He never did answer me that.

He said, 'So the flight attendant? You're talking about Betty Ong, right? Highly experienced, been flying for years. What does she do? Ignores everything she's ever been trained to do. You got an emergency on board, cabin crew don't make calls.'

'How do you know?'

'I know. Don't matter how. Cabin crew do not make calls. They're trained. Don't matter what airline they work for neither. They got procedures, same for every airline.'

'Betty Ong wasn't the only one who made a call.'

Jim Coffin said, 'Yeah, you mean Renee May. She was on the

Pentagon plane, supposably. Called her mom. Cabin crew definitely don't do that.'

'You got this information from your distant relative?'

'Yeah. But it's a well-known fact. Anything goes wrong, cabin crew look after their passengers, keep people calm. Anyhow, Jilly ain't that distant. I get a card from her folks every Christmas.'

Eugene butted in. He said, 'And I'm not done saying my piece about Betty Ong. She picked up a phone and who'd she call? Reservations! She's at thirty thousand feet, says she's got people bleeding to death, says she's got mace gas in the cabin, cockpit's not answering and she calls Reservations? Why the hell would she do that?'

It was one of Eugene's best questions. Why would she do that? You ever called airline reservations, dollars to doughnuts you'd be kept on hold. It can be fifteen, twenty minutes before you get through.

That was how it went with Eugene. Half of what he said was crazy, the other half wasn't. And it was that other half could keep you awake nights.

I went out for a drive to clear my head, and Cort Cooper was picking up his mail. I had to decide real quick if I should just wave or stop and speak to him. I stopped.

He said, 'Good day, neighbour, whose name begins with P but I'm struggling to remember if it's Polly or Penny.'

'Peggy.'

'Peggy, dammit.' He had Herk zipped inside the front of his fleece vest.

I said, 'You spoil that dog.'

'Thing of it is, Peggy, if I don't keep hold of him he'll run off, chasing varmints, and I'll be out here all day searching for him.'

'I haven't seen you since the Fourth. I thought maybe you'd left.'

'No,' he said. 'I'm here till November. I'm a creature of habit. Did we speak on the Fourth?'

'No. You were across the street, at the parade. You had a lady with you.'

'Ah, yes. Faith. How is your . . . Vern?'

'He's okay. A bit worse. I don't really know. You get accustomed to it.'

He was picking at flakes of paint on his mailbox. OPER was all that was left of COOPER.

He said, 'When my wife got sick we moved her bed into the winter kitchen, to save me running up and down the stairs. She was there more than a year. Even now that kitchen looks bare without a bed in it. I believe I still owe you a vodka martini.'

It was eleven in the morning.

He said, 'I also have the makings of a Screwdriver or a Moscow Mule. Or even a Virgin Mary.'

I said I'd go around six, if that suited. He said that suited very well.

Crystal was out back working on a fisher cat. It was a mean-looking beast, a bit like a mink. She said it was her first and she hoped it'd be her last. Vern was perched on a stool, watching her, just like she used to perch at the breakfast bar and watch him polish his dress Oxfords.

I said, 'I'll be going out again later.'

'Okay.'

'I'll only be an hour or so.'

'Okay.'

'I'm invited next door, to Cooper's. For cocktails.'

She put down her trimming knife. 'Did you say *cocktails*?'

'What's wrong with that?'

'Cocktails! What century is he living in?'

'Twentieth, same as me. We're just leftovers, hanging around waiting for our discharge papers.'

'Cocktails! Cort Cooper's time'd be better spent cleaning up his yard.'

'Well, anyway.'

'Yeah. Sure. Whatever. Just don't come home wrecked.'

23

What do you wear for drinks with a neighbour in Kennebec County? I had lovely things that hadn't been out of the closet even once since I'd moved to Maine.

Grice said, 'This is the guy who wears a beanie?'

'Not always. In the summer he wears a straw hat.'

'I reckon you could safely go as you are.'

Well, I had no intention of doing that. I'm a well-brung up Texas girl. Gentleman asks me out, I dress nice and feminine.

Grice asked if I intended walking round to Cooper's. He said, 'Think about this. If you wear a skirt, you'll have to wear heels and I'll bet the track up to his house is uneven. You could fall. It could be dark by the time you come home. On the other hand, if you drive and he plies you with martinis, you'll total the car.'

Such nonsense. I can handle heels and I never crashed a car in my life. The only reason I decided on flats and a fresh pair of pants was we were in Maine. It's an outdoorsy kind of a place and somehow I didn't feel right in a dress.

Grice gave me the once-over. 'Lipstick and a bracelet, nothing too jangly, and you'll be perfect. But first listen to this.' He was reading from his little computer. ' "Cortland Jameson Cooper, born Fairfield, Connecticut, 1928." He's younger than you.'

'Get to my age four years don't signify. What's that you're reading?'

'The story of his life. So far. Graduated Yale, 1950. Married Patricia Wilson of Mainline, Philadelphia, 1964. Senior partner, Strunck, Palmer, Wetherby, 1968–88. They're Wall Street brokers.'

'Crystal thought he taught college.'

'She was fooled by the beanie. Now listen to this. Wife's obituary. "Patricia 'Patch' Wilson Cooper daughter of . . ." Saints alive, Peg. His wife was one of the rubber Wilsons.'

'What does that mean?'

'Rubber. Tyres and stuff. It means they had money. Probably not Carnegie-level money but still. '

'I'm worried about the martinis. They can be real strong, right?'

'Right.'

'What about a Moscow Mule?'

'I don't know. Sounds like a drink that has hairs on its chest.'

'What's the one doesn't have any liquor in it?'

'Shirley Temple?'

'I'll tell him I'm taking antibiotics.'

'Don't do that. Go and have fun.'

I was nervous as a June bride.

I was on my way out of the door. Grice called after me, 'Peggy, if you marry this guy, will you please adopt me?'

Cort was sitting out on his deck. My days, I wouldn't have recognized him. Black polo, black pants, black blazer, tan loafers. I wished I'd worn a dress after all.

He said, 'We'll sit out, if you don't mind. The house is messy.'

I could see the kitchen through the open door and he wasn't exaggerating. I said something like, 'There's not much incentive to tidy up when you live alone.'

He laughed. He said, 'Oh, it was just as bad when Patch was still alive, even before she got sick. She wasn't much of a home-maker either.'

He said a Moscow Mule was vodka with ginger beer but if I didn't care for strong drink he'd make it more like ginger beer with just a whisper of vodka. We sat out for an hour, shared a dish of potato chips with Herk, told about ourselves.

He'd married in 1960. Patch was older than him, a war widow with a teenage daughter. Emily. He said that had worked out fine. He said it appeared to him that teenagers didn't start to be a problem until the late 1960s. I could relate to that. Crystal caught the high tide of the sixties. Cort didn't have any children of his own. 'Just didn't happen,' he said. 'But I've got Emily and her boys, all grown-up now. She's in Palm Springs so I only see her once a year.'

'But you go to Florida too?'

'My sister Faith is down there so I go pester her till the Maine winter has passed.'

'The lady who was here for the Fourth?'

'She was. I don't think she'll come again. She hates to travel.'

He said his sister wanted him to move to Florida and his step-daughter wanted him to move to California but he wasn't ready to settle in one place.

I said, 'These houses are a pile of work. Seems there's always something needs fixing.'

'Oh, sure,' he said. 'Tell you the truth, Peggy, I don't really bother any more. The roof's leaking. I've lost count how many places. When I spy a new leak I buy a new bucket.'

'But you still like to come here.'

'I do. Patch loved this place. She kept chucks and ducks and all sorts. And Herk likes it here. He finds plenty to interest him. Faith's in a condo so there's no critters for him to chase down there. Emily has AstroTurf, which throws him for a loop when he needs to go to the bathroom. No, we'll just hang on here. Once we're gone I guess someone'll pull the house down and build on the lot.'

I liked those Moscow Mules but they certainly go to a person's head. I had to take the steps real slow. Cort insisted on walking me. He said, 'I fear all I've done is talk about myself. Next time you must tell me all about your Air Force years.'

Next time! I said, 'Not so much to tell but I'll look forward to trying another concoction. I might even try a martini.'

'It's a date,' he said. 'Probably be April.'

We were just by the gate to Marvern. He held out his hand. There was me thinking he intended to shake mine but, gosh, darn it if he didn't bend over and kiss it, kinda, hardly touched it actually, but still.

Everyone was in the kitchen. Crystal was dishing up cheese mac.

'Well?' said Grice. 'Show and tell!'

'Nice drinks, no canapés, just chips. House is a mess. Cort's very pleasant. He walked me home.'

'Because you're loaded,' said Crystal. 'Your cheeks are pink and you're not walking straight.'

'Did he flirt?'

'No. He told me about his wife and his sister and his step-daughter.'

'Yeah,' said Crystal. 'I met her, when they had the funeral for her mother. Snooty bitch. Went to Vassar or someplace.'

'Pooh. He should have asked you about *you*. Is he a bore?'

'Not at all. He's a gentleman. He kissed my hand.'

Crystal dropped her serving spoon. 'He did what?'

'Kissed my hand. To say goodbye.'

Crystal said, 'What a creep.'

Grice said, 'Well, I think it was a darling thing to do.'

Vern started eating and burned his mouth. Crystal yelled at him, said she'd told him to let his food cool some, but you can't do that with Vern. Soon as he sees it he wants to eat it.

I said, 'Are you mad at me or just at the world in general?'

'I am *not* mad at anyone or anything,' she said.

Eugene winked at me. And Grice hummed 'Diamonds Are A Girl's Best Friend', but very quietly.

MOSCOW MULE, AS MADE BY CORT COOPER

2 measures of vodka (or 1 for Peggy Dewey)

1 measure of lime juice

Pour into a highball glass of ice, top up with ginger beer and stir.

Good with cheese straws if anyone is willing to make them.

Soon as dinner was cleared Jim Coffin turned up. I sometimes wondered why he didn't just move in. Or why they didn't wait for the official report.

There was an investigation going on, a commission to find out what happened on September 11. Eugene said he looked forward to reading it. 'The day that comes out I'll be on the doorstep of Barnes & Noble before opening time. I'll be first in line.'

When they first announced the inquiry Henry Kissinger was tapped to run it. Eugene said that was akin to putting a fox in charge of a hen house. But pretty soon Kissinger quit. Conflict of interest, they said, because Kissinger was very tight with the bin Ladens. So then Thomas Kean got the job, used to be the governor of New Jersey.

Kissinger had a company that provided consultancy services. That's a new thing. I'm sure we never had consultancy services back in the day. I said, 'What does that mean exactly?'

'He gives them advice,' said Grice. 'Puts out fires. Greases the wheels.' He said the bin Ladens were very, very wealthy, and when people have a lot of money they need consultants to tell them what to do with it. 'Where to invest. What colour drapes to get. Which wars to bankroll.'

'If the bin Ladens are so wealthy, how come Osama's living in a cave?'

'I don't think he is, not really. He's probably got a suite at the Lahore Hilton. Probably got a whole floor. Think of the points he could be earning. But "living in a cave" sounds so much more interesting.'

Crystal didn't like him joking. She said, 'It's not appropriate,

Grice. Thousands of people died because of that murdering bastard.'

Eugene said, 'Who're you talking about now, Crystal? Bin Laden or Kissinger?'

She left the room.

'That's right,' he said. 'Slam the door. Make sure that little mind of yours stays closed.'

Eugene and Jim started working on what they called the Pat Carroll File. Scraps of information Herb had passed along. How Pat and a few others from Otis had been sent to Westover the morning of the attacks but the rest of his wing had been scheduled to rendezvous with tankers and do a refuelling exercise off Long Island. It was part of the Global Guardian war game. They'd been down at the hangar, ready to go, when they saw two fighters scrambled. Pat said everybody assumed it was a 'friendly idiot intruder' alert. They get them all the time. Private-plane owners wandering into the path of other aircraft. People with more money than horse sense.

'What do the fighter pilots do when they find them?'

'Fly alongside of them, apparently. Tell them, "Follow me, douchebag." Get them to land someplace safe.'

After the scramble Pat's buddies had taken off for refuelling practice but then suddenly they were told to lock down the exercise and return to Otis ASAP. They had too much fuel in their tanks for landing, but the base said dumping it would take too long, so to use their afterburners instead. See, afterburners give you extra thrust but they're real gas-guzzlers. Then when they landed they were told to stay on the tarmac with everything cocked for another take-off.

'Which never happened,' Eugene said. 'They just sat there sweating. No idea what was going on. They thought it was all part of the war game, to keep them on their toes. Tell you another thing. Pat Carroll knows some guys who were on duty at Langley that morning. Any threat to DC, Langley's gonna be your first call. Right?'

Vern was listening. '1st Fighter Wing,' he said.

I'd caught him putting Groom 'n' Shine hair product on his toothbrush that morning but he still knew his air bases.

'Correct, Vern,' said Eugene. 'But Pat Carroll's buddies are 119th Wing. They're Air National Guard out of Fargo. They were on rotation through Langley, manning one of NORAD's alert units. According to Pat, when you're on alert duty you practically sleep in your gear. You need to take a crap, you use the bathroom right there in the hangar. The balloon goes up, those planes are supposed to be in the air in under five minutes.'

'So they were scrambled?'

'Oh, yeah. Langley's not far from the White House, from an aviator's point of view. A hundred miles, maybe a bit more. Fighter jets wouldn't take many minutes to get there even if they didn't fly supersonic. Only they never got there. Listen to this. First thing is, Langley scrambled three planes, not two. Know who was up in the third plane? The supervisor. He's the guy meant to stay in the battle cab and direct ops. Vern, you'd know about that. If the supervisor's up in the air, who's in charge? Who's answering the phone? Who's passing on orders to the aviators? Nobody.'

Vern said, 'Supervisor don't fly.'

'Except this one did. And why'd he do that? Says he got orders.'

'Who from?'

289

'He doesn't know. Just somebody on the phone. From NEADS.'

'What's that?'

'Northeast Air Defense Sector.'

'And he didn't query it?'

'You know better than that, Peggy. Military don't ask questions. They do as they're told. Right, Vern?'

'Right,' said Vern.

Eugene said, 'So Langley's got three planes up. But they don't head for Washington. They get sent out over the sea. Finished up further from the White House than when they were sitting in the hangar.'

Vern said, 'Well, hold up now. If you got intelligence of an incoming threat, you're gonna be looking for a submarine or a Soviet fighter coming in over the water.'

I said, 'But, Vern, they already knew they had planes going rogue. Two hitting New York, at least one heading for DC. They hadn't come from offshore. They'd flown out of Boston and Newark and Dulles.'

'Did they?' he said.

He'd forgotten that terrible morning when we'd sat glued to the TV. In his mind he was probably at Drampton, suited up ready to fly out over the North Sea and chase off the Red menace.

Eugene said, 'Peggy's right, Vern. Those Langley fighters could have gotten up to DC, intercepted any plane that had no business being there. But they were out over the ocean, all three of them. Supervisor's plane wasn't even battle-ready, no missiles. And the only people talking to them were navy air-traffic control and they're weren't telling them anything. Meanwhile, back at Langley, nobody was answering the battle cab phone.'

'So a lot of mistakes were made.'

'You think so?' said Eugene. 'No, I'm sorry. Far as I'm concerned that dog don't hunt. A lot of mistakes were made on purpose, more like.'

Pat's friend from 119th said when they eventually headed back to Langley they picked up a lot of radio chatter but they couldn't make out what was being said. They had no idea what had happened in New York. It was only when they saw the Pentagon burning they realized they were dealing with a Real World attack. They thought it must be the Russians.

'Damned right,' Vern said. 'We buzzed a MiG one time, off the coast of Lincolnshire, England. Me and Ed Gillis. We soon marked his card, sent him back to Commie Land.'

Eugene said, 'Three hundred billion a year on air defences, Peggy. Forty billion on intelligence. That's our money. And where the fuck were they on September eleventh? They were stood down, that's what. It's as plain as day.'

Grice said, 'Or maybe somebody just dropped the ball.'

'Somebody?' said Eugene. 'You mean *everybody*.'

'Well, I guess the inquiry'll look into that. They'll make recommendations. That's what inquiries do.'

'Yeah,' said Jim Coffin. 'Like find the guy at NEADS or wherever, the one who ordered that supervisor to fly, and the guy who sent the Langley boys out to sea instead of straight to DC. Then fire them.'

Grice said there were way too many letters. NEADS, NORAD, FAA, FBI, F-16s. He said, 'Why can't they give these things names people can remember? The Big Cheese. The Whole Tamale. The Blip Watchers. The Phone Tappers.'

Eugene predicted nobody'd get fired. 'Leastways, not any-body who was in on it. They'll promote them, more likely. Keep them sweet. Keep them shtum. You heard it here. Yup, I reckon I'll open another file on that. Follow what becomes of all those stand-down generals.'

'And if anybody don't keep shtum,' said Jim, 'they'll probably meet with a accident. Like Lee Harvey Oswald did. Plus, some-thing Eugene failed to mention, you'll recall Bush flew to the Offutt base, 9/11, instead of heading straight back to DC. Guess who else was at Offutt that day? Warren Buffett, that's who.'

'Offutt, Nebraska,' said Vern. 'That's where STRATCOM's at.'

'Right again, Vern,' said Eugene. 'But that's nothing to do with anything. You're muddying the waters, Jim. Warren Buf-fett was hosting a charity golf tournament at Offutt. He does it every year. I'll bet Tiger Woods was there too, but we're not blaming him for anything. Who was pulling the strings? That's what we want to know.'

So a fresh file was opened. Who gave what orders, who messed up and did they get fired.

24

Gayle was sentenced to three years at a low-security correctional facility in Tallahassee, Florida. Everyone said she'd be out in a year, seeing she was a senior citizen and seeing it was what they call a white-collar crime. It made me sad to think of her locked up at all, but Lois reckoned those prisons aren't so bad.

She said, 'I'll bet they got a salon where they can get their hair done. They can probably even order out. You know? Get a Chinese or a pizza? Don't feel sorry for her, Peg. She had a very good thing and she blew it.'

All true, but I still remembered the skinny kid playing house with her First Lieut. Okey, living on TV dinners and love.

I said, 'She's had tragedy in her life.'

Lois said, 'Tell me somebody who hasn't. Didn't make us cook the books, though.'

'So you won't be visiting her?'

'I didn't say that. I'm just not losing sleep over her. I'm losing sleep over this cruise. We need to get things organized. Did you invite Audrey?'

'Not yet. Kath thinks we should decide exactly when we're

going and where we're going first. If we get too many people involved at the beginning we'll never agree on anything.'

'Why's Kath in charge?'

'Because it was her idea. And somebody has to be.'

'Well, I'm not sharing with Audrey and that's final.'

'What's with you? You were so nice with her after Lance Three passed away.'

'I wasn't nice with her. I just encouraged her to have a good cry. It was what she needed. It doesn't do any good to bottle things up, Peg.'

I said, 'Lo darling, how would you know? You never bottled anything up in your life.'

She laughed. She said, 'Fuck off, Dewey. Go tell Kath to organize this cruise. But don't you dare put me in with Audrey.'

When I called Audrey the first thing she asked was had I heard about Gayle. 'So shocking,' she said. 'I heard it on the TV. To think someone we know has gone to jail. And should she even be there, at her age? It's not as though she murdered someone. She's not a risk to society. Why don't they just make her pay back the money?'

I said, 'I think she has to do that too.'

Audrey said the cruise sounded very interesting. She just wasn't sure it'd be her kind of vacation. She said she believed cruises could get very raucous.

I said, 'Well, let me know. We're thinking New York down to Nassau and back. We'll probably book it around Thanksgiving, for next fall.'

'Nassau sounds lovely,' she said. 'But, you know, I might be a liability. My eyes are worse and they're not likely to get any better. I can't manage stairs. I'd slow you all down.' She said there wasn't anything they could do for her. It wasn't fixable, like cataracts.

I told her we still hoped she'd come. I said, 'Those cruise ships have elevators. Don't be a stay-at-home. There'll be enough of us to help you.'

'Bless you, Peggy dear,' she said. 'I'll certainly think about it. Just one thing, though. If we'd be pairing off, I'm afraid I couldn't possibly share with Lois.'

Kath said, 'I could bang their heads together. If they carry on like this, Peg, I reckon just you and me should go, and Grice, of course. Bugger the rest of them.'

Then when I spoke to Crystal about it I began to think none of us would be going.

Crystal said, 'You might have checked if it was okay with me before you started making all these plans. Swanning off on cruises.'

I said, 'We didn't make any plans yet. And it's not *cruises*. It's one cruise. For my eightieth. And, anyway, why wouldn't it be okay with you?'

'And taking Grice with you too.'

'Grice doesn't owe you anything. You're lucky to have him here.'

'I just think you could have asked me first.'

I said, 'I'm your mom, not your employee.'

She'd been getting real testy with me, like I was the one causing her grief, not Marc. First he'd quit his job and gone down to

New York to live with the other woman and her baby. Mia and Quest. He wanted the house sold, equity split 75/25 in his favour because he said he'd put a lot more in than Crystal had, and no lawyers involved because they cost big money. Crystal told him to take a running jump. Then he announced he was coming back to Maine, said he didn't believe the baby was his and he was willing to go to court to contest Mia's claim for child support. So much for not spending money on lawyers. Meanwhile the mortgage wasn't getting paid.

I was sorry for Crystal's troubles. No one wants to see their kid hurting. But Grice kept reminding me that I'd given up my own life to relocate to Maine and help her. To be honest, it hadn't been that much of a life. I'd been retired ever since I sold Swell Parties. Spent my time going through the racks at Dress for Less, watching *General Hospital*, having my first drink of the day too early, maybe.

Grice said, 'So what? Know what most people do at your age? Play golf, go to the podiatrist, meet friends at the coffee shop and compare medical conditions. Some even go on cruises. They don't move in with their ex and help him to wipe his ass.'

Vern was starting to have some bathroom issues and Crystal said it wouldn't be appropriate for her to help with something like that. She said, 'He's my father. I don't want to see him without his skivvies. You were married to him, for Chrissakes.'

He wasn't so steady on his feet either, and I tried to talk to her about what we'd do when we couldn't manage him any longer but she'd just fly into a rage. If I said I was worried he'd fall, she'd say, 'So? If he falls we pick him up. There's four of us.' If I pointed out he was having more and more bathroom accidents, she'd yell, 'He is *not* going into a facility. Over my dead body.'

Grice said, 'This isn't exactly any of my business . . .'

'Correct,' said Crystal.

'But I did relocate. And I do help. So it is slightly my business, and I'd just ask you to consider, what if it's not *your* dead body we're talking about? What if it's your mom's? Then what'll you do? If Peggy dies, I won't stay here. Then it'll be just you and Eugene and a one-hundred-eighty-pound man in a diaper.'

She said, 'We're a long way off that. And Mom's in good health.' But her eyes were full of tears.

Grice said, 'And long life to her. Particularly if she gets proper, restful breaks. Honey, your daddy's a sinking ship. Doesn't mean you and your mom have to go down with him. You've done a great job. Just know when to quit. It might even be better for Vern, you know, somewhere more secure. One of these days he's going to wander out onto that dock and fall in. Then he really will sink.'

She said to him, 'I lost my dad once. I'm not letting go of him again.'

That made me see red.

I said, 'That's BS and you know it. You didn't lose your dad.'

She said, 'I'm damned if I know why you ever got divorced. You get along okay.'

I wasn't going to explain my marriage to my daughter. She was seven, maybe eight when me and Vern split. She wouldn't have noticed him getting paunchy and bad-tempered. I know she missed her daddy when he left but he didn't exactly disappear from her life. He'd call her regular, he'd bring her up to Maine every summer to stay at her gramma Dewey's. Between us we did our best. Then she grew up and repaid us with a few years of heartache.

Some girls, soon as they start developing you have to watch them around the boys. Like Betty Gillis's Deana. Five minutes in a trainer bra and she was like a cat on heat. Crystal wasn't that kind of teenager. She took to wearing dungarees and chewing Hubba Bubba and she was more interested in critters than boys. She bought a lizard, called him Elvis, kept him in her bedroom. If he was out of his tank I wouldn't go in there. I didn't care for the way he blinked at me.

She was going on sixteen when Vern remarried. She came up to Maine for the wedding and she seemed to like Martine well enough. But then she came home to sad news because Perry Kaiser had gotten blown up in Vietnam and lost both his legs.

I date that as the start of Crystal becoming even more contrary. She was anti everything, including me. Whatever I said, she'd say the opposite. She dropped out of veterinary-nurse school and we had a big bust-up. I came home from work one day and she'd gone. Just a note to say she wanted to travel some. I didn't hear from her for more than a year and neither did Vern. I used to cry myself to sleep, wondering where my baby was.

Lois was a good friend to me at that time, when I was feeling low. She'd say, 'Quit beating yourself up. You've been a great mom and Crystal's a good kid. You're just on different tracks right now. It'll work out.'

'If she doesn't get picked up hitchhiking, get murdered by some psycho. Maybe if me and Vern had stuck together, persevered.'

'You think?' she said. 'Peg, look at how I turned out. Do you think that was what my mom had in mind when she used to send me to Bible class? You feed 'em, keep 'em nice, tuck 'em in at night. Then you gotta let them go. Crystal's just trying her wings. Give her time. She'll be back. Betcha.'

I said, 'Easy for you to say. Sandie's never given you a moment's headache.'

'Ha!' she said. 'There speaks a woman whose kid never spent hours practising "Yankee Doodle" on the cornet.'

Christmas Eve 1968 Crystal called me collect from California to wish me a happy holiday. She called Vern too. But she wouldn't give either of us an address. She said she didn't want us laying a heavy family scene on her.

Vern said, 'Well, at least we know she's still alive.'

I guess that was his idea of cheering me up.

If people asked me about her I told them she was travelling, then changed the subject as fast as I could. One day she turned up at Peggy Dewey Weddings. I had an office downtown in those days and Grice had just started working for me. Those were the glory years.

In she walked, but don't imagine for one minute she came back with her tail between her legs. She should have done, the silver hairs she'd put on my head, but she just breezed in and dropped a few bombshells. Like since I last saw her she'd been married, and divorced.

Trent Weaver was a Dallas boy she'd been seeing. Just a friend, she'd always said. He was an anarchist or something, smoked herbal cigarettes, didn't own a tie. They'd run off together, done some travelling, got hitched. I was surprised. I didn't think those types saw the point of marriage. Crystal said she didn't remember too much about it so they must have done it in an altered mental state. They'd been partaking of those funny smokes, I guess.

I remember Grice saying, 'You treacherous girl. Your mom is the best wedding organizer in Dallas County and you snuck off and had some hole-in-the-wall City Hall affair. And not even in Texas. What were your colours?'

She said, 'Khaki and tobacco. And we registered at Wal-Mart.'

When Vern heard she'd come home he said he was just relieved she hadn't married a schwarz and turned up with a coloured baby.

I said, 'Don't let Crystal hear you talk like that. Times have changed.'

He said, 'Not around here they didn't.'

I was so happy to have her back. I didn't care what she did so long as she didn't disappear again. Not even when she built my hopes up saying she was thinking of going back to school but it turned out she meant a taxidermy school in Bend, Oregon. She went through with it too. Well, she is who she is. She works hard, she loves her daddy. She tells me she loves me too. She just seems to choose flaky husbands. Lois was probably right. I don't think Crystal'd have turned out very different if me and Vern had slogged all the way to the finish line together.

Weeks, months even, would pass and I couldn't notice any big change in Vern. He was real forgetful but you could work that to your advantage. He might say he was being held prisoner, threaten to break out and go home. Then I'd say, 'Vern, give me half an hour and I'll drive you.' By the time half an hour passed he'd be throwing a slipper for Banjo or he'd be down at the bait store, yarning with the customers.

Sometimes he'd come out with things and make me laugh, which was strange because I don't ever remember him doing that when we were married. Sometimes I wondered what I was doing there. Crystal could have managed, with a bit more help from Eugene. Then something would happen, a change in him, and it was as though he'd gone down three steps of the stair all at once. And somehow you never saw it coming.

Early October's the prettiest time of year in Maine, when the leaves turn, the sugar maples and the white birches and tamaracks, every one a different shade. One morning I took Vern for a drive. He was so keen to go out he'd put his windbreaker on over his pyjamas. He didn't object when I helped him fasten his seatbelt. He didn't complain when a jack rabbit ran in front of us and I braked so hard the flashlight fell off the dashboard and whacked him on the knee.

He said, 'You shoulda kept your foot down. They make good eating.'

We called at a place where they make a type of bread Grice and Crystal like, full of seeds and stuff, takes you an hour to chew one slice. Give me Wonder Bread any day. Then we stopped off at Merle and Corky's to see their hound pups. They asked us in for a glass of apple cider.

They were in cheerful mood, just got a booking from a company in Newhaven, Connecticut, a group of managers coming for a weekend hunting bear.

Corky said, 'It's called Team Building. These guys sit in their offices all day. Walking to the water-cooler's about the only exercise they ever get. They watch *The Edge* and think they've had a big adventure. Then they come up here, get some mud on their boots. They go home changed men.'

Merle said, 'Pays well too. Couple more gigs like that we can get the roof fixed.'

Vern stumbled a little as we were leaving and I took his arm, to steady him. That was when he turned. 'Get your hands off me!' he snapped. And he knocked the car keys clean out of my hand.

Corky said, 'Whoah, Vern! Peggy was only helping you.'

He said, 'She's been keeping me prisoner and I don't even know who she is. Can you phone Martine? Get her to bring me home?'

Merle said, 'Come and sit on the deck while we figure this out.'

'Don't want to,' he said. 'Nothing to figure out. I want Martine.'

Corky said, 'I don't think we have Martine's number. How about we call Crystal?'

That seemed to satisfy him. He sat, just perched, like he'd be up and off any minute. Trouble was, Crystal didn't answer. We had a lot of fishermen coming in that week and she was getting all the lodges ready. She often didn't keep her cell phone in her pocket, particularly since she'd split from Marc . He was in the habit of sending her messages. Like *WANT 2 COME HOME GIVE IT ANOTHER TRY?* Or *U O ME 75$ BOILER MAINTENANCE.*

Corky said, 'How about me and Merle drive you home, Vern? We can do.'

'Okay,' he said. He shot me a look. Then he spoke real quiet.

He said, 'That woman. She's been stealing from the yarn store. She's took all our money.'

Merle said, 'You mean the store your mom used to run, over Skowhegan? I thought it was sold a while back. We'll have to ask Crystal about that.'

He said, 'But Crystal's only a little girl. And that woman keeps coming into our house and taking liberties. She put a bunch of stuff in the trash, wasn't even hers. Martine's drapes. That ain't right.'

She said, 'I reckon she was just trying to help Crystal. Marvern's a big spread for her to manage on her own.'

'Well,' he said, 'they should ask me.'

Vern got into their pick-up mild as a lamb and they went off ahead. I waited a while, then I followed. When I got back he was sitting in the kitchen eating Cheeze Kurls.

'Hi, Peg,' he said. 'I been out driving.'

The storm had blown itself out but it was just the first of many. After that hardly a day passed without him having an episode. He'd call me a thief. He'd accuse me of murdering Martine and pretending to be his wife. The doctor said we should start to think about the future. Crystal said, 'Yeah, sure,' which meant she had no intention of thinking about Vern's future.

Dr Libby'd come out about once a month to look in on Vern. She needn't have done. We could easily have taken him to her office but she liked to visit people at home, and when she came to Marvern she always bought a bucket of night crawlers. She swore by them for catching bass.

She took me aside one time. She said, 'Vern's going downhill. We need to work on Crystal. Who would she listen to?'

And I couldn't think of anybody. Grice was our best bet and I didn't give much for his chances. She never took him seriously.

Dr Libby said, 'Well, please try. This place is a death trap. You've got all these stairs. He can't even go to the bathroom without negotiating steps. Plus, you've got deep water out there. You've got vehicles pulling in and out, chemicals, firearms too, I'll bet. And what about that trench out back? Nothing ever seems to happen to it.'

I said, 'That was Eugene's project. He was making a tunnel to his survival bunker, only he lost interest.'

'Then he should fill it in. I didn't know he had a bunker. Did he get one of those steel storm-shelters? They're pricey. You can go seventy, eighty thousand for quite a small one.'

I said, 'Eugene's is just a shipping container. You seem to know a lot about them.'

'Husband,' she said. 'He gets the catalogues. It's a guy thing. That trench, though. If it's still there next time I come out I'll have to think about reporting it. '

I didn't have a lot of time for Eugene and his doom-mongering but it seemed to me a man oughta be able to dig a trench on his own land without some clerk coming along with a tape measure and a clipboard, interfering.

I said to Grice, 'So now I'm supposed to persuade Crystal to think about nursing-homes and Eugene to fill in his tunnel.'

'Lordy,' he said. 'And then what will you do the rest of the afternoon?'

25

April came and went and there was no sign of life at Cooper's.

Crystal said, 'Good. Maybe he's decided to sell.'

'I don't think so. He told me he was very fond of the place.'

'Then why doesn't he give it a coat of paint?'

'He doesn't care about such things.'

'Couple of vodkas and suddenly you know all about him?'

Grice said, 'Well, I hope he comes back. It was so good to see Peggy go out on a date.'

I said, 'It wasn't a date.'

'Okay,' he said. 'It was good to see you go out, definitely not on a date, and come home pink and smiling. Out of curiosity, what would have made it a date?'

'Romantic intentions.'

'He did kiss you goodnight.'

'On the hand. That doesn't count. We had a few drinks is all. Get to our age it's just nice to talk to somebody of the same vintage. Somebody who remembers the thirties, say. Or the war.'

Crystal said, 'Yeah, okay, I can see that. His house is still a mess, though.'

*

The dooryard violets were in flower and the bluets and a few lily-of-the-valley. Then one day I smelt cigar smoke and felt glad, but I didn't say a word to anyone because some people don't understand the difference between friendship and romance.

Grice had been into Waterville to fill Vern's prescription. He came indoors and said, 'Visitor for Ms Dewey,' and there was Cort looking over his shoulder. I'd been mopping floors, pair of old ski pants and my hair in a bandanna. I must have been a sight.

Grice said, 'I'll make coffee.'

'Not for me,' said Cort. 'I have arrhythmias and I have a dog over-excited about that trench of yours. I just have a quick question for Peggy.'

Grice made a big fuss about leaving the room.

Cort said, 'I wondered, do you like oddball movies? Something a bit different?'

'Maybe. Not foreign, though. I don't like it when I have to read what they're saying.'

'Okay. Well there's a new movie on in town. *A Mighty Wind*. I'm going tomorrow, to the afternoon show. Be leaving around two, if you want to give it a try.'

Well, of course I did. So that was the start of a summer of movies. Cort paid for the tickets – he insisted – and I bought the jellybeans. Sometimes he said I ought to choose what to see but I didn't care. I was just happy to get out of the house and sit in a nice cool movie theatre for a while. We saw *The League of Extraordinary Gentlemen*, which was weird, and *Finding Nemo*, which was adorable and then I chose *Under the Tuscan Sun* and wished I hadn't because it was sappy and I didn't want Cort thinking I was getting sweet on him.

I came home one time and Grice said, 'I think I've done something I shouldn't. Lois phoned.'

He was under instructions never to tell Lois I was at the movies with a man.

'You told her about Cort?'

'It slipped out.'

'Now I'll never hear the end of it.'

'Sorry. She said she'll call you this evening.'

'Damnation.'

'Yeah. How was the movie?'

'Okay. Bill Murray. He usually makes me laugh but it was a bit depressing.'

Lois phoned, wanted chapter and verse.

I said, 'There's nothing to tell. He's a neighbour.'

'I know. The guy with the dog. But going to the movies! That's dating.'

'We're not dating. And, anyway, he's leaving for Florida next week. I won't see him again till the spring.'

'What am I gonna do with you?' said Lois. 'Guy's only around six months of the year you need to give him some encouragement, move things along.'

'Where I come from we let the men make the running.'

'Where I come from, you find a guy seventy-five years old and still breathing without an oxygen tank, you snap him up.'

'And that's the difference between Texas and New Jersey.'

Lois and Herb were going to Long Island, to Sandie and Gerry's for a big family gathering. Pat's wife was going to be there with the two grandbabies because Pat's unit was deployed to Afghanistan. Gerry's folks were invited too, Mr and Mrs Carroll, plus a sister who never married.

I said, 'Sounds like Sandie needs plenty of chairs.'

'Benches,' said Lois. 'She's borrowed benches. Me and Herb are taking lawn chairs with us. I can't sit on a bench with my hips.'

'Will you stay over?'

'You kidding? Sleeping on camping cots? No, siree, we'll drive home. Half a day of Gerry's mom is as much as I can take. She's bent outta shape because Pat's babies didn't get christened yet. She'll probably bring some of that holy water and do it herself when she's got them cornered. While Pat's not there to tell her to butt out. Also, she brings stuff, for the dinner. I've experienced Mrs Carroll's cooking at previous Thanksgivings. She makes this kinda Jell-O salad, looks like a ring mould of snot. Also a cream of corn pudding, like we're liable to go short on carbs. That pudding, I swear it looks exactly the same going into the body as it does coming out.'

'So what will you be taking?'

'You mean my signature dish? I'm bringing chocolate cookies from the Bake Shoppe, a quart of JD and a stash of sick-bags.'

MRS CARROLL'S HEALTHFUL HOLIDAY SALAD

2 packs lime flavour Jell-O

1 cup mayo

1 cup evaporated milk

1 cup cottage cheese

1 cup canned crushed pineapple

½ cup canned peas

½ cup chopped celery

Dissolve the Jell-O in hot water. Allow to cool a little.

Mix the mayo and evaporated milk in a large bowl. Stir in the Jell-O and the cottage cheese. Then add the peas and celery. Pour into a ring mould and keep in the icebox overnite.

This is good for Thanksgiving or a bring-n-share church supper.

Kath was coming to us for Thanksgiving. Crystal was in domesticated mode, carving pumpkin lanterns to put out on the stoop, looking up recipes for turkey fixings. Grice went to Pottery Barn and bought new serving platters.

I said, 'Well, aren't you a pair of homemakers? It's a pity Grice pitches for the other team. You could get together, look after me when I'm old.'

'Mom!' she said. 'You are *so* inappropriate. And you're already old.'

Kath drove up from Great Neck. She said the drive had been a piece of cake but she looked all in when she arrived. She said, 'I'm all right. I did miss Slick taking a turn but he used to drive too slow.'

I noticed her hearing wasn't so good and she'd gotten into the habit of cocking her head to one side when anybody spoke to her. She said there was nothing wrong with her ears. The problem was, people didn't speak clearly. She said everybody mumbled, even on TV.

As soon as she'd unpacked she was in the kitchen with a pile of cruise brochures all bristling with Post-its. 'Now,' she said, 'we're going to nail this while I'm here, Peggy. If you still want to do it, that is. I reckon we've chewed it over long enough. First thing is, Audrey's cried off. She said she's made other plans. I'm not surprised.'

'Lois won't be sorry.'

'No, but that leaves us with an odd number and single cabins cost more.'

'What about asking May Gotobed?'

'I did think of May. But I don't know if she'd come. She's a terrible worry-wart. She'd worry about getting blowed up flying over here. Then she'd worry about the ship sinking and us all getting drownded. We can't ask your Crystal. She'll be needed here. Do you think Lois'd like to bring Sandie along?'

'I'm not sure we should mix the generations. They don't think the way we do. I don't know what Sandie's like, these days, but I can hardly open my mouth without Crystal telling me off. I'd say Grice is as young as we should go.'

She seemed thoughtful. Then she said, 'I can ask May. And if she says no there's somebody I've got to know at Green Glade as might be interested. How would you feel about that?'

'Okay, I guess. If you can vouch for her. I just want a vacation without getting lectured on what I'm allowed to say.'

'It'd mean you'd have to share with Copper-knob.'

'I can do that. What's your friend's name?'

'Sal,' she said, and she got up from the table, started rinsing cups.

'She about our age?'

'He,' said Kath. 'It's a he. Salvatore. He's a widower. Don't think badly of me, Peggy.'

I was stunned. I said, 'Kath, I'd never think badly of you. You're a widow. You're entitled to a bit of company. Slick wouldn't want you to be lonely.'

She said she was worried people would think it was too soon.

I said, 'At eighty I don't think there any such thing as too soon. What's he like?'

She had a photo. When a person starts carrying a photo you know it's serious. He was a fine-looking man, still had a good head of hair.

311

Grice said, 'Wow! I could go for him myself. Does he have money?'

'I don't know.'

'You sure he's not after yours?'

'I haven't got that much,' she said. 'Any road, there's richer pickings than me in Green Glade if that's his scheme.'

I waited till Kath had gone to bed, but I just had to call Lois. She screamed. 'Talk about hidden depths! Did they have sex yet?'

'He likes to cook. He makes her meatballs and spaghetti.'

'Cooking's okay. Doesn't mean sex is off the menu. She should check he's in full working order.'

'Are you telling me you and Herb still do it?'

'No, no, no. Herb reads *Popular Woodworker* and I do it myself. But a new guy, that's a horse of a different colour. Kath should take him for a test drive.'

'I'll leave you to have that conversation with her. So if Kath brings this Sal on the cruise it'll mean you'll be sharing with me.'

'Perfect. I knew Audrey wouldn't come.'

'She's going to Europe. Mikey's paying.'

'Yeah, Europe's more her scene. Old statues and all that. I couldn't see Audrey going down a water slide, could you? I couldn't see her getting the Spa Experience deal.'

So it was finally decided: we'd take the Ocean Palace, departing from Manhattan September 20, calling at Port Canaveral, Stirrup Cay and Nassau. Me and Lois in a standard outside double, Grice in an inside single, Kath and Salvatore in a balcony state room. I don't believe she ever intended asking May and I can't say I was very happy about it. It was meant to be all friends together and we didn't even know the guy. But I didn't want to rain on Kath's parade. Like Grice said, she might have been a late starter but she was certainly putting up a strong finish.

We went for a walk after dinner, before it got dark. When we got back Jim Coffin had his feet under the table, eating pumpkin pie, Vern was asleep in his armchair and Eugene was back at his 9/11 files. He and Jim were working on why the buildings had fallen down. A professional demolition job. They were absolutely convinced.

Crystal said, 'For crying out loud, the fire from the jet fuel melted the steel. Don't you read the papers?'

'Oh, yeah,' said Eugene. 'The wet-noodle theory. Melting point of steel, 2800 degrees Fahrenheit, temperature of burning jet fuel, 800 degrees Fahrenheit. You understand that? You take science in high school, Crystal? Then there's all those firefighters heard detonations. All the engineers who say there is no fucking way did the steel melt.'

'Not *all* the engineers. Just the ones you listen to. You saying there were explosives? Who planted them? How'd they get in there?'

'On a weekend. Team comes in, says they're laying new cables or something. It wouldn't be that hard.'

'You're crazy. Where's the evidence? Explosives leave a trace.'

'That is true,' said Eugene. 'But, of course, Giuliani had everything shipped out. The steel, the rubble, everything. Had to be the fastest clean-up operation on record. You seen who's

313

parked out front waiting to speak with you? He's been there an hour. I told him you were out walking but he wouldn't come in.'

She groaned, went outside.

Grice said, 'Uh-oh. I guess Black Friday dawned early.'

Kath said, 'Is she still thinking of taking him back?'

That wasn't my reading of the situation. Crystal was very bitter about Marc. I said, 'He keeps pestering her. Thanksgiving, he'll be feeling lonely.'

Kath said, 'Then if she don't want him back, I wonder she harn't divorced him by now.'

Grice thought Crystal was just enjoying a bit of payback time, letting him suffer.

'Well, that's not healthy,' said Kath. 'No good ever come of being vindictive. I shall have a word with her.'

Grice said, 'And so Kath Pharaoh Bonney rides fearlessly across the minefield of Marc and Crystal's marriage. Boom! It was nice knowing you, Kath.'

But Crystal didn't come back in to hear Kath's words of wisdom. When I peeped out she was still sitting in Marc's car, windows steamed up. Next time I looked his car was gone and Crystal's lodge was in darkness.

What's a mother to do? You don't want to see your kid getting jerked around but when they're in their fifties, and they have a tongue like a wood rasp, you tread real careful.

She looked like she'd slept in a thorn hedge. She made oatmeal, slammed a few cupboard doors, yelled at the dogs. Then she said, 'Go on. Ask me.'

'What did he want?'

'Sympathy. Forgiveness. Thanksgiving leftovers.'

'He get any?'

'Ha!' She was jabbing the spoon into oatmeal. She said, 'Okay. He's going back to Mia. Making the best of a bad job, if you ask me. It's because of the kid. It is Marc's. Obviously. And he's getting to the cute age, I guess. Crawling and stuff.'

'Wait till he's a teenager. How old's Marc?'

'Sixty-six.'

'So when the boy's fifteen Marc'll be my age. How's that gonna play?'

'Right. Should be fun.'

'So why did you spend the night with him?'

'I didn't. We went to the house. Spent the night figuring who gets what. So Monday I'll call the realtor. Might as well salvage what I can. I get the dogs. Like they were ever negotiable. Mia's only got a small apartment.'

'Sounds cosy. Miserable old guy, young wife, baby on the move.'

'Stroller in the lobby, bouncer hanging from the door frame, car trunk full of baby gear every time you leave the house.'

'You feel better now?'

'Yeah. I will do, when I've had some sleep.'

'You finished killing that oatmeal?'

She looked at me. She said, 'Did you mind very much when I didn't make you a grandma?'

Like I told her, that was ancient history. I said, 'I didn't ever bank on it, didn't ever sit around waiting for it. If it had happened I hope I'd have made the grade but it didn't and here we are. I can't complain. I'm sitting here getting breakfast with my darling daughter.'

'Love you, Mom,' she said. 'What can I do to make your day?'

'Make me coffee. Mind your dad while I take Kath out for a while.'

'I would have done that anyway. Anything else?'

'Use that anti-tangle conditioner I gave you.'

Grice said he'd never send me into a summit conference. He said, 'You're too easily satisfied. If it had been me I'd have demanded unconditional cruising rights. In writing. And I've have asked her to wash the dogs' bedding. This house is starting to smell like an old boarding kennel.'

26

Lois decided she was going to Great Neck to check out Kath's new beau.

I said, 'You mind your mouth. Don't go spoiling things for Kath.'

She said, 'I have no idea what you mean. I'm just being a pal. I'm looking out for her.'

'Like you've been looking out for me? Trying to push me into the arms of a neighbour?'

'You're different. You need encouragement. Sounds like Kath's going full steam ahead, and sometimes she's way too nice for her own good. Boy Scouts ring her bell, trying to sell her a ticket for a prize draw, she'll buy the whole damned book.'

It was real quiet around Marvern in the winter. You might get a few regulars dropping by the store for a Weekender Bucket but no overnighters. There was better ice-fishing to be had up in Aroostook County. Crystal had an idea for bringing in a bit more money: fly-tying classes. She thought it'd attract the same types who went bear-hunting with Merle and Corky. City workers wanting to get back in touch with the outdoors. But Eugene pooh-poohed it.

He said, 'Folk around here tie their own flies, don't need no classes. Flatlanders buy 'em off the shelf.'

She said, 'That's what I mean. Flatlanders. They'll take classes in anything.'

She had a work bench and a vice but she didn't know much about flies. She needed Eugene to help her but he was too busy. He and Jim were working on their Shanksville File. They had already satisfied themselves that the Pentagon and the Twin Towers were smoke-and-mirrors jobs. Air defences stood down and remote-controlled planes used as missiles.

'Open and shut case,' Eugene said. 'This commission's got any teeth there's a bunch of people oughta be tried for war crimes.'

Grice said, 'Do you mean George W.?'

Eugene said, 'Not really. He's as much a patsy as them towel-heads. No, I mean the ones really pulling the strings. Won't happen, though, not yet. They got everybody by the short and curlies. But folk *are* waking up. Two years ago people thought I was nuts. Now I got plenty of company. Sensible folk asking fair questions because they're done swallowing the official dreck. Are we all nuts, eh, Crystal?'

'No comment,' she said.

'Peggy,' said Eugene, 'tell me something. If you got a call from Crystal and she said, "Mom, this is Crystal Dewey," what would you think?'

I knew what he was getting at. 'This is about that guy, right? The one who called his mother from the Shanksville plane?'

'Just answer me. What would you think if Crystal said "Mom, this is Crystal Dewey"?'

'Well, if she told me she was on a hijacked plane in fear of her life I'd probably think she was so terrified she didn't know what she was saying.'

'Really? Or how about she was trying to tell you, "Mom, pay attention, read between the lines. This call isn't what it seems"?'

'Possible.'

'Okay. That's all I'm asking. Consider what's possible. Don't storm out and slam doors, like some folk I could mention. I'm not claiming to have an answer yet but I'll tell you one thing, Peggy. It ain't Shinola.'

Lois had been to visit Kath, intending to give Salvatore the once-over.

'Well,' she said, 'he's a good-looking guy, I will say. And he's very attentive to Kath. Pulls the chair out for her and stuff. Vern ever do that for you?'

'I wouldn't have wanted him to. Vern never had great timing. I'd have been worried I'd end up under the table.'

'Same with Herb. He hears a plane flying over he forgets everything else.'

'So you approved of this Sal?'

'I didn't say that. I dunno, maybe it's because he just took up with her but it all felt a bit over the top. Know what I mean? And of course there's been ramifications.'

'Such as?'

'Jealousy. I reckon quite a few of the other old broads in there had their eye on him. So now they don't invite Kath when they go for coffee. That's why I'll never live in one of those places, Peg. People twitching their drapes, watching your comings and goings.'

'What about the cruise? Will he be good company?'

'I reckon. He likes dancing, so that's a plus. If Kath gets tired of him he can squire me round the dance floor.'

'They have guys who're paid to do that, because of all the widows they get on cruise ships.'

'I know. Don't mean you can't BYO. So listen up. Lorene Bass went to visit Gayle at the penitentiary. Lorene's in Pensacola, these days, so it wasn't a long trip. She said Gayle looked terrible.'

'I don't think anybody looks good when they're in jail. Is she sick?'

'No. But Lorene said they make them wear these tan suits, like theatre scrubs, and she'd piled on weight.'

'She could afford to. She was never more than a size six even when she was drinking. Sounds like they eat okay in jail. She working? I'll bet they have a chapel. She could do some healing while she's in there.'

'I don't think so, Peg. I reckon she's crapped on her own doorstep healing-wise. Broke the eleventh commandment. Thou shalt not cheat the IRS. You're right about the food, though. Three meals a day, and they got a commissary, if you need a snackette. No schlepping round Stop 'n' Shop, wishing they'd invent a new kind of meat. Maybe I should commit a crime. Nothing big. Just something to get me a year in the slammer. Let somebody else do the laundry for a while.'

THE EARLY BIRDS

'But not until after the cruise.'

'Definitely not until after the cruise. Now, when are you coming down here to get your cruise-wear?'

I hadn't planned on buying anything. I had dresses, I had pants suits.

Lois said, 'Christ a-mighty, Peg, you can't wear a pants suit on Stirrup Cay. Did you see the pictures? That is one beautiful beach. You're gonna need swimwear and a sunhat and something floaty.'

I said if that was the case I'd get them in Augusta.

'I doubt it,' she said. 'I doubt you'll find anything in Maine but camo shorts and lesbo tanks. Get your ass down here. We'll hit the outlets.'

New Yorkers can have a very limited view of the world.

I said, 'I'll make a deal with you. We'll go shopping when you come up here. I'm gonna prove to you I can get everything I need right here. If I'm wrong, I'll come down to New York.'

'Yeah,' she said. 'That was the other thing I wanted to say, Peg. I'm not sure we'll make it up there next month. Gerry's not well. He's getting tests.'

'What kind of not well?'

'He's had a cough for months now. He had it when we were over there at Thanksgiving, and now he can't get his breath. Just walking out to get the mail, he's winded. He was a fit guy, you know. Remember when he ran that race to raise money for the Huntington's people? Sandie's real worried so Herb thinks we should stick around, at least until we know what it is.'

'Sure. You can come here any old time.'

'I know. Still, I'm sorry. Herb's good with Vern and it gives you

321

a bit of a break. We'll get there. We just need to get Gerry fixed up first.'

I'm afraid to say there wasn't much fixing up they could do. It turned out Gerry had fibrosis of the lungs and all they could do was give him an oxygen tank to help him breathe.

Lois said, 'Sandie's in pieces but I said to her, "At least he don't have cancer." Since he got sick he's heard of two buddies, got cancer of the spine. They think it's from when they were searching at Ground Zero. All that gunk they must have been breathing. Asbestos and shit. The union reckons they should get compensation.'

Eugene said he was surprised Gerry had only heard of two cases of cancer. He said, 'Those towers? They were full of asbestos. See, when they were put up, nobody realized it was harmful. Did you know they were supposed to get demolished twenty years ago, when people found out what asbestos could do to your lungs? Know why they didn't do it? Because of what it would of cost. Think about it. They'd have had to take it down floor by floor. Cut through the steel with oxy-acetylene, break up the concrete with explosives, one floor gone, then the next and the next. One hundred and four floors and that's just one tower. And all the while you're doing that you're disrupting life in that whole neighbourhood. Traffic diverted. People's businesses affected. Loss of revenue too, from all those firms got offices in there. So they scrapped the plan. Put it on the back burner until they figured out a cheaper way to do it. Because that was in olden times, Peggy, before they discovered a jet-fuel

322

fire could melt the steel and bring the whole bang shoot down in seconds. Magic.'

Grice helped me to dress Vern. He didn't resist any more. He didn't yell, 'I know how to put a singlet on, Goddamn it.' He'd just stand there like a dummy while we wrassled him into his shirt and pants. It was like having a kid again, only kids grow up and learn to dress themselves. With Vern everything was going in reverse.

Grice said, 'That stuff Eugene was just saying, about the towers? It really makes you wonder.'

I said, 'Do you mean about what happened on 9/11 or do you mean about Eugene's sanity?'

He said, 'I think you know what I mean.'

Well, I did. Only I could never bring myself to say it. I love my country. I've lived overseas and I wouldn't trade places for a big gold bar. All my life I've believed what Uncle Sam told me. Now I felt like I'd walked out onto a narrow ledge and there was no turning back.

I was miserable about Herb and Lois not visiting too. It was the highlight of the year because Lois livened up the house and I could leave Herb and Vern together for hours. I'd been three years at Marvern and I found myself wondering how much longer it'd go on. Dr Libby said the pills Vern took would slow down his deterioration. She said he had the heart of a fifty-year-old. I believe she intended to cheer me up. And Crystal could talk up a storm about them discovering a cure. I tried to point out that her daddy was in his eighties. You get to that point in life you're not looking for cures, you're looking for a peaceful exit. Gerry Carroll, now he was a different case. He was only fifty-seven. He was still a young man.

Crystal came with me to Kohl's to buy a few things for the cruise. A swimsuit with tummy-control panels, sandals, pedal-pushers. I used to live in pedal-pushers when we were at Wichita in 1954. I guess they musta come back in fashion. We all wore them back then, excepting Betty. She thought they weren't lady-like. Actually it was Ed said they left nothing to the imagination and he wasn't having guys looking at his wife's tush.

And Lois said, 'Further proof that Ed Gillis has fresh air between those jug ears of his. Can you imagine any guy ogling Betty? Since she had Carla you could land 96th Bomber Wing on her rear.'

So Betty stuck to her homemade skirts and shirtwaists.

The only thing I couldn't find in Augusta was something to cover me up on the Stirrup Cay beach. Lois had said it should be something floaty.

Crystal said, 'Are you seriously taking fashion notes from Lois Moon?'

'She reads the magazines.'

'She dresses like a clown. All those bangles. All those jarring colours.'

This is what you get from the younger generation now. Don't say 'Red Indian'. Don't say 'cripple'. Don't wear tangerine.

I said, 'I'll tell you a good thing about Lois. She doesn't give a damn what anybody thinks. And her outfits cheer me up. I couldn't wear them but I'm sure glad she does. And I will need something. I don't want to get a sunburn and I don't want folk seeing my thighs. They look like baked marshmallows. They remind me of a dish your gramma Shea used to make for Thanksgiving.'

'Cellulite,' said Crystal. 'Everybody gets it. After you've swum you can just pull on a tee and the pedal-pushers. You don't need floaty. You don't want to look like some wrinkled old relic from a B-movie.'

Wrinkled old relic, my eye. Grice always says I have great skin for my age. 'You and the Queen,' he says. 'Strawberries and cream. What *is* your secret?'

Besides, if we were talking about wrinkles, Crystal wasn't lagging far behind me. It's a strange thing to watch your baby grow old.

I said, 'Maybe I could get something mail order. Like a kaftan or something.'

'Okay,' said my darling daughter. 'Or we could drive across to Bean's, buy you a pup tent.'

27

It was an election year. George Bush was riding high since they captured Saddam Hussein. I don't know why they went after him. I thought the guy getting dialysis in the cave was the one we were hunting. I guess I hadn't been paying attention. So the question was, who would the Democrats put up against Bush? Kerry was the favourite from the get-go. Liebermann dropped out, then Dean, then Al Sharpton. Even when those TV ads started about Kerry's war record, he was still the one to beat.

A group of vets who'd served with him in Vietnam had commenced smearing his name. Kerry had come out of that war with three Purple Hearts and a Silver Star, but one story I read said he got his first Purple Heart for a cut on his arm from friendly fire shrapnel, needed nothing more than antibiotics and a Band-Aid. I don't know. Somehow they always scrape up some mud to fling. Even Bush didn't escape it. Kerry's people said George Bush had been supposed to serve six years in the National Guard, seeing he hadn't gone to Vietnam, but he'd never served anything like that long. I guess his rich granddaddy must have bought him out.

The Fourth of July fell on a Sunday that year. The crowds in

Waterville were getting to be too much for Vern so we decided to take him to the boat parade on McGraw Pond. Jim Coffin had entered his old Boston whaler in the Most Patriotic category. Grice predicted it'd just have a few red, white and blue balloons tied fore and aft but Grice was wrong.

Jim had constructed replicas of the Twin Towers out of grocery cartons and slung a banner across them. It said NEVER FORGET. Actually it said NEVER FORGIT but I still think he should have won. That boat lined with girls wrapped in the Stars and Stripes was an abomination.

Eugene never came to Independence Day parades. He flew the flag every day of his life, lowered it to half-mast when Ronnie Reagan died. He was winding down his investigations, waiting on the commission report coming out. He said if it answered his questions he'd be satisfied. He said if it answered even half of them he'd stand on the steps of the State Capitol and eat his hat.

So on the Fourth, while we went to the boat parade, he turned his attention back to the bunker. Some of the cans and dry goods he had down there needed checking, maybe replacing. Store rotation, he called it.

Grice said, 'Uh-oh. I hope that won't mean beef stew served fifty different ways. I don't care for a lot of red meat when the weather's hot.'

Neither did I. I was making fried chicken. I can't remember a July Fourth when I didn't. I figured if there were cans needed using, Eugene should eat them. Vern'd help him. Put it under a pie crust and Vern'd eat an old boot.

We got back from McGraw Pond and there was no sign of

Eugene or his canned goods. Around six Jim Coffin swung by. He was in high spirits because he'd received a bunch of compliments about his Twin Towers and had his picture taken for the *Kennebec Sentinel* and, like he said, that meant more to him than the opinion of a few college-educated pantywaist parade judges.

Eugene didn't show for my fried chicken. We sat out on the deck. Ten o'clock the fireworks started and Vern didn't even look at the sky.

Crystal said, 'You okay there, Daddy?'

'Yup,' he said.

'What are you thinking about?'

'Stuff,' he said. 'It's getting dark. Wondering how I'm getting home.'

I said, 'Don't worry. You're sleeping here tonight, seeing it's a holiday.'

'Okay,' he said.

When Jim Coffin realized we weren't going to offer him another cold beer he said he'd make tracks. Said he'd look in at the bunker on his way home, make sure Eugene wasn't partying in there with ladies of the night.

Grice said, 'I think you could be on to something there, Jim. I seem to remember he had a stash of Trojans and baby oil. Filed under Recreational Requisites along with the playing cards and the box of checkers.'

Crystal said any more talk of Eugene and baby oil and she was liable to blow her cookies.

Vern said, 'Does Mom know I'm sleeping over?'

We were getting him to bed when we heard Jim hollering at the door. He was bent over, winded from running. He said,

'You'd better get an ambulance. Eugene's had a mishap. Section of shelving fell on him down in the bunker and he's trapped. He's in a bad way.'

Eugene wasn't in a bad way. He was dead. A whole shelf full of canned peach halves and condensed milk had fallen onto him. Grice and Crystal saw him when they pulled him out.

Cort came round. He'd heard the ambulance go up. 'If there's anything I can do,' he said, 'be sure to let me know.'

I'd have appreciated one of his vodka cocktails but it wouldn't have been right to say it.

Grice said, 'Gosh, Peg, it was awful. He was kind of flattened. Paramedic said he probably had a thin skull. I've never seen anything like that before. And it makes you think. All those facts Eugene had in his head, all that reading he'd done. Your brain gets squashed, where's it all go? You could be a genius, you could be like Mozart or Stephen Hawking. Or you could be a moron, like Sawyer Hoose III. Load of canned fruit falls on you and it all turns to the same mush.'

I recommended him to take a pill. Thoughts like that going through his mind, he'd never get to sleep.

He said, 'I might do. There's just a couple of things I need to do first. Clear a few things out of Eugene's room, save any embarrassment to his reputation.'

'What things? What reputation?'

'He had some photos. Girly pics. Strong stuff, some of them. I'll just get rid of them before the police start poking around.'

'Why would the police poke around?'

'Peggy darling,' he said, 'that deputy, when he finally arrived,

329

took one look at what Eugene had in the bunker and sent for back-up.'

There had been quite a wait for a patrol car to come, what with it being the Fourth an' all. They had a trooper up at Belgrade, doing crowd control at the pizza-eating contest, another up to New Sharon, vehicle flipped on its roof, and the only deputy available had gone to a report of indecent conduct in Harmony.

'Back-up? Why? You mean Eugene's weapons? But his stuff was all legal.'

'Yes. But some of the books he'd got in there don't give a good impression. *The Anarchist's Handbook. How to Build a Man Trap. The Bilderberg Conspiracy.* Plus there was a bag of white powder. The deputy was worried it might be anthrax.'

'What was it?'

'I don't know. Not anthrax, that's for sure. Could have been talcum powder. Eugene's idea of a dry shower. Anyway, the deputy made a call. I heard him say Eugene was either mad or up to something bad and it was above his pay-grade to decide which. So I'd say we should expect some questions. I'd say they'll probably search his room. Whatever happens, we better play the he-was-crazy-but-harmless card.'

'Which happens to be the truth,' said Crystal. 'And I've told Jim Coffin to stay away till they've done investigating. Last thing we need is him spouting about the New World Order.'

She went through Eugene's stuff that night too, looking for a will. She didn't find one. I don't know what time they turned in. Monday morning we got a visit from men in suits. They started in Eugene's room and they told us we weren't allowed in there, like it was a crime scene.

Crystal said, 'They'll soon quit. When they start going through the pile of clothes on his floor they'll wish they never started. Eugene took recycling to a whole new level.'

I said, 'I hope those files aren't going to be a problem.'

And Grice whispered, 'Files? I don't remember any files.'

Vern never once asked for Eugene that morning but he got very excited about the suits. He kept trying to follow them into Eugene's room and they yelled at him, even though I'd explained about his condition. In the afternoon they started on the bait store and the worm sheds, but when they saw Crystal's chemicals they decided to wait for back-up from guys in hazmat suits.

She was in the mood for a fight. 'Idiots,' she said. 'It's just borax and acetone and formaldehyde. Tools of my trade. Anybody'd think I'd got a bomb factory out there.'

Grice said, 'Crystal, do not use those words. Ever. Even in jest. Those suits are FBI.'

They said taxidermy was an unusual line of business for a female. She told them she took it up after she quit the pet-grooming business. 'I got tired of getting nipped,' she said. 'The critters I deal with now, their nipping days are done. And I have a good reputation around here. Ask anybody. Ask Trooper Nadeau. I mounted a canvasback duck for him last year, birthday gift for his wife.'

It took them a while to get our living arrangements straight in their minds too. It was because the deceased, as they kept calling him, was Crystal's step-brother and yet she had her mom and dad living with her too. They asked me how come I was living with my ex. I said we were giving it another try.

I asked the guy if he was really FBI.

LAURIE GRAHAM

I didn't get an answer. He just said, 'You're a long way from Texas.'

A state trooper or a sheriff's deputy, they'll call you 'ma'am'. The suits don't call you anything.

He said, 'Are you expecting to inherit this place? That why you're here?'

I could have laughed only I don't think you laugh with the Feds. Truth was, we didn't know where we stood regarding Marvern. Vern's share'd go to Crystal eventually but we had no idea about Eugene's intentions.

He said, 'What about this guy Terry? Where's he fit in?'

I said, 'His name's Grice. Terry's his surname.'

'And?'

'He's a friend and my former business partner. We used to work together and now we live together.'

'So you're in a relationship with him?'

'He's a homosexual.'

'Was he in a relationship with the deceased?'

'No, Eugene wasn't a homosexual. He'd been married.'

'People can go both ways. Terry an anarchist too?'

I told him I hadn't even known Eugene was an anarchist. I told him I wasn't even sure what an anarchist was.

He looked at me. He said, 'Did you ever hear him express anti-government opinions?'

I said, 'He was a patriot. I believe he served in Vietnam.'

'Why did he have a cache of firearms?'

'Because it was his right. And he feared civil unrest.'

'Where's the deceased's wife? Are they divorced?'

*

332

I had no idea and neither did Crystal, although we didn't have to wait too long to find out. After the Feds had decided Eugene had been nothing more than a Sunday-afternoon survivalist and left us in peace, Crystal called the funeral home. They said they had a backlog: July 24 was the earliest they could offer her.

She put a notice in the paper. A graveside service out at Lakeview followed by interment. She said, 'I don't think many people'll come. Jim, Merle and Corky, maybe a couple of Martine's old friends. We can ask them back here for beer and crackers. And I've ordered an economy-range casket. I'm not splashing out money until I find that damned will.'

She was certain Eugene would have written one. She said, 'He may have been deluded but he was too canny to die without making sure this place didn't go to some distant relative he didn't like.'

Grice shuddered. 'Don't,' he said. 'You're giving me an attack of *déjà vu*.'

'Worse yet,' said Crystal, 'if they can't track down any cousins, his property goes to the state. But Eugene'd never allow that to happen. So somewhere there has to be something written down.'

She kept turning out the kitchen drawers but the Feds had already been there. As Grice said, 'Looking for suspicious bomb-making string.' He said, 'And by the way, nobody has thanked me for making sure they didn't find his 9/11 files.'

Crystal said, 'You put them in the incinerator, right?'

Grice said, 'I most certainly did not. All those months of work. I'm looking forward to reading them.' The files were arranged in a neat layer under Browser's bedding.

Crystal said, 'Are you insane? Concealing stuff from the FBI? Why didn't you destroy them?'

'Don't you think they'd have wondered why we'd had the incinerator going in July? If they'd happened to find the files I'd have said Eugene was paranoid, delusional. Always hiding stuff.'

'If they'd found them you could have landed us all in deep shit.'

'But they didn't, did they? Not every candidate graduates top of Spook School. And, Crystal dear, you must admit it was a great place to hide them.'

'Now I know why Browser's not been settling at night.'

'Yes, poor Browser. He's been an instrument of my treachery. But he'll be okay now. I'll put them out on the deck, get the doggy smell off them, then I'll keep them in my lodge. I imagine Jim Coffin will want them but I'm going to read them first.'

I said, 'You're lucky the dog didn't chew them.'

'Not enough teeth,' said Grice. 'Those files are in perfect condition. He didn't even slobber on them.'

It was the day before the funeral. We had fishermen staying in two of the units and that meant Crystal had to be up, with everything ready for their breakfast. My daughter's no great cook but I told her from the get-go if she intended reviving the bed-and-breakfast side of the business she'd have to do the cooking and the laundry. I had enough to do, watching over Vern.

If there were clients in for breakfast Vern liked to sit at the table and listen to the fishing talk. There were four guys in that morning, snarfing down eggs and bacon strips and talking brown trout. They'd been up at North Pond a couple of weeks earlier, using spoon lures. They hadn't had much success.

Crystal said, 'We stock Mooselook Wobblers. They'd be worth a try.'

And Vern said, 'You fish last night?'

They hadn't. They'd arrived around seven, dropped their kit and gone straight down to the Sunset Grill to eat.

Vern said, 'If you go out late you oughta use a Hex pattern. You'll catch a bunch of good-sized trout when the Hex mayflies are hatching.'

Crystal loved it when he perked up like that. Well, so did I. It was a sign the old Vern was still in there somewhere.

She said, 'What do you recommend, Daddy? A nymph?'

'Might do,' he said. 'Nymphs are good. I reckon we got a dry fly too. I reckon Eugene tied a few. Elk hair, that's the secret. It floats real fine.'

Crystal said she'd look them out before evening.

'Ask Eugene,' said Vern. 'Where is he anyhow?'

Crystal said, 'Eugene passed, Daddy. You remember?'

Vern said, 'Oh, yeah. Eugene passed. Only drawback with an elk-hair fly, if you get a nibble on it then the trout gets away, you can't use it again till you've dried it out.'

The fishermen got up to leave.

Vern called after them, 'Leave it till around nine, ten. No earlier. And go prepared. A twelve-pound line. There are some big mommas out there.'

Crystal whispered to me, 'Can you believe this man? Forgets how to use a knife and fork but he remembers the Hex dry fly.'

We drove into town. Grice wanted to buy a black tie for the

funeral. There was no need. Eugene wouldn't have expected it, and the weather was too humid for wearing a suit, but Grice can be old-fashioned about things like that. We bought flowers too, just a few white peonies. Eugene wasn't a flowers kinda guy but, like Grice said, it was going to look too bleak if all we had to put on the lid of the casket was his second-best baseball cap.

As we pulled into Marvern, Crystal came running out of the bait store with an envelope in her hand. 'Goddamn it, I found it,' she said. 'Bottom of the pattern sheet drawer.'

And there it was, in his squinched-up backward-leaning writing. The Last Will and Testament of Eugene Martin Ouellet. I'd never seen his name written before. I'd always thought it was spelled Wellett.

Crystal said, 'I think I need to sit down to read this.'

28

Grice said he'd make himself scarce. He said a will reading was private family business. But Crystal said why didn't he just shut up and sit down or, on second thoughts, pour everybody a cold soda? She was so wound up.

I said, 'Calm down. Whatever it says, your daddy still owns half this place and whatever's his is yours, or will be.'

'I know,' she said, 'but if he's done something crazy, like leave it to Jim Coffin or the National Association of 9/11 Wackos, I'm gonna contest it.'

Her hands were shaking as she opened the envelope. I felt a little sick myself. All I could think of was that awful day we realized we'd be losing Tucker's house.

She looked at it and looked at it. Then she shook her head but not in a bad way. I knew then it wasn't terrible news. I said, 'He's left it to you.'

'Nope,' she said. 'He's left everything to Grice.'

We passed it around. It was just one page, very short and to the point. Grice Terry to be sole beneficiary, *in gratitude for his respectful care of my step-father, Vernon Dewey, and seeing he don't have a place to call his own*. It had been witnessed by Randolph T. Dell at the Harley dealership and Mac McDonald, the bar-keep at the White Birch.

Grice had gone pale. First thing he said was, 'I'm sorry.' Second thing he said was, 'I think I need a Ring Ding.'

We were out of Ring Dings. I found him a Twinkie.

'Anything,' he said. 'My blood sugar just dropped through the floor.'

It was a homemade kinda will. There was no sign of a lawyer's hand in it, no 'aforementioneds' or hereinafters'. Grice wondered if it was legit. If it'd stand up if anybody challenged it.

I said, 'Who would do that?'

And Crystal said, 'I could. It'd have made more sense to leave Marvern to me, seeing Daddy owns half. Grice is just a blow-in.'

I said, 'Are you serious?'

'No,' she said, 'but you see my point? I'm family, Grice isn't. Strictly speaking.'

I said, 'I reckon anybody who helps your dad on and off the john counts as family.'

Grice said, 'Please don't argue. I don't want any upset. I don't even want the place. I had no idea.'

And he burst into tears. It was the shock, I guess. Then Crystal backed off. She said, 'I'm not arguing about it, Grice. It was just a surprise.'

I could see she was still a bit riled but at least there was a will. At least she could put a face to the beneficiary instead of worrying about some distant Ouellet cousin pitching up.

Grice went for a walk. Vern wanted to tag along. Grice said he didn't mind.

Crystal said, 'He wants to inspect his property, I suppose. Lord of all he surveys.'

I said, 'Half of all he surveys. I don't understand you. Grice is like a brother to you. And all you ever did was tell Eugene he was an idiot. You can't be surprised he didn't name you in his will.'

She was scrubbing at the bacon skillet. Crystal hardly ever cleans burned pans. She just leaves them soaking until somebody else, usually me, gives in and scrubs them for her.

She said, 'Did you know?'

'Know what?'

'About Eugene and Grice, of course. There must have been something going on.'

'Going on? You mean "going on"? There was nothing going on. Grice listened to him is all. Grice didn't mock all that end-of-the-world stuff. And he does help with your daddy. I couldn't do it without him.'

'But Eugene didn't know anything about Grice. Three years ago he hadn't even met him.'

'I'll tell you something Eugene definitely knew. Grice is kind to your daddy and he wouldn't do anything to hurt me or you. Besides, he's a cultivated person. He knows about rugs and vases and stuff. Do you really think he wanted to inherit half a worm farm?'

'Maybe I'll buy him out.'

'Maybe he'll give it to you if you quit scowling at him.'

I called Lois.

She said, 'How come you have such an exciting life, Dewey?

A death by canned fruit, then raided by the Feds, then a shocker at the will-reading. It's like something on TV. Well, that's it! When Herbert Moon goes to his reward I'm marrying Grice. Even if he is a faggot.'

She said she'd been trying to get Kath but Kath never seemed to be home, these days. I tried her once myself and then the rest of the day got away from me. We had a person from the Food Bank come to take away most of Eugene's canned goods. Jim Coffin took the batteries and bottled water. He said, 'About the weapons and the ammo? I'll take it all off your hands, if you like. Give you a fair price.'

I told him we'd let him know. I'd already had the same offer from Merle and Corky. Matter of fact, I had in mind to keep the Luger for myself. I said, 'I guess you knew about Eugene's will?'

'Oh, yeah,' he said. 'He did talk of leaving me a slice but I knew that'd piss Crystal, pardon my language. So he said in that case he'd leave it to your friend because he knew he'd do the right thing by Vern.'

Grice wandered around in a daze.

I said, 'Anybody'd think Laurance Rockefeller left you his millions. Half of Marvern. It's hardly going to change your life.'

'But it has changed it,' he said. 'It's upset Crystal, so that's not good. On the other hand it means we don't need to worry, you and me. We can stay here as long as we're needed.'

I said, 'Crystal'll get over it.'

'I know,' he said. 'Because straight after the funeral I'm going to write a new will and leave my half to her. Seeing as I forgot to sire any children. Isn't life funny, though? Whoever would have predicted that a delicate boy from Amarillo would end up a worm magnate in Maine?'

Peace broke out before bedtime. Grice went out and bought a bottle of Californian blush, which is Crystal's favourite, and after he'd told her what his intentions were with regard to his inheritance we popped it open and drank to Eugene's memory.

Grice said, 'Of course, my status here isn't the same now. I don't mean to start throwing my weight around but seeing your mom's too nice to mention it I'm going to. The doggie sleeping arrangements. There's a good reason nobody found Eugene's files, Crystal. Those dog beds are rank. First job after the burying is a trip to Petco to buy new beds. We can go together or I'll go alone.'

She said, 'The dogs won't be happy. Shorty hates change and Browser likes his own smell.'

'Nevertheless,' he said.

She said she'd agree provided he got Banjo seen to. She said Banjo was Eugene's dog, therefore he was now Grice's dog. Grice said okay, but he thought Banjo was probably too old for that kind of procedure.

'No,' said Crystal. 'If he's not too old to screw around he's not too old to get fixed.'

Vern appeared in the doorway. All he had on was his Y-fronts and one sneaker.

Crystal said, 'Did we wake you, Daddy?'

'No,' said Vern, 'I just wanted to tell Eugene, keep an eye on the redworms. This hot weather he oughta bring them in the shed where it's cooler.'

I said, 'Tell him in the morning.'

'Okay,' he said. 'Only I'll be gone first thing. Me and Herb are on strip alert. Where's Eugene at anyhow, staying out after dark?'

Grice said, 'Probably patrolling the perimeter fence. You know Eugene.'

'Yeah,' said Vern. 'Good. Real good. Don't forget to tell him about the redworms.'

Crystal didn't like it when Vern wasn't properly attired. To her way of thinking, bedtime meant pyjamas, not undershorts and one shoe, but I'd learned to pick my battles.

I walked across the yard with Grice to get a breath of air. I said, 'How do you feel?'

'In a whirl,' he said. 'But I can promise you, Peggy, my new-found fortune isn't going to change me.'

The fishing guests were just going out to try the Hex pattern flies.

'Marvern,' said Grice. 'Which half do you reckon is mine, Mar or Vern? Mar, I guess. '

There was a pretty good turnout at the cemetery, considering Eugene wasn't a man who ever socialized. Corky and Merle, Jim Coffin, of course, and a few others from around Waterville. Some of them would have known Martine. They probably didn't appreciate seeing me standing there next to Vern but, like Grice said, they hadn't exactly rushed to help Vern in later years so what kind of friends were they anyhow? I thought Cort would have been there but I couldn't see him.

The peonies had drooped and the officiant had a funny high

voice, which caused Grice to nudge me and nearly make me laugh. I can't say I felt any grief. There was nothing lovable about Eugene. But he was only sixty-three and nobody should die alone under a cascade of canned goods.

We were dispersing from the graveside when Cort arrived. 'Apologies,' he said. 'I was across at Patch's grave and time got away from me. I'm not sure who I should condole with here. Is your daughter chief mourner?'

'There isn't one. Eugene'll be missed but not greatly.'

'Will you be staying on? Will Vern?'

'We'll all be staying on.'

'Good,' he said. 'I'm glad. ' He started to walk away.

I said, 'People are coming by for a drink.'

'Thank you,' he said. 'I probably won't. I don't like those occasions. But I hope it's not bad form to mention they'll be showing *The Alamo* next week. I thought I'd go on Wednesday, if you're interested.'

'Who's playing Davy Crockett?'

'Billy Bob Thornton.'

I was interested.

Then I heard Crystal say, 'Good God, is that who I think it is?' An old lady came up to her, couldn't have stood higher than four ten, face like a little monkey.

Grice said, 'Who's that?'

There was something familiar about her but I couldn't place her.

'Miss Piggy!' she called to me. 'How you been? You don't know me. I got new teeth.'

It was Filomena, Eugene's ex. The only time I ever saw her

before was at Crystal's wedding, 1979, and I don't believe she spoke a word that day. She just kept putting her hand over her mouth when she smiled. Well, now she had a mouthful of shiny big teeth.

She said she was living over Dexter, saw the death notice in the paper.

I said, 'Did you remarry?'

'Oh, yes,' she said. 'Long time. I got big sexy old man. We got swimming-pool. That Mr Vern over there? He got real old.'

I said, 'Yes. Vern's sick. He's got Alzheimer's.'

'Oh,' she said. 'Terrible thing. I tell my husband, "Eat you vitamins, make plenty sex." You don't mind I came today?'

'Not at all.'

'When Miss Martine passed I came funeral. Eugene told me fuck off.'

'He'd have been grieving. He was close to his mom.'

'Oh, yes. Real close. That you boyfriend?'

'No.'

'What's gonna happen to worm business?'

'Crystal's running it.'

'It belong Crystal now?'

'Crystal and another person. Eugene left his share to a friend.'

'Girlfriend?'

'No. A friend.'

'I sure would like to get something. For remember Eugene, you know?'

'He had a lot of books. Do you want some of them?'

She laughed. My days, she should get a refund on those teeth.

She said, 'You joking me, Miss Piggy. I don't want his old books. They boring. He got any cufflings?'

Cufflinks!

Crystal said, 'How about his watch?'

'Okay,' said Filomena. 'Nice gold watch?'

'Waterproof,' said Crystal. 'You'll be able to wear it in your pool.'

Filomena was driving an old Renault. It was burning oil.

She leaned out the window and yelled, 'I come by next week, get watch and cufflings.'

Crystal yelled back, 'Don't bother. I'll mail them. Fucking cufflinks,' she muttered. 'Is she out of her fucking mind?'

Grice said, 'You could throw a selection of his forage caps in with the watch. Gracious, that gave me a fright. I thought we were going to have her contesting the will right here at the graveside. Thank heavens she married her big sexy old man. With a pool too. Who has a pool in Maine?'

Crystal said, 'It'll be one of those ugly above-ground suckers. And did you see those teeth? She must have bought them off-the-shelf.'

Vern said, 'Did we just bury somebody?'

A few people came back to Marvern for iced tea and beer. I could see Randolph T. Dell weighing up Grice. He said, 'Does he know anything about bait supplies?'

I said, 'He doesn't need to. Crystal's up to speed on that side of things.'

'He a bit . . . light on his loafers?'

'Light as a feather, but he's got a good head for business. They'll make a great team.'

'Take your word for it,' he said. 'Course, Eugene was always changing his will. Your friend just happened to drop lucky. Another year and it could have been somebody else.'

Crystal was very subdued. We sat out a while in the twilight. She said, 'Weird without him, isn't it? I guess I was horrible to him.'

'He could take it. You thought he was crazy, he thought you were too quick to close your mind. Funny Filomena turning up.'

'God, yes. Do you know what seeing her made me remember? Gramma Dewey, at my wedding. Remember the teeth?'

Marc and Crystal got married on a sailboat, somewhere off Bar Harbor. It was real nice, very scenic, but there was quite a swell got up and Vern's mom heaved her breakfast and the bottom plate of her dentures into the ocean. Didn't stop her eating a pile of lobster claws, though, and complaining that there hadn't been a preacher or a justice at least, to do a proper marrying. It was a lovely wedding. Funny, really, because I was the mother of the bride and weddings were my profession but I didn't have a damned thing to do with the arrangements. I never saw Crystal look so happy. Pity how things have turned out.

Crystal said, 'When I die do you think Marc'll come to my funeral?'

I said, 'I wouldn't puzzle over that. He'll die before you do.'

'You reckon? Yeah, running round the kiddie park kicking a ball, pushing his brat on the swings. That'll probably kill him. I'm getting Eugene's stupid bunker taken away. Death trap, more like. You okay with that?'

'Nothing to do with me. I'm keeping his Luger. You okay with that?'

'Mom!' she said. 'What is this Texas thing you've got about guns all of a sudden? You used to be into silver patterns and all that bridal registry shit.'

I said, 'That's a long time ago, sweetheart. The world's changed.'

29

I knew as soon as I heard Kath's voice something wasn't right.

'There's been a bit of a change of plan,' she said. 'Salvatore won't be coming on the cruise.'

'Did you quarrel?'

'Not exactly. But when it come time for him to cough up the money he didn't have it. He said I'd led him to believe I'd be treating him. Treating him! So that was that.'

'Damned right.'

'And now, of course, all the old biddies here are laughing about it. I don't know as I shall stay here, Peggy. Everybody knows your business.'

'What about the cruise? You're in a hole now for his share?'

'Well, yes. I mean, I've got it. I can pay it. But I'd be paying for a double and you know me. I hate waste.'

'What about May?'

'I haven't asked her yet. I wanted to talk to you first. See, I thought of asking Sandie. She's always been a dear girl to me. I wouldn't mind bunging for her, give her a little holiday, but her Gerry's ever so poorly. I don't think she'd leave him.'

'What about trying Audrey again?'

'I could do. Copper-knob mightn't like it.'

'Nothing to do with her. You're the one needs a room-mate. Let me call Audrey. I haven't talked to her in a while.'

I'd never heard Kath so subdued.

She said, 'I've been a right old muggins, haven't I? I should have seen what his game was.'

'Wasn't it nice while it lasted? Lois said you were out and about, enjoying yourself.'

'Out and about being a giddy old fool. Whatever would Slick think? And it's spoilt this place for me now. I haven't ate in the cafeteria since I fell out with Sal. Have everybody whispering about me. I drive down to the Seven Seas now, for the early-bird dinner.'

I called Audrey right away. Usually, if she didn't pick up you'd get her nobody-home-chez-Rudman message, but I didn't get anything. It was like her line was disconnected.

Crystal said, 'Maybe Mikey didn't pay the bill. Call him.'

I had no intention of calling Mikey Rudman. I didn't have his number, didn't want his number. So then Crystal went on the Interweb and got me a number for Silver Spring. 'Administration office,' she said. 'They'll know if Audrey's got a new number. Maybe she left. Maybe she's shifted down to Florida.'

The girl at Silver Spring was very cagey with me, wanted to know who was I and what was my business with Audrey.

I said, 'I've known Mrs Rudman since 1952. My husband and Colonel Rudman served together in the Air Force.'

She said, 'Well, Mrs Rudman went to Europe.'

I said, 'I knew she was planning a trip. I thought she might be back by now.'

She didn't say anything for a second. Then she said, 'Mrs Rudman isn't coming back.'

My first thought was she'd gone to England again, like she did after Lance died and she had a funny five minutes, 'finding herself', as she called it. But then the lady said, no, she hadn't gone to England, she'd gone to Switzerland.

I said, 'Do you have a number for her there?'

'No,' she said. 'There is no number. I'm afraid Mrs Rudman went to Switzerland to die.'

I said, 'What does that mean? She wasn't sick last time I spoke to her.'

'It's called euthanasia, ma'am,' she said. 'I'm afraid I don't have any other information. You'd have to speak with her family.'

Well, I had never heard of such a thing. When she said 'euthanasia' I thought it must be the name of a disease. Crystal put me straight. She said it was what people did when they wanted to die. Assisted suicide.

I said, 'Who does the assisting?'

'People,' she said. 'People who believe in it. I do, as a matter of fact.'

'Does that mean you're gonna put a pillow over my face one of these nights, if I get to be too much trouble?'

She said, 'I mean I believe in it for myself. I get old and sick, who's gonna look after me?'

'You plan on going to Switzerland?'

'No, that's for wealthy folks. I'll make my own arrangements.'

Grice said, 'Me too. Advil and vodka.'

'Might not be enough,' said Crystal. 'You might need a big shot of insulin too.'

I said, 'Will you please stop this? So Audrey went to Switzerland. How would she know where to go?'

'They have clinics. You check in, they ask you if you're really, really sure, and if you are they give you something. I don't know if it's pills or a shot, but it's over real fast. It's not hard to find out about those places, Mom. But I'll bet Mikey helped her. He probably went with her.'

'You mean to hold her hand?'

'Or to make sure she went through with it.'

It was a horrible thing to say but Crystal wasn't the only one to say it.

Lois said, 'Mikey Goddamned Rudman. You have his number? Give me his number?'

I said, 'I don't have his number. And, anyway, it's not going to bring Audrey back.'

'Silly cow,' said Lois. 'What a fool thing to do. She wasn't sick. Just her eyes. She should have come on the cruise, like we asked her. She'd have been fine. We'd have helped her.'

Now I think about it, that was probably Audrey's problem. Needing help. She was always bright and breezy, nice straight back, everything squared away. Even when she got the influenza her place never looked messy.

Lois used to say, 'How come Rudman never has dull, lifeless hair? I wish she'd hurry up and get pregnant. I can't wait to catch her smelling of baby sick.'

Audrey did it all. Raised twins, played a mean game of bridge, organized the Red Cross Clothes Closet at the Officers' Wives Club. She made it all look easy as pie. Drumming up volunteers for a fund-raiser was one thing. Asking for help for herself, that wasn't her style.

I felt Audrey's passing more than I remembered feeling Betty's. Betty had put up a fight. When she got real sick some of us went to be with her. We felt useful, washing her nightgowns, dabbing her with cologne, feeding her on Cool Whip. I couldn't sleep that night for thinking about Audrey. Had she gone to Switzerland all alone? Did she get a last meal, like they do on Death Row?

Next morning Crystal got me a number for Mikey Rudman's company, Rudco. 'Here,' she said. 'Call him, find out what happened.'

I didn't call him. I gave Lois the number.

'Good thinking,' said Grice. 'Lois Moon at full throttle. He'll wonder what hit him. I never met any of the Rudmans but I don't much like what I've heard. The least this Mikey should have done is let you all know.'

I went out to the mailbox and there was a package for Eugene. The report of the 9/11 commission. Grice said he planned to read it. I told him he'd better get some new reading glasses and some work boots with steel toecaps. Six hundred pages. Drop a weight like that on your foot, you could do yourself an injury.

Kath called, said she had good news. I felt like I needed some.

'May's coming on the cruise,' she said. 'She's a bit nervy about the flying but I told her to get some pills from the doctor. So now we're all set. You and Grice, me and Copper-knob and May.

Only thing I need is a new sun bonnet. I tried to wash mine and it's shrunk.'

'Did Lois get through to Mikey Rudman?'

'Course not. She left a message for him to call her back. Waste of time. She'll never hear from him. I'll bet he never even got the message.'

But Lois did hear from Mikey. 'Always glad to touch base with my parents' friends,' he'd said.

'Hundred per cent BS,' said Lois. 'Boy, he sounded exactly like his father. That took me back.'

According to Mikey, Audrey had found it very hard to accept her failing eyesight. She hadn't been depressed, she'd thought everything through very carefully and decided she preferred to call it a day, while she could still travel. Leave on her terms. Those were his words.

'Did he go with her?'

'He went with her to Zürich, but he didn't go with her on the actual day. He said she didn't want him there. It was a drink, by the way. First they give you some stuff to stop you throwing up, then they give you the go-to-sleep dose. I told him, half Audrey's trouble was she was lonely, since Lance Three passed. She should have been in Florida with him, not stuck in Silver fucking Spring, groping around the furniture, banging her shins. He said, "Oh, but Silver Spring was very nice. Mother was happy there." And then he said, "And, of course, she always adored Switzerland." Yeah. The mountains, the chocolate, the bank accounts, the coffins.'

I said, 'We're a shrinking band, Lo. Betty's gone, Pearl Petie's gone, and now Audrey.'

'And Ruby Bergstrom,' she said. 'Did I tell you? Out jogging, took a stroke. And Mollie Kowalski. Maybe you didn't know her. She was at Hickam Field. I don't know what got Mollie. I feel like we're dodging bullets, Peg.'

'Makes you wonder who'll be next.'

'Might be me,' she said. 'If friend husband doesn't stop reorganizing his screw collection all over my lounge-room floor I might just jump off the Tappan Zee bridge.'

'But not till after the cruise.'

'Goes without saying. Wait till you see what I got at T. J. Maxx.'

With Eugene gone I was worried about leaving Crystal to manage on her own.

She said, 'You make it sound like Eugene was any kind of help.'

I said, 'At least he was there. Say your daddy fell.'

'Jim Coffin,' she said. 'I'll ask him. That make you feel better?'

And Jim said he was quite willing. In fact, why didn't he move in while me and Grice were away, in case anything should happen? I thought it was a neat idea. He could have Eugene's old room.

Crystal said, 'Just so long as he doesn't get any ideas.'

Grice said he couldn't speak from personal experience but he understood the best way for a girl to deter a guy, if things should get too frisky, was to do something to gross him out, like pick her nose.

'Wouldn't work with Jim,' said Crystal. 'He's quite a nostril-miner himself. He might think it was a mating call.'

The day before we left for New York Jim arrived. He had a

bag full of lager cans, an airplane model kit and a bunch of gas-station chrysanthemums.

Grice said, 'Where's his sponge bag?'

I said, 'He evidently travels light.'

'Ewww!' said Grice. 'No toothbrush?'

Travelling light didn't feature in Grice's mind. He'd been packing for a week and he had twice as much luggage as I did.

I said, 'We're only going for seven nights.'

'Plus a night in New York at each end, plus what if one of my bags goes missing? I don't want to get to Nassau and find I don't have the ingredients for a costume party.'

Vern eyed Jim Coffin. He said, 'Eugene ain't here. Don't know when he'll be back.'

'That's okay,' said Jim. 'I brung this kit. See, there's a Spitfire and a Messerschmitt. I thought you and me could make them up, have ourselves a dogfight. What do you think?'

Vern said he'd fly the Spitfire. He said, 'You'll need glue.'

'I brung glue.'

'It'll take some doing.'

'We got plenty of time. I'm stopping over, while your Peggy and Grice go on vacation. And while I'm here, anything you need a hand with, you know what I mean, getting showered, getting dressed, you can just holler for me.'

Vern said, 'I'm not a cripple.'

'Never said you were, but climbing in and outta the tub, that can be a doozy. No sense breaking your neck when there's a guy around can give you a hand. Okay?'

'Okay,' said Vern. 'But no funny stuff.'

★

Saturday Crystal drove us to the airport. We were flying Portland to LaGuardia, staying the night in the city. She said, 'I'll just go to Drop-off, okay? We don't have to make a big production saying goodbye. You're only going for a week.'

I said, 'Will you be all right?'

'Why wouldn't I be?'

'Jim. You want to know where my Luger is?'

She said, 'If you value your Luger don't tell me where it is because I'll be tempted to get rid of it.'

Then she came over all sentimental and told me I really deserved a vacation and she was sorry she didn't always show her appreciation. She said, 'You take care of yourself now, you hear? Don't be one of those oldsters comes home in a body bag.'

Grice said, 'Well, this is cheerful.'

Crystal said, 'Seriously. They have morgues on those cruise ships. All those old folk. Course, some people probably eat themselves to death. One refuel too many at the All You Can Eat. Remember, just because it's there doesn't mean you have to put it on your plate.'

She dropped us at the kerb.

Kath and May were driving in from Great Neck Sunday morning, and Herb was bringing Lois to the cruise terminal. We had to be on board by one o'clock. I'd left it to Grice to book a hotel in Manhattan.

He said, 'I could only get a twin. I hope you're okay with that?'

I said, 'I shared a bathroom with you at Lake Highlands and survived it. So where exactly are we staying?'

'Oh, just a basic little place,' he said. 'I mean, we're going to be sailing in luxury for a week so no sense wasting money on a fancy hotel for one night.'

'How basic?'

'Well, let's put it this way. They probably don't provide complimentary shampoo.'

'Where is it?'

'Bowery. Is that a nice neighbourhood?'

'I don't think so. Is it a chain?'

'Yes. It's one of the Roach Central group. I have a loyalty card.'

When we got into the cab at LaGuardia he told the driver, Park Avenue at 64th, the Plaza Athénée.

I said, 'Are you kidding? Did you check the price of the room before you booked it?'

'Happy birthday, darl,' he said. 'Or, as dear Lois would say, happy fucking birthday.

'Hey,' he said to the driver, 'can you believe this lady's gonna be eighty?'

'Uh,' said the driver, and he slid the little window shut.

I said, 'Grice, precious, we're in New York not Texas. You get a ride, no conversation.'

It wasn't a twin room. It had two double beds and a marble tub. I just had to call Crystal. She knew all about it, of course. 'Yeah,' she said. 'Well, it's not every day you get to be eighty. And we thought you might pick up some décor tips for upgrading Marvern.'

'Your daddy okay?'

'Yes. Right now we have three hundred tiny aircraft parts spread across the kitchen table.'

'Makes a change from Eugene's 9/11 files.'

'It does. Get off the phone, Mom. You're on vacation. Worst thing that can happen here is Dad swallows a Spitfire propeller cap.'

We went out and walked around some. I couldn't live in New York. I'm not even sure I could live in Dallas again. I've grown accustomed to the quiet country life.

Grice said, 'Well, I'm glad you said it, about Manhattan. Kinda heresy, really. I thought God might strike me down with a thunderbolt if I said what I was thinking. It's just a great big noisy shitbox. Why don't they fix up some of those potholes? And why does everybody look so mean?'

'This time tomorrow,' we kept saying. This time tomorrow we'll be under way.

'This time tomorrow,' said Grice, 'we'll be having our first argument about where to eat dinner. So many choices. And five of us. We'll never agree on anything.'

'We could take turns choosing.'

'We could. Or we could agree to disagree and all do our own thing. I mean, this May, she's probably going to want fish and fries every night.'

We were sitting in the hotel bar when Lois called me.

She said, 'You at the airport yet?'

I said, 'Landed, showered, been out for a walk. Guess where we are?'

'Times Square.'

'Bar Seine. Plaza Athénée hotel. I'm having a Kir Royale.'

She whistled. 'They let you through the door?'

'They let me in and showed me to my triple-glazed double queen.'

'You're *staying* there. Did you come into money?'

'It's my birthday gift from Grice.'

'What a doll. Seriously, what an absolute doll. You got fluffy bathrobes? Splits of champagne in the icebox?'

'I haven't looked.'

'Peg,' she said, 'you're at the Plaza. Open every closet, pocket every freebie. Meanwhile, in White Plains, Lois Moon is sitting on her valise trying to get the stupid thing to close. I guess I'll have to wait for Herb to get home.'

She said May Gotobed had arrived safely, but carrying a suspiciously small bag. Kath had taken her out to buy a few things. 'Jeez, Peg,' she said. 'What is it with these English people? They still got post-war shortages?'

I said, 'They just think different. They have small apartments, small closets.'

'I know, I know. Little cars made for midgets. They got a queen never throws anything away. What's all that about? If I had her money I'd wear a different crown every time I left the house. You ever met May?'

'Years ago, when we were at Drampton. When I was teaching Kath to drive. She's like a timid version of Kath.'

'I'll bet she speaks funny.'

I said, 'Lo, to her we probably speak funny.'

'No, we don't,' she said. 'We speak normal. That's why they

can watch our movies. You ever tried watching anything of theirs? Herb got me a DVD of a TV show, *Absolutely Fabulous*. Great clothes, but I couldn't follow what they were saying. They talk like they got rocks in their mouths. At least if that guy Sal was coming with us we'd know what the heck he was talking about. May starts conversing with me, you're gonna have to help me out, Peg.'

30

We took a cab down to the cruise terminal. We were on board by twelve but our bags weren't brought down right away so we couldn't unpack. We went up to the rail to look out for the others arriving.

Grice said, 'Lois'll be last, just watch. The last of our party and possibly the very last on board, period.'

We spotted Kath and May. Two white-haired old ladies taking their time. Grice tried to do one of those two-finger whistles but it was a feeble effort. You were supposed to be on board by one o'clock. Got to ten to and we were still watching for Lois. I started to feel sick. Grice said if she didn't make it she'd have to fly down to Florida, join the boat at Port Canaveral.

Five minutes to. The guys who man the passenger gangways were down on the quayside ready to close everything up.

I said, 'She's gonna miss it. All those months of planning and she's gonna miss it. I can't bear it. I can't watch. I'm going to find Kath and May.'

I turned to go and Grice said, 'Wait! There's a red-haired mad woman hobbling out of the terminal, waving her arms. Yes, yes, it's Lois. Gosh, what has she done to herself? Sprained her ankle or something. One of the guys has gone to help her. I think I won my bet, though. Last on board. Heavens to Betsy, that woman likes to live dangerously.'

We met her in the Grand Atrium.

I said, 'Don't ever do that to me again.'

'What?' she said. 'Now what did I do?'

'Nearly missed the boat, that's all.'

'I did not. Herb couldn't find the place to drop me. Then my heel broke on my shoe. Look at that. First time I've worn them.'

Grice said, 'You cut it fine. Hadn't been for that deck hand you'd have been left behind.'

'No way. They wouldn't have left without me. And that was no deck hand. That was a two-stripe officer. He was so cute. He can help me walk the gangplank any day. You rendezvoused with the poor relations yet?'

We found Kath and May already at their muster stations with their life vests. Lois wanted to go get a drink.

Kath said, 'There won't be no bars open yet. Lifeboat drill, that's the first thing. You have to go to your station, put your lifejacket on and listen to the safety talk.'

Lois said no way was she putting that vest on, ruining her hair when she'd just been for a blow-out. She changed her tune when she saw our safety leader. 'He's buff,' she said. 'So many cute guys and only a week to enjoy them.'

Kath whispered to me. She said, 'If Copper-knob disappears over the side accidentally on purpose this week nobody'll blame you, Peggy. I'm ready to crown her now and we haven't even left port.'

★

There was a Welcome Hour, with free drinks. Lois had changed into lace cocktail wear. May was still wearing her wind-cheater. She said everything was 'bootiful', which is Norfolk for 'swell'. The drinks, the stateroom, the staff. All bootiful.

Lois said, 'Okay, where are we eating? I thought Houlihan's. It's like an eatery. Something for everybody there and it's open all hours. I can't eat late these days. I get acid reflux.'

'Okay,' said Grice. 'We could try Houlihan's tonight. But of course we don't all need to eat together every night.'

'Sure,' said Lois. 'Be standoffish. It was nice knowing you. I'll bet you like that Japanese shit, right? Raw fish? You watch you don't get a tapeworm. They can get into your brain. Drive you crazy.'

And May said, 'Is that what happened to you, Lois?'

Everything went quiet. Then Lois roared. She said, 'Kath, I think I'm gonna love your friend. May, take your fucking wind-jammer off. Make like you're staying. Okay, Houlihan's. Leave this to me.'

She strode in there, asked for the manager, told him she wanted a nice table for her and her friends. The place was prac-tically empty. When she'd found a table to her liking, she said, 'Good. We'll be in early most evenings. Where you from? What's your name?'

He said he was Jean-Fabrice from Port Louis, Mauritius.

'Great,' said Lois. 'Well, Fabrice, I know I can rely on you to take good care of us.' She slipped him a roll of bills. She wouldn't say how much she'd given him.

I said, 'Why'd you do that? We only just got here. We might not like this place.'

'What's not to like?' she said. 'Cruising 101, Peggy. You tip at the get-go, not when you're leaving. Where the fuck is Mauritius?'

I don't know if Lois felt she got value from that up-front tip. We certainly got a warm welcome every time we ate there. 'My lovely early birds,' Jean-Fabrice'd say. 'And what is your pleasure this evening?'

We were at sea all day Monday, blue skies, calm water. I didn't see Grice until the afternoon. He was lounging by a splash pool, reading *Babycakes*. I said, 'I thought you were going to read that 9/11 thing.'

'Yes, but not in public. It's my dirty little secret. And it's so damned heavy. I'd need to work on my upper-body strength before I could read it lying down.'

'We're booking for *Divas at Sea* tonight, first show. You in?'

'No,' he said. 'Not really my thing. I reckon I'll just hang out in the Topsail Bar. Try to look suavely tan and interesting.'

It was too late for that. He had a sunburned nose. 'You hoping to meet someone?'

He said, 'When you say *meet* someone, I don't think you mean what I'd mean. It's just a vacation, Peg. I'm not looking for The One.'

May and Lois were bouncing on a trampoline together. I sat with Kath and watched them. Sometimes they were in synch, sometimes as one went down the other would pop up.

I said, 'I thought May had bad knees.'

'Me too,' said Kath. 'I reckon she just said that so the council'd give her a bungalow.'

I said, 'She doesn't say much. Is she shy?'

'Not really. She just likes to listen. May never had much of an education. Any time there was work in the beet fields, that's where she'd be. I was in school more than she was and that's not saying much. She reads a lot, though. Large print. She gets them from the library. Did you ask Grice about the show?'

'He said no. I hope he's not going to spend the week sitting in bars.'

'He's missing Tucker.'

'You're missing Slick.'

'Oh, yes. But Slick wouldn't have cared for a cruise. He'd have been fretting to get back to his engines.'

'You been on the trampoline?'

'I did, but it made me feel woozy. I shall be having a go at everything else, though, Peggy. Swimming with the dolphins and all that.'

Watching Lois bouncing around made me feel old. Heck, I used to be captain of Topperwein High softball team. I get out of breath now putting my shoes on.

We figured out how to take a photo with Kath's cell phone. It came out a bit blurry but you can make out the top of Lois's Radiant Auburn and May's tight white permanent.

When Tina Turner came on stage May's face was a picture. Then when Cher appeared I saw her grab Kath's arm, she was so excited. Lois leaned in to me and whispered, 'She thinks they're real.'

Maybe she did. But by the time we got to the Dolly Parton finale she'd gotten the hang of it. I don't know which was better, when she thought she was getting all those stars in one show or when she realized they were guys.

After the show, we went to find Grice. He was sitting alone in the Topsail Bar.

Lois said, 'We've come to ruin your chances. Such as they were.'

'Grice,' said May, 'you missed a treat. You should have come with us. Such bootiful gowns, and do you know, they were all men? I'll bet they're all jessie boys. You might have dropped lucky.'

'Why, May Gotobed,' he said. 'I see there are no flies on you.'

Tuesday, late morning, we docked at Port Canaveral. At first Grice said he was going to stay on board, maybe get a massage. 'Do I want to see the Air Force Space Museum?' he said. 'No, thank you.'

But Kath was determined to try one of those Segway machines and I wanted Grice to take a video.

'Very well,' he said. 'But then I'm coming back to the ship so please don't ask me to go look at manatees. Day three already. At this rate I'm never going to get laid.'

Lois signed up for the Segway too. *Safety helmet and full training provided*, it said. Kath soon got the hang of it, just like when I taught her to drive. Lois was too busy larking around with the instructor. May and I sat and watched them.

She said, 'Lois is a caution.'

'She can be hard work.'

'Oh, yes. Kath's had a few run-ins with her. There's something sad about her, though, don't you think? Perhaps it's because of that baby she had of John Pharaoh. You probably never get over a thing like that.'

'I've known Lo since we were in our twenties. She's always been the same, even before she had Kirk. I'll never understand why she went with John. She has the best husband in the world.'

'Yes, Kath's always said. Well, of course John Pharaoh bewitched her. Kath should have warned her. I would have. He had a demon in him.'

'Did he ever bewitch you?'

'Not so likely. I wouldn't be alone with him. If I seen him coming up the drove I'd say, "Our Father which art in heaven," until he'd passed by. The Devil won't come near you if you've got them words in your mouth.'

'He had that disease, May.'

'Oh, yes. But he had the Devil in him too. I wouldn't ever say it to Kath but I know what I know. And not only me. Thad Chaplin seen him one time, over Waplode, and he had a black demon on his shoulder, big as a tomcat.'

We were sitting in the sun but I felt a chill when she said that. Not that I believe in any such thing.

Grice went back on board and the rest of us got Coney Island hotdogs, even May, although she had a Danish and a couple of bananas in her purse, smuggled from the breakfast buffet. 'All that food,' she said. 'I hate to see waste. And you would too if you'd had rationing.'

Kath said, 'They say we were healthier then, May.'

'Healthier maybe,' said May. 'And blummin' hungry all the

367

time. Anything extra our mam managed to get, a bit of ham or an egg, our dad had first dibs. We used to sit and watch him.'

'Wasn't he in the forces?'

'Too old. He might have had to go if the war had carried on.'

Lois said, 'But then our boys came and saved the day.'

'Saved the day?' said May, sharp as you like. 'They took their blummin' time about it. When was it we first seen any Yanks in Lynn, Kath? 1944? Don't get me wrong, we were glad to have them, but don't you go thinking you won the war. If we hadn't stood firm while you lot were dithering the war'd have been over. We'd have been living under the jackboot.'

'Okay, okay,' said Lois. 'Keep your hair on. I'll bet it was good for morale, though, having our boys in town. You ever date a GI?'

May said, 'Ask me no questions and I'll tell you no lies.'

31

We moored off Stirrup Cay just as we were finishing breakfast. It looked heavenly.

'Like *Desert Island Discs*,' said May. 'Look at them palm trees.'

Grice said, 'Drain those coffee cups, girls. There'll be a stampede for the tenders. Then there'll be a stampede for the sun loungers.'

When you stepped ashore there was a wooden gateway to the beach, with a sign over it. Grice grabbed my arm. He said, 'If I was running this place that'd have to go. Doesn't it make you think of "*Arbeit Macht Frei*"?'

I had no idea what he was talking about.

'Hmm,' he said, 'and I hope we're not going to have a steel band playing all day.'

'Grice,' said Lois, 'stop being a dick and run grab us five loungers.'

Kath and Grice spent the morning snorkelling. May and I just sat at the water's edge and let it lap over us. We could hear Lois's voice, laughing and kidding around with the beach boys. She was wearing a long, floaty thing with parakeets on it, gold espadrilles, giant shades, full war paint.

May said, 'I'll bet they think she's a film star.'

We went for a fish fry lunch but Lois wasn't eating. She just had two Dark 'n' Stormys. She said, 'Only thing I'm gonna fry is my body. I'm stocking up on vitamin D. Orthopaedist's orders.'

All Kath could talk about was the snorkelling. 'Peg,' she said, 'I've never seen anything like it. There's coral reefs down there and fish like you wouldn't believe. Angel fish and all kinds. And do you know? They all look like they're smiling. Did you notice that, Grice? Smiling fish.'

Lois muttered, 'That's because they're living in fucking Paradise.'

Kath said, 'And the colours. I wish Slick could have seen them. Some of them were colours that don't even have a name. I couldn't begin to explain it.'

Lois growled, 'It's okay, Kath. We get the picture. Pretty, smiling fish. Wake me when the last tender's leaving. Second thoughts, don't. I'll just stay here. Tell Herb he can sell my fur coat.'

Around four o'clock people started to head back to the ship. We gathered up our stuff. Lois had sore shoulders. May hadn't even broken sweat. Kath was still sleeping. Grice said it seemed a shame to wake her, to give her another few minutes. But when Lois lifted her sun hat off her face you could see there was no waking her. Her mouth was half open, her eyes were half closed, and she was cool to the touch.

The beach boys came running. Some of the other passengers gathered round, making suggestions, surmising what had happened. Too much sun. Too long snorkelling. Poor May kept whispering, 'Oh, do come back, Kath. Please come back.'

By the time we brought Kath's body on board the word had gone round and there were people on the rail watching our tender dock. Lois yelled up at them, 'Fuck off, you fucking vultures!'

Grice said, 'Lois, we've all had enough of your effing and carrying on. Kath never used language. Be more respectful.'

And for once she did shut up.

They took Kath to the morgue. They said, seeing it was a short cruise, she could stay there till we got back to New York. She was the first death on that trip but she wasn't the last. A man died the following day, in a souvenir shop in Nassau, and another when we were at sea heading back to New York, so Kath had company for the last leg of the cruise.

The crew were so kind. Was there anything they could do, anyone they could contact? But there wasn't. We were Kath's family.

May was in a daze. She said, 'What shall I do now? I don't know how to get to Kath's place. I don't know how to get to the airyport.'

Lois said, 'Don't worry about a single thing. Me and Herb'll look after you.' Then she said, 'Tonight I'm going to get wasted.'

I said, 'Why?'

'Because I've lost a good friend. Fuck. Why'd she have to go and do that?'

I said, 'Look at it this way. She had an amazing life and then

371

she died in her sleep, in the sun, on a perfect white beach, water lapping.'

Lois said, 'But I was horrible to her. When she was going on and on about the damned smiley fish.'

Grice said, 'But, Lois, you're horrible to everybody. We hardly even notice it any more. Kath knew you loved her really.'

Well, then she cried and cried, and when Jean-Fabrice from Houlihan's heard the news, came and found us and said he'd keep a nice quiet table for his lovely early birds because we still needed to eat, she cried even more. 'People are so nice,' she sobbed.

'Yes,' said Grice. 'People are. It's just that some have a hard time showing it.'

It was Pirate Theme Night. Grice had brought an entire costume with him but he didn't have the heart to put it on. Just a bandanna and an eye patch. He called it the Kath Pharaoh Memorial Eye Patch. So then Lois pulled herself together and went swaying off to the atrium mall to get eye patches for the rest of us. She was gone quite a while.

'Got lost,' she said. 'Fucking elevator was so confusing. I ended up by the kitchens. Plus, the only eye patch they had left had broken elastic so I got pirate hats instead.'

We ordered a jug of Caribbean Cooler and a platter of buffalo wings. It was the oddest wake I ever was at. Three old ladies in skull and cross-bones hats and a sixty-six-year-old whipper-snapper in an eye patch, telling stories about their dear departed friend.

Lois said, 'Peggy's better at remembering than I am. We gave Kath a ride home. Was that how we met her?'

'Yes. It was 1952 and King George VI had died at Sandring Ham Palace. Betty Gillis figured out where the Royal Train'd be passing and we went down to watch. We thought it'd be something to tell our grandkids. Of course we didn't really see anything, except fog and steam, but maybe it was the being there that counted.

'There was a small crowd waiting at the place where the track crossed the road. Betty tried to converse with them but they weren't a friendly bunch. Kath was the only one who spoke. And then after the train had passed and everyone disappeared into the fog we saw her striding along with her Union flag poking out of her shopping bag. We drove her home, went in for a cup of tea and the rest is history.'

Lois said, 'Peggy Dewey, you have some memory. You should write it all down. Story of your life.'

Grice said, 'Oh, but she already did.'

Then May said, 'I allus wondered if it'd come out some day, about old man Pharaoh. I used to worry about it. I mean, we still had the hanging in them days. But then when she married Slick and went American I thought she was probably in the clear. You never know, though. You do hear of people raking up stories after donkey's years. Well, she's safe now. They can't come after her where she's gone.'

Grice said, 'Hold on. Am I missing something? Are you saying Kath committed a crime?'

'Oh, yes,' said May. 'She killed him.'

'You mean her brother?'

'Not her brother. She loved her John, even if he was trouble. She looked after him. No, I'm talking about her dad.'

'Kath killed her father?'

'Yes. And nobody mourned him I can tell you.'

'What did she do?'

'Fetched him one under the chin, sent him toppling. He hit his head on the range. Well, he'd been drinking in Lynn, spent all his eel money, come home creating havoc as usual. He'd had a few. And over he went.'

'So it was an accident?'

'It was a happy accident. He was a nasty old bugger. He made everybody's life a misery, specially her mam's.'

'So he hit his head and died?'

'Well, yes, but not straight off. He was on the floor gurgling and gasping for a bit.'

'But then he died? So it wasn't completely Kath's fault.'

'No. And she wouldn't have punched him if he hadn't been picking on her mam. But she did help him on his way, after she'd floored him.'

'What did she do?'

'Pillow over his face. But she sent her mam outside first, so she shouldn't see it. I mean, he probably wouldn't have come to anyway. Or he could have woke up a vegetable and then how would they have managed? No, she did it for the best and I've never faulted her for it. I just didn't want to see her hanged.'

'And the police never questioned her?'

'What police? We didn't see police from one year's end to the next. There was no need. Nobody ever did anything bad. Well, hardly ever.'

'How old was Kath?'

'Fourteen. She was strong, though. She had a good right hook.'

'And she told you what she'd done.'

'Straight after. She knew I could keep a secret. And, you see, I think that's when the Devil got into John Pharaoh. He'd been in the old man and then when he left his body he saw his chance and went into John. He couldn't have got into Kath. She was too strong for him. But John, he had dirty habits. And that's how the Devil gets in.'

'And no one ever said anything about Kath's father? Nobody ever suspected how he'd died?'

'We didn't need to suspect. He was an old bully and he was dead and that was that. Good riddance. Mrs Pharaoh got a few years of peace. That's how it was in them days. We took care of things ourselves up Blackdyke. If anybody put two and two together they didn't say anything.'

Lois said the F-word. Nobody else said anything. Then May suddenly screamed. She said, 'There's a creepy-crawly in my glass.'

Well, then we laughed. It was one of Lois's homemade ginger eyelashes.

Grice ordered another pitcher.

Lois said, 'Well, you all know about my misdemeanours with John Pharaoh so I won't go into that. But I'll tell you something about Kath nobody but me and Herb could really know and that's how much she helped us with Kirk. Sometimes I just couldn't do it any more, but she'd sit and sit with him. Wash him. Feed him. She'd do anything. Sometimes he forgot how to swallow and you could be there for hours trying to get a spoon-ful of ice cream into him.'

May said, 'She blamed herself, that's why. She used to phone me. She used to say, "May, I guessed what was a-going on with John and Lois and I should have put a stop to it. Now look what's happened. That boy's suffering for the sins of the father."'

Lois said, 'It wasn't all suffering, you know. Kirk was a great kid. Wasn't his fault if the schools didn't understand him. Anyway, Kath couldn't have stopped anything. It was between me and John. And as a matter of fact he was really great in the sack. I just wish I hadn't yelled at her today about the Goddamned smiley rainbow fishes.'

Grice said, 'You didn't yell. It was more a rum-fuelled growl.'

I said, 'And, anyway, you're like living under a flight path. We've been listening to it for so many years we don't notice it any more.'

We were due to dock at Nassau the following morning. We'd made all kinds of plans.

'You know what?' said Lois. 'Fuck Nassau. I'm staying on board. I'm not leaving Kath alone in that meat locker.'

Grice was fiddling with his cell phone. 'Oh, nice,' he said. 'Take a look at this.'

And there was Kath. He'd videoed her at Port Canaveral, waving and smiling in that pink crash helmet, like Grice said, 'Segwaying off into the sunset.'

I don't know what time it was. It was still dark.

Lois said, 'You awake?'

I'd been awake for hours.

She said, 'Kath died, right? I didn't dream it?'

She had a hangover. I got up and made her Alka-Seltzer.

'Just you and me now, girlfriend,' she said. 'Betty's gone, Audrey's jumped ship, Kath's gone. Gayle's in the slammer, so forget her.'

I said, 'We're like the ten little nigger boys. And then there were two.'

'Peggy Dewey!' she said. 'Using the N-word in 2004. Wait till I see your daughter. Man, oh, man, am I gonna tell on you.'

I was miserable company on the flight back to Portland. Kath was gone. Our lovely vacation was ruined. Grice was doing his best to buck me up.

He said, 'How about we redecorate your room? Now we don't have to worry about Eugene getting bent out of shape. I shouldn't have said that. He really did get bent out of shape. Or we could remodel the kitchen.'

'You mean ready for my wake?'

'Oh, boy,' he said. 'Remind me never to try cheering you up again.'

Crystal was supposed to meet us. We came through Arrivals and there was no sign of her.

'Great,' said Grice. 'I'm tired, I'm seedy, you're inconsolable and now our ride home didn't turn up.'

I was trying to find my cell phone in that damned so-called organizer bag when I heard somebody calling my name. It was Cort Cooper. He had Herk riding in the hood of his storm-chaser.

'I'm your driver,' he said. 'Crystal's in a fix with her vehicle. Oil pump failed, big end's gone. I'd say the engine's wrecked.'

And, like an idiot, I burst into tears.

Grice said, 'It's been a tough trip. One of our friends passed away.'

'I'm very sorry to hear it,' said Cort. 'Sometimes it's just one damned thing after another. Tell you what, Peggy, why don't you take Herk while I take care of these bags? He's been pestering to see you all morning.'

So I carried Hercules, and Cort pushed the baggage cart out to the car park, and Grice whispered, 'Remember. If you marry him you promised you'd adopt me.'